Dick Swept, M.D.

Dick Swept, M.D.

TOMORROW, THE WORLD

David B. Rosenfield

To order additional copies of this book, contact:
Xlibris Corporation
1-888-7-XLIBRIS
www.Xlibris.com
Orders@Xlibris.com
14017

Contents

DEDICATED TO MARIA

Chapter One

FROM KATHMANDU TO HOUSTON

AN OBSERVER, HAD one been present, might have contended that the lone female trekker uttered a groaning sound. The village lay directly ahead of her. Probably no more than twenty families lived there, perhaps ninety inhabitants, all Sherpas. This time she saw no friendly stares, heard no children saying, "Bon-Bons?" and there were no displays of wares on Yak-cloth. Instead, there were Sherpas lying on the ground, contorted, crusts of saliva and blood at their mouths. The entire village lay dead. All of them.

Diffuse ecchymoses, commonly known as black and blue marks, circumscribed their eyes, decorating each corpse with a raccoon-like mask. The stench of human feces and urine soon enveloped the numb trekker. Stepping back, she became increasingly horrified at the contorted positions of the dead bodies, achieved only by having bones broken. Elbows were hyper-extended in patterns functionally inconceivable from normal body mechanisms. The raccoon-masked heads lay markedly askew, suggesting broken necks. Knees, legs, entire torsos lay so distorted that, combined with the visual and olfactory manifestation of sphincter incontinence, it was clear some incomprehensible malady had to be fathomed.

A few minutes earlier, taking in the beautiful Himalayan scenery, Ricki Hardson had marveled about being so far above the snow clouds, simultaneously feeling the sun's warmth from her highly perched position, while looking at snowflakes below. Now, that had all changed. Despite her years of cynicism and Intensive Care Unit nursing, she vomited. Her knees weakened and vision blurred. The nausea was increasingly powerful as a sour taste cycled repeatedly in the back of her mouth.

Perhaps Ricki Hardson momentarily lost vision, as her heartbeat skipped, sometimes not beating at all for several seconds. She forced herself to stop staring, and to move. She had to move. There was no doubt – the contorted people were dead, emitting the ever-vacuous stare that hungers on corpses and claims itself life's common denominator. She had seen that look too many times in the ICU at one of the hospitals in the Houston Medical Complex, a position she came to abhor, resulting in her transfer to work with the infectious disease team at her hospital.

She touched no one. Trance-like, the woman moved on.

There are no phones in the depths of the Himalaya Mountains. Nor, in fact, many people to call. Sometimes crying, tremulous, horrified, non-believing, almost screaming, she sought to gather her thoughts. Stumbling along the worn Himalayan trails, passing Buddhist shrines to her left, she decided to return to the village of Namche, where she hoped to find a Nepalese official residing near some tourist area.

*   *   *

In the capital of Nepal, Kathmandu, outside Pattan, the man in the dark, navy-blue coat, too heavy for monsoon weather, ate slowly with his fingers. His superiors had explained the task very simply: Put the chemical in the water, give a few verbal instructions and, later, analyze the effects on the Sherpas. He had wondered whether the Sherpas' religious practices would change. Would they still pass Buddhist shrines to their left, would they change how they lived? He reasoned that many of these analyses would take time and come later. He had to do first things first. The man had introduced the chemical into their water supply to test the actual mechanics of administering the chemical to a small human population, as well as to evaluate possible side effects.

He recalled when he and his colleagues had administered the compound to animals. All had survived. Their committee had also given the drug, in a few instances, to some unsuspecting prisoners in the Ukraine. The drug had not seemed dangerous – at least no one had died. His task in the Himalaya was to be certain that the application of the compound to a relatively large group of people could be easily accomplished, was practical, and that the chemical was effective. He had just finished the first stage of his project.

What the man and his colleagues had not counted on was the altered red blood cell chemistry of the Sherpas, an adaptive state of their hemoglobin permitting more binding to oxygen, a necessity for their high altitude survival. The altered hemoglobin had combined with the compound after the Sherpas drank the tainted water. Then, it killed them. All of them, the entire village.

No matter, thought the man. The Nepalese government lacked facilities to perform appropriate post-mortem analyses. He knew they would conclude that the Sherpas perished from some disease, possibly an outbreak of meningoencephalitis similar to the one that had attacked over one thousand people in Kathmandu earlier in the year.

At one time, the man had been a student of existentialism, when he came to realize that most things in life have minimal intrinsic meaning. Everyone lives, everyone dies, everything comes and goes. Even nations. Even a wife and two children, like the family he lost following the train accident in the Ukraine. It made no difference whether the Sherpas died now or died later. In the end, all things die. One's daily goal should be survival, to fight the common denominator that seeks us all. Too bad, he thought, that some lose while others win.

The man momentarily wondered what the female trekker thought when she found the dead villagers. The newspapers had mentioned her name. She was supposedly an outdoor enthusiast, raised in Virginia but currently living in Houston, with a passion for jogging, hiking, and mountain climbing. The article mentioned her winning some type of contest with a Harley Sportster, quoting her as saying that motorcycles allowed her to participate in the environment, not simply view it, much akin to trekking. The man, good at his work, would check all this out later, but doubted he would find much.

Until recently, women considered the man handsome. Now, he was certainly not grotesque, but long exposure to periods of intense emotional strain had produced an ugliness. Casually wiping his mouth with the back of a questionably scarred hand, he paid no attention to the food nested at the end of his sleeve. After consuming more of the local yogurt, he ordered coffee, which he drank black, and lit one of his Sobranie cigarettes, dexterously using his left hand to strike the match. He inhaled deeply, to the full, silently contemplating the changing geometric shapes formed by the lines of smoke. He finished the cigarette, silently cursed the coffee, and exited the restaurant. Since there were no toilets, he relieved his bladder outside, against the restaurant wall, and made his telephone call.

*　　*　　*

Dick Swept's Monday morning had been like most other Monday mornings. The Neurology Clinic was full, with patients complaining of headaches, dizziness, and an occasional radicular pain in their arm or leg. Everyone was doing fairly well on his conservative regimen of treatment, although at times he queried whether his primary function with patients was to babysit, rather than to practice neurological medicine. Swept thought frequently about his patients, believing that he personally had more meaning on this planet if he could make others feel better. He belonged to the small cadre of physicians who truly believed this.

Dr. Richard Michael Swept had been in practice only a few years. Following his Neurology Residency at Vanderbilt, he was a research fellow for several years at Harvard, before joining the Department of Neurology at the Texas College of Medicine. He had not yet become too embittered by the patients who feigned illness in pursuit of narcotics, gave false addresses to avoid billings and, after realizing that he was a sensitive neurologist, complained constantly about their various discomforts. He was no magician and he was no hero. He did the best he could to make his patients well and was fairly certain he made ninety percent of them at least ninety percent better. The other ten percent drove him crazy.

Pushing the memories of the morning clinic behind, he quickly walked down the steps of the Brain Institute and headed toward McIver Auditorium. He felt the hot Houston sun on his face. It felt good. He smiled. The auditorium was one of the more recent additions to the famed Texas College of Medicine. The College was part of the Houston Medical Complex, employing over 80,000 people, laying claim to 14 different hospitals, all but one of which was highly specialized. Thus, the Houston Immunology Institute treated only victims of immunologic disturbances, primarily focusing on AIDS, the Ophthalmologic Institute treated only diseases of the eye, and the Cancer Institute treated only cancer victims. Swept's own affiliation was with the Brain Institute, which treated individuals with Central Nervous System and Peripheral Nervous System afflictions, such as epilepsy, multiple sclerosis, Alzheimer's Disease, pain, numbness, or other neuromuscular disease.

Swept had long ago recognized that doctors, whether patients realized it or not, are the only advocates a sick patient has. He believed that insurance companies wanted patients healthy or dead, and that the hospitals wanted them sick. If the doctor was not the patient's advocate, and sometimes he or she unfortunately was not, then the patient had real problems. Such was the politics of illness, and the finance of health care. The system was a mess.

Thinking about how the practice of medicine had changed over the past several years, Swept walked toward the lecture hall, tightening the grip on his briefcase, a gift several years ago from Louise, as he passed a group of antivivisectionists. He had seen them demonstrating and picketing for three weeks now, since their national meeting, held earlier in Houston, which had received considerable press coverage. Swept nodded to the small group as he passed them on his right, noting that most looked as if they were a product from the Sixties. With reserved, semifeline watchfulness, they returned a similar salutation. They knew he did research with animals and agreed with their main contention, that researchers

should treat animals well. The National Institutes of
Health enforced this treatment by requiring a mul-
titude of forms and evaluations regarding animal care
be filled out for each and every research grant application. Many scientific organizations, including the
Society for Neuroscience and the American Academy of Neurology, had conducted huge public cam-
paigns to convince the public (as well as the researchers) that animal experimentation should be sensitive, but sensible. Swept concurred. He was sensitive
as well as sensible, and he reminded himself, whenever he saw the protesters, that were it not for animal experimentation, human beings would not have
vaccines against smallpox, polio, and other maladies.
Without animal research, most of the research in
AIDS would grind to a halt. Animal research was
necessary for scientific progress, resulting in better-
ment of the human condition.

As Swept neared McIver's domain, he mentally
put the finishing touches on the second part of his
lecture to the Freshman Class at the Texas College
of Medicine. Today's lecture would continue to focus on memory. He had given Part I last week. The
lecture had gone well. Swept hoped that the students had completed their assigned reading and,
perhaps, might even have some intelligent questions,
although he doubted it. Swept held mixed feelings
about medical students, recognizing that some were
more motivated than others and, certainly, some
cared more than did others. He always had considerable difficulty interacting with the lazy ones.

Last year, the medical students gave Swept the
Golden Apple Award. This meant that they thought

he was the best lecturer in the entire medical school. The award transiently impressed his surprised Chairman, Dr. Harold Ranger, but caused petty jealousy among Swept's colleagues. Unfortunately, Swept knew the award held minimal power before the Faculty Promotions Committee, which mainly counted the number of publications and amount of research dollars, especially from the National Institutes of Health, a faculty member brought to the medical school. The Promotions Committee was tough. Tenure was a premium at the Texas College of Medicine.

Swept climbed the hot, white, pseudo-marble stairs and entered through the huge doorway, realizing he was perspiring. Was it the sun, the memories of his own training, the fact that he was about to spend an hour lecturing on memory, knowing that many of the students had crammed data for exams, but truly did not care about the essence of the knowledge he would try to convey? Or, was it that he later had to return to the office and tackle clusters of phone calls, complaints from attorneys representing worker compensation claims, and patients' families blaming him for their 92 year-old grandmother's confusion? These thoughts flickered through the physician-scientist's mind as he stepped into the new auditorium.

It was one o'clock. Most of the students were hanging around the hallway outside the bottom of the huge classroom. Swept descended the steps, entering the lecture hall from the rear, and shut the mahogany doors behind him. After reaching the bottom of the steps, he closed the large green doors at the base of the amphitheater, while the final cluster of students streamed in. Picking up the microphone atop the clear plastic podium sporting the Texas College of Medicine logo (Care, Integrity, Science), Swept inhaled in a relaxed style and looked around the room. He eyed the 135 young men and women, ages 21 to 33, most of them recently out of college, some longer, and some trying to redo high school adolescence and impress others with their being physicians. Hopefully, they were interested in science or interested in knowledge and, God willing, interested in helping fellow humans. However, he knew most would opt for soft living, settling in some fancy suburb, ensconced in their own view of life, the way the country should run, and money. Swept knew that few anticipated the grief that structured health care organizations, PPOs, HMOs, or indemnity insurance companies, would dump on them.

"All right class, let's get started. Last week, we discussed some of the basics of memory. Again, there are three types of memory: Immediate, Short-Term, and Long-Term. Each represents a different anatomic system within the brain, each system is in harmony with the other. Are there any questions about this before we go on?"

A young cherubic-like woman, her black hair tightly pulled back, wearing a bright yellow sweater, raised her hand. Swept smiled and beckoned her question.

"Dr. Swept, how discreet are these memory systems? Are they truly separate, as you describe, or do they, on some level, interact with other parts of the brain? I mean, I would think that memory for the way something looks, like a flower, could also be tied into what that flower is, where it grows, or other things like that? Do you know what I mean?"

At one time in his life, back at Harvard, Swept would have ridiculed her poor grammar and lack of precise language. He had truly softened. "All memory systems within the brain interact with each other, on an anatomic, electrical, as well as neuro-chemical level. Everything in the brain relates to everything. That's because everything we do is a part of a brain function. Being in love, being in hate, wanting something, not wanting something, petting your dog in the morning, in the afternoon, everything is a brain function. Everything is done by the brain and everything within the brain relates, directly or indirectly, to all parts of the brain."

Swept continued, the class listening intensely. "When we speak of a particular memory system, that memory system interacts very strongly with all memory systems within the brain. So, if I look at a flower, say an orchid, and, for whatever reason, want to remember it, I might recall that orchids are highly specialized for insect pollination, that only one of the petals secretes a nectar, or that a particular orchid is the Minnesota State Flower. These points could be tied in to the knowledge that orchids grow in rich moist soil, or that their colors can vary. Or, if I'm less informed, I might only remember the orchid I gave to Patti at the Junior Prom." The class chuckled. "Again, all memory systems within the brain are interrelated."

A few students continued to laugh. The young woman coyly smiled. Swept moved on, acknowledging another outstretched hand.

"Dr. Swept, how do we test these memory systems? Do you test Immediate Memory by asking patients to repeat a string of digits? That's what I read. As I understand it, you test Short Term Memory by giving the patient three or four objects to remember for at least 15 minutes, and then quiz him. And then, you ask people where they grew up and stuff like that for Long Term Memory. Is that right?"

Swept felt inner disgust. The kid was surely a brown-noser who liked to hear himself talk. Swept could only wonder what this guy had been like in college, as a pre-med.

"Bob Dylan once said that the only answer to a truthful question is that question itself. Like, 'What is life?' Well, 'What *is* life?' That's the answer to that question. Now you, you answered your own question. Dylan would have been proud – sort of."

Swept gave an exasperated breath and more than a few students snickered, nodding their heads. Swept, possibly misanthropic, seemed on target. He went on, "But, you're right."

Since there were no more questions, and because he knew the material well enough not to need notes, the young neurologist abandoned the podium and, holding the microphone, paced before the class, the synthetic whiteboard behind him. "Let's talk more about memory. Again, Immediate Memory refers to the ability to recall immediately that which has just transpired. It depends upon input from a reticular system in the lower part of the brain, called the brainstem, and the integrity of at least one of the two hemispheres within the brain, lying above the brainstem. If someone attempts to learn something, that data enters the brainstem and then travels upward to the part of the brain known as the hippocampus, which is involved in Short Term Memory. There is a hippocampus within each hemisphere. From the hippocampus, the information enters the electrical Circuit of Papez."

A tired-faced jock-looking student, chewing gum, raised his hand. "What happens if somebody has disease in those areas? Would they lose just those memory functions, or do they lose more?"

"Actually, I was about to tell you. If someone suffered hippocampus disease in 1954, he could not learn anything after that year. He would not learn the new presidents, nor would he learn that his Uncle George died in 1956. If you tell him that Uncle George died, even if you tell him daily, he can not *learn* that his Uncle expired and, therefore, may break down emotionally each and every time you tell him. He can't remember when he mowed the grass, and may set out to mow it only one day after he already mowed it. He knows how to mow, he just can't remember when he did so."

"As you might guess, his memory would be so impaired that he would have difficulty functioning in society. Certainly, he would have difficulty holding a job. He could never remember what he did, what he didn't do, and would not be able to learn any changes from his pre-disease job routine, whatever that was."

The student, inquisitive for a jock, persisted. "Would that patient be considered demented, like an Alzheimer's patient?"

"No. The patient we're discussing would be able to interpret a proverb and, in that setting, have good reasoning power, unlike an Alzheimer's patient. Alzheimer's patients have difficulty interpreting proverbs. Their cognitive reasoning is poor. Yet, because our patient can't learn, he would not know the year or the month, even though his reasoning was normal. Because of his inability to learn, he would appear demented, because he wouldn't know the date or where he was. He would learn poorly but, unlike demented patients, he could reason well. All demented patients, by definition, have compromise in their reasoning power."

"This might be an appropriate time to comment on Alzheimer's Disease. An Alzheimer's Disease patient does not learn well and does not reason well. Both cognitive faculties are compromised. Further, unlike our patient, Alzheimer's patients often become depressed, making their cognitive difficulties even worse. It is a truly horrible illness, devastating for the patient, but even more devastating for the family. The patients don't know they're demented. Usually, they deny it. The families have to live with a demented loved one and the problems become gigantic, often unbearable."

"Alzheimer's is ten times more prevalent now than it was one hundred years ago, because of the fact that people live longer. Also, our diagnostic tests are better. Victims of Alzheimer's, as well as the other dementias, confront staggering health care costs, insufficient health care services, and health professionals who, more often than not, lack appropriate training to help meet the patients' needs and those of their families."

"The national medical bill for dementia is over 50 billion dollars a year. Patients and their families pay at least forty of that fifty billion. It's a major problem, on a financial level, socio-economic level, and just about any level you can contemplate."

"My own laboratory has a special interest in dementia. And, despite the antivivisectionists outside, we focus primarily on animal research." A few students stirred. Swept detected a hint of disgust in some, while others appeared inquisitive. More hands shot up, stretching for attention.

Swept was amazed at how young they all looked. At 37, out of medical school 12 years, Swept vividly remembered certain romantic crushes he had weathered in medical school. Being thankful that, for the most part, he did not fancy younger co-eds but truly liked women in their 30's, he briefly thought about his current girlfriend, a 33 year-old plastic surgeon who would later join him for dinner. Right now, he was the academician. This was the Neuroscience Course. It was an honor to be chosen to participate in the first lecture series and, despite the shift of the topic more toward Alzheimer's, the neuroscience basis of memory was his focus.

"It may be, that early in this new millenium, we can offer human beings a chemical to help them learn better. Our laboratory is trying to develop such an agent. Hopefully, this compound will enable a patient to remember whatever transpires over a 15 minute time period following its administration. We've already administered our compound to rats. When a rat is injected with the chemical, then placed in a maze and manually shown passage from one end of the maze to the other, the animal pursues that route every time it is placed inside the maze box. The rat will go through this regardless of whether it believes food is at the other end. The rat has *learned*, from a brain chemical standpoint, to pursue this route each time it is in the box. We have run a fairly large number of rats, the mazes are moderately complicated, and the chemical seems to work. Soon, we should be almost one hundred percent certain."

As the lecture hour neared its end, Swept quickened his pace and started simplifying the topic. "One doesn't initially want to eat with utensils, wear clothes, or brush one's teeth. We *learn* these things. We learn that certain behaviors are appropriate and that certain behaviors are not. When we learn, there are concurrent electrical and chemical changes in our brains. Nothing involving the brain is simple. But it is these concepts that I want you to keep in the back of your minds as you attend more lectures in this course, and we cover more details about neurochemistry and neurophysiology. I am going to lecture to you periodically during this semester, just to keep you guys honest. We all have a lot of work in front of us."

Swept turned to erase the whiteboard, wondering what happened to old-fashioned erasers, slate boards, and plain white chalk. He intensely disliked the colored highlighters, always going dry, and whomever the previous lecturer was who put the colored caps on the wrong vials.

The lecture was over. Turning to the class, he lay down the microphone, as exiting students thrust open the lower green and the upper rear mahogany doors, arranging notes as they headed toward the anatomy laboratory located at the other side of the Medical Complex. Swept noticed a good-looking brunette student leaving, the jock not far behind, gum and all. Since the next class didn't begin for ten minutes, a few students with questions trickled down the stairs.

Among them, a beautiful woman of Asian descent approached Swept, holding a diagram of the brain's reticular activating system in her right hand. "Where exactly in the reticular system does memory data travel?" she softly asked. Swept, pleased with himself and with her, identified the location of the nucleus magnocellularis. "It's here that . . ." Swept looked up, seeing the almost wry smile of his girlfriend, who evidently had entered from the back and just descended the stairs. After acknowledging Regina Bruxton's presence with a smile and nod, he returned to the student, showing her the relevant anatomy. Then, after answering the few remaining students' questions, he turned toward Regina, raising his right eyebrow and smiling his usual smile.

Dr. Regina Bruxton, a plastic surgeon at the Institute for Reconstructive Surgery, had an incredibly well proportioned body, which she carried with femininity and style. Her head seemed delicately balanced on a neck that, had it been more thin, would have been too thin. As it was, it was perfect. Her skin was supple, creamy in appearance, and her lips, while somewhat crooked, were more than inviting. Swept knew that those lips, whether Regina was awake or sleeping, were always slightly parted, and never closed. Her brown eyes coordinated their beauty with Regina's beautiful, natural dark chocolate hair. Her perfume, specially prepared at Jean-Michel's of Paris, added a special meaning to her poise and posture. She held a stunning, inviting look. However, as beautiful as Dr. Regina Bruxton was, and as much as she cared for Swept, something kept her from getting too close. Swept had yet to discover what it was. Until he did, he could not love her.

The entire hospital ogled over Dr. Bruxton, but Swept was the only man with whom she would sleep. Swept, also an object of social discussion, until recently had held no such rules or bounds.

The Medical Complex nurses had mocked his rogue stature at their last Christmas party, in a play called "Sweptomania," that asked how many Sweptophiles had succumbed to his manly charms. Swept soon found himself simultaneously lauded and derided by several women. He was not pleased. Swept wanted the Medical Complex to view him as a physician-scientist, not a bag of hormones. Regina, however, had taken it all in good stride. They had only dated for the past eleven months, so what he had done prior to his seeing her was his business. She had never insisted on fidelity, recognizing that she, herself, had sometimes strayed, more often than she cared to recall. However, Swept was the only man she was now seeing. She had gone out with no one else since entering their relationship. Besides, she was proud that such a sexual man was interested in her.

With a twinkle in her voice, Regina reached for Swept's right arm after the last student departed. "One of my patients just died from pulmonary embolism. I was going to do extensive cosmetic surgery on that patient. Now, I'm out five thousand bucks but free for an afternoon." Regina frequently used the term, "bucks" when talking to Swept, knowing that such a calloused orientation disturbed him. In ways, she flaunted her desire for money, almost seeking his disapproval.

At one time, Regina Bruxton had done excellent research in fibroblasts and wound healing, investigating the relationship between estrogen and healing of surgical incisions, but now she focused more on the pecuniary realm of medicine. Her never-ending concern regarding the financial base of her medical practice bothered Swept a great deal.

"Regina, you don't have to taunt me. You don't care that much about the money. Besides, a patient died! And, don't tell me that doesn't bother you. What are you doing? Trying to start an argument?"

"Don't lecture me," her grip on his arm lessening. "And, whatever you do, don't get on me about my practice. Or, why I don't do research. I just came here to talk to you, sort of."

Regina Bruxton smiled, gently twisting his left arm, cocking her neck sideways, and looked directly at Swept, her lips slightly parted, and continued. "What do you say we have afternoon delight at your house, Dr. Swept?" The popular female physician reached under his white lab coat and gently scratched his arm, just above the wrist.

Swept decided against an argument. He would not discuss Regina's avoiding the realm of physician-scientist for the penumbra of money. He had long queried whether her subtle cynicism emanated from her earlier affair with a 58 year-old University of Oklahoma Nobel Laureate, before she met Swept. Swept also wondered whether, deep within, some secret reason kept this beautiful and intelligent woman from love. She had never married but, then again, neither had he.

"Sounds great. Are you woman enough for day-time loving?" he asked, raising his left arm and gently circling her neck.

"I'm certainly woman enough for you," as she smiled into his face and, looking around to be certain no one was watching, gently kissed him on the cheek.

The twosome walked away from the lecture room, went down the hallway, and soon viewed the clear but humid day through the glass doors of the building. Outside, they passed some students whom Swept recognized from his lecture. The students smiled at him, as he surprisingly heard them discuss memory systems with great earnest. They were late for their anatomy class, if they were going at all.

As the two neared the Brain Institute, they passed the antivivisectionists, actively shaking their placards. "What do you think of those people?" asked Regina.

"You know, as we've discussed, they have some good points, some bad. A few are fanatics, who want to stop all animal research. Animal research is important for human progress, but it should be done with sensitivity and care. The standard of care for animals in the labs at the College is very high."

"Would you let someone experiment on Limbic?"

"No, but that doesn't count. Limbic's a pet." Limbic, Swept's beloved Lhasa apso, was almost a close friend. "I wouldn't be happy with that, but that's not a fair question. I have a relationship with Limbic, and he does with me. I wouldn't take any pets from owners and experiment on them. The dogs used in the College are strays. Besides, most animal work is done on rats or mice."

"Well, animals are animals. I sure hope Limbic doesn't stray without his dog tag. Otherwise, won't you be surprised if he winds up in a vaccine!"

"Regina, we're on our way to make love, not to discuss animal research. Okay?"

"I'm not trying to hassle you, I'm just trying to understand those people," pointing to the protestors, still waving their signs."

"Fair enough."

The two physicians walked, now somewhat in silence, to Swept's car, parked in the underground garage below the Brain Institute. They descended the stairs, carefully holding the rail so as not to fall from the narrow steps. The couple then entered Swept's new dark green 456 GTA Ferrari, a modern mechanical miracle, boasting a 12 cylinder 436 horsepower engine that went zero to sixty in under 5.0 seconds. Despite being exceedingly fast and powerful, the car held a sedate, understated appearance, and was so rare that only Ferrari afficionados could readily identify the automobile. Everyone queried how a dedicated physician-scientist could afford such a car.

Swept and Regina exited the underground Brain Institute parking lot, leaving behind a stubble-faced parking attendant, who made a phone call. Had the two doctors been able to hear him inside his glass-encased cubicle, they would have heard a seemingly innocuous report. "This is Tom. Dr. Swept and that girlfriend of his are leaving."

*   *   *

As the lovers approached Swept's home, Swept interrupted Regina's reverie. "I don't want to start an argument, but do you bring up money in order to hold your distance?"

"What distance? Look, I can bring up whatever I choose. What I choose now is to go to your house and make love. Nothing more, nothing less. Okay?"

"Fair enough, but it sure seems you go out of your way to keep me away." At that moment, they arrived at Swept's home and within a few seconds, were inside the small brick house. Limbic, always loyal, circled the pair, wagging his tail, lying on his back, waiting for tummy scratches, now and then dribbling urine from his excitement.

"Limbic's a great dog, but he sure is dirty," Regina quipped. Limbic seemed to sense her criticism, sneezed with a snort, and then went off to the kitchen to scratch himself.

"Dirt? Well, Limbic's got some. He's sort of a walking dust mop, maybe because the way his hair is. It attracts dirt. But," nestling up to her, "Dear lady, I do think that parts of you have touched parts of me that, I am certain, carry more germs per the medical books than my little dog. Besides, don't change the subject."

"Dick, let's not argue. Loads of parts of me feel attraction to loads of parts of you." Her eye then caught a copy of *Penthouse* lying on the couch in the sunroom. "Are you still reading this garbage? What's wrong with you?"

"Nothing's wrong with me. I like the *Forum* section. I like the . . . Look, Regina, you're not happy with Limbic, not happy with my attitude, you're getting on me regarding antivivisectionists, and. . . . this

just isn't the way to begin our afternoon. I don't want
to argue either. I'm going to put on my shorts, jog a
few miles, come back, and then if you want to roll
around, great. Otherwise, let's just go back to work.
Okay? In the meantime, you and Limbic can discuss
his germs."

Before Regina could respond, Swept was down
the hall and in his bedroom, where he donned blue
Gore-Tex running shorts, while Regina stood, looking at him, shaking her head. With a caustic groan,
she put down *Penthouse,* which she was still carrying,
and picked up a nearby copy of *Harper's.* "Fair
enough, Dick. I guess I'm just tired. Besides, it's no
fun when your patient dies from an embolus."

Swept made no comment and left for his jog,
wearing his Walkman, playing a Bob Dylan tape. Over
and over he thought to himself, as his Nikes effort-
lessly paced the dirt track surrounding the nearby
City University, that he wanted to make his relationship with Regina work. Somehow, for some reason,
they couldn't mesh. It seemed as though there was
something, almost touchable, that kept the two apart.
He wondered whether Regina really was as finan-
cially motivated as she made herself appear. Certainly,
she didn't spend much money on personal items,
except that great perfume. Regina dressed well but
never donned designer clothes, and owned little jew-
elry. Perhaps, it was his hang-up. And, now, she was
complaining about animal research. Or was he making an issue where none existed? Swept was amazed
that such a relationship, which certainly wasn't relaxed or *laissez-faire,* had such great sex.

While Swept was jogging, mentally dissecting his relationship with Regina, the plastic surgeon was reading *Harper's*, looking at wriggling Limbic begging for another scratch on his abdomen. She glanced around the den, noticing Swept's trophy collection containing awards for football and wrestling prowess in high school and college, as well as pictures of the beloved Fatboy Harley motorcycle he recently sold, and felt sad that she had no children.

Swept finished his three-mile jog in less than 24 minutes and returned to his home. Regina welcomed him, throwing her arms around his sweaty neck, and gave him a big hug. "Look, Dick, it's nice to be with you. I guess I have a lot on my mind. Shower, then let's go back to the hospital. We'll see each other tonight, okay? Remember, I am supposed to join you for dinner."

"Whatever you like." Swept kissed her, then showered, dressed, and went into the sunroom, where Limbic and Regina, still with *Harper's*, were patiently waiting. "At least I feel refreshed. Let's go."

After saying goodbye to Limbic, Swept escorted Regina to the Ferrari and in a few minutes the two were in the parking lot under the Brain Institute. As he and Regina walked toward the elevator, again the stubble-faced man picked up the phone.

*   *   *

Tom, the attendant, had never understood why Valerie VanDance, the Neurology Chairman's nurse, wanted to know when certain physicians departed and returned from the parking lot. She had told him the Chairman needed to know where these physicians were, especially those important to the well-being of the Department. This never made much sense to him, since physicians had beepers and could be paged. Regardless, Valerie's numerous gifts, including cash, assuaged any worry he had about what he was doing. Besides, what was the harm? And, on the few occasions when he had spoken in person to the good-looking five-foot six-inch blonde, he had felt a tingle.

Following Tom's call, Valerie VanDance sent a message of her own. This was on the so-called Chairman's line, accessible only from the telephone on her desk. The line was allegedly only for patient calls, but Valerie had never heeded that rule. She closed her door, attached a laptop to the telephone line, and e-mailed a coded sequence to her superior in Langley, Virginia.

Chapter Two

THE LONE RANGER

SWEPT, AN HOUR late as he entered his office, reminded himself he was behind in his application for another RO-3 Grant, as well as the RO-1 Grant, both through the National Institutes of Health. The first was easier to obtain but offered little money; the second was more difficult but provided more revenue. He quickly thought about all the work he had to prepare for the NIH Visit, which would determine whether he would receive more funding. He had to meet with his research associates, especially his postdoctoral fellows, order more laboratory equipment, and discuss the Site Visit with his Chairman. He also remembered the Ferrari wasn't driving as efficiently as it should and his mechanic told him the problem was probably the fuel pump. And, of course, there were always the patients in the waiting room. A lot lay on his mind.

Swept called his secretary. Familiar with his patterns, it was not difficult for Tracy to deduce where
her boss had been. She told him that Dr. Ranger, his
Chairman, wanted to see him immediately. Swept
quickly checked his phone messages and then went
down the hall to Ranger's office.

"You're late again. You were supposed to be here
over half an hour ago." Ranger grabbed Swept's mid-
biceps, ushering him to a chair, smiling fatherly as
Swept sank into the deep low-slung chair that always
hurt his back.

Swept had known Ranger more than twelve years,
and greatly respected his scientific acumen and intelligence. He trained under Ranger when Swept was a
Fellow at Harvard. Even at that time, Ranger was intense, primarily interested in scientific research. He
had focused most of his energies on science, too often
overlooking the needs of his son and wife. After his
son, his only child, was killed by a drunk driver and his
wife later committed suicide when she faced her world
alone, her husband ensconced in his scientific laboratory, Ranger had become a near-recluse, focusing even
more of his energies on research, only occasionally seeing patients. Ranger was an expert in cytochrome oxi-
dase metabolism, investigating how the mitochondria
that live within our cells produce energy in normal and
diseased brain tissue. The neurology residents often
poked fun at him, making giddy-up sounds with their
hands slapping at their knees, referring to him as the
Lone Ranger.

Ranger held guarded suspicion for memory research but, for some reason, early on had taken a

liking to the young neurologist. Ranger was especially pleased when Swept decided to join him when
he left the ivy of Boston for the Astrodome and tacos
of Houston, a city where many of Swept's former
Harvard colleagues joked that Houston women wore
their hair in beehives.

Ranger, fifty-four years old, stood five feet, seven
inches, and felt an inner discomfort that Swept was
almost five inches taller. Ranger's thinning gray hair
framed a square face with huge sunken eyes that
always seemed to be busy digesting the surrounding
world and doing a lot of thinking. Too vain to wear
glasses, with a severe astigmatism that thwarted contacts, he spent most of life squinting, wreaking havoc
on the skin around his eyes, etching permanent
crow's feet. His nose had been broken several times
and his thin-lipped crooked smile was seldom lenient
and most uninviting.

Swept wondered whether his Chairman's entire wardrobe came from some New England clothing catalogue. Ranger wore loose-fitting khaki
trousers that always needed pressing, flannel shirts
inappropriate for the Houston climate, and solid
color ties, all draped over with a white coat that
was seldom laundered, as attested by numerous
coffee stains. No woman ever looked at Harold
Ranger twice.

Dick Swept, in contrast, had a poised, masculine
look that attracted most women he met. His firm,
measured way of speaking, near-boyish smile, and
sharp brown eyes could pierce a woman's soul in less
time than it took a neuron in the brain to send a

signal to the foot. Many a lover had caressed his rich brown hair and held tight his muscular frame.

Swept had long felt at ease in his Dunhill garb, which was expensive but wore well. As a throwback to his Harvard days, his tie always had a slash of crimson and, being somewhat sentimental, he never left home without the old LeCoultre watch his mother gave him when he graduated college.

Ranger was furious.

"We have an NIH Site Visit in a few weeks. Are you prepared to discuss your protein work in memory? Funds are tight. I don't need to tell you, you're going to have major difficulty if you don't get more NIH support. Last time, you barely got it, but then it wasn't as important. This time it is. The oil companies no longer provide strong funding because business fluctuates too much for them. The Texas Legislature informed us that the twenty-seven million dollars they give our school each year will be cut to nineteen, because they're cutting back on the number of medical students in this State. Can't say I blame them. And, managed health care is eating us up alive. We just don't have the money. You have to get more NIH funds. Otherwise, you have to see more patients."

Swept, staring at the new mobile hanging over the desk, looked into his Chairman's eyes. Slowly nodding, he indicated his understanding all too well. Protruding his jaw, slightly to the right, he raised his right eyebrow and softly said, "Fair enough."

"That's right. In order to support the lab, you see more patients." Swept cringed. More dizzies, more backaches, more grief. He was continually amazed that, although he wanted to help patients and treat disease, somehow he had difficulty interacting with many patients, especially those complaining of headaches and dizziness. If they did well, they didn't harass him. However, many were depressed, feigned illness for disability benefits, or, simply put, weren't sick. They called incessantly, even bothering him at home, almost wearing him down. Unlike most of his colleagues, he wasn't immune to this. Perhaps it was because he was relatively young, or too sensitive. He believed that many physicians didn't care whether their patients did well or not. They did their best to help them – if the patients did well, fine. If not, most held the attitude that the patient couldn't be helped. So be it.

Swept was different. Failure to make a patient better was taken personally, compounding the frustration of the incessant phone calls. Most did well. But the ten percent who did not seemed to occupy ninety percent of his time, and he just did not like interacting with them.

Ranger looked at Swept, still staring at the Chairman's mobile. "Are you with me?"

Swept's eyes narrowed, and he stared into Ranger's face, seeing what he well knew to be strong cynicism blended with compassion. Turning, he quasi-philosophically sensed the mobile's inanimate presence, hanging above, cutting through space. Inhaling deeply, again arching his right eyebrow, his shoe toyed with a piece of lint on the rug.

"I'll take care of it, Dr. Ranger. We'll get the grant.
I have an outline and it's almost complete. Also, I
have preliminary results that might impress the Site
Visit team with clinical consequences but, for whatever reason, you never want to pursue their clinical
consequence."

Ranger began to move from his sitting position,
placed his hands on both legs, and found himself
canceling an exasperated sigh when Swept continued. "The data's there. The outline's there. All I have
to do is dictate the report. I'll take the dictation to
Word Processing. If you give your approval, they'll
type it in two days. Later, I'll make some changes
after we have more data. Okay?"

As he prepared to leave his Chairman's office,
half-way to the door, Swept turned and chided, "Just
remember, for a guy who gets his work done, who's
received grant funding in the past, and has known
you a long time, I still don't have tenure."

That was it! Ranger approached Swept, stiffened
his posture and raised flaring fingers that reminded
Swept of paws with tension-bitten nails. "Don't bring
up tenure until you not only get this grant, but increase your basic science productivity. Too many of
your papers are clinical. The College isn't interested
in that. I'm not interested in that. And, the NIH isn't
interested!"

Swept retorted firmly. "Clinical issues *are* the major issues. When people have Alzheimer's Disease,
which attacks millions, destroys memory and puts
patients in nursing homes because they don't know

where they live, let alone who they are or how to open a door, those people need help. I don't think I should spend as much time as I do in the laboratory, working with chemicals and animals. It takes years to get these experiments done, and they don't reveal as much about the human condition as we think. Animal models are only animal models. We need to work with humans, with people. Why can't we do my experiments in humans? My drug isn't that danger-ous. It's not that toxic. We can easily monitor the patients and detect side effects. Time and again, Human Experimentation Committees at other insti-tutions approve projects like mine. You won't let me go ahead because you don't think it's as prestigious to publish clinical work as it is to publish animal labo-ratory work. With all respect, you're more concerned with the prestige of an experiment than with what it does for patients. Besides, we both know you don't like the whole field of memory research anyway."

Ranger fisted his hands, the whites of the knuck-les proclaiming their owner's dismay. Swept, strangely, found himself staring at the teeth-torn cuticles. Bristling, Harold Ranger bellowed, "Are you done lecturing me, Dr. Swept? I don't support your doing clinical research but that has nothing to do with prestige. I don't support it because clinical re-search doesn't get NIH grant funding. Private, non-government granting agencies dealing with memory research don't support expensive clinical projects. If you don't get grant funding you don't have a labo-ratory. At all! Then, you can't do anything! Nothing! If you'd do what I tell you, and worked for four or five years with your blasted chemical and animal models, and quit screwing around with half the secretaries and nurses, you might get more done, have a larger lab, and then be able to address these problems in patients!"

Swept stiffened at Ranger mentioning his sex life. Swept's pleasant demeanor had made him popular, too popular, with many women in the Medical Complex. Ranger knew it but seldom mentioned Swept's personal life.

The Chairman calmed himself and placed his arm around Swept's shoulders. "I'm not trying to hassle you. I'm just giving you facts. Funds are tight. Doctors are leaving academic medicine by the droves. You're a good doctor, a good clinician, and a good scientist. But, you are a pain in the ass. Work hard in the lab, get funding, build your lab, and then concern yourself with clinical projects. You'll be more productive if you stick to basic science projects. It's too hard to tell what goes on with human beings in experimental situations. We control more variables in animals because we can operate on their brains and do things we can't do to people."

Ranger continued. "A clinical study that fails to prove something isn't published. Journals don't publish negative results. Should you investigate animals and, even if you don't find anything and your hypothesis is a bust, you can still publish what the drug did or didn't do to an animal's brain, or some other organ, examined under the microscope. Every drug alters something, somewhere. You can find that in animals, but in humans you can only go so far. Animal research is always publishable. Clinical work isn't."

Politely but intently releasing himself from the
Chairman's grip, Swept replied, "I don't always like
working with animals. I'm not happy lopping off part
of a rat's brain and I don't like operating on mon-
keys. I relate to primates, all of them. Sure, I wouldn't
publish as much investigating humans, but I'll tell
you one thing – I would help more people. And, it
would be more fun. Besides, why can't I do both,
experiment in animals and in humans? Or, at least
present my ideas to the Human Experimentation
Committee and let them decide. If you gave permission, I could ask them what they think. Let them
decide whether I should experiment in humans. The
decision would be theirs. Why not let me try? I can't
go before them without your approval, since you're
the Chairman. Give me your approval and let them
decide whether I can work with humans."

Swept continued, wondering if he now held his
Chairman's attention. "I don't publish simply to publish. I am interested in knowledge, even if it sounds
corny. I've been working on a new amino acid sequence that, based upon the goldfish and bird work,
seems to consolidate memory patterns. I could be
on to a really important finding. It's my belief we can
administer this to people without much harm
and. . . ."

Ranger looked at his shoes, a predictable response when he had lost interest in a conversation,
signalling that his attention had flown out the window. Swept paid no heed and persevered. "I think
we could take Alzheimer's and other demented patients and reinstitute memory stores by injecting this
protein into their carotid artery. The artery would

carry the substance directly into the brain, entering the hippocampus and other portions of their temporal lobe. I think they'll remember anything we repeatedly tell them over a short period of time, say fifteen minutes. We could remind them of their birth date, the layout of their home, all sorts of things. We could expose them to various inputs that would then be structurally integrated into their brain. Let me try it. The Experimentation Committee might let me do it. If there are side effects, we'll stop it. What do these patients have to lose?"

Ranger angrily responded. "Look, I don't need a dissertation on ethics. Further, the last thing in the world I want to hear about are the rights of animals. If we didn't experiment on animals, we wouldn't have vaccines, for crying out loud. Why don't you join those damn antivivisectionists out there, if you're so pro-animal? Idiots! We wouldn't make any progress at all if we didn't work with animals. Half those people out there are probably as pro-AIDS research as they are anti-animal research. Tell them, as if they would listen, there would be no meaningful AIDS research if we didn't experiment on animals. Anyway," tightening his hands, "That's another matter."

Ranger continued. "If you follow my advice and continue your work on animals, you'll really know what to do with patients. Besides, you'll publish more. Then, you might get tenure."

"Look, Dr. Ranger. The antivivisectionists do have some valid points . . ."

"You look, Dr. Swept. The antivisectionists are a pain in the ass, despite their temporary good behavior out there. Every place they go, they've demolished laboratories, ruined property, and set a lot of research years behind. Why they haven't done that in Houston is beyond me. As far as I'm concerned, they're a bunch of damn hippies transplanted from the Sixties into the new millennium, worried more about animals than people."

"That's just not fair . . ." arching his right eyebrow.

"I'm not in the mood to hear what you think is fair. If you like the antivivisectionists, hang out with them for all I care. As for me, I'm telling you to do research with animals. I won't allow you to work on humans. Period!"

Despite Ranger's return to staring at his shoes, Swept persisted. "Okay, forget the protestors. But I need to try the drug on humans. Many patients would volunteer for it. Why can't I have your support at least to bring this before the Human Experimentation Committee and let *them* decide how feasible my study is?"

The Chairman, now wide-eyed, looked at Swept. "I'm the Chairman and I'll decide what goes on in this Department. It's my Department, not yours. The College put me in charge, not you. You don't have, and won't have my support for a damn thing until the Site Visit is over and you tell me you have funding! A lot of it! Members of this Department need to have funding! Understand?"

Ranger, annoyed, continued, "Further, you don't like patients – at least on some level. They drive you crazy. They sure as hell make me crazy." Ranger shook his head, turning to his desk, and began busying himself with cluttered papers.

Swept, exasperated, retorted, "Terrific!" He left the office, looking over his shoulder, focusing on the hundreds of books the Chairman kept in a glass-door walnut bookcase, all pertaining to test tubes, petri dishes, and animals. None directly related to aches and pains of human suffering.

Over the bookcase, hung a picture of Ranger's son, killed at age fourteen by a drunk driver. When Ranger's only child died, eighteen years ago, he never displayed grief. Whenever a colleague or a member of his dwindling circle of friends offered words of compassion and sympathy, he politely thanked them, and stared. Death was and yet wasn't a big stick to the Chairman. It was simply a common denominator, having lost his father at age ten, a mother who succumbed to diabetes, and a wife who committed suicide shortly after their son died. No, death was nothing. Just something that pervaded life.

Except, now and then, for whatever reason, he would still dream his dream, the same one he had had for years, although currently less frequent, now occurring only monthly as opposed to every three or four days, as when he was a child. The dream was always the same, always clear and chillingly real. A man in a big black coat walked among many people, all just milling around, while the man took names, writing them down, never looking up.

Ranger sat in his chair, trying to gather interest in the hospital and medical school forms that lay atop his desk, and looked down at his shoes.

As Swept departed the Chairman's corner office, he passed Valerie VanDance. Almost petite, with fierce blue eyes framed by a Midwestern-styled face and blonde hair, her left cheek scar suggested some kind of lost innocence. Valerie's poised demeanor, elegant carriage, and concern for patients contrasted markedly with that of her boss.

Swept and Valerie had occasionally lunched together, with the usual small talk. Nothing serious. Their conversation usually focused on patients, some aspects of Swept's science, and a little load of hospital gossip.

Swept had always respected Valerie's competence. She said her coquettish hello and then disappeared into the file room, but not until she had eyed, unbeknown to him, a butt that she thought should model Wrangler jeans.

Tracy, trying to get through a heap of government forms for her boss, took in Swept silently, eyeing him from behind her desk, jealously wary of Valerie. Tracy had heard the bickering and knew that Ranger would soon exit his office, complaining for stronger coffee. That was always his pattern following an altercation with his favorite faculty member.

Swept was slightly ruffled – the usual after an argument with Ranger. He curtly said hello to Tracy, knowing she heard his argument with the Chairman, entered her office, grabbed his dictating recorder, stethoscope and reflex hammer, and proceeded to walk to the clinic, knowing he would shortly have to deal with the suffering of patients and the difficulties of treating the sick.

Swept, hurrying through the enclosed crosswalk, soon arrived at the Neurology Clinic, located in the adjacent building. Surprisingly, there were only few patients waiting for him. He thoroughly evaluated two new patients with migraines and one with epilepsy, and a few who came in for follow-up. He then poured himself a cup of coffee, which he always drank black, and walked toward the elevator, which took him down to the crosswalk. As he walked back, Swept smiled ironically at the similarity between the rats in the mazes in his experiments and his own shuttling back and forth through the glass-enclosed crosswalk.

Dr. Dick Swept then returned to his office in the Brain Institute.

*   *   *

The Brain Institute was mammoth. Swept had one of the larger offices. His desk faced a large window with a view overlooking a beautiful fountain and garden. To his left, on the wall, hung a street sign, shadow-boxed in green velvet, taken from his home after his parents had perished in an accident, something he never discussed. Swept knew that he and Ranger had both felt the taste of death. Unlike Ranger, Swept had no recurring dreams.

Swept's office was filled with memorabilia, ranging from plants that ex-lovers, all pre-Regina, had given him, a certificate from the Bob Bondurant School of High Performance Driving, two photos of his Harley Fatboy, and two medallions from the Culinary Institute of America for winning a cooking contest in New York for his Italian and Swiss meringue. Bob Dylan's astrological chart, given by a gypsy Swept had sort of dated, hung to the right. There were several texts on evolution, as well as books on right brain/left brain function. All of this was dwarfed by his vast number of books on memory. The physician-scientist had books on the anatomy of memory, physiology of memory, biochemistry of memory, problems pertaining to statistical evaluation of memory paradigms in research, and over fifty texts specifically on various aspects of Alzheimer's Disease.

Relaxing in his comfortable chair, a relic from halcyon days in Boston, Swept viewed his antique roll-top desk with a sense of low-tech pleasure. Earlier, Tracy had placed the *New York Times* on his chair, per her routine. Were it to be placed on the desk, it might become lost in the myriad of forms, papers, and correspondence. An article about an outbreak of meningitis in Nepal was on the front page, adjacent to an article on health care.

Swept had almost specialized in Infectious Disease. At one time, he thought it was the only area, aside from surgery, where a physician could actually cure people. Surgeons cut things out when tissue is diseased and medical specialists in infectious disease place people on antibiotics; both have potentials for cure. Other physicians essentially manage illness as best they can. Swept learned long ago, as a medical student, that one never cured hypertension, one only managed it. The same was true for emphysema, most orthopedic-type aches and pains, diabetes, and just about everything else.

Swept found the *Times* article interesting, reminding him of the intellectually stimulating infectious disease rotation that had almost usurped his entering Neurology. The report came from the Infectious Disease Hospital and Central Health Laboratory in Teku, Nepal:

> A recent outbreak of meningitis in the Himalaya has been reported. Over 90 Sherpas in a local village, several hundred miles from the capital, were killed by a bacteria, probably the strain *meningococcus*. The findings were typical of meningococcus meningitis and travelers have been advised to stay away from particular sectors in the Himalaya.
>
> It is believed that the outbreak relates to the same bacteria strain that killed over 1000 people three weeks ago in Kathmandu. . . .

Swept sighed, sipping his coffee. He wondered why meningococcus meningitis would strike only one village in the Himalaya, and not more. It didn't make sense. Why would meningitis kill over 1000 people in the capital, Kathmandu, and then attack some village hundreds of miles away, and not kill anyone in the villages between?

These thoughts were interrupted when Janos Szeppek entered his office.

"Dr. Swept. It's working. The experiment – it's working! After we altered the esterase fraction, Compound 1040 works unbelievably well, even in the most complicated maze. The rats learn everything we tell them. It's fantastic, absolutely fantastic!"

Swept put the *Times* down and looked at his Hungarian postdoctoral fellow. Szeppek was average height, twenty-five years old, and round-shouldered with hair too short in front, and too long in the back. Szeppek had worked with Swept for eighteen months, having joined the laboratory with sterling recommendations. Swept was pleased, if not slightly surprised, that he had found an individual with such excellent grades and recommendations. Good postdoctorate fellows were hard to find. Certainly, elsewhere in America, there were scientists more prominent than Dick Swept, although within the realm of innovative memory research, consisting of only a small coterie of scientists, Swept knew he held his own. He liked to think that was why Szeppek sought him out.

Janos Szeppek had earlier written Swept, requesting a postdoctorate fellowship. His background, especially training in neuroscience, was exceptionally strong and included chromatographic fractionation, a skill Swept needed in his laboratory. Further, Szeppek was well disciplined in parametric and non-parametric statistics. Given that Szeppek had Hungarian financial support, certainly hard to come by in any academic system, Swept readily welcomed him.

Swept did not have to provide any salary from his own resources, only obtain some additional resources from his Chairman. Ranger was more than happy to comply, being grateful someone would assist Swept with his animal research, at little cost to his Department. This could lead to increased publications, more research, NIH support, all of which would help Swept and certainly do nothing but help Ranger's position in the medical school.

Szeppek continued. "Look, as we know, it takes a rat four to five minutes to figure out how to get from one end of a complex maze to the other, where the food is."

Swept interrupted, asking how many rats they had formally studied.

"We've studied fifteen rats. We place each one in the maze, one at a time, two minutes after it receives injection of Compound 1040. Then, we manually maneuver each rat through the maze, giving it food at the end. This takes about fifteen seconds. We then wait four minutes. After only one of these maneuvered trials, when that rat is placed in the maze again, it immediately takes the same route, even if we stop offering the food. One week later, rats that received the chemical still go through that pattern, even though there's no food. When rats receive a saline placebo, which has no chemical activity, they have considerable problems learning the maze and, when they finally do learn it, they stop attempting to travel through it once they learn there is no longer any food at the end."

Placing the data, including maze diagrams and statistical equations, in front of Swept, the postdoctorate student continued. "If we never offer the rats food at the end of the maze, but give them 1040 before we manually push them through it, they still learn the maze every time and go through it time and again – nothing stops them. All they want to do is go through the maze, and they do it correctly."

Swept, never excited about data he had not personally dissected, stared at the young scientist. "Good, Janos. But this phase of the project still isn't done. We have to autopsy the rats, make certain there are no damaging side effects from the medication and, although we haven't found indication of this in blood analyses, we need to be positive the internal organs aren't damaged, especially the brain, heart, kidneys, and liver. Also, don't forget to follow the National Institutes of Health protocol in killing the animals."

Swept had often stressed to Szeppek the importance of experimenting appropriately with animals. Szeppek had no difficulty accepting humane protocols for animal research, and often wondered why none existed in his own country.

"There's another thing we have to do. Check, again, the part of the experiment, where we put them through the maze without giving them any food or reward, and just administer the chemical compound. That way, we can be certain whether the Compound, followed by maneuvering them through the maze, is enough by itself to teach them the maze, or whether they need something in addition, such as the reward of food in the first trial. If we ever administer this Compound to human beings, we need to know whether we can give them only the chemical and then teach them something, say how to get around in the house, or whether they need some type of associated reward in the beginning. We must know whether the Compound by itself is sufficient. Do you have the rats' learning curve with you?"

Pleased he had everything with him, Szeppek looked at Swept, presenting more graphs and charts. "I agree. For all we know, the chemicals in the food could even interact with Compound 1040. We have to be certain that the chemical does what we think it does, without anything else interacting with it."

"Janos, the probabilities are that the food does nothing. It takes a while before food is absorbed and metabolized. Besides, all we're rewarding the animal with is a little sugar and protein, but we must be certain. Run ten more animals tomorrow, to be certain we have enough data by the time of the NIH Site Visit. Can we do it?"

"Sure. I'm really excited. I think we've discovered a chemical that affects memory. Once we get this published in the animal literature, do you think Dr. Ranger will support our going before the Human Experimentation Committee and working with humans?"

Swept had long been amazed at Szeppek's excellent grammar, figuring that his teachers in Budapest must have been more than demanding. Yet, grammar was not Szeppek's only talent. He was as bright as his grammar was good, energetic as well as intensive and clever. Swept nodded his head, deciding not to rehash his earlier conversation with the Chairman. He arranged the sheets of data, placed them on the left rear corner of his desk, and thanked the excited Szeppek, who assured his mentor he would talk to him later that day.

Swept, pleased, returned to the *Times.* The article on health care addressed the following:

> The Congressional Office of Technology Assessment (COTA) concluded that federal policies must emphasize research, training, and long-term-care services and financing. "The ultimate solution for the problem of dementia would be a 'technical fix,'" according to the report. The study noted that the national medical bill for dementia patients is over forty billion dollars a year, of which victims and their families personally pay all but 8.5 billion dollars. At least three million people suffer from dementia, a complex of symptoms linked to more than seventy physical disorders. Most victims are elderly and as the population of older Americans has grown, so has the incidence of dementia.
>
> The report goes on to state that the disease is ten times more prevalent now than at the beginning of the twentieth century. The number of people with severe dementia has grown by sixty percent over the past one hundred years. In the absence of a cure or a means of prevention, over forty-six million Americans are stricken with dementia.

Most of these patients have Alzheimer's Disease, which strips victims of their mental functions and ability to care for themselves, while leaving them in strong physical health. The long-term care system in the United States is disorganized, incomplete, and poorly adapted to the needs of people with dementia in their families. Care-giving falls disproportionately to women. The late onset of most dementing illnesses often means that a woman in her fifties or sixties is the primary care-giver.

Federal funding of biomedical research on dementia approximates eighty million dollars a year. Although this exceeds the four million dollars expended in 1976, it remains four to five times less per patient than funding for research in patients with cancer or heart disease.

COTA is a nonpartisan agency providing research and analysis for the United States Congress. The report was commissioned by several congressional committees.

Swept picked up his fountain pen and began writing the grants – the RO-3, which was simple and to the point, and the RO-1, which drove him bananas.

Chapter Three

WORLD HEALTH ORGANIZATION

ALEKSANDER KOSTOKOV LOOKED at his passport. Everything was in order, including his arrival into Kathmandu from Delhi, on a Royal Nepal Airline flight. He had been in the Nepalese capital several times, usually entering through Pokhara, sometimes taking a bus from Gorakhpur to the border. After arriving in the airport, he observed the line of bewildered tourists, went through Customs and Immigration, and took a taxi to the Yak and Yeti Hotel where, although a tourist trap, he was assured of clean water and decent sanitary conditions.

Kostokov checked into the hotel, tipped minimally, smoked three Sobranies, and went to bed. He slept well, as he always did, felt refreshed in the morning, and looked out the windows to admire the surrounding 2400 meter hills. After strolling through the old marketplace, where he breakfasted, Kostokov entered the Santa Bhawan Mission Hospital Main Conference Room.

Kostokov was affiliated with the World Health Organization, which met annually in Geneva and had offices at the United Nations Plaza and throughout the world. Their regional office for Southeast Asia was headquartered in New Delhi and included ten Member-States: Bangladesh, Bhutan, Democratic People's Republic of Korea, India, Indonesia, Maldives, Myanmar, Nepal, Thailand, and Sri-Lanka. Supposedly, health-related problems falling within the domain of one of these nations were addressed by these Member-States. However, the Director-General of WHO, an extremely powerful figure, often arranged select committees to address particular problems concerning issues of health that also posed potential political problems, such as biological warfare and terrorism. The meningitis outbreak in Nepal was such a problem.

The Nepalese government, lacking medical sophistication but having appropriate concern for their people, had charged the World Health Organization with deciding what fate had befallen the Sherpas. The government had earlier released an explanation to the press that there had been a meningitis outbreak but, among themselves, the authorities weren't certain. Over ninety Sherpas had been killed, over one thousand citizens were killed earlier in Kathmandu, and the Nepalese government needed assurance this would not happen again. Besides, various dissident groups were adding the problems of poor health in the population to their expanded list of complaints against the government, a monarchy with its own expanding list of domestic problems.

Within this context, WHO had established a special committee, consisting of representatives from America, Russia, Norway, and Austria, but none of the Southeast Asia countries would be present. America, Russia, Norway, and Austria had been involved in similar committees before and worked efficiently with each other, and with considerable expertise. The Director-General once again called them together.

*   *   *

Kostokov entered the conference room, leaving his heavy coat outside on a rack. He approached the conference table, a few paces behind Bradley Serkin, a Cold War freak from America with whom he had had previous bureaucratic interactions on these committees. The two were on fairly decent terms, each subtly knowing that the other did things for his respective government that each government might deny, whether on UN-sponsored or WHO committees.

Serkin trusted no one and never had. He had been paranoid since birth, despite a relatively normal childhood with normal parents. He grew up in New Rochelle, New York, in a nice home on Calton Road, was popular in school, and had good grades in high school and at Syracuse University in Upstate New York, where he majored in political science. Serkin had a wonderful manner of speaking and had been active on the campus radio station for years. After college, he did a short stint in graduate school at Brandeis University, in political science, then enlisted in the army, where he was certain he would be considered officer material. Somehow, while being processed for the army, where he truly believed he could be all that he could be, the CIA obtained his file, knocked on his door, and he was delighted to join.

Serkin had worked hard and was respected by his superiors and small circle of friends. He knew his field well, which now focused on problems relating to health, primarily germ warfare, and had been to Iraq, Sudan, Israel, Azerbaijan, and throughout the Eastern Caucasus, near the Caspian sea.

Bradley Serkin was the point man for the United States government whenever a health-related problem could reflect espionage. He was quick and to the point. His training in political science had expanded his knowledge base of political systems, increasing his love for America. He was always eager to explain the democratic form of government to anyone who would listen. Despite America's problems, he believed it to be the best system the world had ever known.

Serkin's personality, pleasant and seldom complaining, was a positive factor in his interacting with other people in the Company, as the CIA is often called, as well as with the various physicians and different medical schools with whom his job brought him into contact. At age fifty-two, twice divorced, he was a handsome man of athletic build, curly brown hair, and small even spaces between all of his teeth.

Basically, Serkin's job was simple, but important: If people became sick, were there markings of possible biological warfare or subterfuge? He would obtain data and share that information with medical personnel at the Company or with those experts he considered appropriate for the task.

Serkin turned to Kostokov, Russia's point man in these same issues, and the two cordially exchanged salutations with each other and with the other two men in the room, also with whom Serkin and Kostokov had worked in the past.

Serkin sat next to Kostokov, smiling hello to his Norwegian and Austrian colleagues, asking how their flights had been and if they were satisfied with their hotel accommodations. The four men, having long worked together, had a set routine for these meetings.

"Let us get started," Karl Restorf, the Austrian representative from Vienna, said. "As you know, I'm the Chair for this meeting. Everyone here knows everyone. Mr. Kostokov, Serkin, and Lukerson," smiling toward the Norwegian representative as the latter arranged his papers and exchanged smiles with Aleksander, "We have all worked together in the past. This meeting is designed to review medical data. We have all worked before for various WHO missions pertaining to medical data. This particular meeting was requested by the Nepalese government, through WHO. We all know what happened to the Sherpas, but we don't know why. Our job is to find out."

"One more thing. Later, we'll be joined by Mr. Jokhar Gantemirov, a scientist the World Health Organization recommended a few weeks ago. Mr. Gantemirov is from Chechnya and has long resided in Moscow." Aleksander Kostokov looked up. "Why don't I know him?" he politely smiled.

"I don't know. The Executive Board at WHO, in Geneva, called me and asked if he could be on the Committee. If WHO likes him, who am I to argue?"

"We're not going to hear about the pros and cons of Chechnya, are we?"

"I doubt it. He's been in Moscow most of his life, at least according to his resume. Now, can we get started?"

Restorf looked around the table at the three men. All nodded. He could not help but note that Kostokov and Serkin seemed to be ensconced in deep thought. Lukerson just sat, dull faced and expressionless.

Restorf continued. "The Nepalese government told the press the Sherpas died from meningitis – the same outbreak that struck earlier in their capital. But, they are not certain. Here's the formal medical report," pointing to a large pile of paper in front of each man. "It's about four hundred pages thick, not counting photographs and graphs. The reason it's so thick is because all the Sherpas who died, the entire village, had complete autopsies."

Each committee member thumbed through his stack. Restorf continued, "They look horrible. Contorted, with urinary and fecal excrement all over the place. And blood around their mouths. The Nepalese want to be certain there is no danger of this occurring again. Obviously, they're concerned about the tourist trade as well as their own people's welfare. We're to report to Mr. Shahni, the Nepalese representative from the Ministry of Health, after we are done."

"Why is there no official here from the Nepalese government?" Serkin inquired.

Mr. Shahni says it's because they don't want to bias us. Personally, I think they lack expertise and any alleged expert they send us will feel embarrassed. All they could do were the autopsies and who knows how good those are? I don't see any problem with us, the way we are. Besides, we've all worked together in the past, and worked well. After Jokhar Gantemirov arrives," looking at his watch, "which should be soon, we'll have a quorum of five, small enough to be efficient, and we should soon have a final report."

As the men glanced through their stack of information, there was a knock at the door and a thin secretary, with a slight limp, ushered in Jokhar Gantemirov.

"Sorry I'm late," Gantemirov said, as he introduced himself generally to the men in the room, approaching the table.

"Quite all right," said Karl Restorf, standing and motioning the Chechen to sit down. "Let me introduce you. This is Aleksander Kostokov from Russia, Bradley Serkin from Washington, D. C., Hans Lukerson from Oslow, and I believe you and I have already spoken."

Gantemirov shook every man's hand firmly, somehow focusing too briefly on Kostokov's eyes to Serkin's observation, and sat down.

Aleksander Kostokov also found it strange that the Chechen seemed to avoid his eyes, and found the handshake uncomfortably firm.

Gantemirov seemed to be a strange man. Probably in his late forties or early fifties, hair brushed straight back, his forehead was peppered with acne scars, and he had a deep, throaty voice and huge hands with thick fingers. He stood six feet six inches, weighed at least two hundred eighty pounds, and was extremely muscular. For a man whose face appeared so hard and grim, it was strange that he spoke so softly. That told Kostokov, and Serkin, that he was extremely dangerous.

"Now, we have to decide how we're going to tackle this. This medical report," placing one before Gantemirov, "is the only information we have." Restorf continued. "I would appreciate your sharing this only with appropriate scientists or doctors or whomever you need to speak to, but certainly not the press and, especially, not CNN." Everyone smiled and nodded their heads. "Now, we have to figure out what happened."

Kostokov picked up the report and looked around the room. "I don't know about you gentlemen, but I had absolutely no idea the report would be this thick," hand-fanning the seven inch-thick file. "If we're going to do this right, let's meet in a few days, after we each have time enough to review this. Does that sound like a good idea? This looks even more complicated than the epidemic we evaluated in Ethiopia. It's obviously going to take some time."

Excluding Gantemirov, each man had interacted with the others in the past. All had long ago discussed the fact that often, but not always, no physicians were on these committees, whose task it was to analyze particular epidemics. This was because different medical disasters required different types of medical expertise, necessitating different physicians with varying expertise for different situations. But, there was another reason: Governments were frequently concerned that many physicians might be more ethical and too prone to comment about certain observations relating to health problems that could later have negative political consequences. By having government representatives who were not physicians, the committee members could go through "government channels" and seek doctors appropriate for each task. Also, they could withhold "sensitive" information from their respective doctors. This had been a stumbling block in the WHO and United Nations analysis of chemical warfare in the Iran-Iraq conflict, as well as the Iraq-Kurd interaction. Too often, information was withheld from investigating physicians. But, as intended, it kept embarrassing situations to a minimum.

Hans Lukerson, the Norwegian, spoke. "As for me, I have a fair degree of knowledge of medicine but, as we know, I'm no doctor." Sifting through the report, he continued. "I would like to show this to some colleagues. Hermann Bissel, Director of our Norwegian Institute of Research, is expecting to hear from me."

Lukerson continued, looking at the report with near-exasperated eyes. "However, I have a problem presenting this information to Dr. Bissel. He leaves for a lecture tour in Australia in two days. I don't know whether I can get through this data in time to know what it is I need to ask him. And, if I send him the raw report," holding the small tome in his hand, "I don't think he'll have time to go through all this before his trip. Considering the length of the report, I think we should postpone discussing it for a while, until we've all reviewed the data and have something intelligent to say."

Gantemirov smiled. "Don't look at me. I'm not only late, running around with too much to do, but I presume it will also take me quite a while to go through this."

Kostokov turned to him, trying to figure out why in the world Moscow would have two representatives here. Chechnya, my ass, he thought. He's from Moscow. I'm from Moscow. "Well," Kostokov muttered, "I guess we're all busy. Maybe you and I can talk later and coordinate our efforts."

"Fine with me," the burly Chechen replied. "Whatever works for you." Kostokov considered the response too friendly, offered a half-hearted smile, and nodded his head.

Serkin, fiddling with his pencil, had wondered the same. Why would Moscow send two representatives? Why?

Karl Restorf addressed his colleagues. "Why don't we see if we can get Washington and Moscow to agree on this." Addressing Serkin, Kostokov, and Gantemirov, he said, "Why don't you three meet with your respective advisors and then touch base with me? I can relay the findings, after discussing them with my country's physicians, to the Nepalese."

Serkin and Kostokov knew he would do no such thing. The last time Karl Restorf had referred anything to anyone, it was a thank you note for hiding his alcoholism. He was a drunk who had accomplished nothing. His job with these committees was purely titular, the thrust of the work falling to Serkin and Kostokov. At least, that's what had always happened in the past.

Neither one knew what to do with Gantemirov, who sat there, smiling with yellowed teeth.

Kostokov broke the silence. "I have no problem with that. Why don't Mr. Serkin and I," excluding Gantemirov, "take out a few days, review this information and discuss it with anyone we think appropriate, and then he and I will meet. Karl, we'll then give you our report and you can add to it if you like, and," turning to the Chechen, "Mr. Gantemirov, you can touch base with your people and review the report as well. Karl can then present it to the Nepalese authorities." Turning to the men at the table, Kostokov continued. "Is that all right with you?"

Serkin answered. "I've no problem. It shouldn't take too long to get some feedback, maybe one or two days to go over this information."

Jokhar Gantemirov picked up a glass of water with his large hands, virtually encasing the entire glass, and smiled. "No problem here. Whatever works out for you. I'm new at this."

Indeed you are, thought Kostokov.

I'm not so sure, Serkin said to himself.

After exchanging small talk, the men individually departed. Kostokov and Serkin made arrangements to meet in two days at the Himachuli Room of the Soaltee Oberoi Hotel, known for some of the best food in Kathmandu. Both excluded Gantemirov, who seemed not to be offended.

When Kostokov returned to his hotel room, he went over the Nepalese report, reading quickly and thinking carefully, and let his mind wander. Before midnight, he had smoked nearly a pack of his beloved Sobranies, far more that his usual allotment, felt pleased about his plan with Serkin, but had a definite distrust for Jokhar Gantemirov. Who was he and why was he here? What was his relation to Moscow? No matter, being ex-KGB, Kostokov had all the connections he needed to find out.

*   *   *

Serkin, too, went over the report. Then, he decided to contact physicians in the famous Houston Medical Complex. He telephoned Houston and asked for Valerie VanDance in the Department of Neurology, at the Texas College of Medicine.

*   *   *

Jokhar Gantemirov also made a telephone call. Actually, two calls. One to Moscow and the other to a number in the Hotel Kavkaz, in Grozny, Chechnya. Both conversations were from a special cellular phone and he rested assured that his exchange of information was secure.

*   *   *

Three days after the conference, Kostokov was sitting at a table in the Himachuli Room, drinking raksi and soup. He had intentionally arrived before his scheduled time with Serkin. When the latter arrived, Kostokov stood and politely shook the American's hand. "My American friend, you must try this Nepalese soup, *A lu Tama*. But first, a glass of raksi to your health!"

"Likewise, to yours," Serkin replied, taking the offered beverage, drawing his chair to the table.

"Forgive me for beginning without you, but I was absolutely starved and came early."

"No problem. I brought my papers with me and hoped that we might even be able to work during dinner."

"Indeed, we can." The two men each had sliced chicken with bamboo shoots, a tandoori-chicken-type Nepal dish called *Sekuwa*, rice, curry, and *Sikarni* dessert. All of this was washed down with good helpings of raksi, which Kostokov continued to pour.

While Serkin dined on the chicken, he discussed his findings. "I talked to some of our experts and e-mailed and faxed pictures and reports to them. Evidently, the black and blue marks suggest fractures at the base of the skull. Almost all the Sherpas had these markings. The bone fractures, coupled with the urine and stool incontinence, makes my colleagues think that the Sherpas had seizures. I don't know why the Nepalese thought they had meningococcus meningitis. There's no evidence of meningitis and no signs of infection. No actual meningococcus microorganisms were seen in the brain, or anywhere else. The brains did have signs of irritation, but our people think this probably relates to banging their heads so hard they fractured the bones in their skulls, the banging resulting from the seizures."

"Can't someone have meningitis without actually finding any microorganisms in the brain?" Kostokov inquired.

"Yes, in some cases. But, surely, at least some of the villagers should have had them, especially given that about ninety people died."

"What about the skull fracture? Wouldn't that have been picked up in the autopsy?"

"Not unless they specifically examined the base part of the skull, under the brain. The Nepalese evidently thought the black and blue marks around the eyes reflected bleeding from the meningococcus microorganism, and probably didn't look at the base of the skull. But, even if the Sherpas did have meningococcus organisms causing the bleeding, or any other type of significant meningitis severe enough to kill them, there should have been puss in the brain, or at least microorganisms found somewhere in the brain, spinal fluid, or even the blood. The autopsies mentioned none of this. They must have had seizures. The question is – why did they have seizures?"

Kostokov appeared genuinely interested. "Our people weren't certain as to what transpired. Is there anything else you want to say before I tell you their thoughts?"

"No, except for the fact that, for some reason, there were some blood cells that got stuck in a couple of arteries. This was apparent to the pathologist who reviewed the microscope photographs the Nepalese had taken."

Kostokov poured more raksi for Serkin, making certain the American's glass was kept full. "Well, I'll tell you. It took more time for me than I thought. However, at the risk of seeming vulgar, first let me go to the bathroom. Too much raksi." Smiling, almost apologetic, the once-handsome man continued. "I'll be happy to discuss more with you, in just a second." As he stood, turning toward the bathroom, Kostokov said, "Care to join me? You've had almost as much as I."

"Sure. Then, let's finish the report and speak to Restorf. Tomorrow okay? I hope to spend a few days relaxing in New Zealand. I've never been there more than a day and I understand it's beautiful. I'd like to take in some of the sights."

"Never been there either, but I hear wonderful things as well."

Kostokov stood from the table, followed by Serkin. The two walked to the small bathroom, down the hall, to the right. Kostokov entered a stall, began noisily relieving his bladder while Serkin stood at the urinal, and then departed his stall almost as soon as he had entered, cutting short his sphincter enterprise. Kostokov then returned to the table, waiting for Serkin.

When Serkin returned, both glasses of raksi had been refilled. "I think we both have probably had too much of this. No?"

"We did, but it's good my friend. Here's to international relations and to New Zealand," holding up his glass, Kostokov looked at his cocked wrist. "One gulp for relations and one for New Zealand." The two men then put down their glasses.

It was now Kostokov's turn. "We disagree. There was evidence of meningococcus meningitis, as well as puss and inflammation. Our physicians are certain of this. The photographs confirm it. We disagree strongly with you and believe that the Sherpas died from meningitis. We agree with the Nepalese that they died from meningitis. There was meningitis, the same type of meningitis that earlier killed people in Kathmandu. That's what it was, meningitis. They died from meningitis. All the Sherpas died from meningitis, meningococcus meningitis. None had seizures. Only meningitis."

Serkin looked at him, with an almost puzzled look on his face. Kostokov continued. "It was meningitis. Meningococcus meningitis killed the Sherpas. No arguments, okay?" Almost taking advantage of Serkin's stare, Kostokov said, "Let's go. I'll hail a taxi and put together the report. You sleep well."

Serkin looked inquisitively at Kostokov. "Be that as it may, I'm tired. Why don't we go now and put a report together tomorrow?"

"I'll put the report together, tonight, and show it to you tomorrow. You approve it. They died from meningitis. Meningococcus meningitis. The Sherpas died from meningococcus meningitis. It was meningococcus meningitis. There were no seizures."

Serkin continued his strange stare and mumbled something incomprehensible.

Aleksander Kostokov paid the waiter and the two men left the restaurant while the owner looked at them, placing turned chairs over empty tables, simultaneously admonishing the young boy sweeping the floor.

Kostokov hailed a taxi and dropped Serkin off at his hotel. Kostokov continued on to the Yak and Yeti, where he put together the report, smoking his Sobranies. He would take the report to the conference the next morning. Pleased but cautious, slightly tired and extremely curious, he retired to bed.

The following day, Serkin, Kostokov, Gantemirov and Restorf sat at the conference table in the Santa Bhawan Mission Hospital. Lukerson had returned to Norway. Kostokov placed the two-page report in front of Restorf. Restorf silently read it, and then looked at his companions.

"We have our report," said Kostokov, looking at Gantemirov. "And you? Is yours ready?"

"Actually," Gantemirov said apologetically, "mine isn't ready. I should have the final analysis soon. I'm happy to listen to you and then contact Mr. Restorf later regarding possible additions." Kostokov was surprised at this, but said nothing. Serkin seemed to pay it little attention.

The four men then digested the analysis. The ceiling fan above them softly hummed and the secretary, with the limp, brought in some weak tea.

Approximately forty minutes later, Restorf announced to the group, "Well, gentlemen, thank you for your time." Turning to Kostokov and Serkin, he continued. "I take it you both believe that the Sherpas were exposed to meningococcus meningitis and that the Nepalese were correct? And, there should be no future outbreaks, this particular type of microorganisms having reeked its toll and no longer being present. Is this correct?"

"Yes, you are," Aleksander Kostokov said. "I don't think we have to worry any more about meningitis. Our two governments respectively agree."

Serkin drank his tea, put the cup down, and quietly stated, "Yes, we do agree. They died from meningitis, meningococcus meningitis."

"Indeed," said Kostokov, reaching for one of his cigarettes. "I hope no one tells WHO about this. Smoking is one of my few sins of health."

"Good for you," Gantemirov smiled. "Sobranies are a good brand. I smoke too, but nothing as fancy." After seeming to wait for a Sobranie, which Kostokov failed to offer, he continued. "As for me, I'll look at the report and contact Mr. Restorf only if I have additional suggestions. Also, my apologies for being late the other day," Gantemirov smiled, taking in the people in the room, while Kostokov and Serkin looked at him inquisitively.

"Well, gentlemen, thank you for your time," Restorf replied, as he sipped his tea laced with cognac, reminding himself to thank personally, maybe even provide a gift, to the secretary outside.

Chapter Four

OPERATION HIPPOCAMPUS

As ALEKSANDER KOSTOKOV sat in the hallway, waiting for his superiors to call him in, he looked out the window, watching black limousines carrying government officials. The Federal Counterintelligence Service, mistakenly referred to in Western media as the Federal Security Service, is one of the KGB's successors, known by its initials FSB. The *Federalnaya Sluvhba Besopas* is headquartered in an ochre-colored neo-renaissance building, at what used to be 2 Dzherzhinsky Square.

The interior of the building was damp. Kostokov often wondered whether the environment in the hallways, where one waited for one's superiors, was intentionally kept that way. Higher level officials had perfect temperature control, as well as humidity control, in their private offices. Hallways on the first and second floors were another matter.

*   *   *

Despite recent changes in the building's structure, the names on the offices, and the name outside, whether KGB or FSB, Kostokov ruminated at how little had actually changed in his beloved KGB. The only difference now was who did what to whom. Under the Soviet Union, the KGB was sectored into different components, all of which worked closely with one another. All that supposedly changed after the Soviet Union disintegrated in 1991, when the KGB allegedly dissolved, but did not.

The KGB was formerly assigned the task of security within the Soviet Union's borders, as well as espionage outside her borders. Whereas, in the United States, the FBI focuses on internal security matters and the CIA concerns itself with foreign-related matters, the KGB did both. The National Security Administration, another intelligence agency, hooked into the Treasury Department, is also involved in national security. Tracking all these organizations, the FBI, CIA and NSA, was included within the umbrella of the former KGB, making the organization formidable and powerful.

Following the dissolution of the Soviet Empire, the KGB broke up into the FSB, SVR and FAPSI. The FSB functions similarly to the FBI, the SVR (*Sluzhba Vneshnyaya Razvedka*), "Russian Foreign Intelligence Service," similar to the CIA, and the "Russian Federal Agency for Government Communication and Information", the acronym of which is FAPSI, similar to the NSA. Adding the arm of military intelligence, "Main Intelligence Directorate of the Russian General Staff," or GRU, all the sections of intelligence gathering reign once again in modern-day Russia.

Unlike the CIA, the KGB, now the FSB, functions both abroad and home, doing for the former Soviet Union and the current Russian system what the CIA, FBI, and NSA, as well as the Secret Service, do for the United States. And a good deal more. At one time, the KGB chief commanded an army of 700,000 agents and about as many informers. The United States intelligence and counterintelligence network numbers 130,000. Most of the KGB had kept watch on their fellow citizens within the former USSR. Today, approximately 60 years after Stalin's reign of terror, the Russians are still reluctant to refer to the KGB by any name, preferring euphemisms such as "the Committee," or "the Office," not unlike the Americans referring to the CIA as "the Company."

When the Communists ran the Soviet Union, which included Russia, they exploited a centralized economic system and instituted a dictatorship similar to that of the Czars. Under the Communists as well as the Czars, the merit of aristocracy overrode the aristocracy of merit. Only the denotation of "aristocracy" had changed. Czarist blood lineage was replaced by the elite lineage of the Communists. The KGB was the Communists' nobility. Following the dissolution of the Soviet Union, many Russians longed for the old days of Communist rigor, accounting for the Communist plurality in the lower house of the Duma.

*   *   *

Aleksander Kostokov, an agent in the FSB and a former KGB agent, was a good agent and longed for the old days.

Kostokov entered the old Moscow building one hour ago, having arrived from Nepal three days earlier. His satchel, at his feet, carried the newspaper clipping about Ricki Hardson's dead Sherpa discovery, as well as a copy of the article in the *New York Times*. There were some other articles in other newspapers concerning the death of the Sherpas, as well as a copy of the report filed by his committee to the Nepalese government. That report, submitted to Restorf and, subsequently, to the Nepalese, had been officially accepted by the Nepalese government. Kostokov's own report had earlier been delivered through high-frequency radio signals, using the Russian NALYD Code sequence.

He could not hear the conversation down the hall, behind the adjacent double doors, but Aleksander knew they were discussing him. He now waited, alone, in an empty office.

"He smokes too much," the woman commented. "It shows lack of discipline."

Another man, in the corner, his voice shaking and eyes constantly blinking as a result of a nervous system disorder, spoke. "Discipline has never been a problem for Comrade Kostokov. Besides, Sobranies are probably the best cigarettes there are, certainly better than any we make. However, he does drink

too much, especially since his family died in the
Ukraine. But, he holds it well. I believe that he's one
of the best. Now, we need to hear what he has to say
about those mountain peasants."

"I agree," said Jokhar Gantemirov. "When I saw
him in Nepal, he seemed competent. At least, Serkin
did what we anticipated. Bring him in."

In a few minutes, Kostokov was ushered through
the security system, taken through an anteroom and
then, going through another set of doors, his voice
triggered the power-spectral analytical electronic device insuring his identity. Kostokov entered the room,
noticed the conference table in the center, and stood
at the side of the table.

He had been in this room before. At a different
time, before the FSB and SVR and FAPSI, when the
KGB was KGB, and Russia was the USSR, before that
traitor Gorbachev dismantled the Soviet Union,
where his beloved family had died.

The room held little light, one small overhead
fixture being the only source of luminescence. The
temperature was pleasant. The trapezoid-like conference table, slightly off balance, briefly rocked
when he placed his satchel, with permission, on the
old wood. Hands of the people in the room, except
those belonging to the man blinking in the corner,
rested lightly on the table. The participants stared at
him, exchanging polite but subdued smiles. The one
in the corner walked over to Kostokov, outstretching
his hand. As he passed under the light, Kostokov realized he had forgotten how noble, in ways, this man

appeared. Kostokov had always held him in high regard, especially after Yuri Lyachin visited him in the Ukraine hospital when Kostokov's family was killed.

Yuri Lyachin's face was filled with contrasts. He had Grecian, noblesque features, but these somehow did not blend with his big nose and eyes that were reminiscent of some character in a scary movie. His mouth, jaw and eyes all twitched, sometimes in synchrony and sometimes not.

More than once, Lyachin had complained to his colleagues that President Putin was well-intended, but incompetent. Russia was no longer a respected world power, the world had lost its respect for Mother Russia, and the lack of proper naval maintenance had led to the death of his son, his only child, in the Kursk submarine disaster. Were it not for Mikhail Solokov, the esteemed Moscow physician-scientist who treated Lyachin's facial movement disorder, the stresses in his life would have markedly worsened his neurological condition. As it was, the stress had somewhat worsened his voice tremor, creating stacatto-like catches whenever he spoke, but the remainder of his abnormal facial movements had improved.

*   *   *

Lyachin had forever been with the KGB and, despite his holding a position of prominence within the FSB, longed for the days of his former Soviet Union. When his son died in the Kursk submarine disaster, where 118 members of the crew were killed outside of Vidyayevo, the Kursk's home base, Lyachin confided to his former employee, Aleksander

Kostokov, how disgusted he was that President Putin had so ill-equipped Russia's nuclear submarines, much akin to the poor state of repair of the railroads. Kostokov agreed and the two commiserated over the inadequacies of the current-day Russian system.

Two years ago, Dr. Mikhail Solokov personally examined Lyachin for his voice and jaw problems, diagnosed oromandibular dystonia, and prescribed medication, including chemical injections into the afflicted muscles. Mikhail Solokov helped him considerably with his medical expertise. A small but brilliant man, with a near-concave face, Solokov bemoaned to Lyachin his concern regarding the low level of financial support the Russian government gave scientists. Solokov emphasized he was especially disturbed because he believed a new medication that could help people with memory disease would have to be shelved, due to lack of research funds.

Lyachin, impressed with Solokov's expertise and his own response to Solokov's treatment, immediately recognized the potential for controlling people's thinking – after all, if a medication could alter memory patterns, why not give the medication to people, either individuals or groups, to control them. Think of it, he mused, one could give it to Chechen dissidents and squelch their revolutionary movement in a short time.

Lyachin told Solokov that he had access to personnel who might find Solokov's project intriguing. Solokov more than welcomed the opportunity, introduced other scientists interested in the project, and the two soon met with Liubov Usova, one of the ugliest women in the KGB, but more competent than any man in the world, and the best strategist and tactician in the Russian espionage network. The three gradually developed a plan.

Shortly, they brought Aleksander Kostokov into that plan, assigning the veteran agent the task of administering the chemical compound on which they were working, a chemical that was effective but needed perfection. They also needed money and weapons. Jokhar Gantemirov was the perfect source. He was a mixed breed, half-Russian and half-Chechen, with allegiance to both. His major allegiance was to power and, as a fighter in the Chechen underground movement, he had access to money and guns.

Thus, Mikhail Solokov, Liubov Usova, and Yuri Lyachin had financial resources, access to scientists, and a good field agent, Aleksander Kostokov. Luri Lyachin and Liubov Usova both had contacts within the old KGB network, many of whom now worked in the new divisions (FSB, SVR, FAPSI), as well as contacts with the military intelligence unit, the GRU. Only recently had Lyachin met Gantemirov, an ambitious Chechen with connections outside the usual Russian FSB resources.

*　　*　　*

Kostokov was the point man, so to speak, the one who would deliver goods and services. Throughout many years, he had demonstrated loyalty and exceptional trust for his mentor, Yuri Lyachin. One year earlier, after the explanation of their attempt to work with the memory-altering drug, Liubov Usova, all three hundred-plus pounds of her, offered Kostokov some ill-tasting coffee, while Solokov sat at her side, as they sat and talked about their project. She then turned to the scientist, who excused himself, and she remained behind closed doors with the point man. When the two emerged, some forty minutes later, she slyly nodded at Solokov, and a stone-faced, sexually-abused Kostokov walked alone, down the hallway, having just provided oral sexual comfort to his behemoth master.

*   *   *

Muffled hellos were offered Aleksander Kostokov from Yuri Lyachin, Liubov Usova, Jokhar Gantemirov, and Mikhail Solokov. Lyachin, obviously in charge to any newcomer, moved back to the corner, resting his body on a small stool. Kostokov was offered a seat, with little friendly talk.

The voice from the dimly lit corner, failing to hide the underlying vocal tremor, emerged.

"Comrade Kostokov. It is good to see you again. How are you?"

"Fine, just fine. It is good to see you again." Looking at Gantemirov, Kostokov was somewhat startled. "Well, I believe we have met." Then, turning to Yuri Lyachin, he said, "How can I help?"

"How can you help? Well, first, tell us what happened? Obviously, things did not go as planned. We consider you one of our best and await your explanation. What happened?" Kostokov digested the man's abnormal voice, still wondering about Gantemirov, and tried not to think of the multiple sexually disgusting encounters he had suffered with Usova.

All the field agents, especially those from KGB days trusted to work beyond the confines of Eastern Europe, knew about Lyachin. Those who had worked with him before also knew that the man's jaw moved inappropriately while speaking, although recently there had been improvement. Listening to the shaky tremulous voice from the mouth that moved inappropriately, with the eyes that kept blinking, Aleksander Kostokov deftly opened his satchel, exercised a well-learned feigned confidence, and pulled out various papers. The room was not friendly, and he knew it. Yet, somehow, he knew he belonged to these people. He felt some degree of ease. Relative ease. No one asked him to sit and he was still standing.

Kostokov's report was brief, to the point. The people in this room did not care for extra phrases, extra words, or meaningless hype. Everything was bottom-line.

Aleksander Kostokov made his presentation to the disgruntled agents and scientist in the room. "Comrades, the Sherpas from this village obtain their water twice daily. I placed the compound upstream, as instructed. It was to leak from the specially designed container over a period of forty-eight hours, ensuring everyone would consume some of it over one to two days. I camped a few miles from the village, planning to return twelve hours after the project began, to make certain everything happened as planned. Meantime, an American woman," showing the newspaper article, "found them, all dead. Evidently, the entire village drank the water several hours after the project began and they all died. I found them after she did."

Kostokov's superiors curtly reviewed the newspaper clipping. Each had already seen it, and all held little regard for any Nepalese newspaper as a source of reliable intelligence data. Then, they looked at the *New York Times* article, but said nothing. They wanted information from the source.

"Proceed. What else?" Gantemirov politely inquired.

"Sherpas briefly boil their water prior to drinking. Our scientists," looking at Dr. Mikhael Solokov, "earlier found the compound resistant to boiling. Thus, the boiling should not have caused the compound to become poisonous. So, why did it kill them? We had tried it on a few prisoners, certainly under different circumstances, but they had no major side effects and no one died."

"I discussed this matter, following permission," looking at Yuri Lyachin, "with the scientists who work with Dr. Solokov." His attention now focused on Mikhail Solokov, the famous Russian scientist. "They believe the altered red blood cell chemistry of these mountain people, an adaptive state of their body's hemoglobin that permits more binding to oxygen at high altitude environments, was responsible for the deaths. The red cells bound to the chemical, depriving the body of appropriate amounts of oxygen. A few experiments in Moscow, exposing the compound to blood cells stored at low oxygen pressures, confirmed this hypothesis. The red cells stick to one another when, after being stored at low oxygen pressure, they are exposed to the chemical compound. The villagers probably died after ingesting the water, due to blood cells sticking in their arteries, damaging their brains and other organs. We assume this caused severe convulsions, so severe that they broke bones."

Kostokov placed the laboratory report, still in its sealed envelope, on the table. No one touched it.

"After the Sherpas' death, I asked permission for further testing, but was refused. Then, I was summoned back to Kathmandu where I carried out the plan with Bradley Serkin. That plan was tested and successful. The Nepalese believe that the Sherpas died from meningitis, a bacterial infection. Had the Serkin plan not worked, I would have had to kill him, making his death seem accidental."

Thinking as he spoke, knowing that Solokov as well as the beast Usova did not know him well, he realized that Gantemirov must have been placed on the committee in Nepal to check up on him, to make certain all went well. As far as Kostokov was concerned, all did go well.

"What about the other men on the health committee?" Usova asked.

"There were three others, besides Serkin and myself. Karl Restorf is from Vienna, an alcoholic, who does nothing. He doesn't care, just an incompetent bureaucrat. Hans Lukerson, from Oslow, needed much more time. Had he stayed, and if I had to kill Serkin, Restorf would have digested the conflicting data from me and Lukerson. I would have tried to make it seem that Serkin, had he not died, would have agreed with me, thus placing the Russians and the United States together, against Lukerson. It might have been tricky but I could have handled it. As it happened, though, Lukerson left."

Uncertain what to say, Kostokov continued. "Also, Jokhar Gantemirov," motioning to the Chechen, "was there. I was not aware he would be and we had not earlier met."

The man with the tremulous voice interrupted. "You didn't have to."

Gantemirov, standing, smiled at Aleksander Kostokov, motioning his hand in a semi-handshake, and then sat down. No explanation of Jokhar Gantemirov's presence was given. Kostokov tried to pay this little notice, and continued.

Kostokov was pleased he did not feel nervous. He provided the information as best he could, citing the details, intentionally trying to relate the events as would a schoolboy reciting declensions of grammar to his headmaster. That was his style.

Kostokov had long ago lost fear or concern of death, for anyone, including himself. He had been this way since the Ukraine train accident erased the lives of his family. After that tragedy, somehow, he had lost a baseline matrix of feeling, the sensitivity all humans at one time or another possess, unless they allow the world's events and interactions to drain it from their souls.

Aleksander Kostokov's philosophy of life was known to all in the room. All had seen his file – psychological test results, essays, past performances in the field. Aleksander believed that most people spent the majority of their lives dealing with, planning for, hiding from, or anticipating the moment before their death. He no longer cared how one felt the moment before dying, that moment when one queries various delineations. He believed *Homo sapiens* pushed this from their mind on a daily basis, hence the heavy attendance at revival meetings, reading books on politics, fighting for ideals, or engaging in anything that somehow provided meaning for empty lives. People strung together the dots of the moments in their lives, trying to form some continuum, so that when they thought about that moment before death, before equilibrating with the entropy of the universe, whether or not it entails heaven or hell or both, they felt substance and relief.

Kostokov relished his not having fallen under this spell. He did not need to provide himself meaning. He had it. He did not need to find value in his daily existence. He had it. He needed nothing. His job, his life, his entire *being* was defined by providing quality work for the intricate Russian system. True, at one time he had been different, but not now. His per-

sonal meaning emanated from his performance for
the KGB, now the FSB.

Creating a crevasse into this morass of cognition,
this labyrinth of defense mechanisms, could only
bring torment. Thus, the man was a good agent, as
everyone in the room understood. He was not disturbed by occasional rumblings from colleagues that
he might be too reckless, or that at times he tempted
death too closely, perhaps almost wanting it. Nor did
it bother him that some thought him borderline crazy.

Yuri Lyachin, walked toward Aleksander Kostokov,
still standing. His facial countenance broadcast neither displeasure nor disbelief regarding the agent's
report. "Aleksander, sit down."

Kostokov sat, an empty chair flanking him on both
sides. He listened with focus and with care.

"As you know, your mission was special. Strictly
MK-6, Priority Red. Only a few are aware of our task.
Only a small sector of the FSB is aware of our mission. Some would surely find our project almost jocu-
lar, others totally unrealistic. But, it can be done and
will be done. We are certain. That is why we are here
and why you were selected."

The blinking, voice-tremulous Lyachin stared
hard, without apparent feelings or compassion, and
looked directly into Kostokov's face, constantly re-
evaluating him as he spoke, as he re-evaluated everyone and everything on a daily basis. Friendly as he
was to Alekesander Kostokov, Lyachin trusted no one.
Nothing was secure. Nothing was forever.

Yes, he thought to himself. He had made the right decision in selecting Aleksander Kostokov as their field agent. And, Jokhar Gantemirov had agreed.

The aging man remembered how Kostokov had grieved following the death of his loved ones, how he often daydreamed at his desk, staring out over what was then Dzherzhinsky Square. Kostokov had been with the Office for many years, but now began to change his patterns, exercising considerably, obsessing over his body, and reading incessantly about anything he could get his hands on. It was then that Lyachin and Gantemirov incorporated him into their special mission, Lyachin explaining to Kostokov that only a select few in the FSB were familiar with the project. Strictly MK-6, Priority Red. Kostokov accepted, feeling important and having purpose as long as he was tied to the KGB, or FSB, or Lyachin. He was defined by his profession.

It was all in Kostokov's dossier, the dossier that only those in that room, except for the Division Secretary, had seen. Aleksander Kostokov was strictly undercover.

"Aleksander, there are some who might think our project naïve. As we have discussed," looking solemnly at each of his colleagues, cementing his gaze into each of their eyes, "It is not. Improvement for the people in the world, including Russia, lies not through obstructions at the Persian Gulf, nuclear war, concepts of 'openness' in our society, or these trivial terrorist games different groups, some supported by our own organization, others not," looking at Gantemirov, "engage in, but through the control of people's thinking."

"People *are* what they think. The human brain is a series of electrical circuits that make us believe certain things, want certain things, and need others. Make no mistake, Comrades," looking at each individual in the room, "the brain in our heads is no different from the brain of those entertained by watching lions eat Christians, or Nazis shutting oven doors. Or, for that matter, the beliefs of Chechens, Czars, or those craving caviar. Nor is it different from some cowboy in America, a bushman in Australia, an Arab in the Middle East. What matters is how an individual interacts with his culture and how that culture affects his thinking. Whether someone is happy or is not happy with communism, capitalism, Chechnya, whatever, depends solely on how that person's brain processes available information. That information is processed by electrical circuits, circuits that depend upon learned experiences and what society has taught that person. The main reason people throughout the world do not believe a particular philosophy or religion is because they were not appropriately exposed to it or not exposed to it early enough. Had they been, they would believe it. And, although we might dislike admitting it, the same is true for all modes of thinking, even that propounded by the Americans. Had any of us been raised in the United States, we would be die-hard capitalists. Earlier, we were members of the Communist Party. Now, who knows what we are. But we do know one thing: We are what our brains are, and our brains are what our society tells us. To be sure, there are variations, but this thesis holds: Children enter the religion of their parents or, for many of us, the non-religion of parents. Everything, I repeat, everything, is a reflection of what our brain tells us!"

No one smiled, since all held respect as well as fear. Lyachin continued. "I am pleased to lead this committee. As per your approval, I have had to make certain decisions. We must not lose our pace, nor our lead. We are two years, at worst two and one-half years, from total success. It will all be done through mind control."

No one stirred. All were listening.

"We have some scientists," looking at Mikhail Solokov, "working hard at discovering the intricacies of the human brain and how it functions. We are on the verge of knowing what chemicals, of which there are probably several, alter a person's thinking. If we can find a chemical that controls that person's thinking, we can end wars, end battles, and propagate our cause."

What did not need to be stated was that, were this true, the men and one woman in the small room, functioning virtually on their own, would become extremely powerful figures in the world. All would be formidable geopolitical adversaries.

The group's leader continued. "On a few occasions, we believed we had a drug capable of altering one's thinking. We were wrong, but close. Our plan was to place the substance in the human system, and then expose those human beings to a new line of thinking over the next several days. We hoped that material to which they had been exposed would become a part of their own system of belief, forever."

Pacing, carefully looking and studying each person at the table (and their response), he continued. "It is unfortunate the Sherpas died, but their death is trivial to our project, arrogant but noble, and, most important, correct. We had planned to introduce the Sherpas to a new concept in their religion: Comrade Kostokov was to enter the village and simply suggest that they pass religious shrines on their right, not their left. This would have been a simple change, but contrary to centuries of custom. The change would have offered ample evidence of the efficacy of our project."

"Aleksander, following their ingesting the chemical-containing water, was to appear as a trekker, simply telling them to pass shrines on the right, not the left. He would reiterate this statement several times. Had they followed his instructions, thereby going against their teaching since childhood, it would have been fantastic! It was our belief, certainly our hope, that they would follow Aleksander's suggestion – each Sherpa being testable with the numerous shrines surrounding the village. Another concern was to be certain the compound would not drastically alter other aspects of their behavior."

"As you know, the chemical killed them. I am sure the Nepalese have no idea why these people died. What this article," pointing to the newspaper on the table, "states is probably correct, namely that Nepalese officials believe the Sherpas perished from meningitis. As you know, the Nepalese king frequently uses meningitis as an excuse to disperse crowds that gather for political demonstrations. Crowds help propagate meningitis due to close hu-

man contact, and the government uses fears of meningitis as an excuse to disband protestors. Consequently, many people in the Nepalese government
truly believe meningitis is common in Nepal, which,
as it happens, our sources tell us is probably true."

Kostokov was surprised at hearing the recapitu-
lation of the scheme. He quickly reasoned that perhaps not everyone in the room (Gantemirov?) knew
all the pieces that fit together into the project. He
heretofore thought they did, but perhaps not.

Aleksander Kostokov had previously met all the
people in the room. What bothered him was that if
there were individuals in this room who were not
aware of the entire project, and the current speech
was designed to link them, to make each more aware
of the entire project, it could mean one of several
things. First, perhaps he, himself did not know the
full extent and consequences of what he was doing.
That could certainly explain Gantemirov's presence.
He had known of other agents duped by superiors
into tasks more treacherous than the agent expected. He had known of agents who had mistakenly believed they were doing good for their country but, in reality, were helping the enemy. This "false
flag" trick was frequently used in different settings,
placing an unwitting government employee under
the impression that he was working for one cause,
while working for another. It was frequently used by
the South Africans during the days of apartheid, as
well by Israel and America. But, what distracted him
more, was that if some in this room were not aware
of the full scope of the project, there might be elements in the plan not sanctioned by appropriate lev-

els of FSB authority. He might be doing something not approved, for which he could be punished. Kostokov felt a twinge of uneasiness. These thoughts were soon interrupted.

"We heard Aleksander Kostokov's report regarding the blood cells of the Sherpas. Regardless of why they died, they died. The compound didn't work. Still, we are close to the correct formulation. We must ascertain the final chemical structure as soon as possible."

"Although it sounds preposterous, if we can have a compound such that we can expose people to it and then tell them what to think, we can easily attain our goal. We can put the compound in the water or even vaporize it so that people inhale it. Once we determine the chemical structure, we can explore these possibilities. It sounds like science fiction, but it is possible."

The man was selling his point, not merely stating it. He checked his colleagues' expressions, whom he knew feared him, but whose support he still needed. Each person there had contacts necessary for the project.

"I am aware how hard our scientists have worked on these experiments. It is difficult to run these experiments on animals, since human brains, certainly in terms of thinking and thought patterns, differ considerably from non-human animals. I am also aware that one of the thrusts of the Sherpa experiment was to see how people behaved following oral administration of the drug. Before now, most of our experiments involved intravenous injection of the chemical compound. We need to be able to give the compound orally if our plan is going to succeed. We gave it orally to Serkin and it seemed to work. However, it is all still experimental."

"We are very close to discovery. We must pursue this swiftly, especially because the Americans are not focusing on this line of thinking."

"Our CIA contacts tell us only a handful of people in the world do research on mind-control drugs. This type of research in America fell out of favor because the section working on mind-control drugs had too many dim-witted ideas, such as putting thallium on Castro's shoes, hoping it would make him lose his hair and beard. That absurd idea and others, coupled with the American penchant for what they term mental freedom, keeps them from mind-control research. However, a small group of scattered scientists in America investigate this area, although we do not yet know who they are. We must learn about them and find out their level of knowledge."

"I tell you, it is not far off. We shall soon have the appropriate drug. Again, the possibilities are multiple. We can use it for interviewing politicians by the media, asking them what their beliefs are after we tell them what they are. Representatives in disarmament negotiations could be cajoled into doing what we want. Perhaps, we can give the compound to individuals and make them terrorists, or make them cease terrorism. We could use it in individuals or groups. While the West is busy with new missile defense plans, thinking we care more about it than we do, we can focus our major efforts not on missile defense but on mind control. This is not science fiction. The proof is Serkin. Aleksander, tell us what happened to Serkin."

Kostokov, now wondering whether none, some, or all these people knew about his report, which certainly included Serkin, was surprised at this request. Why didn't everyone already know about Serkin? Had his earlier communications not been dispersed to all? Was this a power move, some type of manipulation?

Was Lyachin deranged, preaching to an already believing audience, or did he have to sell his point to some nonbelievers?

Kostokov gave his report, presumed Serkin's identity was known, but what transpired in the restaurant was not.

"Bradley Serkin told me his sources told him that the Sherpas did not die from meningitis. He was aware they all had seizures, which was probably true," turning to Solokov, who nodded his head, "according to our physicians and scientists. The compound, I am told, probably bound hemoglobin in the red cells, causing decreased blood flow to the brain. This, coupled with the chemical itself, must have caused severe seizures, breaking their necks, bones, and the base of their skulls, and made them lose control of urine and stool. Evidently, a fracture at the base of the skull is very difficult to see on X-ray or at autopsy. Still, it can cause hemorrhages into the skin around the eyes, resulting in black and blue marks. That's what the Sherpas had. The fractured base of the skull, which was near vital areas of brain function, together with the decreased blood flow, is probably what killed them."

"Tell us about Serkin. How did the compound work with Serkin?"

Serkin and I were in a restaurant. I put the compound in his drink and told him, repeatedly, that the Sherpas died from meningitis. He just sort of looked at me, while I repeated this. He had just told me they had seizures and no evidence of meningitis. But, there he was, not arguing with me, as I continued to tell him the Sherpas died from meningitis."

"Did he have difficulty accepting that? Did he disagree at all?" inquired Usova, whose arms were so big that they could not rest at her side. Aleksander tried to avoid Usova's gaze. The KGB, or the FSB, had no American rules regarding sexual harassment. He remembered his earlier performance on this physically disgusting woman who held power over him, and hoped she would not demand more satisfaction from him. He could not believe he had consented, but yet he had wanted to. Trying to be professional, he steadied his countenance.

"As amazing as it sounds, no. He just looked at me. Normally, he is rather talkative. He hardly said anything. He just sat there, looked at me, and later agreed."

'Were there any side effects from the chemical?"

"I saw him a short time later the following day, at the conference. He appeared normal, perhaps a little quiet. He appeared to believe what I had said. He just sat at the conference table and didn't say much. He had no objection when I presented our report to the Nepalese government, confirming what they thought, that it was meningitis. He agreed with me. So, it appears our compound worked."

"I don't doubt it does," Usova responded, smiling at Dr. Solokov, who nodded his head. Solokov had a question.

"How do we know Serkin wasn't simply going along with this? How do we know he wasn't pretending, simply to see what you were up to?"

Lyachin interjected. "Actually, we don't. But, bear in mind, he would have no idea why these Sherpas really died. Why would he not have disagreed with Kostokov when Kostokov told him that he thought the people had meningitis? Serkin gave no argument, he simply accepted what Aleksander said. The only way Serkin might have faked being duped would be if he wondered whether something strange was going on. But, remember, no one knows about the chemical compound, except us. Further, you would think Serkin would find no advantage in saying whether these people did or did not die from meningitis, when Aleksander initially disagreed with him at the dinner table. There is no proof you are wrong, but the odds are overwhelming in our favor." Turning to Aleksander, "Do you agree?"

"Yes. Also, the fact that he seemed a bit tired, and quiet, makes me think the compound really did something to him, altering his thinking. I can't be certain. Our scientists still haven't worked out all the chemical mechanisms of action, nor all the side effects. But, again," Kostokov looked at Mikhail Solokov, hoping for approval. "I think it worked."

Solokov nodded his head. "It does. I have worked on it for years. It does."

Kostokov continued. "One thing strange, and it was certainly true in our earlier experiments with the prisoners, was that when we gave someone the chemical and gave them a single 'new memory,' if you will, they did not recall they had been given the new memory. Thus, no one said, 'You kept saying something to me over and over again and I now believe it.' Rather, they just believed what they were told, and had no recollection they had gone through some type of learning process to acquire that information. I know it sounds amazing, and hard to believe, but from what I understand this all has a basis in how brains function."

Again, Solokov nodded his head. Lyachin not far behind, said, "I am not saying we are ready to use this compound now. We need to know about long-term side effects, and how to utilize and plan the most effective use of these chemicals. But, we're on our way. If there are no further questions, I would like to bring us to my main point. Any questions?"

Everyone was attentive. There were no questions.

"It is imperative that the West not know we are working on this compound. In this setting, we need to discuss another man, someone different. His name is Dr. Richard Michael Swept."

The blinking man, voice tremulous, poured himself a glass of water. Kostokov mulled over in his mind the fact that his superior had just given a policy speech. Why? Yuri Lyachin and Liubov Usova at one time had held great powers within the former KGB structure, and now held them within the FSB. Kostokov was increasingly uneasy regarding the legitimacy of this committee. Yuri Lyachin and Liubov Usova had been instrumental in helping the North Vietnamese defeat the South Vietnamese, in fighting Afghanistan, and helping Latin Americans establish drug routes for smuggling cocaine into America. But, he knew, the Soviets had not survived as an empire, and the KGB had changed. And, regarding Chechnya, nothing helped the Russians there. Chechnya was a cesspool from which Russia could not extricate itself.

So, why was Gantemirov here?

The committee had no formal name. It had evolved over years, its projects were major, and its importance was considerable. Outside the room, in hushed tones, they referred to themselves as "Pi-Two," after the famous numerical symbol, having special mathematical significance and always having additional decimal places. Just as the numerical concept, infinity, could always be a larger number, *pi* could always have another decimal fraction. Both numbers could always be better defined and more extensive.

Yuri Lyachin continued. "Janos Szeppek is an Hungarian student who works with Dr. Richard Michael Swept. Swept is an American neurologist, investigating mind-control drugs, although I don't think he perceives them that way. Our routine checking of postdoctorate applicants to work in the West culled out Szeppek's application. Swept has not published a great deal, and, like most scientists, his publications do not always reflect his specific research projects. He has written articles pertaining to Alzheimer's Disease and some other articles as well."

"Swept may not realize the full implications of his work. Evidently, he wants to expose demented patients to his drug, and then give them information as to where they live, how to get around their house, how to get into town, and other information necessary for daily living. He believes he is on the trail to help these people, not by curing the disease itself but, rather, by laying down memories that permit them to function more normally. At the moment, he is investigating animals and not allowed to experiment on humans. The reason for this involves his Chairman, Dr. Harold Ranger, a prominent American scientist who investigates energy metabolism, focusing on small organelles called mitochondria, in cells, and whom our sources find stubborn and ill-adjusted, having never recovered from the suicide of his wife and the death of his son." The blinking man, thinking of his own son killed in the Kursk disaster, looked at Kostokov, who momentarily fidgeted, making Lyachin wonder whether it was a mistake to mention Ranger's tragedy. All three men, Lyachin, Kostokov and Ranger had lost children. Regardless, he continued.

"Szeppek gathered this information and has mentioned it, in passing, to the Hungarian Consulate. Szeppek knows nothing about our plan, and has no knowledge of our interest in mind-control. He was accepted for the postdoctorate fellowship position in Dr. Swept's laboratory as a result of our impeccable recommendations and providing funding through Hungarian channels. As do all Hungarian students in America, he periodically reports to his Consulate while in the United States, although we have him report more frequently. Hungary is most cooperative. Through him, but without his knowledge, we're gathering information about Swept, to learn where Swept and other Americans stand in their knowledge of mind-control drugs."

"The important thing here is that by following Dr. Swept, seeing what scientific meetings he attends, and what colleagues he interacts with, we can learn which American scientists are doing research in mind-control and, hopefully, what they are doing."

"Swept has government funding, from the National Institutes of Health, the NIH. The people who review his grant must have some knowledge in this area, so we presume these reviewers have some expertise and interest in mind-control as well. By maintaining our contact with Szeppek, we hope to find out who these people are. It shouldn't be difficult. Besides, there aren't many of them."

"It is mandatory the Americans not reach our level of sophistication and knowledge pertaining to these drugs. The potency of this field simply has not occurred to them. We must learn who are the people working in this area, and their current level of knowledge. Again, the FSB's Washington sources state that the CIA has no strong interest in this area of research, but we must be certain. Szeppek's information is very important. We may bring him in with us, later, but I'm not sure. I hope not, not only because we don't think his background is appropriate but, more important, we should keep Pi-Two as small as possible."

Everyone at the table, including Gantemirov, nodded approvingly. The committee was important and powerful. They had little intention of diluting it. Each held power ranging from the field to scientific research to espionage, but that was miniscule compared to the synergism wielded by the group of them, together.

"Here is Swept's dossier," passing several manila envelopes, each marked "MK-6" in red ink. "Dispose this into the shredder when you leave."

Each person opened their envelope, tearing through both seals, and removed the crisp papers inside. They glanced through Swept's dossier, then looked at their leader.

"This is not yet complete. Swept is slightly under six feet. His picture is enclosed. He is thirty-seven, right-handed, and evidently rather complex. On his college transcript, a copy of which is before you, there is a space for church preference. Swept stated 'red brick'. He was Phi Beta Kappa and a member of Alpha Omega Alpha, both prestigious academic organizations, and served in the Army Reserves for six years, spending summer camps at Ft. Bragg, in North Carolina, with the Special Forces, the Green Berets. For all we know, he had formal interaction with the Central Intelligence Agency, although I doubt it."

"He sent letters of inquiry to the Army Rangers, asking whether he could take their six-week training course. This shows interest in being in good physical shape and, as Americans say, being tough. However, we have a copy of a letter from the Ranger Commission to Swept, stating one doesn't join the Rangers simply to get into shape. Their curt and abrupt letter seemingly dismissed his inquiries as facetious, suggesting little previous interaction with him. We have no evidence that he contacted them again."

"Swept did his neurology residency at Vanderbilt, where he won every academic award offered by the University, and was Chief Resident, a position of prestige. Following that, he spent several years at Harvard, working on the neuroscience basis of memory, where he interacted with Dr. Harold Ranger, his current Chairman at the Texas College of Medicine."

"Getting back to the army, we have no more knowledge regarding his army experience. Our information was obtained from Reserve Headquarters in St. Louis. One of our agents posed as an employer, asking to see Swept's evaluation before considering him for employment. It wasn't difficult to microfilm the file, especially after a sergeant excused himself for coffee, leaving the file on the desk."

"He's not married. At one point, during his neurology training, he lived with a woman, Louise Konos. Evidently, he was very committed to her and, for whatever reasons, their relationship dissolved. He currently dates a physician, Regina Bruxton, a plastic surgeon, but doesn't appear to care about her that much, nor she about him."

"We can find out more. It won't be difficult. I don't want to push Szeppek too hard, by discussing too many activities in the laboratory. Remember, he doesn't know our plans or the possibilities of his mentor's research activities. He reports to the Consulate at prescribed intervals. In the course of discussing his various activities, he also comments about the social structure of the laboratory. On one or two occasions, he heard Swept comment to Dr. Bruxton that she was more concerned about money than about him."

"Aleksander," turning to the field agent sitting quietly at the table, "find out about Dr. Richard Swept, who he is, and what he knows. Be certain we get as much information as possible from Szeppek, without raising his suspicions."

Kostokov did not twitch, budge, or relate his own experiences to those of Swept. He was a field agent, and a good one. The job, at the moment, was to listen. "Is there any particular plan I should follow? Or do I act this out on my own?"

"First, read Swept's entire file. According to our sources, he was a tough guy as a youngster. Find out more about Louise, if you can, and this girlfriend,

Regina Bruxton. Also, read about memory. I'll see to it that the FSB Reference Section supplies you with books and articles. Learn as much as you can about the newer theories. Following this, you will hear from me our final plans. Liubov Usova," turning to the stone-faced whale of a woman, "will inform you of the details. Following that, we'll devise a plan, code name Operation Hippocampus. You will later be informed about appropriate details, on a need-to-know basis."

Aleksander Kostokov looked up from the dossier, at which he had been staring, and noted that the others were looking at him. "Will I have particular constraints?"

"No, just get the project completed. You have full license." Aleksander Kostokov knew that full license meant a lot. He could kill.

Although not his fault, Kostokov somehow felt responsible for the failure of the mission in Nepal, not to mention the death of the Bedouins in an earlier mission in Israel. That failure had not been mentioned, yet it involved the same drug under discussion, in an earlier and less refined state. Perhaps Lyachin did not want to discuss that in front of his colleagues. Perhaps, these others weren't aware of that failure. Certainly, Liubov Usova knew. He shuddered when he thought of her. She was huge, obese, powerful, and he was now a victim of the tales of bizarre sexual pastimes he had heard she inflicted on her male underlings. Lyachin interrupted his thoughts. "Learn everything possible about Dr. Swept. We'll continue to let Szeppek spend time with him, and then do whatever is necessary."

Kostokov looked at his leader, and the dossier with the torn seals. He thought a moment, then asked, "When shall I see the entire dossier for Operation Hippocampus?"

"Now. Thank you for your time, Aleksander." He walked Aleksander Kostokov to the door. As he unlatched it, Kostokov turned and nodded good-bye to his colleagues at the table. The man in charge turned to those at the table. "Gentlemen, this must be successful."

As Kostokov passed the security system, he was met by a woman wearing a brown dress, who evidently had been waiting for him. He reached into his pocket for another Sobranie. He had long wondered why the Turks made better cigarettes than the Russians. The two turned down the hallway on the right, and then took the elevator to the Sub-Ground floor. His thoughts were interrupted by the woman. "I am to show you several dossiers. When do you want to see them?"

"I'll look at them now."

"Fine. Follow me."

The woman ushered him into a room, the interior of which contained one desk, two chairs, and a bed. There was a box of records on the desk. Within a few minutes, Liubov Usova entered the room and smiled at the now-nauseated agent.

"Good to see you. Read the dossier after we are done. Do what I tell you and do it now."

Liubov Usova proceeded to remove duct tape from her purse and taped the amazed agent's hands behind his back. The huge woman then applied pressure to his shoulders, lifted her dress, and moved his head toward her groin. She looked down at him, directly into his eyes, and sadistically whispered, "Do it! Do it now!"

Chapter Five

NIH GRANTS

JANOS SZEPPEK LOOKED forward to dinner with Swept and his girlfriend. He was always pleased whenever he was invited to join Dr. Swept for dinner, an invitation seldom bestowed upon an academic subordinate in his native Hungary. Swept was usually very busy, socially and academically, making social interactions with laboratory personnel less frequent than he preferred. Although the purpose of the dinner had academic overtones–they were to discuss the forthcoming Site Visit, as well as future research directions of the laboratory–Szeppeck was delighted at being socially accepted by his mentor.

Social familiarities were seldom bestowed upon people such as Janos Szeppek in Hungary, certainly not to someone whose mother was Croatian and whose father was half Jewish, half Magyar. His Magyar blood had allowed him to get into the school system and, through hard work and feigned loyalty to the country, so he believed, obtain a passport to the United States where he could investigate memory at the Texas College of Medicine. He had read some of Dick Swept's articles and welcomed the opportunity to work with him.

Szeppek had not always disliked his native land. He had two siblings who had taken part in the nation-wide uprising in 1956. During that Hungarian Revolution, workers demanded worker management of factories, a government consisting of representatives from trade unions and the youth, withdrawal of Russian troops, and other changes. Being too much for the Russians, Moscow deployed 6,000 tanks and tens of thousands of troops to put down the Revolution, re–establishing Soviet control. Following the Revolution, during which two hundred thousand Hungarians fled their homeland, the Soviet-approved Hungarian regime went to great lengths to please the people on a material level. Rather than institute a markedly repressive regime, they allowed more private ownership, a slight increase in "verbal" criticism of the massive bureaucracy, and permitted some Hungarians to depart freely. After the 1991 dissolution of the Soviet Empire, regulations were even more relaxed and Janos Szeppek was allowed to travel.

Szeppek's professors had been encouraged by the higher-ups, still very much under Russian influence, to show him and certain other students articles pertaining to how brains process memory. Recognizing that Szeppek was bright and energetic, they encouraged his desire to travel to America for further study.

The Hungarians and their Russian colleagues both wanted Szeppek to have a position in Swept's laboratory. This necessitated outstanding letters of recommendation. Swept was working on mind-control and it had come down, from the mighty Russian scientist Mikhail Solokov himself, that Szeppek should get this position. He was to be given full Hungarian support, with monies secretly channeled from FSB funds, provided through Yuri Lyachin. It wouldn't cost Swept a dime for Szeppek's salary support. The Hungarian government was paying the full bill. Swept, digesting the Hungarian's excellent letters of recommendation and broad background in chromatographic analysis, plus his impeccable English, was delighted to have him join the laboratory.

Szeppek had been instructed to report to the Hungarian Consulate, or his representative, at particular intervals. Slightly insecure and an over-achiever, ever anxious to please, he was perfect as an unwitting *stukashki*, an informer.

Szeppek was 30 years old. Being three-quarters "Hungarian" in the eyes of his countrymen, school-mates, and professors, but one-quarter Jewish, he knew he could never be a major figure in his country's government, let alone one day be elected to the National Assembly. His only chance in life lay through his intellect. He had to perform well intellectually if he was going to please the University Faculty Committee and administration. He had solidified the rules of do's and don'ts in his government-run institutions and knew the government could make him return to Hungary and could cause hardship for his family. He remembered what the Communists had done to his now-ailing sister when they were in power. That memory burned with an incessant glow.

Thus, when asked questions by the Consulate regarding his research, he sought no reason to consider this other than routine. He was frequently asked what papers were submitted for publication, what abstracts had been submitted, what kind of research was going on. He always cooperated fully, answering as best he could, never considering that the information had any significance other than to a fellow scientist.

Szeppek thought of his family's love, as he walked down his apartment stairs to meet Swept and Regina. The three were to have dinner at Oscar's, one of Swept's favorite restaurants, and one of Houston's most expensive places to eat.

The young Hungarian entered the Ferrari, commenting on the soft interior, and sat in the rear seat. "What a nice car, Dr. Swept. As you Americans say, mighty fine." He nodded his head to Regina, "It's nice to see you again."

"It's nice to see you Janos. How is everything?" the handsome plastic surgeon said, her lips remaining slightly parted after she was done speaking. "I hope all is well."

"No complaints. Working with Dr. Swept has increased my knowledge considerably. I only wish I worked with him earlier. I would have learned even more."

"Don't let that go to your head," Regina said wryly, poking Swept in the ribs, who until then had been driving silently.

"Nothing goes to my head except you, darling," the neurologist remarked, as he raised his right eyebrow and smiled. "I'm glad you were able to join Janos and myself this evening. Hope you don't find our conversation too technical," looking at Regina, "but I need to speak to Janos about the NIH system and our Site Visit, and of course spend time with you. What better place than Oscar's? So, if we can all function as one big happy family, let's have a good dinner and talk a little shop."

As the neurologist finished those words, he pulled into the driveway fronting the restaurant, pleased with the quality of the repair of the automobile. Swept was greeted by the ever-present valet, who had been there since Swept began frequenting the establishment. The valet now had his son parking cars, when the young man was not attending Houston University classes. Oscar's was a Houston landmark, with excellent food and high prices, and big tipping for the valets.

As usual, the valet parked his car in front. Oscar, himself, had more than once offered to buy the automobile, aware that only a few hundred had been produced.

The threesome were seated by the *maitre d'* at Swept's favorite table, in a corner booth facing the entrance, where Regina relished observing high society people enter the establishment, most of whom had undergone facial cosmetic surgery resulting in skin so tight their face appeared abnormal, fostering the pecuniary-oriented cynicism within the surgeon.

Swept tried to keep his love for food, and his greater love for talking about it, to a minimum. After exchanging greetings, the *maitre d'* returned with menus, first providing Swept the wine list.

Despite Oscar's simple nomeclature, the restaurant served a broad spectrum of food. Being single and because he frequently ate alone, Swept had made food and wine a favorable pastime, assuring added enjoyment during solo evening meals. His culinary relish was not superficial. Every meal held a lesson. Every meal was a lesson.

The threesome dined on grilled Swordfish steak, pan fried brook trout with bacon, *Homards grilles au beurre blanc*, broiled tomatoes provencale, creamed squash with basil and parmesan, and a bottle of one of Swept's favorite wines, Chateau Montelena Chardonnay, '97.

While the threesome enjoyed their dinner, Swept talked shop. "Janos, let me explain something. Although you're funded through your government, our National Institutes of Health, the NIH, in many ways is responsible for your being here."

"I thought Hungary paid my way."

"It's true your government paid for you to come here, including your salary. But they didn't pay for equipment in my laboratory and don't pay my salary or the technicians'. It's a complicated system. Let me explain how it works. It is so important we do well on our Site Visit. You might have funding for working with us but, if there's no money for the laboratory, we've got misery."

Seeing that the wine was near empty, Swept ordered another bottle of the Chardonnay. He smiled at the wine captain, with whom he had had numerous delightful conversations, and continued. "The NIH is part of the United States Department of Health and Human Services. It has two main divisions, an Intramural Division and an Extramural Division. Each Division has several Institutes. One of these institutes is the National Institute of Neurological Disorders and Stroke, the NINDS. This is the Institute that supports my laboratory and to which we applied for additional funding."

"You've received funding from them before, right?"

"Yes. We have funding from them right now, through what is referred to as an RO-3 Grant. However, funding is now more difficult to obtain, and we are asking for considerably more financial support. We're applying for what they call an 'RO-1' and, the fact that the antivivisectionists are complaining about working with animals doesn't help matters."

Regina interrupted. "I'm not against animal research, but don't forget, Dick, you wouldn't want anyone tackling Limbic."

"Is Limbic that dog of yours, Dr. Swept?" Szeppek inquired.

"Yes, he's my dog."

Swept, annoyed, turned to Regina. "Let's not get into this again. I wouldn't want to operate on anyone's dog. Dogs scientists operate upon are usually strays. Look," aiming his displeased glance directly toward Regina, " let's not get off on a tangent about Limbic, dogs, or the antivivisectionists. Let's talk about the Site Visit. All right with you?"

"Sorry, Richard. Just asking." Regina smiled coyly, scratching her right index finger under the table, against her boyfriend's thigh.

"The NINDS primarily focuses on research pertaining to diagnosis, treatment, and prevention of nervous system disorders. This includes the neuromuscular system, the ear, and some elements of communication, although many aspects of that are handled by the National Institute of Deafness and other Communication Disorders, the NIDCD. The NINDS funds particular types of programs, aimed at particular diseases. For instance, they have an interest in brain tumor, stroke and other diseases, such as dementia. They have a program in neuroscience that sponsors funding in dementia. This is the program that funds us. We receive $150,000," Szeppek's eyes almost fell from his head, "but this is divided over a three year period. " The eyes fell back slightly, but the exophthalmic stare remained.

Swept continued. "That funding soon expires. As you know, our laboratory does research in the neurochemistry of memory, investigating substances that promote the formation of new memories. The approach our laboratory has is very different from that of most memory-oriented scientists. This helps us, in that we're unique. But it also hurts, because we're not the norm."

"I'm aware of that, Dr. Swept. I think your approach is fascinating. Most scientists working in memory try to find where the focus of abnormality is, and how the disease comes to be there. You, on the other hand, have been trying to develop new ways of building memories within what remains of the old system. Why would the NIH not want to help you?"

"Simple: Most scientific investigators don't do it. It's not good to be too different in academia."

Swept drank more of the Montelena, commenting on its oaky crispness. He smiled at Regina, "Are you having a good time, sweetheart?"

"Certainly," looking off in the distance, trying to figure out who the society high-brow was who just entered the restaurant, creating quite a scene of adulation, as well as wondering what plastic surgeon had done her horrible eyelid job. She smiled, and squeezed Swept's hand.

Swept continued. "It's just that! We have a very different approach. If our laboratory can figure out how to make *new* memories, we can take individuals with brain disease, who have difficulty remembering how to do various things, and re-teach them. Maybe we can't bring their ailing brain back to its normal baseline, but we might be able to re-teach them many things they need to know. Maybe we can even access parts of the brain that have never been used before. This isn't an untenable concept."

"Does the NIH not want to continue your funding? Since they've already funded it in the past, wouldn't it be silly if they didn't continue? Wouldn't that mean that they had wasted money already spent?"

"That's true, and it isn't. They want to see us productive, completing our projects. If we do that, they should be pleased and continue funding us, although, as I said before, funding is ever harder to come by. On the other hand, if we don't have enough data, haven't accomplished what we earlier said we'd accomplish, they'll drop us."

"But we're well along in our research, aren't we?"

"Yes, but we need to be even further. We need to complete the experiments that prove we can put rats in a maze and teach them how to get through that maze easily, after giving them the chemical compound with no other reward. We need more trials, to prove our data. That's why we have to run the rats we discussed the other day. Our thinking, experimental design, and data must be well laid out and impeccable. The data needs to be reliable as well as valid."

"Have you told Dr. Ranger about our data?"

"He's aware of most of it. The problem is, he hates clinical research. All of it. He thinks researchers get more funding and have more prestige in science if they work with animals. There's no way I can change his thinking. He and I discussed this the other day, and I got nowhere."

"It's the same in Hungary. Probably, the same all over the world. Animal work is more basic-science oriented, or so people think. Scientists respect animal research more than clinical work, which always seems to have too many uncontrolled variables."

"In some ways, I don't disagree. Whatever you do to an animal, there's always some data you can publish. If you give an animal a drug and the experiment fails, you can cut open the brain and show whether there were or weren't microscopic side effects. That data is publishable. In animals, you can look at tissue under a microscope and show whether or not there's any damage. You can't go around biopsying every organ in humans, searching for side effects. It is always easier to publish animal research than clinical experiments. And, as far as journals and funding opportunities, they prefer animal research any day of the week."

Swept toyed with Regina's hand, trying to keep the surgeon from being too bored. "The problem with this type of thinking is that most science should be hypothesis-driven. If the hypothesis in an animal experiment fails to work, it may be you can publish the findings in terms of what abnormalities were noted in brain tissue, but if it doesn't relate to the hypothesis, as far as I'm concerned, it's all a bust. But that's another matter in terms of how scientists derive hypotheses and, actually, gets into the philosophy of Reductionism. However, that's for another time."

Regina interrupted. "If I may say, perhaps it is a valid issue the antivivisectionists have. Too much work with animals has little meaning. It's done only to publish."

"I don't disagree. If people couldn't publish as much negative results as they do, they probably wouldn't be operating on as many animals, and everybody would be happy. Limbic and his animal brethren would certainly be more safe."

Swept turned to Janos, wondering whether Regina's comments had bearing on her earlier leaving the field of fibroblast research. "Look, Janos. We've a lot of work to do. We must complete our data analysis on whether the rats, after receiving the injection of the chemical and being manually led through the maze, go through the maze many times on their own, even when there's no reward at the end. I know we've discussed this before, but we must be certain we have completed enough trials."

"I think they do. At least our preliminary data supports that. But, the experiment isn't quite finished. It will take a few more days."

"The data must be precise, accurate, and reproducible. If there is any question at all, let's run everything again. We need to show whether the Compound can do it by itself. When we present that information to the NIH Site Committee, it must impress them and drive home our legitimate need for funding. Once they're impressed, and if they provide funding, then Ranger is going to be hard put not to give approval to go before the Human Experimentation Committee. All we're asking is permission to present our data before them, and let them decide whether we have a legitimate case to run it on humans."

Swept put down the Chardonnay. "Go over the data again and discuss it with me in the next day or so. Everything must be in order."

"Dr. Swept, what if the data doesn't support the hypothesis?"

"If we're wrong, we're wrong. Under no circumstances, fudge the data. But, so far, the data support our hypothesis and it seems we're right."

"I agree. I was just wondering."

"Wonder no more. The data will speak for itself."

Swept paid the bill, adding a generous tip, and the small party exited the restaurant. Swept bid goodbye to the owner, handsomely tipped the valet, and the threesome drove off. After dropping Szeppek off at his apartment, Swept turned to Regina. "What do you say you and I have a little investigation of our own?"

"Not tonight, Dick. I have an early case in the morning and I need to be well rested."

"Okay. You can still get rest. We'll hit the sack early. We don't have to make love."

"I'm doing two blepharoplasties tomorrow, as well as a liposuction and a cosmetic skin graft for a burn injury to the lip. I need to start early. I can't stay with you."

"Why not spend the night? I get up at six. The Operating Room doesn't open until seven."

"I can't."

"You're kidding. What's wrong with you? Cram as many cases as you can into one day, make your money, but stay away from me?! Is that it?"

"Look, I don't need a lecture on money or the Operating Room schedule. These patients want my services and I'm going to operate. The fact that I'm well paid doesn't make me evil. I want to stay with you, but I can't. I won't be rested if I spend the night. You know it and I know it."

"The fact that you structure your day so that you're so packed you can't spend time with your lover, who allegedly is me, and which you would be able to do if your day started later, which you could do if you didn't have so many cases. . . ."

"I like to be with you, hold you in my arms, but I'm a surgeon and this is what I do."

"What you do is cut and make money!"

"You will never understand, will you?"

"*You* will never understand. You'd rather spend time with your practice than me. You do whatever you can to keep from being too close. You win, lady. Go home." With that, Swept exited Highway 59, went down Bissonnet, and drove to Regina's townhouse.

"You don't need to be angry."

"Why should I be angry? Your practice is more important than I am. I accept it."

The couple spent the next several minutes bickering, then in silence. Swept remembered a Bob Dylan line, *"If I can be in your dream, you can be in mine."* He looked at Regina, raised his eyebrow, and rolled his tongue against the upper back of his mouth. "I don't know what it is, Regina. So many things about us go so well. But we don't have real intimacy."

Regina gave no response and walked away from the car.

Swept returned home, alone, gave Limbic an under-the-chin scratch, placed him outside, and thought about Regina's distancing maneuvers. Never one to worry about mixing grape and grain, having a cast-iron system, he opened the freezer and poured himself a chilled Ketel One Vodka, straight up, adding a single drop of Highland Park Scotch to remove the bite.

While the two Medical Complex physicians each thought about their respective lives, Szeppek was in his apartment, making a call. He had been told to phone the Consulate that evening, and saw no reason not to do as instructed.

"Sir, there's little to report. We have a forthcoming Site Visit important for our funding."

"Any problems with that, Janos?"

"I don't think so. I have to do more experiments and tabulate our data. Hopefully, we'll obtain funding. If we do, do you think I can stay an additional year?"

"I don't see why not. By the way, have you men made any earth-shattering discoveries? Anyone going to win the Nobel Prize?"

"You never know. We inject this Compound into a rat, take that rat through a maze, and then that rat goes through that maze, in that direction, in that pattern, every time it's in there. It is truly amazing."

"Have you discussed this yet with the NIH, with the Site Visit people?"

"We're supposed to meet with the NIH soon, I'm not sure when. Dr. Swept is in charge of that."

"Is there any danger in your being exposed to this Compound? Any harmful effects from the medication?"

"I don't think so. We're still evaluating it. We should know soon. Dr. Swept is a good man. Brilliant. For all you know, we will win the Nobel Prize."

"I hope so, but don't let it go to your head. I'm glad your work is going well. Give me a call after the Site Visit. I'm excited for you and would like to know what's happening. Let's be certain that our prize students are happy and doing well."

"Thanks."

"These are just formalities, you know. To be certain you aren't exposed to anything harmful and that the Americans don't whisk away our best scientists."

"No need to worry about that. I'll talk to you later."

"By the way, one more thing, Janos. As you know, all our students talk to us on a periodic basis. Americans sometimes have a hard time understanding this. It isn't necessary, unless you think otherwise, that Dr. Swept or anyone else know about our routine conversations."

"We've discussed that before. I agree. I'm happy to do whatever you want."

"Fine. Have a nice evening."

"Thanks. Good night."

Chapter Six

HIMALAYA BLUES

THE FOLLOWING DAY, recesses of his mind holding thoughts of Regina, Swept sat in his office overlooking the fountain. A firm knock on the door broke his repose, causing him to turn in his chair. It was the Chairman's nurse.

"How are you this morning, Dr. Swept?" Valerie's query held a crisp, refreshing air about her.

"Fine, Valerie. You're in good spirits. What can I do for you?"

"Not much. I was taking care of some errands for Dr. Ranger, saw your door open, and thought I'd say hello."

"I appreciate it but, to be frank," as Swept thought about patients, grants and Regina, "between an NIH Site Visit and everything else, I'm pretty busy." Just then, the intercom on the phone rang. Swept depressed the flashing intercom button and picked up the receiver.

It was Tracy.

"Dr. Swept. I'm sorry to bother you, but a Ricki Hardson, some nurse, is really vexed and absolutely insists on seeing you today. She isn't making a lot of sense. I'm not certain whether she wants to be seen as a patient. She insists on talking to you and has called several times. What do you want me to do? Do you want to see her?"

Looking at Valerie, wishing her out of the office, Swept released an exasperated sigh. "I'm planning to work on research and grants all day. Have her come over a little before noon. How long do you think I'll have to spend with her? Five minutes?"

"I have no idea. All I know is that she is unbelievably insistent about seeing you."

"Tell her she has ten minutes. It may be she has some neurological disease and is terrified of someone knowing," thinking perhaps she had AIDS. An increasing number of people in the Medical Complex had contracted AIDS, many of whom presented with neurological symptoms. If she had AIDS, she might not want to go through the routine clinic scheduling system. Swept would see her in his office, rather than in the clinic. Ten minutes would suffice for ascertaining any bona fide neurology emergency. If she had major disease, he would admit her to the hospital, or place her in the Outpatient Unit. Otherwise, he would schedule her for a routine clinic appointment, and do his best to protect her privacy, which could well be a major issue for her.

Swept replied, "I'm hers from eleven-fifty to twelve."

"I'll tell her. Have a nice day," Tracy responded. Swept could mentally see Tracy's sarcastic grin.

"Thanks. You too." Swept returned the phone to its cradle and turned to Valerie, leaning against the door jam. "Someone can get you for ten minutes in the middle of the day? Lucky her." Valerie grinned, and went down the hallway.

Swept sat in his chair, clasped his fingers behind his head, extended his chest and pushed back his neck, similar to extension maneuvers he practiced as a wrestler in high school. Now, he had work to do. As he began busying himself, someone else appeared at the door. It was Szeppek, starry-eyed and excited.

"Dr. Swept. Look at this data," handing over graphs and tables. "Look. I came in early this morning because I wanted to run more rats, putting them through the maze without any reward. Eleven more rats, given the Compound, placed in the maze and taken through it, with no food at the end of the maze," emphasizing the last phrase, "go through that maze from beginning to end every subsequent time they're placed in it. All we have to do is give the chemical to these rats, then put the animals in the maze once, manually push them through it, and they travel through it every time on their own. They learn the route after only one trial. Unbelievable!"

"Janos." Swept again clasped his hands behind his head, applying an isometric maneuver to a now tight neck. "Let's go over this again. Beginning to end." He motioned to one of the three chairs in his office, offering Janos a chair.

The two spent the next forty minutes discussing the data. There was no doubt: The chemical was effective.

"Janos, we are really on to something. This is potent data. As simple as it seems, the way to help people with memory deficits probably is right in front of us. We have to bear a few things in mind, though. Patients with abnormal memory systems, such as Alzheimer's patients, have underlying brain disease. They might not react the same way that a non brain-damaged patient reacts to the chemical. Also, let's not forget, human beings aren't rats. We'll proceed with our work, obtain more data, and continue to look for side effects. Then, I'll show these results to Dr. Ranger and get our presentation ready for the Site Visit."

"What do you think Dr. Ranger will say? Do you think he'll let us try it in human beings? If not, I don't mind trying it on myself."

"Under no circumstances do that! As for Dr. Ranger, he still won't be interested in working with humans. But, he might be forced into it, following the Site Visit. Perhaps, at the Site Visit, we can ask what they think about our working with humans. If they support it, and think it's a good idea, Ranger's got to go along. After all, these are the guys who provide the funding."

"I can't tell you how excited I am, Dr. Swept. This is terrific! Unbelievably terrific! This is great science!"

"Science doesn't dwell on believables or unbelievables. Nor on whether anything seems terrific. True science is only concerned with asking questions and dealing with alternative models. But, that discussion's for another time. Who knows what's believable, real, or known. Science asks questions and provides models that provide and test answers. That's what science is."

Szeppek said nothing. He respected Swept, but occasionally queried whether the neurologist was too much an academic. No matter. His respect was immense and the recently attained knowledge, believable or not, real or not, known or not, was exciting. The laboratory was tapping into how the brain actually functioned. Szeppek left the neurologist's office and returned to the lab, confident that he could run the remaining experiments over the next two to three days.

Meanwhile, Swept labored at his desk, putting together necessary information for the grant. His concentration was intense and he accomplished a great deal. Now and then he looked out the window, noticing the attractive fountain, seeing the antivivisectionists sitting on the fountain's edge. He could not tell whether they were looking at him. It was difficult to see his office interior from the outside, certainly with the sun projecting on the window. He turned to page six of the grant application, and noted the section on vertebrate animals. There it was:

> No federally funded award for research involving vertebrate animals will be made to an applicant organization unless that organization is operating in accord with an approved Animal Welfare Assurance and provides verification . . .

There were four paragraphs on the rights of animals. There was one on the civil rights of humans, one paragraph on the rights of handicapped individuals, and another on sex discrimination.

Swept failed to see so many of the points of the antivivisectionists. He knew that some weren't satisfied, even when animals were appropriately treated in a laboratory. They didn't want the animals in any laboratory setting at all. How could he, Dr. Dick Swept, ever hope to discover a compound that could help Alzheimer's patients if he were not allowed to work with rats? Yet, many individuals had mistreated animals, prompting these NIH guidelines.

Another complication in life.

At 11:50 a.m., there was a knock at the door, the third for the day. Swept knew who it was, without turning. Swept rose from his chair and walked to the entrance. He smiled graciously at an obviously nervous young woman. "You must be Ms. Hardson."

"Yes, Ricki Hardson. Dr. Swept?"

He clasped her hand, noticing the firm grip in this nervous woman and motioned her to enter his office. "I understand you want to see me. Please, sit down."

Ricki Hardson sat in front of Swept, facing him. "I really appreciate this, certainly on such short notice. I've got a problem and was hoping you could help me. Today, I decided to stop mulling this over and see someone I respected."

"Thank you, I'll try. What's on your mind?"

"This." Opening her pocketbook and removing a folded newspaper article, obviously worn, she carefully unfolded the article, consisting of two pages, and placed it before the neurologist. "What they say here isn't true. It isn't. I was there."

Swept briefly looked at the article. He recognized it as the article he had earlier seen in the *New York Times*, addressing the death of the Sherpas in Nepal.

"Why are you showing this to me?"

Dr. Swept, I'm an Infectious Disease nurse. Not only would it surprise me that meningococcus meningitis broke out in the middle of the Himalaya, but I'm the person who found the dead Sherpas."

Swept looked at her, in amazement.

"Yes. It was me."

Swept arched his right eyebrow. "Wow! That must have been something."

"It was. They were incontinent of urine and stool, as well as being in a whole bunch of contorted positions. I think they had seizures, but not from meningitis. I've seen a lot of patients with meningitis, but I've never seen meningitis make people look like that!"

Swept interrupted. "I earlier saw that article and was sort of surprised myself that meningococcus meningitis, which usually attacks people living in crowded conditions, you know, like army barracks, struck a village in the Himalaya. But let me get back to my question. Why are you here, seeing me?"

"Because I don't know who else to see. I spoke to the Chief of our Infectious Disease Unit, Dr. Hibbing, and he agreed with me, but didn't want to get involved. He said he was too busy."

"Involved? Involved with what?"

"If those people died from something, then there's a danger others can die from it. The Nepalese government obviously dismissed major concerns by saying this was meningitis, so they're not doing anything. For all they know, there's another disease lingering out there, in the mountains, and it will strike again. What about tourists going through? What about people like me, who were there? I could have been killed, as could thousands of tourists each year."

Swept nodded his head. "But, I still don't understand why you're seeing me."

"I wrote to the newspapers and they dismissed my concern. I called the Nepalese Consul in New York, who also dismissed my complaints. When I phoned the Embassy in Washington, D. C., all they wanted to know was whether I was a doctor. When I said no, they hung up. After that, I spoke to Dr. Hibbing but he wouldn't call, he was too busy."

"For the last time, why me?"

"Because, you're respected, intelligent, and a neurologist. I can't conceive you wouldn't think these people had seizures, once I give you more details. They had broken bones, all over. Also, maybe you can get hold of data the Nepalese government has. I'll bet they didn't find evidence of meningococcus meningitis."

"Ms. Hardson, I think it's noble you have concern about the suffering of humanity, and I appreciate your compliment, but I'm not the person to whom you should speak. Why not contact the Communicable Disease Center in Georgia?"

"I did. They weren't interested in anything I had to say. They wrote me off with a form letter. I have no data, at least no actual medical reports and, besides, they don't review reports that pertain to other countries, unless it involves the United States. They suggested I contact some branch of the United Nations or the World Health Organization."

"And. . . ?" Swept was smiling, impressed with this woman's tenacity.

"I did. There was a meeting in Kathmandu involving representatives from Norway, Austria, Russia, and the United States. They all agreed these people had meningitis. I tell you, it's impossible. People with meningitis don't look the way they did. Certainly, not meningococcus meningitis. They would have had blotches all over their skin, not just around their eyes. And why would they all have seized? Something other than meningitis caused this. It's made me a wreck. I even started smoking again."

"Sorry to hear that. Look, I appreciate your speaking to me, and I wish you luck. But, frankly, I'm tied up with research grants, getting ready for an NIH Site Visit, busy in the clinic, busy in the lab, and, maybe at one time I was somewhat of an idealist, but not now. Dealing with the Establishment in America is one thing. Dealing with a medical establishment in Nepal, and the Himalaya, is a totally different matter. I'm sorry, but you've got the wrong guy."

"No, I don't."

"Yes, you do," Swept said with a polite, apologetic smile, initiating his rise from the chair and beginning to motion the young nurse to the door.

Ricki Hardson picked up the newspaper article

that Swept had placed on his desk and proceeded to put it back in her purse. "I guess I was wrong. Sweptomania was on target after all."

The right eyebrow arched.

"I won't trouble you again, Dr. Swept."

Swept was not pleased when the nurses poked fun at his amorous adventures in their play, "Sweptomania." At one point, he had slept with nearly every attractive looking woman in the Medical Complex. Indeed, before the widespread prevalence of herpes and AIDS, he sometimes had concurrent relationships with women. As time went on, certainly during his seeing Regina, his concept of romance changed. Regina, somehow, altered his view of himself. Whatever the reason, whatever the cause, he was not as "easy" as at one time he had been. Swept wasn't certain whether his sexual drive had diminished, but he didn't care. Another factor curtailing his amorous encounters was the fact that various "Sweptophiles," as they were called in the play, were now aware of the short-lived nature of the relationship Dr. Swept offered, and wanted little to do with him. Even Ranger, with his near-pariah attitudes, had made some comments to Swept.

"Ms. Hardson. First, I take personal offense at your bringing up a nurses' play at my expense at the same time you're asking me for a medical favor. If you're trying to goad me into doing something for you . . ."

"I'm not trying to goad you into anything, Dr.

Swept. I'm not even asking you anymore. I thought that you, as an intellectual, an academician, and a physician-scientist that, despite 'Sweptomania,' you would be interested in this." She momentarily hesitated as she inserted the folded article into her purse. "I'm not trying to coerce you into anything. I'm just concerned more people will die, and I ought to be doing something about it. I just don't know what to do. That's all. If you want to help, fine. If not, I'm sure someone else in the Complex will be interested. I won't give up. Something killed those people and it wasn't meningitis. If I offended you with 'Sweptomania,' I apologize."

"I take my hat off to you. You are committed."

"So, do you have a change of heart. Will you help me?"

Swept studied the woman, a look of earnest concern mapped on her face. "I may not be able to get to it for a week or two, because of the Site Visit, but I'll look at the article again and, if I can get hold of the Nepalese reports, I'll go over their data."

Ricki smiled. "That's all I'm asking. I think I should go over, in as much detail as I can recall, which isn't too much, considering that I almost passed out when I saw all those dead people, everything I saw. Do you want me to write it down? I've started to, and have some notes, but I think it would be easier if we just sat and talked about it."

"Fine."

"When?"

"When?" The woman was certainly persistent.

"When? If we're going to do it, let's do it. If you want to wait awhile, then wait awhile. But I'd like to do it as soon as possible."

"Okay. You've got it. How much time will you need?"

"Probably not more than an hour. I just want to describe everything I saw. Then, you can decide whether you want to contact the Nepalese authorities regarding getting hold of the actual medical reports or, maybe all you have to do is to send a letter to a newspaper and point out the discrepancies between what you think meningitis does and what happened to the Sherpas."

"Saying what? Saying that I spoke to someone who was in Nepal and based upon that information I have something to say to the news media?"

"No. Obviously, you couldn't do that. But you could sign a letter with me. Actually, I would be happy if you just got hold of the medical reports and looked at them. I'll bet you can do it, if not on your own, then possibly through Dr. Hibbing, because he'll probably work with you. He's a hotshot in this Medical Complex and runs several floors in his Institute. And, I happen to know, he respects you."

"Why doesn't he help you?"

"I told you. He's too busy."

"And I'm not? Besides, you don't strike me as a woman who can work for a man who doesn't want to 'get involved.'"

"He's the Chairman. Actually, I don't work a lot with him directly. Besides, how close are you with your Chairman?"

"Case closed. Mine's a pain in the neck."

"Dr. Hibbing isn't a pain. He's just busy and, I guess, doesn't care."

"Good for him."

"But, you'll help me?"

"Yes."

"When do we meet?"

"Tell Tracy, my secretary, when you want to meet with me. She's probably at her desk right now, next door, wondering what in the world was so important that you had to meet me."

"I can't tell you how happy I am you'll do this."

"You aren't becoming a Sweptophile, are you?" Swept said, smiling.

"Hardly," Ricki did not smile. "This has been on my mind for some time and I just want to discuss it.

Don't worry about my being a Sweptophile. Why don't I meet you here in your office at the end of the day and we can discuss this and then I'll be out of your hair. How about 7:30?"

"Can't. I have to be home before seven o'clock to put my dog out. Otherwise, he has incontinence of his own, inside my house."

"You have a dog?"

"Yes, a dog. Is that surprising? I take it he wasn't mentioned in Sweptomania."

"Look, I'm sorry I brought that up. I just don't meet many men who have dogs. Most don't have time for them. Certainly, not professional men working here in the Medical Complex. Besides, most men aren't that emotionally inclined."

"How about if we make a deal, Ms. Hardson. You forget Sweptomania and Sweptophiles, and I'll forget your conclusions about emotional juxtapositions within my brain, based upon my having a dog. Sound good?"

"Sure." Ricki thought a second, then gathered her composure. "How about if I meet you later this evening? It shouldn't take too long. I'm dying to get this off my chest and discuss it with someone who's neurologically knowledgeable. I tell you, Dr. Swept, something happened to those people that all the authorities are missing."

"Fair enough." Swept gave her his address, writing it down. "Be at my house at 7:30. If I'm not there, it's because I haven't returned from my jog. Wait outside and I'll be there in a few minutes. You'll get to meet the famous dog and show me whatever data, letters, correspondence, you like. See you then?"

Smiling, Ricki Hardson said, "Great."

Swept walked Ricki Hardson to the door, thinking about his evening plans. He had initially hoped to see Regina, but her distancing maneuvers were doing just that, distancing him. So, he had planned to work that evening on the grant, going over data from Szeppek's experiments. But now, he thought that speaking to Ricki Hardson could prove interesting, and the respite might be good for him.

Swept went through more of the papers on his desk and then went to his laboratory, eager to speak to Szeppek about the day's projects.

*   *   *

After reviewing more data with Szeppek, discussing the exact configuration of the maze, how the rats were killed, and searching for side effects, Swept returned to his office. As he did so, he ran into Valerie VanDance.

"How was your Nooner, Dr. Swept?"

Swept knew no reason why Valerie should assume familiarity. Without cracking a smile, looking into her eyes, the neurologist responded, "I don't discuss patients."

"I beg your pardon, Doctor. Just trying to be polite."

"No you weren't. You were trying to be too familiar."

"My apologies."

"Accepted." Swept returned to his office and worked diligently for the next several hours. Coffee was his lunch. He saw some in-patients in the hospital, whose physicians had requested he personally evaluate them. One had lumbar spine disease, one Carpal Tunnel Syndrome, and another a small but surgically unresectable tumor in the upper part of the spinal cord. After examining these patients, feeling good he could help two, but miserable that the other was doomed to quadriplegia and, ultimately, death, he returned to the office, gathered his papers, put them inside his briefcase, and headed toward the parking lot. After placing the worn briefcase in the rear seat, he started his car, and passed the parking lot attendant.

The attendant smiled at Swept and picked up the telephone as the Ferrari disappeared around the corner. The phone rang four times before a voice answered.

"Hello."

"This is your downstairs man. Dr. Swept just left. Doing my job, lady."

"Fine. Thanks." The phone disconnected. Valerie hung up. The parking lot man snickered slightly, put down the phone, and returned to collecting money from those who had parked in his domain.

Chapter Seven

A COMMITTED WOMAN

AFTER ARRIVING HOME, Swept greeted his dog and went out to jog. He took a favorite Dylan tape that, although not good for jogging, placed him in the mind state that supported his jogging. Good jogging music was disco music. Swept hated disco music. He loved Dylan, not so much for the music but for the words. The words altered his state of mind. As he softly pounded the dirt in his Nikes, running three miles around City University, he readjusted the tape to hear "It's All Over Now Baby Blue." The anti-materialism lyrics reminded him of Regina.

Swept returned home, showered, and had just finished putting on his Wrangler jeans and T-shirt when Ricki Hardson knocked at the door.

Swept opened the door, expecting to see a woman appearing the way Ricki Hardson had earlier appeared – somewhat nervous, light brown hair tucked in a bun, thin lips, with a firm handshake forecasting some level of confidence. Now, she looked totally different. He almost fell through the floor.

Ricki Hardson wore a loose fitting T-shirt, which said "New Orleans Jazz." Tight black jeans tapered toward her Greek sandals. With no makeup, she looked fresh, almost virginal. Her hair was no longer in a bun but now flowed across both shoulders. For the first time, Swept noticed how she moved. She obviously had physical prowess, certainly consistent with her hiking in the mountains. For some reason, her lips now appeared almost inviting.

"Well, Ms. Hardson. Come in. This creature over here," pointing to Limbic, sniffing at her heels, "is Limbic. We can sit in the den and, if you like, I'm happy to pour you a drink."

"Thank you, Dr. Swept. Actually, club soda is fine."

"Sure. Some lime?"

"Thank you."

Swept walked toward the kitchen, after escorting Ricki Hardson into the den. He said in a pleasant demeanor, "Rule number one – call me Dick, not Dr. Swept."

"Thank you. 'Ricki' is fine for me."

Swept went to his kitchen, announced that he had no club soda but did have Perrier, poured two glasses, each with a slice of lime, and returned to the den, finding Ricki still standing.

"Please, sit down. Here's a Perrier. Close enough to club soda?" Swept picked up his glass, smiling a toast to the nurse, and continued. "Now, Ricki Hardson, what is it you want me to hear, see, or believe?"

"You can believe what you choose. I want you to understand the postures that these people were in when I found them. Then, I'd like to show you my correspondence."

Ricki Hardson spent the next twenty minutes carefully describing the distorted postures of the dead Sherpas. She regretted not taking pictures. Ricki did not remember as much as she would have liked, but was certain about one thing – the bodies were incredibly contorted. The only way to achieve this distortion was through broken bones, or so she thought. She described the incontinence of the dead mountain people, making her query seizures. Last, she showed Swept her correspondence, consisting of letters that had mostly elicited responses of two to three sentence dismissals.

Swept leaned back and put down the drink. "I appreciate you telling me this but let me toss out something: The bones could have been broken by something other than seizures."

"What?"

"Well, to begin with, if something happened to the bones, they might not have been strong enough to support the normal mechanics of body movement. That can cause broken bones and contortions. Now, I grant you, the likelihood of this is remote, assuming that they were all walking and moving around normally with normal bone function before they died. But, you haven't excluded the possibility of diffuse bone disease. Second, people usually don't have multiple broken bones from seizures. They may break some vertebrae, or their hip or skull, especially if they fall down hard, but it's rare to break limbs."

"Are you sure?"

"I'm sure. However, there aren't many things that break multiple bones, certainly not acutely. Someone can be osteoporotic and, if they fall, have multiple fractures. But, unless the Sherpas were all osteoporotic, they wouldn't be predisposed to bones breaking. Further, the fact that they're all living in mountains, walking around on what I presume are inclines and declines, makes me think they have enough physical stress on their bones such that they're less predisposed to osteoporosis. You don't see, usually, significant osteoporosis in individuals engaged in significant physical activity, for all sorts of reasons pertaining to bone metabolism."

Ricki Hardson listened attentively. She was pleased. Obviously, Swept had listened to her and was processing her input, offering concepts and ideas she had not considered.

"Second, or third, I agree that meningococcus meningitis shouldn't strike a remote village in the Himalaya. Meningococcus meningitis strikes peoples in close quarters. But, even if they had meningococcus meningitis, why should they all have broken bones? The only way that meningococcus meningitis could cause broken bones, would be if they did seize. And, again, seizures usually don't break bones that often. Further, seizures aren't that common in meningitis. Besides, they wouldn't *all* seize."

Swept continued. "This doesn't make a lot of sense. Now, having agreed with you but having nothing intelligent to add, what do you want me to do?"

"I'm not certain, but I do know something happened we don't understand, and that it can happen again."

Swept looked at Ricki Hardson. She was a good-looking woman. He took in her sensual posture, and he now thought she had gorgeous eyes and a compelling smile. Swept found her attractive. Limbic walked over from the corner of the room and readjusted himself across her right foot, without Ricki seeming to mind.

"Why don't I write the authorities in Nepal and ask for the medical report?"

"I bet they won't send it. You can try, but I bet they won't."

"Well, we do have another alternative. Why don't you and I together write a letter to the *Houston*

Chronicle, the World Health Organization, the Nepalese Embassy, the Surgeon General, the Communicable Disease Center in Georgia, the King of Nepal and anybody else we can think of?"

"I thought you said you didn't have enough time to spend on all this?"

"I don't, but it won't take long. Not to a man with access to a computer and a good secretary. I'll put together one or two letters, show them to you, and in the meantime you decide whether anyone else should receive the letter."

"Thanks. Can I stop by your office tomorrow at the same time as today? Noon?"

"You are a persistent woman. I'll dictate the letters. It shouldn't be that difficult for my secretary to type them tomorrow. Noon will be fine."

"Thanks, I appreciate it. I'm not trying to push you too hard on this but, please understand, this has been bothering me a lot, especially since I saw the article in the newspaper. They're wrong."

Swept was impressed with Ricki Hardson's concern for human suffering. He couldn't help but compare her to Regina's strong financial orientation, as he walked the nurse to the door, and then found himself walking her further, to her car, an old maroon Toyota.

"Thank you very much, Dr. Swept. I really appreciate your interest and your time."

"Isn't it supposed to be 'Dick'?"

Smiling, the woman got into the car. "Thanks, Dick. See you tomorrow."

Swept returned to his den and dictated two letters, brief and to the point. One was addressed to the Infectious Disease Hospital in Nepal, politely requesting medical records of the dead Sherpas. He referenced the *New York Times* article, a copy of which he would enclose, and commented on their alleged findings of meningitis. The other letter he would send to the *New York Times* itself, as well as to the *Houston Chronicle*, commenting about the *Times'* article and his suspicion, as a neurologist, that the Sherpas did not have meningitis. Both letters highlighted that he was a faculty member in the Department of Neurology at the Texas College of Medicine, and that his reason for writing related to a possible international health problem: *Why* did a whole community of people die?

After finishing his dictation, making a mental note to give the tape to Tracy first thing in the morning, Swept called Regina to say goodnight. He hoped she would be interested in spending the night with him, perhaps to push aside some of the misgivings he had about their relationship and to counterbalance his pleasant time with Ricki Hardson. Instead, he found himself speaking to an answering machine. He called Regina's answering service, identified himself as a physician, and asked where she was. She was in the Operating Room.

Swept did his exercises, poured himself a glass of Chateau Fontpinot cognac, read Lewis Lapham's curmudgeon editorial about the medical establishment in *Harpers*, and went to sleep.

*　　*　　*

The following day, Swept found his thoughts periodically interrupted by his anticipation of seeing Ricki at noon. Tracy promised to have the letters done by then. Ricki's commitment and apparent enthusiasm for humanity, an enthusiasm in recent years he knew had diminished within himself, was exciting and reminiscent of what he used to be. What he used to be was something he no longer was – committed. Now, somewhat older, at 37, trudging through the rigors of academia, he found himself making increasing number of compromises. Sometimes, they were to the hospital administrators. Other times, to his Chairman.

Swept would not compromise his science. His methodology was good. His experimental designs were good. His hypotheses held meaning. He had never pursued quick, easy projects in order to publish more, thereby expanding his Curriculum Vita. As he put the finishing touches on his grant application, and readied his data for the forthcoming Site Visit, Swept felt pleased with his laboratory's work.

He was thinking of Ricki, but he knew he should be thinking of Regina. The contrast was compelling: both women were attractive, physically and biologically, but Ricki *cared*. Regina, on some level, cared but always had some distancing maneuver about her.

Swept could never love a woman who was not loyal to him, and Regina wasn't loyal. Indeed, she seemed to lack the quality of loyalty altogether. She certainly hadn't been loyal in the concept of marriage, when she had her love affair with that married Nobel Laureate. But, perhaps, his intelligence dazzled her, although Swept never found him that exciting a conversationalist, at least not when he had met him on one occasion. Regina held no loyalty to her scientific domain, having left behind her research in wound healing. And, she had no loyalty to Swept – she was constantly changing plans with him, placing her medical practice, especially its financial aspects, before him.

On one occasion, while making love to Regina, Swept remembered saying, "I need you. I really need you." Regina smiled for a moment, only to reply, "If you need me, then there must be something you want. What do you want?" The coldness of that comment made his interest plummet, disastrously so, for the moment. The two argued about insensitivity. How could Swept love a woman who spoke like that? How could anyone?

Somehow, Swept knew those words would never be spoken by Ricki Hardson. Or, was that just wishful thinking?

No matter, Swept had to be certain everything was ready for the Site Visit and that his ideas would sell well. He needed the funding. If he received funding, he would stand a good chance of receiving tenure, as well as having more financial resources to pursue his scientific endeavors. So, money was also important to him.

Relinquishing this thought process, Swept returned to his experiments and data collection. When the neurologist concentrated, he was incredibly productive. He had always been able to do in one hour what most people could not accomplish in less than two. This was not because of his being brighter than his colleagues but, rather, his inordinate concentration skills. It was in this edifice of concentration, working on his grant, that the hours passed and he found his thoughts broken by Ricki Hardson's knock at the door.

"Dick? Sorry to interrupt you, but it's noon."

Rising from his chair, simultaneously being gestured not too, he beckoned Ricki Hardson to enter his office. He showed her the letters, explaining that he would send a copy to the Infectious Disease Hospital in Nepal, the World Health Organization, the United Nations General Consulate, and the Communicable Disease Center in Georgia. Another letter, addressed to the *New York Times* and the *Houston Chronicle,* would be copied to Dr. Hibbing, as well as the *Washington Post* and anyone else she could think of.

"I'll even send it to the *National Enquirer* if you think that's appropriate."

"This isn't a joking matter. If everything fails, perhaps you can write to the *New England Journal of Medicine.* They accept letters, don't they?"

"Yes, they do. That might even increase my Curriculum Vita, help me get promoted."

"This isn't a jocose matter. I'm serious."

"Look, Ricki. I'm serious too. If I weren't serious, I wouldn't interrupt my day to do this."

"Sorry. It's just that this has been welling up inside me for so long that, after I finally got it out, talking to you, I guess I feel a little bit of a rush."

"That's okay. I'll ask Tracy, my secretary, to send these out. I need to get photocopies of the *New York Times* article so that I can enclose it in the correspondence. That way, people will have a better idea what I'm talking about."

"Fine. I have the article here."

"I'm not surprised." The two walked, found the photocopy room empty, and Swept made copies of the article.

"Dick, thanks again. Let me know what people say in response to your letters. Thanks ever so much." Ricki Hardson extended her hand, and kissed Dick Swept on the cheek.

Swept contained himself, surprised at the kiss, but enjoyed it. "My pleasure. Besides, I also think we should get to the bottom of all this."

Swept and Ricki left the copy room, and Swept started to return to his office. He somewhat hoped Ricki would follow him. She did not. The nurse had to get back to work and walked toward the elevators. Swept accompanied her until the elevator arrived.

When the elevator door opened, Valerie VanDance was inside, and exited on the floor as Ricki entered the elevator, waving good-bye with understated hand movements. "Thanks again. Let me know what happens."

"Sure. Talk to you later." The door closed.

Valerie, smiling, looked at Swept. "Well, Dr. Swept. Another Nooner? With the same woman?"

"I don't know what your problem is, but I can assure you my own realm, academic or otherwise, poses little interest to you." Swept tried to restrain himself, realizing he was talking to the Chairman's nurse.

"Well, you never know." Her eyes then noticed the copies of the newspaper article he was holding." What do you have here? Photocopying articles about how famous you are? Certainly, not at Department expense, I hope."

"Hardly. It's an article about a meningitis outbreak in Nepal."

Valerie VanDance seemed a bit startled. However, trained not to lose composure, looking squarely into Swept's eyes, she asked what the article contained.

"Here, see for yourself," handing Valerie a copy. "That woman is a nurse who found the dead bodies in the Himalaya. She doesn't think they died from meningitis. Nor do I. If you want, take a look. Now, I've got to go."

Valerie VanDance thanked Swept, and took the copy of the article to her office. Actually, she had no need to do this. She had seen it before and was familiar with its contents. What she couldn't understand was why Dr. Dick Swept was involved with the Sherpa outbreak. She closed her office door and, using her private line, phoned one of her Washington contacts.

After going through appropriate check channels, the labyrinthine patterns of which reminded Valerie of fairyland gimmicks, she reached Bradley Serkin. Serkin's main office was in Washington, D. C. . Valerie was pleased he was in.

"Bradley. How are you?"

"Fine, Val. How's everything with you?"

"Everything's good here. I have a question. Do you have a minute?"

"Shoot."

"There's a neurologist here who contends that the Sherpas in Nepal didn't die from meningitis. What was the formal conclusion?"

"Well, I contacted you – uh – after that meeting in Kathmandu. I telefaxed the documents and you – uh – showed them to a pathologist in Houston for my report. Right?"

"Yes. He gave me a lot of medical jargon, said that most of the findings suggested brain damage. I thought he didn't say meningitis, just a lot of hemorrhage. But I sent that data to you. Right?"

"Absolutely. Those poor sons of bitches, as well as the ladies, they all died from meningitis. Everyone on the Committee agreed."

"Okay, Bradley. Thanks a lot."

"Any time."

Valerie VanDance was puzzled. First, why was Dick Swept involved with people dying in Nepal? Perhaps it was by chance, perhaps not. It was also strange that Ricki Hardson, a nurse in the Medical Complex, was the one who found the dead Sherpas. Valerie was not aware that the nurse who found the dead Sherpas worked in such proximity. Why was she now speaking to Swept? Most of all, she was puzzled over Bradley Serkin. He had always been a gentleman, polite, with perfect grammar and diction, without any "uhs." Only on one occasion, when both were very lonely, had he called her "Val." His demeanor now seemed different. She needed to find out from the neuropathologist who had reviewed the data for her what disease, if any, had killed the Sherpas.

Valerie VanDance phoned Dr. Luke Patterson, the neuropathologist to whom she had given the information. Patterson wasn't in. His secretary said he would call when he returned from the Operating Room Disease Control Committee meeting.

Meanwhile, VanDance pondered the *New York Times* article.

One hour later, Patterson returned her phone call. "Ms. VanDance. How can I help you? Does that grouch of a Chairman you work for have some problems?"

"No, Dr. Patterson. Actually, I'm calling because of a favor I earlier asked you. Remember?"

"You mean reviewing that voluminous stuff about those dead people?"

"Yes. What were your findings? I thought you said there was some type of hemorrhage. Was there any meningitis?"

Valerie VanDance had earlier asked the neuropathologist for his review, and sent her analysis to Bradley Serkin, who was to have amalgamated the information with data from other sources, had he deemed other sources necessary, in preparation for his report. She had no way of knowing, and would not follow up on what Serkin did with the information or what the committee in Kathmandu had decided. Her job was to provide Serkin with Houston input regarding the neuropathology findings. She had looked at the summary of Patterson's findings, and the details of the report, and did not recall evidence of meningitis.

"What I found was evidence of small strokes and some hemorrhage throughout the brains. There was no evidence of meningitis, no evidence of purulent exudate or any infection. Those people had, as best I could tell from the reports and the photographs, evidence of microinfarctions of their brain."

"What exactly does that mean?"

"Many of the arteries in the brain were blocked off, especially the smaller ones. This resulted in damage to the grey matter, which is probably why they had seizures. At least I assume they had seizures, because that would be the only way they could have had all those contorted positions, but they would have to seize extremely hard."

"So, you never said there was meningitis? You thought that they had small strokes and hemorrhages, not meningitis?"

"Yes. If you like, I can send you another copy of my report."

"I'd appreciate it. Can I get it now? I can pick it up, if you like."

"No problem. I'll have my secretary copy it and take it to you. Anything else?"

"No. Thanks again."

After Valerie VanDance received a copy of the report, she went over it in detail and called Bradley Serkin. Serkin insisted that the Sherpas died from meningitis.

"Bradley, I have the report in front of me. There is no evidence of meningitis. Dr. Patterson just told me on the telephone there was no meningitis."

"Well, the Sherpas had meningitis. Besides that's what everyone else on the committee thought too. They died from meningitis. Why else did they die?"

"Do you have a copy of the report Dr. Patterson sent you?"

"No. But I don't need it. I distinctly remember– uh – that's what the report said. How many times do I have to tell you?" They died from meningitis, meningococcus meningitis."

"Sorry to bother you. Talk to you later." Serkin bade goodbye and the respective phones disconnected.

Serkin's personality certainly had changed. Valerie should have had no reason to doubt him, considering the number of Inservice Awards he had won in the past, awards that could never be revealed to the public or press. Bradley Serkin was an excellent agent who had been with the Company a long time. Either his memory was incorrect or he was lying. Why would he lie? Perhaps, Patterson had changed the report. Perhaps, Patterson was lying. But, why would he do that? The Chairman's nurse decided to see Swept, who was in his office, putting finishing touches on the research protocol description.

"Dr. Swept, I'm sorry to bother you. But I have some questions about that newspaper article."

"About the newspaper article? Fire away, but I'm busy and have only a few minutes."

"It won't take much time. Why do you think those people didn't have meningitis?"

"I don't know much about this, only what Ricki Hardson, the young woman I just saw, told me. She said they were incontinent of urine and stool and in contorted positions. The only way to lose urine, and stool, and be in multiple contorted positions is to have had seizures, severe seizures, unless someone has ongoing bone disease, or unless they were hit by a truck. Fractures are rare with seizures. Also, if those people all had seizures, why would meningitis be the cause? Meningitis usually doesn't cause seizures and, if it does, why did the meningitis affect everybody? And, if they had meningitis, why would they have meningococcus meningitis, especially in a village high in the Himalaya? Now, why are you interested?"

"Just interested. You're pretty sure these people didn't have meningitis?"

"I don't think they did."

"Thanks. I was just curious."

*   *   *

Valerie returned to her office. She had been a CIA operative for over a decade, having been recruited while in nursing school. Her job at the Medical Complex was fairly simple, at times almost boring: She was to keep tabs on research that might be important for defense, or the nation's well-being, and, at other times, was asked to analyze data. She had many contacts in the Medical Complex, most of whom were cooperative. Considering that research published in journals was usually two years old, due to publication lag time and the time involved in reviewing the article prior to acceptance by the journals, this was how the Agency kept tabs on newer developments. The CIA's major interest in the Houston Medical Complex was on recombinant DNA and the Human Genome Project. Phones weren't tapped and laws weren't broken, but Valerie kept her ears open as to what people were doing.

One of the people Valerie VanDance closely followed, at times moreso than others, was Dick Swept. Swept's work pertained to memory research and she found it not only interesting but, conceivably, important. After all, didn't it broach on the area of mind-control? Her thoughts about this had been criticized as naïve, but she harmed no one by watching Swept. It was fun, although at times she wondered whether it was meaningless.

Another role of Valerie's was to obtain medical information that agents requested. This was not too frequent. She reasoned that her task was not alone in this domain, and that many hospitals and Medical Complexes had their CIA watchdogs.

Now, she was puzzled. Serkin's personality was not what it used to be. No matter, Valerie thought. People do change. But, here she was in the Houston Medical Complex with a neurologist now interacting with the death of the Sheupas, which already involved Serkin, and the nurse who found the dead Sherpas was also here in the Medical Complex. How did that nurse fit in? The paper had not identified her as being in the Complex. And, why would Serkin give information other than that found in Patterson's report, unless Patterson was lying?

Valerie telephoned Patterson, who again affirmed the accuracy of his original report. Perplexed, she decided to think more about this after she went home, passing the attendant, Tom, to whom she gave a bottle of wine for his troubles, politely fending off his advances.

Chapter Eight

NO HUMANS

DICK SWEPT SAT in Harold Ranger's office. "This is how I see it, Dr. Ranger. Our substance, Compound 1040, has a complex arrangement of amino acids, thirteen in all." Swept laid an outline of his research before the Chairman.

Ranger looked at it, grumbling about having to attend too many administrative meetings, and commented that the structure of 1040 appeared similar to growth hormone. Swept agreed, noting that the man truly could think about more than one thing at a time.

Swept broke the momentary silence. "When a rat that hasn't been exposed to any chemical is placed in this complicated labyrinth," showing Ranger the maze diagram, "it takes eight trials before it learns how to go from point A to point B in order to get food." He outlined the path with a retracted ballpoint pen. "Our placing a rat at point A, then manually taking it through the appropriate route, does almost nothing to facilitate its learning the maze. However, if we inject substance 1040 into the animal's system, then manually take it through the correct path, it not only spontaneously travels that route every time it is placed in the maze, but it resists any attempts to unlearn, if you'll permit the term, that route. We give it Compound 1040, which alters memory-related proteins, and thereby establish a behavior that becomes an indelible part of the animal's memory system."

Ranger was not impressed. He seldom appeared otherwise. The powerful Chairman had learned long ago that one held more respect from underlings and peers by never getting too excited about anything, good or bad. To get excited was to hint dealing with the unexpected. The Chairman of Neurology, positioned in one of the country's leading medical schools, thus never seemingly encountered anything unexpected. He never gave an inch.

Deep inside, Ranger was aware that Swept's discovery might actually have merit. Further, he was pleased that Swept would probably be approved by the Site Committee. Still, the dishevelled academician said nothing.

Swept, unphased by Ranger's silence, continued. "We've done preliminary studies in which the animal, under influence of 1040, is taught to go through particular portions of the maze, eat certain foods, avoid others, avoid certain geometric shapes, and to approach others. It's a large array of tasks." He placed several outlines of experimental paradigms before Ranger. We've discovered something major. I would love to try this on humans and . . ."

"Absolutely no humans, Dr. Swept! You do *not* have my approval to propose this before the Human Experimentation Committee. Stick with the animals, get the data together and leave humans out of this for the time being. Get funding. Get your feet on the ground, then worry about humans. Everything will be totally blown if anybody gets hurt by your new substance. You haven't used it long enough to know whether it produces deleterious effects after a few years. Maybe it's carcinogenic. Maybe it alters sexual function, appetite, weight, whatever! It's happened to others. What about Harrison in New York, or Williams and that crazy group of his in San Francisco? I don't want to hear any more about humans!"

Swept stared at his Chairman, in the eye, to the face. Trying to be polite, he expressed only some of his anger. "You say that with an almost misanthropic pleasure. Look, we're physicians. We're here to help people. I don't think demented patients and their families would mind trying a drug that has an even remote chance of helping their memory. We can always inform them about risks. Why don't you at least let me give it a try? At least, let me present this before the Human Experimentation Committee and see what they think. They might not find the risk as pronounced."

"I don't want to hear about it. This is *my* Department, *my* fiefdom, and I say no! After you've done follow-up studies for several years in animals, then and only then can you try it in humans. Until then, no!" Ranger's eyes rolled toward his shoes. The conversation was over. Swept rolled his eyes toward the ceiling, in exasperation. His transiently expanded nostrils and increased respiratory rate betrayed his emotional angst. Ranger, not having attained his position of power without feeling comfortable at trying to manipulate people, spoke.

"Dick, if I may change the subject, are your laboratory personnel ready for this? That postdoctorate fellow from Hungary seems to be working out well. He seems energetic, stays here late. Highly motivated. If his visa permits, I wonder if we should offer him a position on faculty. That is, if you're pleased with him."

Swept's emotions intensified, angry at Ranger trying to manipulate him. Surprised his Chairman would even consider bringing in someone else to work on memory and, perhaps, being slightly paranoid, concerned about the status of his position, he replied he was not certain what type of visa Szeppek had. Swept knew that the Hungarian, having worked in his laboratory and having been exposed to Swept's idea, was fairly knowledgeable. Szeppek might be more acquiescent at the Chairman's scientific whims, and thus more pleasing to Ranger, and perhaps to the medical school.

Swept responded that Szeppek had done good work but that his staying on at the medical school at this point in time would not be a wise move on the part of the College, regardless of his visa status, since he had not been in the laboratory sufficient time.

The point was made. Swept could be replaced.

As far as laboratory personnel being ready for the Site Visit, Swept explained his multiple rehearsals as to how they were to present the data, using Microsoft PowerPoint, and how they defined their research goals. Then, Swept had gone over it again – alone. Multiple times. He had planned to discuss this more with Harold Ranger but now lacked some of the energy necessary for that enterprise.

Swept left the Chairman's office. He did not enjoy situations in which he had little control. Nor did he like being manipulated. The neurologist entered his own office and donned his sacerdotal garb, the long white coat. He cautiously disappeared down the hallway, en route to the clinic.

Dick Swept examined two patients with occipital neuralgia, one with cervical spondylosis, two with atypical migraine, and one with epilepsy. The epileptic patient's seizures were well-controlled. Another patient had myotonic dystrophy. All the patients were doing well, all pleased. He felt good. Swept was pleased when patients did well. Always, he took it personally when they did not. After finishing his clinic at four o'clock, he rounded on his patients hospitalized in the Brain Institute and the neighboring Community Hospital. He then went home, exhausted.

Swept and Limbic had their three-mile run outside City University. For whatever reason, he decided this time to take Limbic with him. As he ran, he concentrated not so much upon the Site Visit but how he didn't fit into the rigors of academic medicine. Research was exacting and, being as thorough as he was, never settling for less than excellence, everything took its toll on him. Despite the near three mile daily run around City University, fine meals at Oscar's, and quasi-romantic evenings with Regina, he realized he was having increasing difficulty unwinding.

Swept returned home, showered, and ate alone at Oscar's. He returned home, poured his favorite cognac, and went to bed. The Site Visit was soon.

Chapter Nine

SITE VISIT

THE MORNING OF the Site Visit found Dick Swept refreshed. He arrived at the office early, reviewing his data one more time. When Harold Ranger knocked at his door, Swept was ready, his old brief-case in hand.

"Dick? Ready?"

"Yes. Where are these guys?"

"Upstairs in the conference room. They're already up there. This can take anywhere from thirty minutes to ten hours. I'll take you up there, introduce you, and then I'm off."

"Thanks. But, if you don't mind, why don't I just go up there and introduce myself? I'm a big boy."

"You got it. Good luck." Ranger departed down the hall, returned to his office, while Swept took the stairs and entered the conference room.

Swept introduced himself to the four men, including Dr. Nathaniel Chippers, the Director of the NINDS, and two women. Chippers was 67 years old, stood six feet two inches, trim, with a full crop of gray hair, a squared jaw and wore tortoise-shell glasses. His voice was firm. The exchanges were polite, brief, and formal.

Richard Michael Swept, M. D. excellently presented his data to the Site Committee entourage. After four hours, ignoring lunch, they asked him to leave while they discussed his proposal. They told him they had no need to meet with his laboratory personnel, a decision that surprised him. The information he had provided was sufficient for their decision process.

Swept returned half an hour later.

"Dr. Swept, on behalf of this Committee, I congratulate you. Your work is excellent and your approach to memory certainly unique. As Director of the National Institute of Neurological Disorders and Stroke, this is the most impressed I have been for quite some time in the field of memory research. If you ever decide to leave this school and want to work at the NIH, we're happy to have you."

Swept breathed a sigh of relief. He had made it. Then, Chippers continued.

"We have a meeting of fourteen prominent scientists doing research in memory, from the United States, and Western Europe, on October nineteenth, not too far away. Although these researchers are full professors and slightly older than you," Swept took this as meaning more experienced, "I would be most pleased if you joined us and discussed your experiments, especially your ideas and concepts. They're brilliant, absolutely brilliant. Many of the researchers working on memory and brain behavior could benefit from your concepts. And you, in turn, from theirs. All of us would be delighted, I'm sure, if you'll join us. I'll send a formal invitation."

Swept was delighted, and stunned. Finally, he thought, someone had something nice to say about his work. Yes, Harold Ranger respected his research in animals, but not enough – he wouldn't recommend his project to the Human Experimentation Committee. Interacting with established colleagues in memory research, exchanging information and ideas, all in the setting of the mighty National Institutes of Health complex, was indeed a great opportunity.

"Thank you very much. It's kind of you to say these things, but I really can't take all the credit. Many people in the lab have been extremely helpful. Thank you very much. I'll make the arrangements after I hear from you. I am truly honored."

"My pleasure," Chippers replied. The two shook hands. Swept walked with Dr. Chippers to the door when the Director, suddenly becoming more formal, was steps ahead of him. The Director of the NINDS departed with his entourage, a few glancing wistfully at the elevator, hoping their boss would not take stairs after the tiring day. Those hopes were soon dissipated since Chippers seldom took elevators, unless to ascend more than ten floors. Descending, he might tackle fifteen. The man was incredible. He firmly believed that taking stairs improved the quality of his currently excellent health and helped prolong life. Chippers stopped outside the stairwell, turning to Swept. "By the way, who are those antivivisectionists protesting out there? What's your Chairman, or the medical school, doing about them? Is there a large antivivisectionist movement in Houston?"

"No, not really. Frankly, I'm not sure what the College or Dr. Ranger are doing about the protestors. As far as I know, everything the protestors are doing is legal. All of us here in the medical school certainly follow the animal research guidelines. The antivivisectionists held a national meeting here for pro-animal people a while ago, and they're still here. I'm surprised they still are."

"Some laboratories have had major difficulties with the antivivisectionists, with major destruction of property. Have you had trouble here, in Houston?"

"No. They haven't caused any damage here. At least, not yet. For me, I have long thought that people concerned about the use of animals in biomedical research fall into two general categories. One group is concerned with animal welfare. They're not opposed to biomedical research, all they want is assurance that the animals are treated humanely, and that the number of animals used is the absolute minimum required. The other group is concerned about animal rights. They have a more radical position, totally opposing the use of animals in biomedical research. I support the first group." Thinking about his conflict with Ranger, and his desire to work with humans, Swept made a giant leap forward: "If you want to know my feelings about this, I think we should try my experiment on human beings."

"It might not be a bad idea, once you're certain about everything you're doing with the animals. We might fund human experimentation, but not now. What does your Chairman think about this?"

"He's against it."

"I'm not surprised, tough guy that he is. Tell him I said he's not right about everything. It might not be a bad idea in the future."

Swept felt good. He had not been inappropriate and had made his point. He took the stairs with Chippers and his entourage, and walked them to the entrance, where a limousine was ready to take them to the airport. Again Swept extended his thanks.

Chippers said good-bye, congratulated Swept and, once inside the limousine, used the car phone to contact Harold Ranger.

"Harold, that's a good man you've got there. He gets full funding. Smart, to the point, on top of things. Treat him well, otherwise we might take him."

"He'll get funding?"

"All of it. You run a good Department."

"Thank you. And, thanks for your support."

"Our pleasure." The limousine, now on Highway 59, headed north toward the airport, bucking Houston traffic.

Meanwhile, Swept met with his anxiously awaiting laboratory personnel. They were delighted and impressed. So small a window in time had been so important. Funding was now a sure thing. They put together a party in one of the conference rooms where Szeppek and the others, mostly technicians and a few undergraduates, interacted with their mentor with even increased deference, and obvious joy. Flowers and pizza materialized from nowhere, along with a bottle of Dom Perignon, which Swept only sipped. Others were more indulgent. Swept, obviously pleased, toasted his colleagues. "Here's to all of you. Thanks for your help, your hard work, and your energies. Here's to us. All held their glasses high, toasted the director of their laboratory, and felt good.

Swept tried to be similar to his Chairman, never allowing himself to become too excited, trying to keep his level of excitement under control. He did not enjoy having people control his life, having long believed that the way to keep people from having power to make him sad was never to permit them enough authority to make him happy. He did not apply this to his interpersonal relations, but did apply it to personal interactions within the medical community and his laboratory. Pleased that the Site Committee appreciated his research, still his main delight centered on the fact that he had funding and Ranger would not be on his back. However, he reminded himself, he could not allow Chippers' impression of his work to influence his own mind's validation of his scientific merit. The work was good, regardless of what anyone thought. Had the Site Committee not liked his research, perhaps it would have been because he had not presented it appropriately, or perhaps because they were fools. But, unless there were cogent arguments against the data, his work was good and his scientific method was exact. Swept would not give the Committee much hold over him, be their input complimentary or one of misgiving. However, for whatever reason, all that philosophical machination fell by the wayside as he held his glass high and said, "To us! To us!"

Following the small laboratory party, to which no one thought of inviting Ranger, Swept went directly to Ranger's office, bypassing the Chairman's secretary, and knocked firmly at the door. After stating he had full NIH funding, eliciting polite congratulations from Ranger, Swept told him of his invitation to the meeting at the NINDS. Then, to goad him, announced, "What do you think about my working at the NINDS?"

"Wrong person, wrong time, wrong place." Swept had too often heard that memorized statement. He had heard it all before. Ranger employed this little phrase several times when good people thought of leaving for a better job. He silently wondered whether Ranger would again bring up the possibility of Szeppek's staying on as faculty. He doubted it. Swept left Ranger's office, and noticed that the Chairman did not stare at his shoes.

*   *   *

One week later, Tracy placed an important letter from the NIH on Swept's desk, the invitation to the special conference on memory disturbances of the NIH, on October nineteenth. In addition to Swept, there were fourteen scientists, each well recognized in his or her field, each a pioneer doing research done by no one else. The NIH, through Chippers, believed that Swept's area of expertise overlapped with their investigations.

Chippers attached a list of those expected to attend. Swept immediately phoned Szeppek, asking him to obtain a Medical Complex Library database search on their articles, so that he could review and be familiar with everyone's research. He recognized the names of all those attending, had met several, however briefly, and wanted to be as knowledgeable as possible about their research when he interacted with them in the nation's capital.

*   *   *

Szeppek continued his diary every night, a pastime acquired years earlier from emotional frustration. His bookstand back home held written memories of all that had transpired since he was nine years old, a compendium of factual debris about his day, but seldom about the feelings in his life. Perhaps, one day, when he would be a great man, his diary would have great meaning. Until then, it was a superficial repository of indices of frustration.

The Hungarian student recognized that Swept's laboratory was doing outstanding research. Szeppek was a part of the project. He *felt* it. In more than a sequestered parcel in his mind, the Hungarian believed his role in developing Compound 1040 would place him, and his family, in good standing back home. Szeppek made his call to the Hungarian Consulate. It began as small talk but soon included the Site Visit.

"Our work is outstanding and the NIH realizes it. Dr. Swept was given full funding."

"Good, Janos. That must be really exciting. What did they say about it?"

"They thought his work was unique and creative. As a matter of fact, he will present his research, our findings, to fourteen other scientists working in overlapping areas, at a meeting of the NIH in Washington D. C.."

"Soon?"

"October nineteenth. We're all very excited."

"Are you going?"

"No. It's only for the hotshots."

"Come on, Janos, you're a hotshot."

"Not like Dr. Swept."

"I'm not sure about that. Who are the other

scientists? Any of them have Hungarian students working with them?"

"I don't know. There are fourteen other people. Dr. Swept just received his formal invitation. I've heard of most of the people coming, but not all. I have to run their names through the library database system, get a printout of their publications, and pull their articles from the library so he can review them before he goes to the meeting. It will also be a learning experience for me, to read those articles."

"Do you think any Hungarian students work for these people?"

"I don't know."

"Well, we can find out. Presumably they'll call us. We have many students working in the United States. Who are the scientists? Maybe I'll recognize some of the names as being mentors to some of our students."

"Just a minute, let me get the list." Szeppek went to his kitchen, where the list lay on the table near the stove, and read the names.

"This must all be quite exciting for you, Janos. I'm so pleased."

"Yes. Thanks. It is an honor."

"It's an honor to have you represent our country."

"Thank you."

"Have a good evening, Janos. Dream of goulash."

"Don't worry, I do. Goodnight."

Janos felt good. The representative from his country was happy, Janos was happy, and there was funding. He could stay longer in America, and maybe one day have his own research laboratory back in Hungary. Janos took the liberty of pouring himself a glass of wine, given to him as a Christmas present by Swept. As he settled to bed, he was aware that his calls to the Hungarian Consulate, as requested, had increased in frequency. He dismissed concern, having learned long ago not to question requests from officials of state.

Janos Szeppek thought that the Consulate personnel, like the people back home – faculty, administrators, and government officials – might be able to help him in his career. Certainly, all could pose bureaucratic threats. The phone call made him feel important, despite his not viewing the conversation as having immediate import. However, Szeppek could not have conceivably predicted the important consequences of his actions. He could not know that the polite secretary who had put him through to the Hungarian Visa Liaison Office tape-recorded everything he said and, per routine, forwarded the information to the Hungarian Embassy in Washington, on Shoemaker Street. The Houston liaison officer had a list of questions for all Hungarian students in the Southwest sector of the United States and, he too, thought little of it. The questions were fairly rou-

tine: Who are the individuals with whom you work?
Describe the laboratory. What is the goal of your research project? What work is done by you, personally? What scientific hypotheses are you investigating? Do you miss your home? Your loved ones? The
liaison officer had no way of knowing whether other
liaison officials in other cities had similar instructions.
Nor, would he think to ask.

He had been told to find out the names of everyone with whom the students or their laboratory personnel came in contact. This had been his instructed
routine for a long time under the Soviets and, later,
under the Hungarians. He did as told.

As per instructions, this low-level bureaucrat who
had worked in the Consulate for over fifteen years,
forwarded the information to the Embassy. When the
FSB Hungarian Lieutenant, Larek Xpolinok, received
the information, he personally delivered it to the
Russian Embassy at 2650 Wisconsin Avenue. In a short
time, a pudgy Russian, Joseph Petsh, listened. Forty
minutes later, the tape was taken to a room in the
basement, where it was received by a man who had
been expecting the data. Within ninety minutes,
Aleksander Kostokov had the tape and digested it.
In certain matters, the *Federalnaya Sluvhba Besopas*
was efficient.

Aleksander Kostokov had made the necessary arrangements with the Hungarian Embassy and the
Hungarian Consulate. He did not speak directly to
any of the Hungarian officers, making his contact
only with the liaison officer at the Russian Embassy.
He saw to it, three times, that appropriate commu-

nications had been established. Kostokov was a field
agent, accustomed to working on his own. He did
not like delegating too much responsibility, especially
on a mission as important as this.

The liaison official, ensconced in his easy desk
job, had taken an almost immediate disliking to
Aleksander Kostokov. He had heard of the man before–pushy, arrogant, but accomplished. Yes, he
would make the appropriate arrangements with the
Hungarian Embassy and the Consulate. Yes, arrangements had been made. He answered Kostokov's re-
lentless questions, until the agent was satisfied.

"Thank you for your time. Please understand, I
do not question your abilities in these matters, I am
merely making certain things run as smoothly as possible. I'm sure that this is our mutual concern."

"Indeed it is." The two shook hands, Kostokov
disgusted at feeling such smooth soft palm skin, the
signature of a man who was a pansy. However, he was
also certain that his comrade-in-arms was rebuffed
by the calluses on his own hands. The two men departed stiffly but formally. Aleksander Kostokov was
ushered to the door and gazed down the streets of
Washington, D.C..

Chapter Ten

AN EXPERIMENT THAT WORKED

THE AUTUMN WEATHER was pleasant in Moscow but predictions were for a hard Russian winter. Familiar with fall as well as the glorious spring in Washington, D. C., a tired Kostokov considered how seasons differed around the globe, as did the people. His thoughts became less weather-oriented and less philosophical as he approached the door to the building three miles west from what used to be Dzherzhinsky Square. The building contained a room about which he had heard, especially after the multiple fiascoes with Chechnya. The room was not bugged by other ex-KGB or current FSB agents. One could speak in total privacy, so it had been rumored.

The room now belonged to Yuri Lyachin and to Lyachin alone.

The interchange transpired seventy-two hours after Szeppek's last call. Following the knock and the
voice print security system, the field agent entered.
This time, small talk was exchanged. The somewhat
barren room, warmed only by two fireplaces spewing flames behind glass screens, had as its center-
piece a bust of the powerful figure, Yuri Lyachin himself. Lyachin, proud of his Grecian-looking appearance, never discussing his abnormal voice and blinking eyes, seated himself, after asking Kostokov to do
likewise.

"Aleksander, thank you for the tape and your
work. As you know, Richard Swept does not know
that we, too, work on a protein similar to his. Neither Swept, his medical school, nor scientists at the
NIH have any idea we work on such a compound.
That is why Solokov has kept most of our scientists'
work out of the literature."

"We must know the exact chemical sequencing
of Compound 1040, not just the amino acids in it.
Swept has never published his theory or the structure of his chemical. Indeed, it's still somewhat em-
bryonic, from what I understand. Otherwise, we
would know more about his research. Szeppek must
obtain a copy of this in the near future, but we must
not create suspicion."

Kostokov, despite fatigue from long sessions of
reading about disorders of memory, his recent
Aeroflot sojourn to and from the States, and his investigating Swept, understood the nonsequitors,
knowing the signs all too well. His superior was covering his tracks. Surely, others would wonder why

the FSB, with its vast source of personnel and money, did not know more about Swept. The alleged reason, as emphasized, was that Swept had not published his theories, had not yet completed all the experiments, and had not earlier applied for a large NIH grant specifically focusing on his current hypotheses. So what, thought Kostovov. Surely, the FSB with its multiple contacts among the former KGB officials and agents, most of whom were disgruntled and hated the new non-communist system since the demise of the Soviet Union in 1991, could have had more information by now. They had obtained more information about individuals with projects less conspicuous, and less to gain. Perhaps, not all the KGB and FSB resources had been utilized, perhaps because only a small sector knew of this project. Who were the agents who knew about Operation Hippocampus? Who knew about 'Pi Two'? Were Lyachin's activities approved by the government, or was this some renegade group?

"You said earlier that this neurologist works for a chairman, Harold Ranger, who refuses to allow the Human Experimentation Committee at the Texas College of Medicine to review the project."

Kostokov momentarily cogitated, but only for a moment. The Russians had no such procedures for human experimentation. He remembered the dead Sherpas. They were the experiment. For another moment, he thought of his dead family, the train, the chilling Siberian breezes in Eastern Ukraine, and whether his loved ones were aware of their imminent death, as they were hurled into the oncoming train. Did they see it coming? Probably not. Were they thinking of him? Were they angry at his having asked them to go to the FSB's secondary headquarters near the Carpathian National Natural Park, the vacation home for former loyal Communist Party members and their families?

"Aleksander?"

"Yes, sir," his reverie broken, "I was just thinking about the implications of the drug. Dr. Harold Ranger refuses to authorize Dick Swept to present his data to the Human Experimentation Committee. Evidently, Swept has done his research well, investing a great deal of time and effort."

Lyachin responded. "We have unsuccessfully tried various amino acid sequences on different subjects, in fact over 800 combinations. As you can tell from Szeppek's discussion, Compound 1040 has several amino acids. We need to know exactly how they are chemically linked to one another, and what is the carrier compound in which they are immersed. This should not prove too difficult. Aside from the fact that Dr. Swept doesn't consider his information classified – for all we know, he doesn't know even know what that means – he will soon present his data at a meeting at the NIH, and then many others will know. We can't allow that."

Yuri Lyachin, speaking with a tremulous cadence, somehow seemed almost not to know whether he was addressing one man, several, hundreds, or thousands. "Richard Swept has actually discovered how to alter a rat's memory pattern. He injects the chemical into the animal's system, then forces the animal through a maze, which results in the rat learning that maze very well. So well, it automatically goes through the maze the moment it is placed back in the maze box, even if there is no food reward at the other end. Our scientists are confident that the compound will work on humans."

"However, let me emphasize a major concern. When scientists at the NIH meeting hear Swept's ideas, many may alter the focus of their own research. That is not in our interest. We could then lose the lead in the race for mind-control drugs."

"Swept's chemical could be more potent, and far more deadly, than nuclear weapons. There would be no need to deploy bombs in cities and destroy populations if we could control people's minds. It is not inconceivable to administer the drug to large numbers of people and expose them to an ideology, our ideology. It would be better for all mankind."

"The problem is that Swept's formula, unlike ours, has to be administered through an injection. To assure efficiency in humans, and evidently Dr. Swept has agreed with this concept in discussions with Szeppek, the compound might even have to be injected into their arterial system, possibly the carotid artery, the main artery in the neck."

"We have used our compound orally, as you well know, ranging from Sherpas to Serkin. For all we know, Swept's Compound 1040 could also be used orally, although it might be more potent when injected into an artery. All that has to be worked out."

"Dr. Solokov has reviewed this with several members of the Russian Academy of Sciences. They believe Swept has made a major discovery and, although they are not certain, it might be several years before we can administer his drug orally, without side effects. The enzymes in the stomach digest amino acid structures, rearranging the molecular architecture."

"Ours worked on Bradley Serkin, at the restaurant," Kostokov replied.

"Yes, but that was just one person. We need to test it more. It did not work very well when our people gave it orally to rats. Some learned the maze well, others didn't. Swept's chemical might be better, perhaps not. But it certainly seems to work well when directly injected into the peritoneum of the rats. That is a part of their abdominal system, and medication injected there is rapidly absorbed into the arteries, bypassing the digestive processes in the stomach. The important point is that the rats are not given the medication orally."

Lyachin continued. "We need to obtain a sample of Dr. Swept's chemical and ascertain whether it works in humans after it is injected into the carotid artery. We can use patients in Asylum Number 54-B, in the Ukraine. If it works, we're on the right track. Then, we can investigate whether we can administer his substance orally without compromising its efficacy."

"Now, another matter. I assume that you weren't that familiar with the total operation involving the Sherpas or the Bedouins. You were a field agent following orders. I do not hold you totally responsible for those mishaps. However, you are totally responsible for this mission, and have total authority. I think you are one of our best. As I said before, you have 'Full License.'"

Walking around the table, placing his right hand on Aleksander's shoulder, Lyachin continued. "We'll give you all the help you need, all the data you need. Make this work. The Americans had a chance after World War II of controlling the world. They were the only ones with nuclear armament. They could have done it but they did not. They were soft. The only one with any guts was Churchill. Thank goodness no one listed to him regarding marching on us. The West would have annihilated our country, probably for good."

"Now, we have a second chance. We're the only government actively pursuing mind control. Some may work with rats, but we shall work with humans. We can end war, devastation, and solidify the human race."

"Just think of it. We could erase prejudice. We can erase many human frailties. All we have to do is administer the medication, giving it to large numbers of people orally, and then tell them what to think. Certainly, this could be dangerous in the hands of some, but when one considers the problems that exist in the world today, it couldn't be much worse. Regardless, we want it. You are the one who can get it for us. Get the Compound so that our scientists can analyze it and see to it that we stay in the lead. The West must not be permitted to advance in this

area. I shall later discuss possible plans with you. Any
questions?"

Kostokov, not having said more than a few words
since he had been called into Yuri Lyachin's office,
had little to say. Yes, he was a good agent. Yes, he did
his job well and, he believed, had he been given total control over the Sherpa and Bedouin projects,
they would have faired well. However, in the back of
his mind, he wasn't certain. Would there still have
been dead Bedouins in the desert? There certainly
would have been little opportunity to predict what
had happened to the Sherpas due to their altered
blood cell chemistry. And, he wondered, was Lyachin
not aware of the same? Further, could Lyachin provide all the support that this failed agent might need?
He would soon find out.

However, Aleksander Kostokov was not without a
background in espionage. Why was Lyachin meeting him here, outside the main headquarters? Who
was involved in Operation Hippocampus? Who was
involved in Pi Two and had these been sanctioned?
And, still, what about Gantemirov?

Aleksander believed he was being praised to
make him feel better, to help him do the job well.
However, he needed none of this. He would do his
work well because he was good, not because of any
sycophantic hype. "I appreciate your confidence in
me. I'll take care of it, Comrade Lyachin."

The man left as he had entered, passing the security system, responding to the barely discernable
salutations from some officers waiting outside. One

of them escorted him to a room, third on the right, down the hall, where he was provided instructions to contact Dr. Mikhail Solokov . . . at a later time. As he entered this room, turning back toward Lyachin's office, he saw the old man standing in the doorway. That one could simultaneously look both pathetic and noble struck a chord in Kostokov's mind.

Kostokov was aware that this powerful man had been the official liaison between the KGB and the Soviet Academy of Sciences, as well as the leading member of the Supreme Anti-Terrorist Group. He was livid when Gorbachev *de facto* dissolved the Soviet Union and disgusted when Boris Yeltsin tried to diminish the KGB's power. Lyachin had also expressed his doubts about President Vladimir Putin. Truly, Yuri Lyachin was a remarkable man. Soon, if Lyachin's plan succeeded, he would have enormous power.

*   *   *

The following day, Yuri Lyachin, large hands occasionally wiping hair from a twitching brow, met with Liubov Usova, Jokhar Gantemirov, and Mikhail Solokov. This meeting transpired in a dacha forty miles outside FSB headquarters. The drive had been boring, passing familiar half-dead trees and underfed cattle.

These four members of the select committee, which met very infrequently, were impressed. The break that the Russians had been seeking was at hand. If only they could administer the drug orally, they could place it in water supplies, rivers, lakes,

spray it on foods, mix it with fertilizer. Who knew
what ends could be accomplished? That was what
they had tried with the Sherpas, but how were they
to know that the high altitude would alter the hemoglobin, itself a protein, and result in death? So,
they must stay away from high altitudes.

"*Dobryy den,* Good afternoon," turning to Liubov
Usova and Solokov and the Chechen. "We have an
interesting situation on our hands. I think we should
move with great speed towards seeing whether this
drug can truly perform what we hope. Considering
other scientists will soon know about Dr. Swept's
chemical, coupled with the fact that his compound
is effective on rats, we must move as quickly as possible, analyzing whether the American's chemical is
capable of doing what we think. But, there are several constraints."

"At the moment, we do not know the exact structure of the chemical. However, this should not be
difficult to ascertain. It is not guarded and, hopefully, we'll have it soon. Also, there are probably
records of its structure in laboratory books. We do
not anticipate this to be a major issue."

"What we do anticipate to be a major issue is
whether the drug will work on humans. We must
see. After we have the chemical, the testing itself is
rather trivial. We simply inject it into some subjects
and analyze whether we can alter their behaviors,
teaching things they might not otherwise want to
learn or to do." He was not certain whether he detected a slight smile on Usova, who looked at Solokov,
but then dismissed that concern.

"As you know, we were close to this with the Sherpas and, possibly, with the Bedouins. I am told by Dr. Solokov," the scientist-turned-politician nodded in acquiescence, "that once our scientific investigators see exactly what Swept is working on, coupled with their own knowledge, it should not be long before we have the chemical we need."

"Another problem is that it might be longer, perhaps years, before we can administer the drug orally. Our own is effective, and we have used it orally, on Bradley Serkin, for example, but we still need to do more work. What we do know is that our own chemical, given orally to rats, is not nearly as effective as is Swept's, which is injected. Further, what must not happen is for non-Russian scientists to investigate what this man Swept is investigating, and share in his major discovery."

"As we've discussed, his Chairman, Dr. Harold Ranger, undervalues his work and, although Ranger is pleased that Swept will receive financial support for his research from the National Institutes of Health, he absolutely refuses to permit Swept to present his data to the Human Experimentation Committee, seeking experiments in humans. As a result, the big question, whether the chemical works in humans, is unanswered, at least for the time being. We must answer it."

"The name Richard Michael Swept has only recently entered our files. As we earlier discussed, he is bright, tenacious in his research convictions, has a penchant for physical activities, is single, and is romantically involved with a plastic surgeon, Regina Bruxton."

Liubov Usova, not only the only female in the
room but the only female in any of the top Russian
international committees of covert operation, spoke.
Everyone here, including herself, had long ago forgotten her gender. "At the risk of impertinence, I
should add that a great deal of our information
evolved from excellent operations within my Section.
It was our idea to pursue academic exchanges with
the Americans, hoping to keep up with particular
areas of their science. Were it not for us, Szeppek
would never have been accepted into Swept's program. His recommendations and credentials
wouldn't have been strong enough. With all due respect, were Comrade Solokov more persistent in his
demands on our scientists, we might not be behind
in Russian knowledge of memory. Our Section . . ."

Lyachin interrupted. "We shall have no disputes
over the efficiency of our espionage system versus
our scientific capabilities or infighting between Sections. I'll tolerate none of it. We are meeting here
on behalf of the goals of Pi Two and are to decide a
course of action. Let us continue."

Usova, shifting her weight with nervous arrogance, chose silence. Solokov long ago had come to
terms with Usova's love-hate relationship toward him
and toward all scientists. She hated him, even though
she needed and respected his intellect. Solokov did
not know whether Usova felt uncomfortable around
him because she was insecure of her own intellectual prowess, or because she could not follow a scientific dialogue. The woman seemed to be a control
freak who did not like being in any situation in which
she lacked control. Placing her in a room with a

bunch of scientists, which he had done on several occasions, promptly put her in that predicament. Regardless, she was to be feared.

Solokov had not believed that the Bedouin project was ready. Usova insisted it was. The project failed. When Solokov was not prepared to proceed with the Sherpas, again Usova insisted the project be pursued. Solokov had wanted to pursue testing in the Ukraine, experimenting on political prisoners. Usova insisted otherwise. Why run the risk of causing disturbance among the prisoners over brain experimentation? she asked. "They occasionally have riots over these matters. Let us not check Russian citizens, even the dissidents, when we can check people in third world countries, running the experiment on a much larger scale."

Solokov's objections were muted against the powerful female. For some reason, she had enormous faith that one could give the Russian compound orally to individuals and that it would work. It was striking how certain she seemed regarding this, yet she was not a scientist and could not analyze the data as well as the investigators.

What Solokov had no way of knowing was that she had given the chemical to Aleksander Kostokov, in a glass of tea, and told him repeatedly to do her sexual bidding. "Whatever I tell you to do sexually, do it." She repeated that sentence a dozen times to a seemingly bewildered Aleksander Kostokov. Ever since then, whenever she picked up her dress and ordered the stone-faced Kostokov to bring her pleasure, he did. Liubov Usova's own experiment, on a scale of one, had worked successfully. Aleksander Kostokov always responded to her sexual commands, no matter how she degraded him. And, degrade him she did.

Solokov knew another reason why she wanted the drug tested outside Russia: the woman wanted the glory. If the experiment succeeded outside Russia, she would be given credit. The compound would then totally be in her jurisdiction, even though the details of the experiment and the delineation of the drug were managed by Solokov and the scientists under his direction. If the project was done in a formal experimental setting within Russian bounds, the glory would go to the scientists, glory that would be attributed neither to her Section nor to Usova.

The whole thing made Solokov sick. Deep in his craw, the idea of injecting humans against their will was morally unethical. But, long ago, he had come to terms that his whole life was morally unethical, doing what was necessary to survive under the shadow of the first Soviet State, then the current Russian system, and, finally, Pi Two.

Solokov, accustomed to long monologues as well as reveries, found his thoughts interrupted by Lyachin.

"There is going to be a meeting in the United States, in Washington, D.C., with the scientists working on memory and related cognitive behaviors. They meet at the National Institutes of Health, in the main NINDS building itself. Dick Swept will be one of the scientists. We cannot allow him to exchange information with his colleagues. We cannot let the Americans see the results of his work. We cannot let them realize the importance of this type of work. Once they focus on his line of research, building new memories, it is only a matter of time before multiple laboratories are working in this area in the United States, as well as other areas in the world."

"It is imperative we interrupt the meeting. The scientists meet October nineteenth. Swept must not present his data to these researchers who, in all probability, may pursue similar and possibly even more extensive work in their own laboratories. At the moment, our sources are certain no one else is pursuing his kind of research."

"Killing him immediately is not an option. That would not keep other scientists from learning about his project. The NINDS branch of the National Institutes of Health has already received some information. The Director, Dr. Nathaniel Chippers, along with a few others, primarily those on the Site Committee that granted Swept funding, have already seen his preliminary results. Knowing how the American system works, they will not pay much attention to it until this forthcoming meeting, because the data has not yet been published or formally presented at a scientific meeting. I have a much better plan, one that will set the West decades behind us in memory research, and in many aspects of power as well."

Lyachin, muffling a faint cough, looked around the room, waiting for his laryngeal muscle tone to relax to appropriate pitch, before making a statement with appropriate force and certitude. His la-

ryngeal tremor always worsened with emotional excitement, and this was such a time. He relaxed, trying to overcome his body's own physiologic mechanisms, and spoke. "My colleagues, I suggest we destroy everyone present at the October nineteenth
meeting, eliminating all the scientists, including Dr.
Swept and Dr. Chippers. All researchers with expertise in areas of memory, especially those relating to
Swept's work, should be at this meeting. The United
States takes little security precautions at scientific
meetings of this sort. It should not be difficult."

Usova smiled, the I-told-you-so smile. Solokov,
stunned, held his comments but was dumbfounded.
Destroying the NINDS, a major branch of the National Institutes of Health, certainly would compromise research in America. However, what would be
the repercussions? What would be the interactions
between Russia and her dwindling array of allies in
the western nations at future scientific meetings?
Would Americans employ similar tactics on the Russians? Solokov was not oblivious to the fact that he
directed the Soviet counterpart of the American
NINDS, the Supreme Russian Scientific Institute. He
favored research in mind-control drugs and more
money for his research, but killing fellow scientists
made him feel nauseated.

Several Western scientists working in neurology,
scientists with whom he had frequently interacted at
international meetings, might be killed. He had no
idea whether they might be there, since some of
them worked in areas overlapping with memory. The
idea was repulsive.

But, what bothered Solokov most was the arrogance of the idea. It was one thing to seek world domination, a concept that these power-crazed leaders (Yes, he thought, they were crazy.) believed, but they had also tried to convince him of the possibility. True, he had rationalized this by telling himself that one country controlling the world could end wars and international bickering, but he knew it wouldn't happen. Had his colleagues forgotten that when the Catholic Church ran all Europe, just about everyone in Europe was Catholic, as well as Caucasian, but there were still battles between religious factions and different political groups. People still killed each other. There were hundreds of other examples. Human beings would always disagree. No large faction was forever homogeneous. Even individual families, sharing skin color, religion and, for that matter, DNA, had major battles.

Yes, it was the incredible arrogance. How could a pig like Usova have anything to do with any type of plan to "take over the world." Usova's answer to everything was death. That was why her PLO objectives frequently failed, why her Afghanistan work had been a fiasco, and what about Chechnya? Russia was still mired there.

On one occasion, Usova, in an effort to find out what Solokov was doing with his scientists, invited him to her home for dinner. The woman lived alone, her house a pig sty without a single work of art, not a single recording of any great Russian composer. On the kitchen table stood a singular bottle of vodka, not even good vodka at that, from Poland no less. Her personality was mirrored in the behavior of her dog, who continually stared at the door of the oven.

An amazing woman, thought Solokov, and even more amazing that she had been able to achieve a position of prominence within the State. Further, and equally repulsive, was the fact that this woman also had a position of power. And, now, she was involved in a committee planning world domination. At least, that's what the focus seemed to be.

Solokov kept his silence. He accepted himself for what he had become – weak, an academic whore, now listening to and doing what he was told. Regardless, he felt sick. It was one thing to have to work with Usova, but another to be involved in a plan that took human lives, destroyed scientific investigation, and, carrying good and bad points, might actually work.

Lyachin continued. "Our main source, this easily manipulated postdoctorate fellow Szeppek, is the only other individual who comes close to understanding Swept's work. After the plan is complete, we shall return him to Hungary, then Moscow. Only a select few will know the composition of this Compound, Number 1040."

Usova, Solokov and Gantemirov looked at Lyachin, nodding their heads.

"So be it. We agree. Dr. Solokov and Aleksander Kostokov will give Liubov Usova full cooperation. Operation Hippocampus will soon be in full operation."

Jokhar Gantemirov sat there, silent. He knew his job provided opportunity to siphon funds from Muslim-directed bank accounts intended to support

Chechen rebels, but now earmarked for Pi-Two. No matter, thought Gantemirov. If the plan worked, he would run Chechnya, if not more, and glory would come to his people. He was active in the Chechen underground, had contacts in Moscow, and redirecting the money was easy. After all, his compatriots trusted him.

Usova smiled again, that same smile. "Aleksander Kostokov has been working in this area. I shall keep him. As per your request, Comrade Lyachin, the task will be done. I shall see that he is given appropriate instructions and that Operation Hippocampus is a success."

Solokov spoke. "I have already told him to obtain 1040 for us. I met with him earlier this week"

"I know," responded Usova with confident arrogance. "My officers met him outside your office. He has been appropriately instructed."

Solokov began to protest. However, when his peripheral vision revealed that Lyachin was not upset, he felt prompted to act otherwise. The silent man thought about a Western poem he had read long ago, something about old warriors who succumb to the new, which was exactly what he was doing now.

In a few minutes, the faded yellow meeting room was barren. There was no remnant of any conversation or altercation having transpired. There were no notes, no paper, no scribbling. No writing implements had been allowed. A table and five straight-back chairs stood alone, naked.

*   *   *

At that moment, Regina lay in Swept's arms. Their lovemaking had been passionate, deep, without bickering. They looked into each other's eyes as their passions exploded, and melted into a deep sleep which they both needed.

*   *   *

Also, at that moment, Aleksander Kostokov rested during his British Airways transatlantic flight. He would enter America through JFK International, an airport he had visited on multiple occasions. He had previously gone through customs at Heathrow, arriving on an Aeroflot flight, and rested overnight in London. When he worked under the KGB, agents frequently traveled outside the Soviet Union, often with no mission at all. This was to make them feel comfortable, enable them to practice skills in dealing with cabbies, police officers in case they were in an automobile accident, to learn colloquialisms, and to know how to deal with the vagaries of the average day in America. Now that the Soviet Union was no more, the practice seemed to have been a waste of time, but had certainly left him well skilled.

Chapter Eleven

HOUSTON BOUND

KOSTOKOV ANTICIPATED NO problems when passing through United States Customs. He had nothing to conceal. He was to meet his collegue, Yorky, in Louisiana, who would provide any equipment he needed. In truth, he currently needed none.

The conversation with Usova's officers, and two days later with Usova herself, had been brief, but exacting. There was no doubt in his mind, the woman was a despicable human being. He doubted she ever held any femininity or sweetness during her entire life. Again, he performed cunnilingus. She just picked up her dress, looked him in the eye, and said, "Do it!" Somehow, he did. As disgusting as it was to him, he brought her to orgasm and could never understand why he agreed to such an act.

Aleksander had had no difficulty with female agents. In fact, he usually found them methodical, clever, and usually more adaptable and with a stronger learning curve than their male counterparts. But, Liubov Usova was different. It wasn't that her personality and demeanor just lacked womanhood. Nothing about her implied that she had any feelings at all. The woman bordered on being non-human.

It was evident that she truly enjoyed killing, especially killing women. Kostokov had seen her conduct interrogations, torturing young women with sadistic delight. He knew several interrogators whom she had trained, most of whom later entered interrogation rooms with brutal conviction of Russian superiority, and an unnecessary inclination to inflict pain as they conducted their work.

An interrogator's goal is simple: Get the information. Nothing more, nothing less. Since the early 1970's, medications available to both sides of the Cold War conflict were such that obtaining information from unwilling subjects was usually not as difficult as the lay public might believe. Individuals were simply injected with these drugs which, coupled with sleep deprivation, chemically altered their cognitive states. Nine times in ten, they were unable to monitor what they said. Obtaining information from unwilling subjects is seldom so difficult as to require physical torture.

However, no one ever told this to Usova. She still used older methods, relishing their application. She continued to instruct students in different methods of psychological as well as physical pain, methods

Aleksander found unnecessary. For some unexplained reason, the woman had taken a strange liking to him, which not only gave him an eerie feeling but also resulted in her sexual domination.

Kostokov had never understood Usova's attitude toward him. Perhaps it was because he stayed clear of most of the political games within the KGB and was trying to do the same in the FSB. Indeed, he never understood, and still did not, where Pi Two fit in, and who ran it. He held loyalty to the KGB, FSB, Russia, and even the former Soviet Union, but felt little toward Liubov Usova.

The woman and her officers had instructed him in the necessities of the mission, supplying whatever personnel and financial support was needed. The plan was straightforward. Kostokov had considerable authority in the planning. He felt certain Operation Hippocampus would be successful.

As Kostokov mentally rehearsed the details of the plan, over and over, he gave himself the luxury of wondering on what he would dine after arriving in America. He enjoyed the wide variety of foods in the States, as well as his visits to museums, noting to himself that many interesting objects of art had been plundered from other countries. He never stopped to think the same about the Hermitage Museum in Leningrad, now St. Petersburg, or the Pushkin in Moscow, both of which had plundered art from other countries as well as taking paintings from private families at the time of the Russian Revolution.

On some level, Kostokov queried whether he enjoyed the freedoms in America, most of which his Russian colleagues considered damaging to American security. He had long ago noted the carefree demeanor of how Americans walked – their gait was carefree. He also noticed a similar gait in other so-called Western democracies.

For the time being, the agent tried not to think further about these issues. Although he had no family in Russia to whom he could return, he did have his work and his profession, both requiring diligence and concentration, supplying him with meaning, tying together the dots at the moments that detail one's daily life, offering a mental infrastructure from which he could operate. He would see to it that Operation Hippocampus was successful.

While resting on the plane, he dozed. He dreamed that his wife was Liubov Usova's illegitimate daughter. That was the reason for her allegedly feeling close to him and her having sexual relations with him. In his dream, he found the idea repulsive. The Russian woke and ordered two Bloody Marys, mumbled that he wanted "real vodka," and drifted back to sleep. This time, there were no dreams, just an alcohol-induced sleep woken by announcement of the landing.

The plane arrived on time at Kennedy.

Kostokov was totally at ease when he deplaned in the foreign land. He had been there only a short time before. He walked with other British Airways passengers to Customs, going through the sector for those with nothing to declare. He was in New York City, in the United States.

Changing terminals, he freshened up in the men's room, and boarded a Delta Airlines flight to New Orleans. He wondered why the FSB had not had him fly directly into New Orleans, or, to be safer, Orlando. Regardless, it was England to New York and then to New Orleans. He was sure they had their reasons. But, he wondered, if they were so efficient, why had they erred with the Bedouins and Sherpas?

Kostokov arrived in New Orleans, rented a car, and drove north to Homer. Although he knew the itinerary, he politely asked the woman at the car rental desk the route to Homer, Louisiana. She misunderstood him, thinking he was saying Houma, a misunderstanding Kostokov knew many made, and that it did not reflect any accent. Homer and Houma were frequently phonetically confused. The Russian knew that from his training. The cities were totally different, but only a handful of Russians, primarily those in Pi Two, understood why.

After arriving in Homer, despite exhaustion from his trip and needing more sleep, Kostokov was to touch base with his colleague, Yorky. Kostokov and Yorky held a long relationship, both having trained and shared many field missions. Yorky, full name Rimsky Yorkahow, was called Yorky by fellow agents and his few friends, and held great respect for Aleksander Kostokov. Kostokov had always sensed that Yorky was too inquisitive of his relationship with Usova, whatever that was, but never held Yorky in ill light because of this.

As Kostokov approached Homer's city limits, he saw Yorky outside the local convenience store, adjacent to the Claridge Freeway. Yorky was hitchhiking, according to plan. Hitchhiking with the thumb at waist level signified all was well. If the hand were higher, he was to be picked up, but United States agents were watching. If the hand offered no hitchhiking gesture, Kostokov was to drive on, return to the airport that day, and wait for further instructions after returning to New York.

The hand was at waist level. Aleksander Kostokov stopped the automobile for the hitchhiker.

Entering the rented car, Yorky turned to his companion, "You old son-of-a-pig-headed-farmer, my friend. How are you? It is good to see you. How is everything?"

Both agents knew not to mention Russia or to use Russian terms, such as "Comrade." One could always be bugged, or followed, or both. It was reckless to take chances.

"It is good to see you, too, my friend. It is good to see you. We have much to talk about."

The two drove to an apparent hippie colony, where eight or ten long-haired, skinny, head-banded men walked about in cotton T-shirts, wearing faded denims, looking like hippies from the Sixties, now and then working in Claiborn Parish in construction-type jobs. All recognized Yorky. A few of the hippies fleetingly glanced at Kostokov, but no one seemed to pay him much notice. At least, it was not apparent. The hippies were professional agents, clever and well trained.

Yorky escorted Kostokov into a little bungalow in the northeast part of the colony. His Vodka, Smirnoff, certainly wasn't Stolichnaya, but at least it was kept in the freezer, as all vodkas were in Russia.

"You must be tired. Why don't you rest?"

"I will, but first I need to know whether you received my instructions. I take it from the road signal all is well? Is our operation running smoothly?"

"Some of it is tricky, but there should be no problems. We had some difficulties making one or two contacts, but we straightened that out. Our agents went through the Houston hospital. Everything is set."

"Yorky, I know I haven't told you much about this operation, and I can't. It's Need-to-Know. If your part goes well, and I'm sure it will, things will run smoothly. We've been through a lot together. We were involved with the submarines off Finland. As you know, we did well there, received medals, although I think only you deserved them. I don't know whether we'll get any medals for this, but we are doing the world justice."

Yorky, deep in thought, looked like a philosophy graduate student. He was thin, average height, had deep eyes and sculpted facial features, and always appeared to be thinking. His thin frame belied immense muscular agility and the fact that he had killed scores of men and women on behalf of the KGB and FSB.

"Justice? Certainly, a philosophical term with different meanings for different people. For me, whatever you and Usova want is fine. And, as for Homer, everything is doing well here. We've infiltrated the area and everyone leaves us alone, except for a few run-ins we had with some local high school students, but that quickly ended. Now, they're terrified of us. They think we're a bunch of hippies working in construction, which is fine."

"Here's to us, my friend. Here's to us!" *Nasdarovye!* Both men drank a half glass of Smirnoff.

Following some small talk, Yorky ushered Kostokov into a separate bungalow, where he drifted to sleep, sleeping soundly, forgetting in the morning that a brief restlessness had ensued when he dreamed about a Ukraine train crash.

Both men breakfasted the next day on sausage, strawberry pancakes with biscuits, pomegranate juice, and Columbian roast coffee, amid small talk and memories. Following a warm embrace, Kostokov drove back to New Orleans, returned the car, then flew into Houston. The project was underway.

*   *   *

Aleksander Kostokov arrived at the Houston Marriott, tipping the taxi driver an exact 10 percent. He had scheduled an appointment with Dr. Richard Swept through the Office of International Relations at the Houston Community Hospital. This was not difficult to do. The Hospital, closely affiliated with the Texas College of Medicine, was pleased to evaluate individuals from other countries, especially since they required a $5,000 deposit were they to be admitted. Were they not admitted, patients were often scheduled for multiple tests, since they had to be fairly ill to decide to make the trip to the Medical Complex. The Hospital made out like bandits, charging full fees that HMO's and PPO's always discounted. Foreign patients had big bills and paid them. The hospital seldom turned these patients away.

The Russian agent, using the name Mohammed Abdul, employed an Arabic accent and told the Office of International Relations that, while visiting friends, he developed a severe headache behind his right eye. He had had that headache before, but this time it was more severe. His friends stated that Dr. Richard Swept was a good neurologist for him to see. Could the Office kindly arrange an appointment? He gave a false London address, which he was certain the Office would not check since he was happy to pay cash.

Following a few phone calls to the Department of Neurology, finally able to get hold of Tracy, the influential Office of International Relations confirmed the appointment with Dr. Swept. The next day, Mr. Abdul appeared.

Aleksander Kostokov, alias Mohammed Abdul, had donned a small amount of makeup to darken his skin. He patiently sat in the Department of Neurology Clinic waiting room, disdainfully gleaning through copies of *People*. Turning his attention to *The Smithsonian*, he was slightly startled when a poised figure appeared, looking more self-assured and handsome in person than Kostokov had anticipated.

The neurologist, wearing a light blue Dunhill shirt with a slash-crimson tie, covered by a starched white coat, politely introduced himself, although somewhat curtly. "Mr. Abdul, I am Dr. Swept. Please follow me into the examining room." The handshake was strong and, under different circumstances, might even have been considered somewhat friendly. Dr. Swept was confident, offering a slight smile. Could he possibly know Abdul's true identity? Certainly, not.

"It is a pleasure to meet you, doctor," said the patient, with his disguised Middle East accent. "I was sent by the hospital to see you. I apologize for the short notice, but my headache came on all of a sudden and then disappeared, and occasionally it comes back. The pain is very severe when it is there and I was hoping you could help me."

The two entered the examination room, Swept pointing the way, following his patient. Abdul related a classical story for occipital neuralgia, stating that the pain began in the posterior portion of the right side of his neck, was associated with numbness over the back of his head, on the right, and that he had right eye pain. Swept spent a full hour taking the history and performing the physical examination, spending more time with the patient than would any Russian doctor. The exchange was formal, Swept explaining the disease and appropriate medical treatment.

"Mr. Abdul, I am placing you on two medicines, Klonopin, an anti-spasm medicine, and Vioxx, designed to cut down inflammation." Swept then explained possible side effects, which were minimal.

The prognosis for recovery was excellent. Mr. Abdul could not help but be impressed with Dr. Swept's manner.

At the end of the explanation, Swept opened his old briefcase, removed a prescription pad, gathered his stethoscope, sphygmomanometer, reflex hammer, and ophthalmoscope, all originally on a small desk in the corner of the examination room, and placed them within the briefcase. After writing the two prescriptions, he returned the prescription pad to the briefcase, closed it, and then placed the small briefcase on the floor.

A rather complicated series of events for a mere prescription pad, noted the patient-spy. "I'm grateful you think you can help me, Dr. Swept. I appreciate it."

"Frankly, I normally don't see patients today. I'm a physician-scientist and do research. However, I am happy to extend a hand to needy patients and friends of the hospital. It's a pleasure to meet you." The neurologist rose from his chair, extended his right hand while simultaneously picking up the briefcase with his left, waited for his patient to leave the room, and followed. Kostokov, seemingly momentarily pensive, angled a cocked head, and posed a question.

"Forgive my asking, doctor, but I thought most American physicians had black doctor bags, not briefcases."

Something struck Swept, which, in turn, jolted Mr. Abdul, the trained Aleksander Kostokov lurking beneath. "Just a gift from an old friend. Just a gift." Swept waited for his patient to leave and momentarily thought about Louise, who gave him the briefcase years ago.

Endeavoring to think what he might have touched upon, Aleksander Kostokov kindly thanked the physician again as he left the room, and walked to the cashier. As he thought about the briefcase, an idea struck. Yes, he now knew how to finalize Operation Hippocampus. Everything would be tight. The plan would work elegantly. He would later make a seemingly innocuous phone call to his Embassy in Washington, informing them, in code, of his change in plans. Only he, Aleksander Kostokov, would know the final details.

Kostokov paid for the physician's services, impressed with the pleasantness of the clinic cashier. Just in case he was being followed, which surely he knew he could not be, he meandered carefully to the pharmacy and obtained the prescribed medication. He was also impressed with the efficiency of the hospital pharmacy, waiting no longer than eight minutes for his medicine, less time than Russians waited in line for anything. Later, in his hotel room, he discarded the pills, flushing them down the toilet. The Russian placed calls to Shreveport, Monroe, and Homer, all cities in Louisiana. Then, Kostokov telephoned Washington, D. C..

Lying in bed, Aleksander Kostokov turned on the local news and watched an advertisement with some guy jumping on waterbeds.

Chapter Twelve

THE LAST JOG

SWEPT SAW REGINA every night that week. Her technique of pulling the frenulum forward with her teeth, while simultaneously pushing the skin of the shaft away from her mouth with her hand, drove him wild. He had never before paid much attention to technique, but could not deny the explicit delights the plastic surgeon offered. She had recently pulled back from her busy operating schedule and was spending more time with him. Her inconsistencies in this domain drove him crazy and kept a distance between the two lovers.

Swept's being with Regina every night mollified her unhappiness over his recent decision to take her home following their nocturnal lovemaking, rather than going to work the following morning with her. He did this because he now had a new routine –

running in the morning. Swept believed that his thinking was more clear during the day if he could run in the morning. Regina did not understand this new rationale, but there were many things about Swept that had never made sense to her. Although she enjoyed waking in his arms early each morning, she acquiesced. It was not a major matter. She was busy herself.

On Monday, following perhaps too many margaritas but exquisite moments with Regina, Swept rolled out of bed. The time was 5:45 a.m.. Donning a purple and white running outfit cut wide at the thigh, he tucked his jersey into the comfortable running shorts, laced his Nikes, staggered into his car with his Walkman and Dylan tapes, and drove to City University, certainly within walking distance but time was of the essence at this hour.

His stretching maneuvers seemed to take longer than usual. Following these, now feeling fully wakened, Swept donned his Walkman, carrying Dylan's "Empire Burlesque," and began his usual jog around the block, going east on University, north on Main, west on Rice, south on Greenbriar, and then east on University. Only, he never got to Greenbriar.

It was as he turned the corner from Rice to Greenbriar that it happened, just past the bus stop. He vaguely recognized the odor of chloroform enveloping itself around his mouth. He began to gag, simultaneously noting a strange metallic taste. After that, everything blurred, including his being lifted into the Ford, blindfolded, hands tied behind his back, and the pricking of a needle entering his right antecubital vein, inserting chloral hydrate, Demerol, and Phenergan into his system. These injections, together with the chloroform, put him out cold.

*   *   *

At 3:30 that afternoon, Swept awoke in a field within the confines of City University. His face slightly bruised, his body aching and a slight pain in the right side of his neck, he felt as though he had been hit by a freight train, having the worst hangover in history. The gag in his mouth prevented him from effectively calling for help, but some passing graduate students exiting the chemistry building heard his muffled cries.

Thirty minutes later, the campus police were talking to the victim. All he could recall was that he had been jogging. After that, everything was a blur. His watch, his old Le Coultre, had been taken, as had the Walkman with its Dylan tape. The police queried whether robbery was the motive, but doubted this since joggers usually don't carry money, are seldom mugged, and the watch, although possibly valuable, was certainly no Rolex.

An antivivisectionist card had been attached to Swept's jersey, with a copy of the *Houston Medical Complex News*, the front page article announcing Swept's funding award. A large black X crossed the page and the note read, "Save our animals."

The campus police reported the incident to the Houston Police, who accomplished nothing. The Houston Police spoke to a few of the animal lovers, still picketing the Medical Complex, all of whom had alibis and witnesses. The authorities had no idea what to think about the antivivisectionist card and the crayoned newspaper article. Besides, no researchers in the Medical Complex had had trouble with them. The Medical Complex had not had one act of vandalism since the protestors had begun their protests and their picketing.

*   *   *

Ranger and Szeppek wondered all day about Swept's whereabouts. It was unusual for Swept not to report to the Institute, certainly not to tell anyone, especially Tracy, that he would be absent.

At first, Ranger was furious that Swept did not come to work. He was angry that patients filled the waiting area, interfering with clinic flow and complaining incessantly that the neurologist was late. Then, more late. Then, absent. Who would see these people? Who would monitor their seizure medication? Who would check their muscle examination? Certainly, not Ranger. The Chairman considered himself too busy with administrative matters and his own laboratory research.

Finally, after multiple unsuccessful attempts to reach Swept, an exasperated Ranger removed two neurology residents from the affiliated James Montgomery County Hospital and arranged for them to see the patients. It mattered not that they, too, had patients needing attention. The neurology residents, specialists-in-training, were tired, overworked, and angry at having to walk the one-quarter mile to get from the County Hospital to the posh Brain Institute. The patients were angry that neurologists-in-training, which is what the young man and woman were, were to examine them. Some of the patients had driven from places as far away as Lufkin and Lubbock to see Dr. Swept. That they were seen without charge meant little to them.

At 4:40 p.m., Dick Swept, confused, hung over, and now home, phoned Dr. Harold Ranger. Ranger was aghast. He, too, initially assumed that robbery was the motive. But, why rob a jogger? Was it for the watch? And after some caustic remarks, why an animal lover card?

Swept recalled what he could for his Chairman. "I feel strange. I don't know whether this is a result of the robbery, the – uh – abduction, or what. I still remember smelling chloroform. Why was I chloroformed instead of smashed on the head if all they wanted was a non-existent wallet? Or – uh – my recorder? Swept assumed that his "feeling strange" related to the chloroform. He did not know he had been injected with Phenergan, Demerol and chloral hydrate, and paid little heed to the ache on the right side of his neck.

Swept apologized for missing his clinic. Ranger, lying, said it was no problem.

For the next two days, Swept felt ill. His appetite was down and he was slightly disoriented, a symptom especially pronounced when he was driving and needed to turn his head quickly to check surrounding traffic. He constantly felt that he had a hangover. He had difficulty, at times, focusing on the small print in scientific journals and noticed his speech was occasionally dysfluent. His grammar and pronunciation had always been excellent but now he had occasional "uhs" and "uhms," although these had decreased over the past few days.

As the neurologist's sensorium gradually cleared over several days, he became increasingly angry. What happened to him? Who caused this unconsciousness? What was done to him? The better he felt physically, the angrier he became. Swept did not like being out of control and especially did not like being abused, mentally or physically. His persona had been tampered with. His realm had been poached upon, and he didn't like it.

After several days, Swept's anger dramatically increased, despite his feeling better physically. He believed his mental faculties had returned to normal. His anger was certainly not quelled by the campus police's continued questions, being obviously more concerned about bad publicity regarding the University than with what happened to Dick Swept. Finally, a local sergeant stated, "Look, Doc, you're all right. All you lost was the watch and the recorder and that Bob Dylan tape. We'll do what we can, but these things are kind of tough. We've got a lot of low-lifes down here, some of whom aren't even citizens. We got real problems in Houston. We'll do what we can. My advice is to relax and forget the whole thing."

The Houston Police were no better. Swept couldn't really fault them. What clues could they go on? He knew little would come from their investigation and wasn't certain what more he himself would do were he in the officer's place. He had a few conversations with the protesting antivivisectionists, almost daring them on, but all were officiously sympathetic, saccharin, and of little help.

Regina commented to some of Swept's friends that he had changed since the jogging incident. One week following the incident, his interest in Bob Dylan decreased. No longer did Regina's teasing that Dylan was a superannuated relic from the Sixties annoy him. Regina also noticed that Swept's lovemaking was different. He no longer squeezed as hard. He lacked his former stamina. Not only was he different in lovemaking, but he no was no longer as fond or interested in Limbic.

Swept had earlier taken great pains to explain to everyone in his office that the Lhasa apso breed was from Tibet, bred to watch over the temples. These excellent watchdogs barked whenever someone entered the temple. People had heard this monologue scores of times. Now, Tracy had to remind Dr. Swept that the veterinarian had called twice, stating that Limbic had failed his appointment for the rabies vaccination, as well as for his parvovirus injection.

Ranger, too, was taken aback. On one occasion, when the two were riding in an elevator, Swept, leaving his morning clinic, failed to comment with his usual bitterness about patients who feigned illness for narcotics.

When a patient entered the elevator on a stretcher, Swept and Ranger both in the elevator cab, Swept said nothing. Nor did he even smile. Ranger was surprised. The popular neurologist was known for his exceptional courtesy to patients. Yet, Swept said nothing to this patient.

Ranger noticed something else. Swept's creativity had not changed, and Ranger still found him intelligent, but the nuances that made up Swept's personality had changed. Regina, particularly, noticed this.

When Regina and Swept had Sunday brunch at Oscar's, although Swept had eaten there on numerous occasions, he asked whether their Hollandaise was made in a blender or on the stove. The waiter, having interacted with Swept for some time, was surprised and replied in a supercilious tone, "Dr. Swept, you know our Hollandaise is never made in a blender. It is always cooked on the stove. On one occasion, sir, you even helped us because you thought we used too much lemon juice, affecting the quality. Our sauces are cooked, never blended."

Swept normally would be annoyed at the waiter's haughty demeanor, but was nonplussed. Yet, minutes later, he turned to Regina and crisply retorted, "I - uh - don't think I like that jerk. Besides, you never know when a restaurant is going to go downhill and start making the sauces inappropriately. Anyway, I like Mornay." He muttered something about the role of a slurry in making sauces, then returned to his meal.

Regina found the interaction bizarre.

Things came to a head when Swept ordered a California Chenin Blanc. Swept always contended that Chenin Blanc white wines were too variable to insure quality, and never ordered them. His favorite California white wine was Chateau Montelena, 1997. Now, he was ordering Chenin Blanc! Regina knew something was wrong.

"Dick, we've been seeing each other for some time. You're different. Something has happened to you."

Swept replied, "What do you mean?"

"I don't know whether it's me, the jogging incident, or what. You're just acting differently. You're different in bed, different in discussing affairs of State, you don't even push Limbic on me anymore. Your taste in wine has changed, much for the worse I might add. Even your speech is a little different. Is there something I should know?"

Swept, with a look of insouciance, replied indifferently. "No, I don't feel any different. I don't think any differently. I'm not different. Everyone keeps looking at me as though I were. I'm not. I'm not pleased I was abducted and it's disquieting not to know what happened, but what can I tell you? I'm Dick Swept, I work hard, and I like you. Now, when are we going to my house?"

Perhaps Regina did love Swept. She didn't know. She knew she was no match for his facile way of changing subjects, avoiding that which he cared not to discuss. But, the surgeon was concerned. Swept had never been this aloof. She did not know whether it was something she had done or whether he was depressed over the jogging incident. Maybe, he was on drugs, or seeing someone else.

She dismissed the drug hypothesis. Swept simply did not like the idea of being controlled by anything, especially a drug. She dismissed his not being interested in her – they were seeing each other too often. Besides, they had no recent fights. It must have been the jogging incident. But, why? What had happened?

Something was different about him, she was certain. Dr. Regina Bruxton was very concerned. She decided against raising the issue of his personality change again for the time being. Later that night, placing her consternation aside, she gently oriented her mouth and the two physicians entered their own Valhalla.

As the lovers briefly awaited sleep's magical transport, Swept digested Regina's comments. He didn't like criticism, unless constructive and valid. He knew Regina meant no harm and wasn't certain whether her comments were even critical. Perhaps, he had changed. The points about his behavior could be valid. Again, anger seethed within. What happened to him? How long was he unconscious? How long did he lay on the grounds at the University? What had transpired?

Meanwhile, Regina realized that another change had occurred. Swept no longer enjoyed morning jogging. The old Dick would have jogged twice a day, hatchet in hand, ready and almost hoping to meet another intruder. He had given up jogging. Given up! It wasn't like him. Dr. Regina Bruxton decided to speak to Harold Ranger.

Regina and Swept fell asleep, embraced in each other's arms.

Chapter Thirteen

ACID PHOSPHATASE

IT WAS NOT without hesitation that Regina made an appointment to meet with the Chairman of Neurology. She was in private practice at the Houston Community Hospital and Ranger was a full-time academician. An ongoing town-gown conflict frequently caused a rift between the Medical School physicians and the private practitioners. More than once, several physicians had commented to her about her dating someone affiliated with the power-mongering Texas College of Medicine. They thought that private practitioners should stick with their own.

Private doctors complained that the Medical School physicians were snobs, but she knew the real reason for this schism. Many private physicians mistakenly perceived that, in an effort to keep funds within the Medical School, their doctors seldom sought private physicians for consultations. Consequently, the more Medical School physicians there were in the hospital, the less referrals to the private community. That was the main basis for the town-gown conflict – money!

Swept and Regina often discussed this rift. Swept fervently maintained that were it not for the scientific research performed at the College, ranging from genetic investigations to new drug therapies, and a lot of neuroscience in between, the private physician community would be just that, another private community. In this context, Swept highly respected the President of the College and also the Board of Directors, which continutally sought scientific excellence.

Swept paid no attention to town or gown affiliations, consulting only the doctors whom he thought best for his patients. Swept was as demanding in his own realm of clinical expertise as he was in his scientific sphere. Regina respected him for this, as did the entire hospital community. Within the confines of the Houston medical community, Dick Swept was near-legendary. More than once he had solved a difficult diagnostic dilemma for local physicians, specialists or otherwise.

The Chairman of Neurology welcomed Regina Bruxton into his office. Yes, he was busy, but was happy to give her a few minutes of his time. Ranger was aware that the plastic surgeon had been dating Swept, but not aware of the extent of their involvement. Regina told him about her concern, asking that their conversation be confidential.

Harold Ranger rose from his mahogany chair, walked across his three generation-old tattered Persian rug, a gift from the Harvard faculty upon his departure to Houston, closed the door and, in his coffee-stained flannel shirt, disheveled pants, and scuffed shoes, sat beside Dr. Bruxton.

"I agree. There is something going on. He no longer looks me in the eye when he talks to me. He blows up at Tracy. His work is excellent but his demeanor is different. It's as though he's doped up on something. I asked him about it once but he sloughed it off. I agree with you. I'm concerned."

Ranger continued. "To tell you the truth, the man is brilliant and interesting, but a bit bizarre. I wouldn't be surprised if he's taking some of that stuff he's been using on the animals. I wouldn't be surprised, knowing him as I do, if he were smoking it. Well, I'll get to the bottom of it. I'll have a chat with him. I'll also keep your confidence, Dr. Bruxton. Good-bye." Ranger stood, motioning Regina to the door.

What a haughty, supercilious bastard thought Regina. Ranger never asked Regina her feelings, never inquired how she felt, never asked whether she had any ideas, and never even directly looked at her. She absolutely had no persona with the Neurology Chairman. All he cared about was his own reputation in the medical school. She hoped one day Dick would leave him. It would serve the creep right.

Regina bade formal good-bye, took the stairs down to the second floor, crossed over to the Houston Community Hospital, turned right, and went into the Sopwith Building, fifteenth floor. Her office hours would soon begin. She didn't like being late.

At mid-morning, the Chairman called Dick Swept into his office.

"Look, Dick, you're not the same man you were prior to the incident, or whatever the hell that was. What's going on? Are you doing drugs? Is there anything I can do to help?"

Swept was amazed. It was for this that he had been taken away from his laboratory, to speak to the Chairman of Neurology about drug abuse? Prior to this, Ranger never raised a hair, let alone fired a single brain cell, on behalf of Swept's personal matters. Now, here he was, prying into his personal realm. On one level Swept was flattered; on another he was most annoyed.

Swept explained that although others had said similar things to him, there was nothing wrong. And, he wasn't "doing drugs," and never had.

Ranger continued. Something drove him.

"Look, I've known you over ten years. I met your parents before they died. I even met Louise." Swept felt a slight cringe. How dare he mention Louise?

The man continued, oblivious to Swept's concerns or his altered respiratory pattern. "I even met your sister, your nephews, your brother. I know you. Something's going on and I intend to find out what it is. Now, if you're doing some kind of drug and you're afraid that the hospital Medical Ethics Committee is going to find out, I'll do what I can. Roger is a good psychiatrist and deals with a lot of drug problems. If, on the other hand . . ."

Swept interrupted. "Look, what's wrong with you? I appreciate your concern. I appreciate everyone's concern. I'm telling you, there's nothing wrong. I'm being gaslighted. Nothing's wrong with me. Nothing. I'm productive in my laboratory. I'm productive all over. Nothing has changed."

Swept knew he was lying. He was lying in a way that seemed easy, yet difficult, the easy kind of lying chronic prevaricators use when they want to solve a problem at hand, lying without conscience. The Chairman's concerns, and Regina's, were valid. He knew it as he spoke. He had changed. Not a lot, but some. What had happened to him?

Ranger continued. "I don't believe that for a moment. In the years I've known you, have I ever called you into my office to address personal issues? Do I meddle in your personal life? Personally, I thought you were doing cocaine a while ago. I heard rumors about it from the nurses. Yet, you never heard from me."

The upper right corner of Swept's mouth twitched. It must have been that blond, Londerberg, who opened her mouth. She took him to a wild party once. He noticed people – her friends – snorting cocaine, and insisted they leave immediately. "The last thing I need to do," he told her, "is have my Class

Five Narcotics License revoked. We are gone, and gone now." He never called her again and she never forgot.

"I don't pry into your personal realm. I'm not trying to be an ass, but I will if I have to. You're part of this Department and you're well-being is important to our stature and growth. You're in the process of receiving funding and I don't want anything to happen to you. Besides, we're friends," Swept looked at him in a puzzled way, "at least in some ways. I'm concerned something happened to you and it happened around the time you were jogging. Maybe you were just hit on the head and that caused some changes. I don't know. Maybe it's the long-term effects of the chloroform you said you smelled."

"Chloroform doesn't have any long term side effects."

"Maybe it does in you. Bottom line, I want you to undergo a neurological examination, get an EEG and an MRI of the brain. You let me arrange this. I also want some blood tests, including a sed rate, thyroid profile, collagen screen, and some others."

Swept did not have to guess whether "others" included a drug screen. Putting principles aside, wondering whether anything had happened to his brain, the neurologist acquiesced.

"Okay, if it will make you feel better. Do whatever you want. When do you want to do this?"

"How about right now? Let's walk over to the Neurology Clinic. Phone the lab, your experiments can wait."

Swept's neurological examination was normal. The motor evaluation, consisting of Ranger examining Swept's extensors, flexors, distal, and proximal muscles, was normal. Fine motor control was normal. Stretch reflexes, reflecting brain and spinal cord integrity, were also normal. Likewise, his coordination, subtended by the cerebellum, was perfect for both legs and arms. The cranial nerve examination, including eye and face muscles, was normal. Pupils were equal and the back part of the eyeball was normal, signifying an absence of brain swelling. The sensory system was intact. Blood pressure and pulse were also normal.

Swept's neurological examination failed to reveal any evidence of neurological dysfunction.

The Radiology Department's Magnetic Resonance Imaging machines were located in the Brain Institute, on the ground floor. The Neurology Chairman, bellowing into the phone, insisted on an appointment for Swept later that morning.

Swept felt at ease as he lay on the table appended to the giant circular magnet. Without touching him, the magnetic resonance machine could delineate minute areas of brain compromise, from head trauma, tumor or otherwise. His feeling of relaxation momentarily dwindled as he was stripped down and placed inside the tunnel that covered him, from his head to his abdomen.

Swept had never experienced a claustrophobic episode in his life, but now had one. Swept concentrated on standing on the shores of Lake Michigan, his favorite beach, and counted to two hundred. He soon felt relaxed and made a mental note to query, in the future, whether phobias had a biologic basis.

As he lay in the claustrophobic-oriented hole, he heard the metal wings rotate about his cranium, feeding split-second molecular information about his brain into the computer, telling the digital and analogue system how his brain molecules were arranged. The computer, digesting this piecemeal data, constructed a picture of Swept's brain, to be interpreted later by the neuroradiologist.

After the study, Swept went to the EEG laboratory. The sign on the door – Electroencephalography Center – now held new focus for him: He was the patient. Swept exchanged familiarities with the technician, whom he knew well. He once dated her roommate, taking her out several times. His memory momentarily lingered on supple skin and pulsating charms, then no longer. Perhaps he *was* different, he mused, more so than he cared to consider. Prior to this, he would have briefly relived the entire sexual act. Now, he didn't. Regardless, he concentrated on the task at hand, preparing himself for the electroencephalogram.

Swept lay still, permitting the technician, Mary, to secure more than eighteen small metal disc electrodes to his scalp. He knew that he would have to wash his hair diligently that night to remove the EEG paste. He didn't care.

After the discs were attached, they were connected to a series of wires, and then to the sixteen-
channel EEG machine.

The brain, being an electrical organ, emits electrical energy that an EEG machine can record. Too
much electrical activity can cause epileptic seizures.
Too little activity can reflect disease in metabolism,
or stroke, or tumor in the brain.

Following the test, Swept walked to the laboratory for his blood studies. The technician had no difficulty accessing the blood within the physician's ropy
veins. She filled four tubes, telling the neurologist
that within a few hours she would have the results.

One of the blood vials was a screen for drugs.

Swept thanked her and returned to his own laboratory. Later that afternoon, as scheduled, he would
meet with Harold Ranger.

When the Chairman met with Swept, he told him
the results of the studies. The EEG and magnetic
resonance scan of his brain were normal, with no
evidence of tumor, stroke or infection. The blood
tests, including sedimentation rate, metabolic screen,
drug screen (which Ranger admitted requesting),
hemoglobin level, and the white cell count were
normal. Ranger ignored the report's statement that
the staining of different types of blood cells revealed
orange stippling in Swept's white cells, the cells used
for fighting infection. Ranger dismissed the staining
abnormality, attributing the stippling to an error in
staining technique. Besides, he had never heard of

orange stippling. Ranger told Swept that although the studies were normal, he still believed something was amiss and wanted Swept to know he would help in any way he could.

Swept was tired of these monologues, finding them almost boring. If he had changed, what was the cause? He semi-politely thanked his Chairman and showed himself to the door. As he was leaving, he noticed the lab slips. His eyes took note of the orange stippling. "What's this? Do I have orange stippling in my white cells?"

"Yes, probably a result of those newfangled machines that automatically do the staining, which you and I used to do manually when we were interns and residents. I don't put much stock in them."

"That's puzzling – it's never been reported in humans. We recently saw that, just the other day, in some of our rats given Compound 1040. Janos and I discussed it. It seemed to be a minor, insignificant finding."

"It is. Don't make much of it," Ranger said. Swept, furrowing his eyebrows, exited the office and returned to his laboratory.

Swept drank a cup of black coffee with Szeppek, telling his student what had transpired, and that his tests were normal. Szeppek commented that he, too, thought Swept was acting differently, but had kept this to himself, and thought that Swept should not readily throw away the orange stippling finding. The Hungarian had never heard of this finding in white cells until he worked with Compound 1040. He was surprised, very surprised, that Swept had the same abnormality.

Szeppek, staring into Swept's face, somewhat ill at ease, showed true concern. "This just doesn't make sense. You are acting differently. Dr. Ranger thinks you're acting differently, too. Everyone who knows you thinks you've changed. Even your speech was a little different before, although now it's back to normal. They do a medical screening and find abnormal staining of granulocytes in your white cells, the same staining abnormality we find in animals treated with Compound 1040, although we didn't know what to make of it and considered it trivial. Could you possibly have taken some of this yourself, accidentally, or maybe even on purpose, to test its effects on humans? Don't be offended, I'm just asking."

Swept, finding the Hungarian inappropriate, was indignant. "Absolutely not. Were I to take it, I would certainly tell you, because I'd engage in defined experiments. To tell the truth, the thought crossed my mind, but I stayed away from it because of the transient increase in acid phosphatase it caused in some of the rats. I stayed away from it for that reason, if not for others."

"Perhaps you accidentally ingested some or even inhaled it. Is that possible?"

"Don't be ridiculous. What do you think I do? Sneak in here at night and inject 1040 into myself? And, there's no way that any of us could have been accidentally exposed to it. It's a liquid, with a low vapor index. There aren't any fumes to inhale."

Swept, with mixed feelings about Szeppek, was struck by something. Like most academicians, he held a mild degree of paranoia. Academia was a competitive realm. Swept had personally known, and had heard of people who had gone off the deep end. He had long realized that many colleagues were jealous of him. Being a physician-scientist, many scientists were jealous of his income as a physician and, on the other hand, many physicians considered him too academic because of his scientific work. Also, more than a few were jealous of his relationship with Regina Bruxton, a beautiful and intelligent woman in her own right.

Swept's practice was small, but substantial, and the physician-scientist was well respected. His research was good and, were his Chairman to allow him to pursue injecting patients with his medication, he could become better established and possibly help millions of people. But, a new thought now struck him. Could Szeppek have a role in his bout of unconsciousness? Suppose someone had tried to kill him, leaving him at City University for dead. Could Szeppek be behind his quasi-tragedy? He dismissed the notion as absurd, but the thought lingered.

Szeppek continued, unaware of the thoughts in his mentor's head. "Let's just say somehow it got into your system because of some laboratory mishap. Things like that can happen. Isn't it true that at one time when your country was engaged in working with the Venezuelan Equine Encephalitis Virus, some laboratory workers became infected?"

"I don't need any negative innuendoes about 'your country.' "

"Dr. Swept, I meant nothing by 'your country.' This is what I mean about your being different. Little things bother you that never did." Swept, harboring thoughts of whether he had changed, remained silent about these possible misgivings. He wanted to attribute any possible changes to the stress of the abduction, but he know that wasn't enough. Why was he abducted? Was he now diseased?

Swept said nothing and gazed through Szeppek with an angry, distant stare.

"Look, Dr. Swept. I owe you a great deal. I only say these things because I'm concerned. You're not what you used to be. I tell you, you're not. You act differently. It may be you were accidentally exposed to Compound 1040. Why not draw some blood and check your own acid phosphatase? If you were exposed to the 1040, then perhaps your acid phosphatase will be elevated, as it transiently was in many of our animals exposed to it. It's a simple test and might help confirm whether the Compound entered your system."

Swept concurred, begrudgingly. Acid phosphatase levels were ordered primarily when physicians suspected prostate cancer, which explained why Ranger had not requested the study." Swept was too young to have prostate cancer. Swept again entered the outpatient laboratory, smiled at the technicians, and more blood was drawn. Again, his large veins were easily accessed, this time for acid phosphatase.

The following day, Swept was startled when he was informed his acid phosphatase was 7.6 microunits, five times the normal value. He decided to see Dr. Evelyn Graham, a superb urologist, who examined his prostate, told him it felt normal, and ultrasounded the organ, only to arrive again at the diagnosis of a normal prostate. She ordered a bone scan, repeated the acid phosphatase, which was still elevated, and told Swept not to be concerned about prostate disease. There was no evidence of cancer in his prostate and no evidence of cancer spreading to the bone. The next step could be a prostate biopsy but she suggested he wait a few months and see whether his level remained elevated. Dr. Graham very much doubted that he had prostate cancer.

Swept was worried, not simply because others thought his behavior was different, but because he now had abnormalities in his blood chemistry. He not only had an elevated acid phosphatase, but also orange stippling in his white cells. Maybe he had contracted a new type of disease, a new leukemia, possibly related to Compound 1040 side effects. Things like that were not unheard of. It happened to scientists quite frequently, especially when scientific investigators are exposed to yet-unheard-of carcinogens. He wasn't certain why the rats had an elevated acid phosphatase; their prostates were normal. Besides, in a majority of the animals, after a few weeks, their values returned to normal. However, elevated acid phosphatase was also found in female rats, and females have no prostate. In the female rats, the acid phosphatase level returned to normal after three to four days, taking a much shorter time to return to normal than in the males.

To his chagrin, and against some internal feelings, he returned to Ranger's office.

Ranger seldom involved himself in anyone's personal life, including his own. He believed himself to
have been an inadequate father, a belief that made
the untimely death of his son more intolerable. He
had known Swept a long time and, despite differ-
ences in their personalities, Ranger being abrupt and
non-compassionate, Swept sincere, kind and popular, the two held a bond. At least, in Ranger's mind.
Maybe so, in Swept's.

The Chairman was worried.

After Swept told Ranger about the acid phosphatase level, Ranger smirked that was why experiments had to be done in animals before humans.
Swept retorted that he had done the work in animals, not humans, which was why he knew they had
elevated acid phosphatase levels. Further, he had
been careful, which was why the fastidious researcher
was aware of the acid phosphatase elevations nor-
malizing. Regardless, the acid phosphatase in the
animals had not been shown to be associated with
serious damage.

Again, Swept denied his Chairman's ridiculous
thought that he had taken the drug. The necessity
of denying this almost reached a point of comedy.
Swept wasn't certain whether his Chairman believed
him, but the issue seemed to matter less with each
conversational exchange, the first with Szeppek, and
now with Ranger.

Perhaps Swept had a bizarre illness, an illness totally independent from Compound 1040. An indolent illness, only affecting certain aspects of behavior, of which he himself might not be totally aware. He certainly seemed to be getting better, at least his transient speech hesitations had improved and were now gone.

Ranger suggested Swept have a complete medical evaluation, not just a neurological examination. After Swept concurred, he made an appointment to see the most respected internist in the Houston Medical Complex, Dr. Michael Drake. The internist was out of town, but his office said that he could see Dr. Swept as soon as he returned, in a few days.

After thanking Dr. Drake's staff, Swept went to speak to Szeppek, who was busy in the laboratory, patiently awaiting the readings on chemicals being analyzed by the gas-layered chromatograph equipment.

The Hungarian heard Swept enter the lab and knew in a moment that anger was at hand. Before he could say anything, Swept was upon him. "Look, what the hell is going on? First, I want *you* to have a sample of blood drawn and see whether *your* acid phosphatase level is elevated. If not, it means I was exposed to that chemical and you weren't. And, if that's the case, I want to know why! If both of us were exposed, then we're doing something wrong, exposing ourselves to 1040, and it's somehow entering our system!"

Swept was not smiling. "Something weird is going on here and I intend to find out what it is. So, if you don't mind, go downstairs, tell the technicians to draw your blood and run an acid phosphatase level, and have them check your white cells for stippling. They'll cooperate. Use my name as the doctor ordering the test and tell them to bill our lab. If they have questions, tell them to page me."

Szeppek considered telling him to go jump in the lake. However, knowing better, he reasoned a refusal could prompt a return to Hungary. Besides, if he had the chemical in his system, he needed to know it. Somewhat miffed, Szeppek acquiesced and went downstairs. As he left, the Hungarian student mumbled, "I work for you and respect you. It's not my fault if you have problems. But, I'm happy to do what you want."

"Good." Swept turned, cleared his small laboratory desk, and paged through a laboratory manual, trying to occupy himself with details about flasks, beakers, and micropipettes.

After Szeppek left the laboratory, Swept was alone in the lab since the technicians were out on break. The physician-scientist released a parcel of energy, smashing his fist against the blackboard over his desk. A few thumbtacks fell, his hand hurt briefly, his mind hurt, and the pain stayed. Mumbling to himself, he wondered why he was so angry at Szeppek?

After the Hungarian returned, Swept could not concentrate as well as he wanted on the experiments. His relationship with Szeppek was becoming testy.

When the laboratory called Szeppek's results at 4:45 p.m., the ringing of the phone sliced through the atmosphere in the quiet laboratory. Szeppek's acid phosphatase level was only slightly elevated. It wasn't very high but it wasn't normal either. The result was indeterminate. The white cells were normal, without any orange stippling.

Swept looked at Szeppek with a steady gaze. "For some time, you've been trying to seek a position of favor in Harold Ranger's eyes. I don't have trouble with that. But, and you'd better believe this, if you in any way, shape or form, are trying to cause me trouble, or had anything to do with what happened to me that day at the City University track, I'll send your sorry ass back to Hungary in a sling in the baggage compartment."

Szeppek stifled his resentment as best he could. "Dr. Swept, I don't know what you're talking about. My work is nothing without you. I have family back in Hungary and I do want to go back there, but certainly not now. Your being ill or compromised in any way does me absolutely no good. I'm not your enemy and, if you want, I'm your friend. Regardless, I'm your student. Don't blame me for something out of control that happened to you. I've no more idea what happened than you do."

Swept stared. Following a long inhalation, he pursed his lips and exhaled slowly through his nares, extending his neck against clasped hands. "All right, maybe I owe you an apology, maybe not. Mind you, I'm going to find out what happened. When I do, someone's life is going to be turned upside down. I can promise you that."

Swept shook Szeppek's hand and left the lab for his office. It was now almost six o'clock. He telephoned Regina, who was still seeing patients. No, she couldn't see him that night. She had consults to see in the hospital and would be there for several more hours. She had several operative procedures to perform tomorrow.

Swept left the hospital and drove home. The attendant, who left promptly at five o'clock, was gone. There were no calls to Valerie VanDance. After arriving home, he opened the door, only to find dog-torn mail on the floor.

He picked up Limbic by the scruff of his neck and shook him. Limbic whelped, not knowing what he had done wrong. For years, the dog had tried to dissect mail and, when possible, even the mail carrier. Fortunately, his teeth were small and damage was minimal. Limbic had done this for years. As Swept held Limbic level to his own eyes, shaking him and hearing him whine, he became disgusted with himself. He had given up punishing the dog for this years ago – the dog was steadfast in his anti-mail behavior and Swept recognized that damage was minimal since Limbic's teeth had considerable difficulty piercing most envelopes. Now, here he was, punishing Limbic for the dog's routine offense.

Swept recognized he truly was different. He had changed.

Apologizing to Limbic, Swept place the dog outside and reheated some Fettucini Alfredo he made earlier that week, drank some wine, and then went to bed. He looked forward to seeing Dr. Drake.

*   *   *

Szeppek returned to his apartment, somewhat upset. Had he angered his mentor? Was someone trying to hurt Dr. Swept? He did not want anything to happen to Dick Swept, whom he admired and liked, and certainly did not want anything happening to anyone whose role in his own life was important. Phoning the Consulate, Szeppek told them what had transpired, relating the account of Swept's abduction, and his behavior change. He thought that discussing this with the Consulate might relax him and possibly help focus his thoughts. Szeppek was nervous and, deep within, thought that calling might make him feel important and in control. Again, he was wrong. He still felt lousy.

"Yes, he is different. He gets angry rather easily. . . . Yes, he has changed. . . . No, I don't know exactly what that change is, but he no longer is as friendly as he used to be. . . . I'm not sure, but I think that he wonders whether I had something to do with this. . . . No, I don't discuss my calling the Consulate. I know that is not a good idea. . . . Yes, I see him every day. . . . The chemical he is using is the same one I told you about before, Compound 1040, the one we've used for some time. The Compound isn't dangerous and I don't know the exact structure. It's composed of a simple sequence of amino acids, somewhat related to growth hormone. I don't know exactly what it is. . . ."

The bureaucrat had more questions. "Well, to be certain all our students stay in good health, I'd like to know the exact structure, so that you're not exposed to anything some of our other scientists might believe has a possible cancer-inducing effect. We don't want Dr. Swept to think we believe he doesn't care about the safety of people in his lab, so I suggest you not discuss this particular issue with him. But, let us know what the structure is."

"I can't find that out. Once, I asked Dr. Swept and he stated it was an amino acid sequence but wasn't certain of the exact structure himself. He said he worked with so many different structures that he had gotten them confused. He wrote it out for his presentation for the Site Visit I told you about, but then he threw those records away. He tried to look it up the other day in one of his logbooks, but was unable to find the exact delineation. Both of us tried to look this up a week ago, while preparing his manuscript for presentation in Washington. We couldn't find it. We know the amino acids, but not the sequence. And, as for the carrier substance, forget it."

The questions continued. Szeppek did not have all the information available and figured that Swept would know this information by the time of his presentation in D.C.. "Actually, now that I think about it, he's also not as organized since that episode at the University. And, as for my safety, I don't think I have much to worry about. But, regarding his disorganization, maybe that's the reason he doesn't know the exact structure.

"Janos, you said that Dr. Swept's acid phosphatase was elevated?"

"Well, maybe. At least that's what I understand. Mine wasn't. Well, it was slightly high but basically within normal range. Maybe his elevation reflects whatever chemical he was exposed to when he was abducted."

The voice on the other line seemed annoyed. "Janos, don't be too much of an investigator. It will probably take up too much of your time. If you could find out the structure of the Compound, fine. Otherwise, forget it. On another note, please be well. We want our students to be in good health and make us proud, which you are certainly doing. Thanks for your concern. Have a good night."

The tape went to Petsh, at the Embassy.

Szeppek sat down in front of the television and watched the news, drinking a Dr. Pepper. At the same time, Petsh wired the tape to Kostokov. It would be in Kostokov's hands within 90 minutes.

*   *   *

Aleksander Kostokov reviewed the text several times. It had been rather easy to obtain information from the student, all too willing to share information, showing how important he was in the laboratory. Evidently, he truly did not know the exact formula of Compound 1040. At one time, according to the increasing amount of information that Kostokov had gathered about Swept, Swept had kept meticulous records. Evidently, following the incident that occurred when Swept was jogging, his record-keeping system had become sloppy. But, although the exact molecular structure was not known, a large bottle of Compound 1040 was available, as Szeppek had mentioned numerous times before.

The inquiry had not been pushed too hard, lest Szeppek become aware that he was truly being interrogated.

Szeppek earlier related a great deal: Prior to the jogging incident, Swept scrutinized all records in the laboratory and compulsively maintained an excellent record-keeping system. However, following the jogging incident, not only had his behavior changed in his social life, as his friends and colleagues had observed, but his behavior changed in the laboratory. As a result, although he was still scientifically creative, many attributes, such as good record keeping, had fallen by the wayside. Although Szeppek knew the general structure of the Compound, he did not know the exact molecular arrangement, since Swept made several alterations during the preceeding years. He also did not know the duration of the interaction of the free radical-initiated cyclization of the omega-phenyl-1-alkenes, an interaction essential for the production of 1040. Nor, was he certain what procedure he initially pursued when placing the mixture through the gas-layered chromatograph. Swept was aware of this, slightly annoyed that his own record keeping had interfered with having this information available, but did not find it too important at the time. When questions about the structure had arisen at the Neurology Department Research Subcommittee, Swept stated he would later outline the Compound's complex chemical structure, since the data was probably somewhere in his briefcase, stuffed with papers and medical equipment.

Again, thought Aleksander Kostokov: the briefcase.

Chapter Fourteen

TRUTH SERUM

MICHAEL DRAKE'S OFFICE was remarkably different from the medical offices of faculty physicians at the Texas College of Medicine. Drake, a private practitioner, had an office with comfortable high-backed chairs. His receptionist politely greeted each patient. A tasteful rug covered the floor and magazines in his office were current, not months old.

By contrast, offices of physicians affiliated with the Texas College of Medicine were cramped with old peeling linoleum floors, outdated issues of *People*, *Time* and *Sports Illustrated*, and, given that Department administrators decreed well-designed offices to be unnecessary accoutrements, having nothing to do with the quality of medical care, the offices and patient waiting areas were a mess. What Swept could never understand was why the administrative offices were furnished with plush carpeting, Chippendale-style chairs, original oil paintings, and watercolors by contemporary artists.

Following a detailed medical evaluation, the experienced Dr. Drake returned the stethoscope to his jacket pocket. "Dick, I'm flattered you asked to see me. However, I find nothing wrong, nothing at all. The only observation of note is a mild swelling, which might be a lymph node, although I doubt it, at mid-position over your right carotid artery. Also, you have a slight degree of tenderness there."

Swept nodded, feeling the area Drake described. "I never noticed it until you pointed it out. It's too low for me to recognize while shaving. As I think about it, though, I remember when I awoke in the field I had a slight pain in the right side of my neck. It's kind of cloudy and difficult to remember, probably not a big deal." Swept continued, "What do you think I should do about all this?"

"I don't think you should do anything. Perhaps a virus infected tissue there. It would be unheard of for a blood disease to form at mid-position of your right carotid. If you had an aggregation of abnormal cells, you should have other evidence of abnormality. You don't."

Drake continued. "I don't think it's much of anything. Your examination is normal, including your prostate. I don't know what to tell you about that elevated acid phosphatase. I called the lab after I spoke to you yesterday and asked them to repeat the test on some remaining blood they still had. The value came down a bit, but it's still fairly high."

With the look of a concerned colleague, the internist posed a direct question. "Is there anything at all you can think of that might have bearing on your health?"

Swept, looking at the floor for a few moments, muffled a statement. "I tell you one thing I've noted," Swept said, looking seriously at Drake. "I get depressed when I drink alcohol. I used to drink between two and three Oferitas a night over at Ofelia's, but now I can't because I get depressed."

Drake was familiar with the branch of Ofelia's restaurants in Houston, noted for their Tex-Mex food. Drake especially liked the *carne asada*. The Oferita was a strong Margarita. Usually, two or three of them knocked anyone out, and Drake was surprised that his patient had previously been able to handle two or three.

"What do you mean?" Drake said.

"Well, when I have that drink, whereas I used to tolerate two or three Oferitas, I now get depressed. Not a lot, just a little. Sometimes, I might even get a little confused. It's reached a point where I hesitate to have an Oferita at all. Never thought much about it until now. I've just stayed away from them. Do you think that means anything?"

"It's easy to find out. As you know, alcohol suppresses activity of the nervous system. Often, it makes people feel high for a while, but sooner or later, it depresses nervous system electrical activity. It may be that it's depressing your cerebral cortex, which contains emotional feelings, causing depression to emerge. However, considering you don't have other signs of depression, like early morning wakening, loss of appetite, crying spells, or a decreased sex drive, I doubt you're clinically depressed."

"But, I agree that something peculiar's going on here, Dick. Something. Now, I've never considered you a crock, one of those patients who fakes illness or has symptoms from psychological problems. It's not that those people aren't sick in their own way; you just aren't one of them. I don't know why you have that granulocyte stippling, the increased acid phosphatase, or the change in your reaction to alcohol. But, I think we can test it and test it well."

The internist removed his white coat and placed it on the hook next to the statue of Osler, the legendary physician. "Why don't we do an Amytal Test, the old-fashioned truth serum? That will depress the action of your brain cortex cells, just like the alcohol. Maybe we can get a better handle on what's going on in your brain. I'm not sure, but it's worth a shot."

Swept was slightly stunned. He had frequently administered intravenous Amytal to patients, jokingly telling himself, but telling them in a serious vein, that it was truth serum. Actually, it was. Amytal slowed down the action of the cells in the cortex and, by so doing, interacted with the underlying memory system. If the patient were employing brain activity to hide certain memories from their own consciousness, such as hating a mother, or hating a father, hating a wife, hating a job, not loving one's children, or other stresses, these issues sometimes surfaced. Sometimes it worked, sometimes it didn't. The efficacy of the Amytal truth serum varied, which is why it never achieved widespread clinical acclaim.

Swept agreed it was worth a try.

"Okay, Michael, happy to do it. How about tomorrow morning?"

"How about later this evening? Six o'clock?"

Swept inhaled deeply, answering cautiously. "Sure, Michael. See you here?"

"Yes."

Dr. Richard Swept entered Dr. Michael Drake's office at 6:20 that evening, October fourteenth. Swept had earlier mentioned to his Chairman he was going to undergo an Amytal study. Ranger insisted on accompanying him. Swept was concerned that some memories pertaining to his private life might emerge, memories he did not wish to make public. On the other hand, he had no major memories to hide. He had never made love to a married woman and had never done anything illegal. Yet, his private life was his private life. Since the neurologist was going to be injected with a drug that affected brain function, it wasn't a bad idea to have someone there who knew how the brain worked, and knew what to do in case anything went wrong, a doubtful occurrence. Ranger was a neurologist and, although his clinical skills were rusty, they were good enough to provide Swept assistance if he needed it.

Also, for whatever the reason, Swept was pleased that Ranger cared enough to come.

Ranger arrived at the office shortly after Swept. Except for the three physicians and a nurse stapling records together, Michael Drake's office was empty. The three physicians went into the examination room at the end of the hallway and Swept sat down, rolling up his right sleeve. Drake commented, jokingly, "Still wear Dunhill? Well, I must admit it looks good."

"Yes, Dunhill clothes are expensive but they last forever and maintain their style. Besides, I like them, probably a hangover from Boston days. Okay with you?" Swept sarcastically smiled. Neither Ranger nor Drake responded.

Drake was aware that Swept, like other Boston-trained physician-scientists, never mentioned the word "Harvard." It was always "Boston." Somehow, it bothered the Texas-born internist, but not enough to compromise his friendship with the locally prominent neurologist.

Michael Drake picked up the syringe, sucked saline from the sterile vial, and mixed the liquid with the barbiturate crystals. The solution was ready. Two hundred milligrams of truth serum was prepared.

Swept winced when he felt the stinging needle enter his forearm vein. His veins, having recently received multiple punctures, were becoming slightly tender. Drake injected ten milligrams of Amytal, then twenty, then fifty, then more. Soon, the full dosage mixed with Swept's body chemistry.

Swept lay supine on the examination table, aware of Ranger at his right. Impatience hungered on the Chairman's face. After three minutes of silence, Drake spoke.

"How do you feel, Dick?"

"A little woozy, just a bit. It's uncomfortable being here, in the patient's position, on the other side of the fence." He looked at Ranger's face, which was slightly blurred, but Swept was able to discern a countenance of restlessness. Swept felt somewhat tense but simultaneously felt somewhat at ease, as he waited for the effects of the medication to take hold. He soon experienced slight vertigo. "Real strange, real strange."

Within seven minutes Swept developed abnormal eye movements noted in patients who have succumbed to the effects of intravenous Amytal. As his gaze sought to follow Drake around the room, his eyes moved with jerky movements rather than with smooth pursuit, resulting from Amytal affecting brain coordination centers for eye movement. The drug had taken effect.

In some respect, Swept was not a willing subject for this procedure. He hated the idea of releasing anything locked within his brain, at the behest of someone else's commands. Swept's orientation was what many people derogatorily describe as macho. He disliked anything being done *to* him. In fact, it was for that reason that Ranger and Swept had maintained such a long-standing relationship. It wasn't that the two were close. They were not. Ranger knew how to deal with Swept. He knew never to confront him in a manner too aggressive; otherwise Swept would uncoil. Ranger had long recognized that Swept was reasonable and would do anything his superior wanted, as long as Swept never felt directly challenged. Thus, he was easily manipulated by the Chairman.

Long ago, Swept recognized this shortcoming, if it were a shortcoming, within his emotional matrix. Being aggressed did something to him. It delivered some kind of hormonal rush that released an anger within, almost unreasonable in nature. The way to Swept was through reason. Ranger recognized this and had thereby succeeded in producing a loyal member for his Department.

Drake, judging from Swept's irregular eye movements, thought that he should now pose questions. "Dick, how do you feel?"

"Not normal." Swept's speech sounds were slurred. Glancing around the room, eye movements again demonstrating the barbiturate-induced oscillating movements referred to as nystagmus, indicated to the two standing physicians that the patient was now under the influence of the drug.

Drake interceded. "Dick, tell me the date."

"Monday, October fourteenth." Swept's speech was considerably slurred.

"Where are you?"

"Sophwith Tower, part of the Houston Community Hospital, Houston, Texas."

"Are you aware why you are here?"

"Yes, it's to see whether I'm doing drugs. I'm not."

"It's not just to see about drugs, Dick. It's to see why your behavior has changed. Further, you said sometimes you feel ill at ease when you drink alcohol. It's occurred to your friends and colleagues that, perhaps, there's something wrong which this so-called truth serum might help elucidate. All right?"

"All I can tell you is that there is nothing going on. All I can tell you is that there's nothing special. . . ." Swept's slurred speech lost volume, his eyes glistening at the colleagues-turned-investigators. Swept blinked, sensing himself drifting through forests, sailing off the coast of Maine. Then, train wrecks went through his mind. First one, then two, then countless. Her face was on the engines, all of them.

With a tone of remorse, he mentioned her name. His pulse, despite his heart being bathed in barbiturate sedation, missed a beat. "The only thing special for me is Louise. I really thought we'd get married. I felt committed to her. She felt it for me. The rigors of being a resident in an intense program, being on call five nights out of seven. . . . too much. She chose a different lifestyle . . ." His slurred speech ceased, the ocular oscillations accentuated and then returned to their earlier-induced level. "From what I understand, she's never married, I guess. I don't even know where she is. She took a piece of me—with her."

Swept, staring into space, knew he had discussed the anathema – Louise. Even in his altered state, he felt annoyed he mentioned her, slightly accepting, knowing that his letting her interfere with his life was his doing, and no one else's. He had trained himself to be independent, to think independently, to be a survivor. She made it difficult. Or, rather, he let her.

The train returned, wearing her face.

Ranger stared, a vacuous stare. The Chairman was aware of Louise, but had no idea Swept still carried any feelings for her. However, in fact, he had no idea whether anyone carried feelings about anything. Ranger had never been one to understand feelings. He was not what one referred to as a sensitive man. The Chairman was here, with Swept, primarily because he cared about Swept's emotional milieu interfering with publishing, grant support, matters affecting Ranger's Department, thus affecting Ranger. At least, that's what he told himself.

"I wondered if I'd talk about Louise. Actually, I don't mind. It used to be that I thought about her every half-hour. Now, sometimes, I can go a day. But, always, always . . . ," Swept's voice faded again, the barbiturate's soporific effects compelling drowsiness, Swept still seeing train wrecks.

"Who's Louise?" asked an astonished Michael Drake.

"Let the matter drop." Ranger knew enough to let sleeping dogs lie.

Swept became slightly more alert. "I don't mind, Mike. I really don't. It's just that. . . ." The speech with decrescendo volume slurred further. He had to be roused from his stupor.

Ranger abruptly interceded. "What happened to you the day you were abducted?"

Swept, rising from the drug-induced sleep responded. The barbiturate's somnolent effects were decreasing. Without particularly trying, or tending to the task, he responded.

"I have no idea. I remember I went for my morning run. I turned at one corner, then another, as I've done multiple times. The next thing I know, when I approached Greenbriar, I smelled chloroform. That's all I know. Then I awoke with a gag in my mouth. I have never understood it. Why chloroform? If they wanted money, why rob a jogger? If they just wanted the watch, why not just use a gun? Joggers don't carry a wallet, let alone money. . . . No place to put it. . . . What about the animal lovers card? Why did they drug me? I don't understand it. It doesn't make any difference. I didn't understand Louise either. . . ." His eyes stared at the ceiling, speech again slurred, soon unintelligible. The physician-patient drifted into sleep.

Again, Ranger interceded. "Wake him up."

"Why?"

"Because I said so. We're not done. Something's going on with this man and I damn well want to know what it is."

"Very well, Harold." Ranger tensed at the unexpected, unearned familiarity of Drake using his first name. Drake, sensing the Chairman's unease, felt pleased. Supercilious bastard, he thought.

Drake shook Swept, waking him.

"Dick, is anything bothering you?"

"Nothing that anyone can help me with. Only Louise, and I've resigned myself to that."

Ranger interjected, "The hell with Louise! You've been strange, Richard, real bizarre. You don't complain like you used to, don't have that carefree snicker in your voice. Hell, you even walk different. You're not leveling with me. Have you been doing drugs, anytime at all?"

"No. I told you before. Once, maybe. But that was years ago. I don't do drugs."

"Have you taken any of those chemicals you work with?"

"No! Nothing, not even aspirin."

"I think you do."

Swept, half-awake, half-sleeping, disagreed. He had nothing more to add. He then fell into the blanketing canyon of deep slumber.

"All right, let's call this thing to an end," said a reluctant Harold Ranger. "I never much trusted things popularized by the press anyway. Truth serum, my ass. How do we wake him up?"

"We don't. We just let him rest. He can stay here for a while. He'll soon be awake. Amytal is a short-acting barbiturate, rapidly metabolized. It will be out of the system soon." Drake, checking the bandage over the antecubital vein, turned to Ranger. He decided not to reveal his anger over the obnoxious man's interference with the Amytal interview.

Ranger chose otherwise. "I damn well know what Amytal is. I'm a neurologist, in case you forgot. As I said, 'truth serum, my ass.'"

"Well, on a more pleasant note, I agree with you, Dr. Ranger," employing the appropriate appellation for the Chairman. "If there's one thing I've learned as a physician, it's to trust my feelings. Something is wrong. Richard doesn't act his normal self. He gets a little depressed when he drinks, has strange stains in his granulocytes, an elevated acid phospatase, and pain around his carotid artery, as well as a bump there."

"What? What kind of bump is near his carotid?"

"Here, over the right carotid," pointing to the outside area of Swept's neck.

Ranger looked at the area, then felt the small swelling. "Hmmm, I must have missed that on my examination. Why does he have swelling over his carotid? Probably means little. Still, it looks like a needle puncture. Even Swept isn't crazy enough to try to puncture his own carotid."

Ranger picked up his doctor's bag. "Well, I hope whatever's going on doesn't interfere with his research, certainly not his funding. He's been looking at medication that lays down memory, some crazy idea of his. I must say it certainly impressed the Head of the NINDS. He was so impressed he invited Dick to present his work at a meeting of scientists at the NIH."

"Yes, he told me something about that, said he wanted to work with patients but that you wouldn't let him. Personally, I think it's a splendid idea. I don't think it makes a difference what you do to those patients, as long as you don't cause unnecessary pain. Some of them are so demented they don't know how to get from the bedroom to the bathroom. I have a mother like that. I can see her at two o'clock in the afternoon, but at four o'clock, when my sister calls, she says she hasn't seen me for weeks. She doesn't recall that I was just there. It's all very sad."

The Chairman retorted. "I know it's sad, but we don't do experiments on human beings just because somebody is sad. We do experiments on human beings after studies have been appropriately done on animals, after scientific hypotheses have been appropriately tested. I've been fighting this issue in my Department for years. But, sure as hell, I'm not going to argue with some damn private practitioner about it." Ranger began to exit.

Michael Drake winced. Sarcasm was on the verge of spewing from his mouth, but he decided against it. Once again, the town-gown conflict. "Well, we can't be that bad. After all, one of your famous gown people here, Richard Michael Swept, came to see me. Me! Not any of the geniuses in the College's Department of Medicine, people who have interns and residents do their work. He came to see me. And I don't see that you objected."

"All right, my apologies," Ranger muttered. "I've got to go. Are you able to stay with him until he's more alert?"

"Yes. Apologies noted."

Both physicians, one an egomaniac, left Dick Swept resting on the examining table, belted down. Ranger exited. Drake caught up on his office paperwork, eyeing Swept through the open door. His nurse had gone home.

When Swept awoke, one and one-half hours later, Drake recounted what he had talked about, including Louise. Swept, vaguely recollecting something similar, expressed concern that he had discussed matters too personal while under the drug, but knew it did not make considerable difference.

"Who was Louise?"

"Louise? Just someone I knew."

The neurologist was tired, the barbiturate causing a hangover. Swept was not certain he should drive. Drake agreed and offered to drive him home.

Swept climbed the four steps to his front door, feeling slightly shaky. When he opened the door, he was glad that furry little Limbic greeted him with his step-bouncing demeanor, always happy to see his master. Again, the mail was torn, but this time Swept was not angry.

In his own way, Swept loved Limbic. Swept was especially proud of the style and focus with which Limbic approached the world. Few dog owners considered their pet's cognitive strategy for dealing with the world. Swept did. He admired Limbic for being up-front about what he wanted, whether it was another dog's bone, more food, or wanting to go jogging. Many a time, when Swept used to jog, irate that Swept had run several days without taking him along, Limbic would soil one of the oriental rugs. Following an ensuing yelling that made the dog actually shake, when Swept exited the front door, the undaunted Limbic, having been punished only minutes earlier, barked and snarled at the window as Swept entered the car. Limbic wanted to run with his master and cared not that he had just been punished. He wanted what he wanted. Lhasas were a good breed.

Swept prepared for bed, exhausted. He fed the dog, placed him outside, slipped into an old pair of scrubs from the hospital, and then poured himself

some cognac. As it mixed with the barbiturate remaining in his system, he entered sleep, his scrubs
still on, Limbic outside for the night.

A message from Regina lay within his answering
machine, asking to see him that night. He never
played it.

*   *   *

The drugged neurologist slept, dreaming
about standing in the middle of a deserted island.
He could see all surrounding shores, the entire
island. And, as dreams have that strange capacity
to do, he simultaneously saw the world from afar.
He was soon at a faculty meeting, hearing a colleague maintain that insurance companies were
responsible for the health care mess. He was then
back on the island, but could no longer see the
shore. A ship came and rescued him. He was taken
back to the faculty meeting.

Swept woke the next morning with a slight ache
in his head. He took two aspirins and walked to the
Institute, since his car was still there from the previous day. The short walk refreshed him.

After arriving at his office, Tracy told her boss
Ranger wanted to see him.

"Dick, I've been thinking."

Swept arched his eyebrow, trying to forget his
headache.

"Look, I don't want any complaints or wisecracks until I'm done. And don't give me those blasted hair-brained stares. I think you should take a vacation. Yesterday, you were talking about Louise, acting bizarre and, somehow, I still can't help but think you've been exposed to some of that crap you're giving those animals. I'm saying this for your own good, understand?"

Swept had a blank expression on his face.

"Your acid phosphatase is up. You've got abnormal staining in your white cells. Those same abnormalities occur in your rats given Compound 1040, by your own admission. Further, that conceited Michael Drake says you've got something going on over your right carotid artery. You do. I know you contend you haven't injected yourself and I'm sure you haven't, but. . . . Look, how about taking off a few days to relax? It would be a good idea. You need to be in shape, which includes being relaxed, for your conference at the NIH."

Swept's mind raced back and forth, between anger at Ranger's mentioning Louise's name, to gratitude for his concern. He knew the man was self-oriented, caring about Swept only because of the prestige he gave the Department. However, he wouldn't mind a few days vacation. He could use the rest.

Swept's head ached from the Amytal.

"To tell the truth, I don't mind. I could use a vacation, but we're too close to the NIH meeting. I know that one of the airlines offers inexpensive packages to the Cayman Islands, and I wouldn't mind taking it, but I'd miss the NIH meeting. I also know I'm the 'wrong person, wrong place, wrong time,' person for the NIH job with Dr. Chippers, but I can't miss that meeting. Not only is it a great honor, but I want to know what other people in the field are doing. Every American and European scientist with any prominence at all, the number not being that large, in the field of memory will be there. I must attend that symposium."

Ranger briefly glanced at the floor. Swept noticed the prominent scuff marks on the old leather shoes. "Look, I know Chippers well. Those scientists he wants to bring together for this meeting don't number more than fifteen, including you and Chippers. There aren't many people doing direct work in your area. The meeting is set for Saturday, October nineteenth. Today is Tuesday, the fifteenth. What's the difference if they move it back a week? When I last spoke to Chippers, Thursday, he told me four people from Europe were invited but couldn't make it. European funding for transatlantic trips, evidently, is nonexistent. Caput! It shouldn't make any difference to you – none of those Europeans work directly in your area of *new* memories. Of the remaining participants, five are from the NIH itself, all within the NINDS. They can attend any time, since they work right there. Therefore, all he's got to do is to contact the remaining handful. There might be some others I don't know about or whom he's recently invited, but he can change the time without much difficulty or inconvenience to most of them. People hadn't planned to miss weekday work to attend. It's only on one day, Saturday. They can put it off a week. It's not as though they're going to have hundreds of people in the audience. Just a handful of folks who think memory's important." Ranger smiled and winked. Swept did not.

"They're not *folks*, they're scientists. The fact you don't think memory research holds merit doesn't for a moment legitimize being cavalier, even if it's just to get a rise out of me. Anyway, why were you discussing this with Dr. Chippers?"

"Because you're in my Department and I can do what I want."

Ranger reflected a moment, then continued. "Meant nothing by that, Dick. Don't be offended," noting that perhaps Swept was beginning to feel better and act like his former self. "Just this old Boston fart's way. Take off some time. I'll call Chippers. He'll put off the NIH meeting for a week. I guarantee it will not be an issue with him. He'll do it. He and I go back a long way. These small conferences are very malleable and, besides, who would argue with the head of the NINDS? Take off more than a few days, leave today, if you want. Stay in the Caymans until next week."

Swept consented, believing the rest would do him good. In front of Swept, Ranger called Nathaniel Chippers. It wasn't difficult for the powerful Chairman to get through. Ranger told him some important Department matters had arisen and he would personally appreciate the change in schedule. Chippers agreed to postpone the meeting one week. It wasn't a problem at all. The Director told Ranger he thought that some of the invited scientists would actually appreciate the delay, since several had complained they might not have some of their presentation data ready in time.

Swept thanked Ranger for his time and effort, then returned to the laboratory. He was amazed at how prominent his crusty Chairman must be, being able to access so quickly a man as important as Nathaniel Chippers and getting him to rearrange a meeting. And, here he was, Dick Swept, liked by both but seemingly supported much more by the man whom he had met only once, rather than by the man whom he had known for so many years.

As soon as he entered his lab, Szeppek approached him, stating something was on his mind. A thought had struck him, and it was that thought he wanted to discuss.

"Dr. Swept, I know you're concerned about your elevation of acid phosphatase." Swept thinned his upper lip, quelling incipient anger. "Since your acid phosphatase is elevated and mine is essentially normal, perhaps there is something that happened to you but didn't happen to me. You told me you recall smelling chloroform at the time of the incident. Isn't it possible that both of us have been exposed to Compound 1040, resulting in our acid phosphatase enzymes being slightly elevated, but the interaction between the chloroform and whatever amount of Compound 1040 was in your system at the time, is responsible for the pronounced elevation in your case? Is that reasonable?"

Swept looked at Szeppek, deeply and carefully. Yes, it was a good idea. He was impressed. Perhaps, he should have thought of it first. Perhaps he would have, prior to the entire incident. He wasn't thinking as well as he should. This confirmed his needing to take the trip to the Caymans.

"I agree. I'm going to spend a few days in the Cayman Islands. I just had a discussion with Dr. Ranger about it. The NIH meeting has been delayed for a week. Why not take some of the rats and give them chloroform? You know the technique. Then, inject Compound 1040. Analyze some in a few hours, the rest in two days. You probably won't need more than six or seven animals. There's a fair amount of the Compound left," pointing to the bottle labeled 1040 over his desk.

Swept hesitated for a moment, then turned to Szeppek. "It seems as though we had more chemical in there. No?"

Szeppek, looking at the bottle, agreed. "I think so, but I'm not sure. The meniscus of the fluid seems to be lower than I recall. The last time we removed some was three weeks ago, when we placed one hundred milliliters in the smaller bottle near the animal cage. The smaller one is the bottle we use for our experiments. We haven't taken any from the large bottle in a while."

Swept began to feel overwhelmed. "Look, I'm taking off a few days. If I've been inappropriate with you, I'm sorry. Run the rats. See whether chloroform interacts with the Compound, making the acid phosphatase elevated. Also, see what it does to their white cells. For all we know, there are other interactions with this Compound we should know about. As for both bottles of 1040, let's start marking the level of the fluid. Maybe I'm having hallucinations." Looking again at the larger bottle, Swept muttered to the floor, "No matter, I'll think about it in the Caymans."

After Swept left, Szeppek felt pleased. His idea of testing the possibility of interaction between chloroform and Compound 1040 was a good idea. He dismissed the possibility of a lower level of the chemical. There was over 2000ccs of the mixture in the large glass container. Perhaps one of the custodians had taken the bottle off the shelf to dust it (something they were not supposed to do — they were never to touch the chemical reagents) and spilled some. But that could happen only if the top were removed. The top was firmly corked.

No matter, thought Szeppek, he had work to do. That night was the night he had to phone the Consulate. Surely, they would be pleased to hear about his idea of checking the reaction between chloroform and Compound 1040.

*   *   *

What bothered Aleksander Kostokov, obtaining the tapes within his 90-minute time-frame, was that Szeppek and Swept had noticed the decrease in the level of the fluid. He cursed himself for his stupidity. He should have placed some type of inert chemical back in the container to make up for the fluid he removed, but was concerned it might alter results of experiments. If Swept found error in his experiments, which could result from contaminants in the bottle, he might not attend the conference and the NIH might put it off. He had weighed the risks and, thinking that the amount he had taken was so small, decided to leave the bottle as it was, minus the small aliquot he had removed. Had he taken the liquid from the small bottle used for the experiments, the amount taken would surely be noted. Well, no matter. What was done was done.

Chapter Fifteen

CAYMAN MAGIC

SWEPT PHONED REGINA. She was surprised at his sudden decision to vacation in the Caymans. No, she was too busy with her practice to join him, but wished him well. She agreed to water his plants, especially the *Dieffenbachia*, and take care of Limbic. Swept went home, upset that Regina would not join him, although he was well aware he had only given her short notice. He packed. While packing, he had to decide whether he would take swimming trunks, which were, in actuality, his jogging trunks.

He decided to go jogging. He hadn't jogged since the "incident." A slow run around the City University perimeter might do him good.

Swept donned his jogging outfit, until recently dormant, and decided to take Limbic, who was delighted. He drove to the University, Limbic pawing at the car's window. He stopped the car, stretched and, with the happy dog at his side, minus the Walkman and Dylan tape, he began what had earlier been a common routine.

As Swept thought about Regina, he realized the relationship was truly falling apart. Was her concern for her practice (Was it the patients? The money?) so great she couldn't spend time with him? Regina certainly cared; otherwise she wouldn't have seen Ranger regarding Swept's recent behavior. Further, and he felt no reason to doubt this, he was the only man she was dating.

Yet, something kept Regina from being close. Until she was, and had more loyalty to him than to her practice, whether due to ego or money or power, he could hold no loyalty to her. And, he knew, he could never love someone for whom he felt no loyalty.

This time, when he arrived at Greenbriar, a sense of anger, tension, and fear agitated inside, as he remembered his last experience at this location. His thoughts were interrupted by a familiar voice.

"Well, hello Dr. Swept. I haven't seen you in a while."

Swept turned to see Ricki Hardson, jogging alongside, having come from behind. Pleased at her presence, he responded, "I've been around."

"Not jogging, or I would have seen you."

"No, not jogging. How have you been?"

"Okay. Any word from the papers, embassy, or whomever on our mission of justice?" The woman wasn't out of breath, had come up from behind, and obviously was in good shape. As Swept realized this, he also realized that his thinking was improving.

"None. They could be ignoring us."

Swept was now jogging alongside Ricki. The two runners kept pace with another well. The conversation, kept to short sentences and phrases because of the exercising at hand, despite both runners being well fit, soon turned to Limbic, who stayed at his master's side, ignoring passing canines. The two completed running the square block, stopping at Swept's Ferrari.

"Can I drive you home, Ricki?"

"Actually, I'm going to run two loops, six miles. I'm not done."

"Good for you. Well," he hesitated, "It was nice to see you."

"And you, too" said the well-bodied woman, bending down to scratch a panting Limbic, exposing some of her breasts.

An idea struck the physician. "Listen, without going into this, and I know we've really never socialized, but how would you like to join me in the Caymans for a few days?"

Ricki looked at him, startled.

Swept proceeded. "It's a long story. We don't have to make this heavy. We can have separate beds," smiling, "if you like."

Ricki looked at him, smiled, and said, "Here's to Sweptomania, Doctor," raising her right hand as if she were toasting a glass.

"Is that a yes? Come on, join me. There's a special package. We'd leave Thursday and return Sunday. What do you say? It's only for a few days."

Limbic lay on the ground, wiggling for an abdominal scratch. "See, even Limbic thinks it's a good idea. The treat is mine. I need the relaxation and would truly enjoy your company."

Ricki looked into the neurologist's eyes. "Done. I'll tell Dr. Hibbing."

"Will it be a problem for coverage? Can he do without a wonder woman nurse like you for a few days?"

"He felt embarrassed, probably humbled, when you interceded on behalf of the Sherpas. He'll approve it."

"Well, here's to you, lady." The out-of-breath Dick Swept reached out to shake Nurse Hardson's hand. He was surprised when she smiled and kissed him on the cheek. "To a man who appreciates commitment."

Limbic stopped wiggling and stood on all fours. "I'll call you tonight with the arrangements," Swept said.

"Great. My number is in the book."

"Talk to you later."

Ricki went off, jogging, and Swept drove home, Limbic at the window.

*   *   *

The NIH, including the NINDS, has a weekly calendar release, listing events for the coming two weeks. That calendar is released each Monday. Today was Tuesday. Since the calendar was distributed each Monday, the forthcoming Saturday meeting scheduled for the neuroscientists working in memory was already listed in the preceding week's calendar, as well as the calendar for that week. There was no formal announcement of the cancellation, because the meeting was not open to everyone at the NIH.

All Chippers had to do for his friend Ranger was to have the NINDS Chief's secretary contact the scientists who were to be there. None of the researchers objected. None would have objected to a personal request from the Director of the NINDS. Were one to antagonize him, one could have major problems in funding, although Chippers was never rumored to be a vindictive man. But, why take chances?

*   *   *

The Russians, continually monitoring NIH calendars, publications, and whatever they could get their hands on, had no idea that the meeting was cancelled. On Friday, October 18th, they phoned Swept's favorite Washington, D. C. hotel to make certain he was staying there. Was their plan working? They were told he had not registered. Curious, an agent phoned the NIH, allegedly to ascertain the location of the meeting, posing as a graduate student doing research at the University of Maryland who had been given special permission to attend the meeting on memory. He was told the meeting had been postponed until the following Saturday, the 26th of October.

The Russians needed a new course of action. A back-up plan was immediately set into play. They would simply kidnap Swept again, going through the same routine, but change the dates.

The wheels were set into motion. Agents in Houston were ready. The van was ready. The Russians made some calls around the hospital and, to their surprise, found that Swept was out of town, in the Cayman Islands. A few well-placed calls to the appropriate airline revealed Swept would return October 20th. Were he abducted again, a few days before leaving for Washington, he would probably cancel that trip. The plan was not without risk.

The Russians had no further back-up strategy.

Why had Szeppek not known of the cancellation?

Perhaps he did, but had not mentioned it. Aleksander Kostokov wondered.

Liubov Usova wanted one of her seductive female FSB espionage agents, all cold-hearted, ruthless murderers, to seduce Swept in the Cayman Islands. They could then proceed with the same plan they had executed in Houston. Yuri Lyachin was more sensible, realizing that this carried major risk. First, the Russians did not have a main base of operations in the Caymans. The colony, stubbornly loyal to the Queen of England, never had a strong leftist faction and the Russians, during the days of the USSR, had never established a foothold there. Second, Lyachin was hesitant about abducting Swept from his room or from the beach, the two places he would probably spend most of his time. There were too many tourists wandering around. Finally, even if the kidnapping were successful, it still might prompt Swept to cancel the trip to the NIH. Lyachin discussed this with Kostokov; both were convinced that the plan would not work smoothly.

Kostokov decided upon a new approach.

*   *   *

Swept registered himself and Ricki for a Cayman Island package, one slightly different from the one he had initially selected. They would leave Houston at 4:45 p.m. Thursday afternoon, and return at 4:15 p.m., Sunday, October 20th, arriving at Bush International Airport.

A few days to relax. Also, he planned to think about his NINDS presentation. He wanted it to be good, to be excellent. His anger over the abduction was gradually decreasing, but still lay within his mind. He had begun to feel more normal, or less abnormal, and looked forward to spending time with Ricki. He packed two Dunhill classic blazers and slacks, some shirts and swimwear, as well as a few Turnbull and Asser sportshirts.

Swept met Ricki as planned, at the Cayman Airways counter. He explained he did not trust the airlines. They lost his luggage too many times. That was why he carried everything in his Mark Cross soft leather valet, with compartments for folded clothes, hanging clothes, and anything else for a serious traveler. He was permitted to carry it on the plane, either hanging it in the garment section or placing it in the overhead compartment.

However, the woman at the Cayman Airway ticket counter told him there were no garment closets on Cayman Airways. She also doubted there was room in the overhead compartment for his bag since the flight was full. She advised Swept to send his luggage through regular baggage. Begrudgingly, Swept acquiesced, concerned it would be lost like so many times before.

Swept and Ricki went to a bar, Airway Heaven, where he ordered a Ketel One Vodka, chilled, straight up, with a single drop of scotch. He meticulously explained to the barmaid that he wanted only one drop and did not want to taste the scotch in the drink. Ricki, witnessing this conversation, jokingly said, "Meticulous, are we? You've got to be kidding." Turning to the exasperated waitress, Ricki made a simple request: "Perrier, any way you want."

The twosome drank their beverages and left for the plane. After going through the metal detector, they walked down the corridor lined by disconcerting geometric patterns, heading to Gate D-9. The aircraft was at the gate and passengers were boarding.

When the two entered the plane, Swept was miffed. The plane wasn't full at all. There was considerable room overhead. He told himself to relax, trying to believe the woman at the ticket counter may have been right in other ways. Although the plane was two-thirds full, with much room in overhead space, it was probably true that were everyone to bring garment bags on board, there would not be room for all. Thus, no one had been allowed to bring them on board. Never mind that the overhead bins were empty.

The reasoning didn't work. He was perturbed.

Swept hoped his luggage would arrive safely. He expressed his concern to Ricki, who up until now was fairly silent.

"I never realized how intense you were," she said. "I thought you were laid back."

"I am, and I'm not. I just hate incompetence, at any level, in any job."

Grabbing his arm, the nurse gently spoke. "Look, Mister. You relax and I'll see that you have a nice time." Ricki kissed him on the cheek, lingering considerably longer than when she had kissed him post-jogging. Swept smiled.

During the flight, Ricki removed her *Field and Stream* magazine from her purse. Swept commented, "Is this what women who hike in the Himalaya read?"

"Actually, I read a lot of outdoor magazines. I especially like this because it covers fishing and hunting."

"Don't tell me you hunt?"

"Not recently, but I used to. A lot. I even field-dressed the animals. My dad hunts elk every year, in Vermejo Park, up in New Mexico."

"I'm familiar with that area. It's in northern New Mexico, near Raton, just south of Colorado."

"Do you hunt?" Ricki asked.

"No. I've never been against it but, for whatever reason, I don't. But I know about Vermejo. It's a class act. What kind of rifle do you use?"

"I don't have one. I use my Dad's, a Remington 700, .270 caliber."

"Isn't that a bit small for elk?"

"Is there anything you don't know? Yes, it is slightly small but he uses 150 grain bullets. It's good enough for deer and elk. Do you know about guns?"

"A little, from army days."

"Anything else I should know about, like being weird, really weird?" Ricki asked with a smile, taking his hand and looking into his eyes, wondering whether she saw a bit of cruelty.

"Sure," Swept replied, his eyes holding a mystique. "But, nothing illegal." With that, Swept opened his *Economist* and began to read, turning occasionally to admire the beautiful woman at his side.

After the three-hour flight, and a landing that conspired whiplash, the two took a taxi to the Holiday Plaza, supposedly one of the better hotels in the area. It offered good music at night, allowed its occupants to access the majority of the water-sports facilities in the vicinity, and provided many other recreational activities as well.

Swept had traveled to the Cayman Islands several times before. He especially enjoyed the snorkeling. Swept had not learned how to scuba dive, perhaps due to some claustrophobic fear the magnetic resonance scan had uncovered. If a true phobia, it was one of his few weaknesses.

Swept had snorkeled a great deal on the island. He particularly enjoyed swimming among the reefs, reminding himself that coral was an animal, not simply stone. He had attended two Pirate's Week Festivals and once even attended a Scuba Bowl activity. The only bad memory he had was eating at a local pizza parlor, touted as having the finest pizza in the British West Indies. He not only became ill from the overhead fan's strong draft, but was annoyed at being given garlic bread that he thought was complimentary but was then charged for it. It wasn't the money, but the principle. But, he knew in his heart, that it wasn't the principle. It was the idea of being pushed around and having something done to him. He didn't like it.

Regardless, he loved the Caymans. The islands were inviting, beautiful, and relaxing. Ricki exponentiated their splendor.

*   *   *

Swept registered at the Holiday Plaza and was given a partial ocean front view, which they called a Superior Room. Although exacting, he was pleased with the internal accommodations, which included two queen-sized beds. It was too dark to appreciate the view. In a short time, the couple unpacked, Ricki being somewhat modest as she placed her clothing in the dresser closest to the bathroom, and the two were soon ready for dinner.

At the hotel bar, Ricki had a piña colada, Swept his Ketel One. Afterwards, following a brief dinner at the hotel, they walked along the beach, soon finding their way back to their room. Despite the air conditioner's droning noise, the couple was soon asleep, each in a separate bed.

Swept did not dream of an island.

The twosome woke in the morning to the noise of men outside, hammering and painting. Peeking behind the drapes, now for the first time since arriving in Cayman, Swept noticed the view of the pool and a barely visible ocean. So much for having a partial ocean front view. However, his head felt clear and he felt good. The workers outside were swearing, arguing, but appeared to be having a good time. He felt relaxed.

Ricki, similarly, was well spirited. "Nice night?" she jokingly smiled.

"I've had better."

Swept showered first, washing himself down with his Vinolia soap and Crabtree and Evelyn lemon oil shampoo. The soap, with its boric acid and cold cream base, had an invigorating capacity. It always refreshed him, as did the shampoo. He then shaved with his Crème A Raser a L'huile d'Amande, the only shaving soap he used, despite his believing it responsible for the occasional slight rash on the underside of his chin. Leaving the bathroom with a towel wrapped around his waist, his chest exposed, he turned to Ricki.

"Your turn, woman," he smiled.

"Really?" she chuckled back as she entered the bathroom, still wearing the extra-large T-shirt in which she had slept.

Ricki returned, hair wet, only to gather some clothes and return to the bathroom. In a short time, the refreshed couple were breakfasting at the hotel coffee shop, Swept sourfully taking note of the laid-back demeanor of the waiters.

The menu stated papayas were available, when in season. He asked the waitress whether they were in season. When she said yes, he requested a papaya, but was told they were not yet ripe. Swept settled for a raisin muffin and cheese omelet.

When the muffin came, he took a bite and noted there were no raisins. After hailing the waitress, she stated they only had fruit muffins. Thinking to himself that, as he was growing older he was, somehow, becoming more relaxed, he accepted it. A few years back, he would have asked why she had not told him they were out of raisin muffins. No matter, he was here to relax, and relax he would.

Ricki laughed at his intensity. "I never would have believed it! You're not laid back at all. Sweptomania was wrong."

"Come on. Knock it off about that play."

"Never, you playboy of the western world." Giggling, the nurse, hair still wet from the morning shower, placed her right hand on his face, cupping both sides of his lips, and kissed him, following which she removed a sliver of muffin from his lips.

Wolfing down his cheese omelette, raisin muffin *sans* raisins but with fruit, Swept smiled at her. The twosome returned to the room to change into bathing suits, Ricki changing in the bathroom, Swept in the bedroom. While Ricki was changing, Swept went to the lobby to purchase a newspaper. It was in the lobby that he recognized someone. He couldn't believe it.

"Valerie VanDance!"

Valerie hailed him, extending greetings. "Hi there. I thought I'd take some time off myself and enjoy the sun, and the Islands. Maybe . . ." pointing her right index finger, now waving it, ". . . . I can even enjoy you." She smiled, that smile possessed by many women over forty, the one that beckons, warms and soothes, simultaneously carrying the potential of leading a man to emotional doom, or the sexual time of his life, or both.

Swept had never sexually touched Valerie. At one point, it had crossed his mind, but he thought it unwise. One should never mess around in the kitchen, as his uncle used to say. Valerie was the Chairman's nurse. Swept wasn't certain whether she had been married at one time, but he knew she was currently single. She was a few years his senior, brimming with almost as much energy as he had. He often wondered what she would be like in bed, but the thought of finding out never seriously crossed his mind. Besides, he was not certain whether she was interested.

"What a surprise," Swept politely said. "Is Dr. Ranger aware you're here? How did you get him to give you time off?"

"Who cares about Dr. Ranger? The Texas College of Medicine states I'm allowed to have four weeks of vacation a year, Doctor, and I seldom take it. The school probably owes me seven or eight weeks, if not more. Besides, I don't have to ask Dr. Ranger anything regarding my personal life. I tell him. I told him I want to take off some time and visit my relatives in Louisiana. That was it. Nothing more, nothing less. He said 'Fine.' Right now, he's tied up trying to figure out how to get nominated to the National Academy of Science. That's all he cares about, his scientific prestige. He doesn't care what I do, as long as I show up for work forty-eight weeks a year."

"If you're asking me whether he knows I'm down here with you, the answer is 'No'. And, if you're asking whether I'm going to tell him I met you here, the answer is still 'No.' "

"He'll know by the tan, Valerie."

"Then I guess we'll have to spend a lot of time indoors," she cooingly responded, almost laughing with wanton abandon, the over-forty smile on her face.

Swept was annoyed. "I wouldn't get carried away with myself. What's this about anyway? I must tell you, I'm here with a friend." He politely dorsiflexed his left hand, walking away.

"Who?"

The right eyebrow elevated. "Ricki. Ricki Hardson. And that's it, she's just a friend."

"The woman who found the dead Sherpas?"

"Yes, that woman. Okay with you?"

"Sure. Besides, it's none of my business. I guess it's also none of my business whether you're still dating that plastic surgeon."

"Right."

"You are?"

"No. Right, it's not your private concern." Swept's voice was becoming increasingly testy.

"Well, I just never knew that you were seeing Ricki Hardson."

"Well," he mocked, "I guess that proves my private life is not a part of your personal purview."

"My apologies. Have a good time." The nurse smiled, poking her finger at Swept's sternum. As she walked away, the Chairman's nurse turned, facing Swept. "Look, I'll be frank. I thought I could spend some time with you. I saw Dr. Bruxton, whom the whole hospital knows you date, on the fourteenth floor of the hospital the other day. I asked her whether she planned any recent trips, knowing from Dr. Ranger and the secretaries you were leaving town. She knew I was referring to whether she was travelling with you. She gave me some song and dance about how busy she was and that she couldn't go. So, I figured, not to intrude in your realm, that either she's too money-hungry or you guys stopped seeing each other. Either way, she's out of her mind not to be here with you. So, I decided to come here, hoping we'd both have a nice time. If it worked out, fine. If it didn't, then it didn't. Besides, I wanted to get away and relax from that tyrant I work for."

Swept defended Ranger, not permitting a nurse who worked for the Chairman to attack him. Swept simultaneously remembered his loyalty to Ranger was probably less than Ranger's loyalty to him.

Valerie knew, as did others in the Department, that Swept was different following the jogging incident, although he was certainly returning to his baseline. When Ranger commented to her that Swept was going to the Cayman Islands, she decided to meet him there. Aside from her fantasy of extracting pleasure from his body, she hoped to learn what was transpiring in Swept's life. Something had made him different. Since he was somehow involved with the Sherpas, just as Ricki Hardson was, Valerie VanDance wanted to find out what was going on. Information never hurt, and she welcomed a vacation.

Valerie silently respected Swept's loyalty as they walked outside, continuing their conversation, bordering on bantering. Walking toward the rooms, Swept having forgotten the newspaper, they saw the ocean waves pulsating forwards and backwards, reminding Swept of childhood summers in Union Pier, Michigan, where he had met Louise.

Valerie poked him gently, "Penny for your thoughts."

"Nothing, really nothing." He was here to vacation and vacation he would. Forcing himself to push Louise from his thinking, still occasionally thinking about his abduction, he found Valerie's touching his arm a pleasant respite. Then, playing again with his chest, she whispered something in his ear. Swept almost went through the floor.

In some ways, Swept was a simple man. Actually, in most ways. Only a few friends understood his true complexity. However, once they understood, they also understood his simplicity. He believed in God and honesty, believing all people should be honest and kind. People lacking belief in God were acceptable as long as they were good and honest. Some of the finest people Swept knew were atheists. He did not share their disbelief, recognizing people either believed in God or they didn't. He respected them as long as they were good, sincere human beings. Swept did not tolerate dishonesty. Nor, adultery. In many ways he was straight. He never lied, even on his taxes.

Sex was another matter for the handsome neurologist. Where there was sex, there was pleasure. It was not a usual type of pleasure. He wasn't certain as to its description. At times, he thought sex provided a release of fantasies, knowing that he usually had little vignettes cross his mind during intercourse.

He eyed Valerie's body as she disappeared down the coastline, remembering the intense sexual innuendo she had just whispered. He returned to his room, and kissed Ricki Hardson hello. "You look great in that," eying her two-piece suit. "Purple does you well."

"We'll see," smiled Ricki. She took the neurologist's hand and the two walked toward the beach.

The sky was becoming slightly cloudy as the two left their room for the beach. Swept hoped that the clouds would provide a mild sunscreen. To be safe, he purchased some lotion, and was baffled by the increasing complexity of suntan lotions. One simply used to buy or not buy a lotion. That was it. Suntan lotion was suntan lotion. Now, there were fifteen different levels of sunscreen. He purchased a sunscreen lip balm, and, not knowing what number rating of suntan to choose, bought the one in the middle, No. 8.

Stopping walking, instigated by Ricki's gentle tug, she rubbed lotion on his back. Her smearing the lotion side to side on his chest, coupled with her whispering how happy she was that he had asked her to join him, made the veteran lover pleased. He temporarily relinquished other thoughts.

Hurrying to the hotel room, where they exchanged a few pleasantries, the couple soon lay naked in bed. Ricki was experienced, lithe, and confident. She ran her tongue along the furrow between Swept's scrotum and thigh, simultaneously pushing upwards at his perineum with her thumb. Then, licking the man's skin, she unexpectedly, and without mild degree of discomfort, forced her index finger against his prostate. Fairly hard. When her finger found its target, an orgasmic-like sensation soared through Swept's body. That, coupled with her mouth's activity on his genitals, soon completed the orchestration. A confident loving look appeared on her face, and Swept kissed her to the full.

The two spent the latter part of the afternoon learning about each other's bodies. They made love with passion and tenderness, leaving their respective worlds behind.

Chapter Sixteen

SEX, FOOD AND WINE

AFTER THE AFTERNOON of intense sex, during which Swept discovered, or rather had discovered for him, that he was sensitive in previously non-explored areas, the two lovers showered and dressed for dinner. Again, the invigorating Vinolia and Crème A Rases. Ricki changed her clothes in the bathroom, while Swept waited for her near the bed. Together, they walked to the lobby.

Swept and Ricki took a cab from the hotel to the Large Old Home, a noted restaurant where, surprisingly, Swept had not previously dined. They were fortunate to obtain a table without reservations. The atmosphere was delightful.

The restaurant was in an old Georgian-styled home overlooking the water. Numerous overhead ceiling fans created many nuisance drafts. These, coupled with the sixty-degree air conditioning, made Swept uncomfortable. His concern about drafts stemmed from his awareness that they could cause Bell's palsy, a paralysis of facial muscles. Ninety-five percent of those afflicted did well. Five percent did not. These thoughts lurked in the back of his mind as he held Ricki's hand, which felt so good that he soon forgot about Bell's palsy.

The two drank a *negociant* Pouilly-Fuisse, certainly not excellent, but the best available. Although the best wine from the Mâcon area, Swept explained it was only good if domaine bottled, certainly not a *negociant.* However, the allegedly best restaurant on the Cayman Islands had no domaine-bottled Mâcon wines. So much for fine restaurants in Cayman, he thought.

Following the Pouilly-Fuisse, they had Conch chowder. Swept, ever the gourmet researcher, explained that the chunky seafood soup was a descendant from the Bouillabaise French fish soups. The term "chowder" paid homage to that descent, being derived from the French *chaudiee*, translating to "heater," the heater being the vessel in which fishermen's soups were cooked.

"Like the famous French soups and stews, chowder can include a mixed catch of seafoods. The best version, clam chowder, has two distinct types. One, New England style, has a mild milk or cream-based broth with cubes of potato, onion pieces and salted pork. The other, Manhattan, has tomatoes, water, potato and vegetables. Conch chowder is similar to that of New England, with conch instead of clams."

Ricki looked at him as though he were an idiot. "I appreciate all this information, darling, but I never asked you anything about it. It sure doesn't impress me. You, on the other hand," wiggling her index finger and smiling, "certainly do." Smiling gently she said, "I'd much rather hear about you, your thoughts, and your feelings."

"You're right, forgive me. First, you are fantastic. It was wonderful to hold you. And, please excuse me if I seem pretentious. It's just that, being single, and eating so many meals alone, I've made food a kind of hobby. It makes dining more enjoyable. I probably would have muttered aloud what I just said, even had you not been here. It's a habit. Besides, there may be something interesting about a man who knows that Conch chowder looks like New England chowder." He smiled faintly, arching that right eyebrow, grabbing her still extended right index finger, and kissing her.

Ricki mildly contorted her face but broke into laughter when the Conch chowder arrived. The chowder was not the New England type but, rather, was red. It looked like Manhattan. She asked the waiter whether this was the way Conch chowder always looked, glancing sarcastically at her accompanying gourmet. The waiter replied it had been that way for centuries.

Swept, docile but strong, chose to be quiet about food for the rest of the evening. He ate his assorted vegetables, homemade potato bread and cheese-covered snapper without much conversation. Not that he was unhappy or embarrassed about being wrong.

Perhaps it was due to his fear of ruining a good time with this woman who, certainly, was all woman. Perhaps his little monologues were unnecessary. The waiter brought a combination plate of papaya with lemon juice, which was outstanding and also highlighted to Swept that papayas *were* in season. He made no comment to Ricki. He finished the snapper, ordered expresso, exchanged small talk about the Brain Institute and Ricki's past experiences in nursing school, and inquired about her multiple excursions, most of which involved camping, that had taken her to various places across the globe. They discussed their past motorcycle days, and their individual reasons for selling their bikes. Swept also found Ricki's stories about elk hunting with her father fascinating.

Swept paid the bill and the couple entered a cab waiting outside the Large Old Home and returned to the hotel. After another barrage of love making, Ricki and Swept held each other in deep embrace, kissed and said goodnight, sleeping in one bed.

*   *   *

While the two newly discovered lovers slept, Valerie VanDance placed a telephone call.

"Alfie, Valerie here. It was nice seeing you."

"Nice to see you. The ride was fine. No problems, but nothing new."

"Basically routine with me. Although, I have to tell you, it could have been more fun."

"That may be, but it's not good to mix too much pleasure with business. It dulls the mind, even for a woman."

"Don't be a chauvinist," Valerie said teasingly, but firmly. "Anything new on our man from Nepal?"

"No. Solid as a rock. That's all I can say."

"Well, it's still bizarre. Talk to you later."

"Fine, good-bye."

Valerie was pleased with herself. Had someone heard the conversation, they would not have known that the topic was Swept and Serkin. Nor would they know that Valerie VanDance had met the Louisiana businessman after he disembarked a boat earlier that day. He was from a special subdivision of the Agency, a subdivision that included domestic surveillance, which was illegal for the CIA to pursue, despite their doing so daily.

*   *   *

The following day it rained. All day. Some upset tourists relinquished time playing guitar, while others ineptly hovered over video games. Swept showed Ricki his knowledge of the small eating monsters on the video screens. Not only had he learned patterns of their movements, but he knew what strategies each monster employed to get his man.

Ricki seemed to take in (how, she was not certain) this meaningless panache of knowledge. "I'm astounded at your knowledge about food," holding his arm and laughing, "automobiles, motorcycles, science, neurology, video games, and mind-control drugs. There must be something screwy with you."

Occasionally, he had thought of implications of mind-control, perhaps had even discussed it with Szeppek at dinner. But it was the phrase "mind-control" that threw him.

"There are many things to know in this world, but I can assure you I know only a few. But, if I may ask, I've never heard anyone, even in our Department, use the term 'mind-control.' I don't work on 'mind-control,' I work on medication that could improve people's memory. I don't try to control anyone's mind." Swept was almost annoyed. Irritated, he continued. "Speaking of mind-control, I don't suppose you had anything to do with my jogging incident, did you?" asked Swept. He had earlier discussed with her his misfortune.

"Dr. Swept, had I abducted you for half a day, you would have had no complaints and would have come out of it a better man, awake and performing ever so well," said Ricki, looking at his lower abdomen, a twinkle crossing her eyes. Although Swept welcomed sexual innuendoes, he had misgivings about this.

Ricki continued. "Dick, I don't know what happened to you. I know it bothers you a lot. You often bring it up."

Of course, Swept had no idea he was working on mind-control drugs. On some level, he knew he was, but on another level he did not. He was too absorbed in the task at hand to think about mind control. His concerns related to memory, how medications might alter memory, and how medications might improve people's memory function. It had not occurred to him that he could actually alter people's *thinking* or that some might try to turn his good-oriented knowledge to destruction.

Ricki, as can be done by more than a small fraction of women, smoothly changed the subject as the couple now sat inside the glass poolside enclosure, watching the soft rain persistently assault the water. Something about rain pleased Swept. It always had. He felt eased when the weather appeared sad, a milieu painted by the rain clouds. Sadness in weather somehow made him feel things were stable within himself. When the outside was sunlit and cheery, he thought he should feel more cheery. Although he never felt sad, he never felt cheery. He felt solid, and truly believed he was one of the more emotionally strong people he had known.

Whatever the reason, Swept did not like good weather, but was not pleased to learn that the day would be overcast and raining. The couple was scheduled to return to Houston tomorrow. They opted for a sexual respite in the shower.

On Sunday, the airport was crowded. The taxi driver, negotiating the road in the rain, shaking from alcohol, having made a brief pass at Ricki only to find his forearm torqued by Swept, had placed the couple in no mood for the massive airport bureaucratic disorganization. They checked their luggage, and Ricki commented how pleased she was that Swept was without complaints.

Their plane landed in Houston in the late afternoon. Swept thanked Ricki for a truly wonderful time, walked her to her car parked in the airport, and returned to his home, taking Highway 59. They both decided to go to their respective homes. He unpacked, telephoned Regina, anticipated thanking her for keeping an eye on his house and feeding and caring for Limbic but, not to his dismay, encountered only her answering machine. Swept left his thank-you message on the machine and went out for a walk with Limbic, feeling no sadness and not missing Regina. She was probably at the hospital, operating on patients and making money.

Swept missed Ricki. He earlier was not certain whether Regina might show up at his house. Now, that he had made the call, he doubted it.

Looking up at the sky, Swept noticed rain clouds gathering. He felt slightly sad, yet he felt good. Turning the corner, he re-entered his house, showered, had his cognac, and went to bed.

It began to rain.

The tired neurologist lay in bed, alone. He had been struck with Ricki's term, "mind-control." It was the last thing in the world to which Swept had intended his research be oriented. He was a scientist, a physician-scientist, concerned with memory and how the brain functioned. He viewed his job, and all tasks, with serious glint, without any desire to enter any aspect of biological warfare, germ warfare, or mind-control. These all lay beyond his bounds. He believed God placed physicians on the planet to help patients, a fact frequently forgotten by many other physicians, and certainly by many hospital administrators. One's approaching knowledge in its true form brought one closer to God. Mind-control drugs, biological warfare and any facsimile stepped out of the domain of the physician. He felt strongly about these concepts.

Maybe Regina did too. He wasn't certain. Soon, he fell asleep.

Scientists would have noted that his rapid eye movements, the eye movements associated with dreaming, soon appeared and were pronounced. He dreamed about animals. He dreamed about humans. He dreamed about God. In his dream, he asked why it was that God had created living creatures that killed one another. He could not understand why an all-good God created animals that suffered and maimed one another. Why did animals have to devour one another, instead of eating vegetative plants? Then, it occurred to him that plants were living organisms as well.

Perhaps, he thought, the fact that animals kill one another is not emotionally disconcerting to the animals. Animals differ from humans in one major respect: they do not know one day they will perish. Animals do not query whether, one day, death will intercede that animal's running the herd, or watching its young pups grow, or accomplish any particular goal. Many humans believe that they must accomplish certain things in their life before dying, and that death can interrupt these goals. Therefore, animals, unlike humans, are less vexed, not because humans are so intelligent and have conflicting thoughts within themselves, but because humans know that one day they will die. Animals do not.

Chapter Seventeen

BACK AT WORK

When the alarm rang at 6:00 a. m., Swept found himself trembling and feeling mild anxiety, but this soon dissipated. Looking outside, he could see it was a clear day. Pellets of rain rested on the deck that circumscribed his outdoor spa. He soon felt more relaxed, remembered little of his dream, something about animals or humans, knowing that one was going to die. He looked down at Limbic, the dog's feet chasing rabbits while he slept. Swept stepped over the furry body and prepared for his day.

When Dick Swept left for work, he was in a good mood. He ran into Valerie, the two exchanging subtle innuendoes. Valerie was coquettishly formal. Thinking about Ricki, he had already decided not to mention anything to Regina, at least not for the time being.

There were no hospital inpatients on whom he had to round. Everyone had gone home prior to his respite in the Caymans. He stopped at his office and then went to the lab.

Swept looked forward to reviewing more data with Szeppek. The Cayman trip had been enjoyable. He felt good. Feeling relaxed, he greeted Szeppek, the two exchanged greetings, and got down to nuts and bolts.

"Before we go over the data for the NIH presentation, what did you find in the rats given chloroform?"

Szeppek, unable to curtail his emotion, showed him. "Here's the data, Dr. Swept," placing several graphs and charts in front of him." Each rat that received chloroform and Compound 1040 had a markedly elevated acid phosphatase. I took the liberty of administering it intravenously, as well as intra-peritoneally. Every rat, each one, had a huge elevation in acid phosphatase! When we gave it orally, it had similar but not as pronounced effects."

Szeppek rearranged sheets of data. "I also analyzed the white cells in the animals. The chloroform, when combined with Compound 1040, has even greater effect on the animals' white cells than we noticed before. I don't know what it means and I don't know whether it's dangerous, but it's there."

A piece of the puzzle had unraveled. Chloroform, combined with possible exposure to Compound 1040, had caused the abnormalities in Swept's system. Then, an idea struck the neurologist.

"I still don't know how I could have been exposed to Compound 1040. Maybe, I inhaled some vapors. But, then, why wouldn't your acid phosphatase level be as high as mine? Yours was only slightly elevated and you had no stippling of your white cells."

Szeppek responded, "Maybe its because you were exposed to this chemical for a longer period of time than I was, having worked on it before I got here."

"But you're around it more often during the day. This just doesn't make a lot of sense." Swept glanced at the data sheets and shook his head. "Also, we can't forget that different people can certainly react differently to the same chemical."

Swept continued. "Let's go over this again. You have only a borderline elevation of acid phosphatase. When the rats are given Compound 1040, they have no elevation of acid phosphatase, unless they concurrently receive chloroform. You have no change in your white cells. I do. The rats, which certainly received more of this than you or I have, all have changes in their white cells. Perhaps I was exposed to more of the Compound than I realized, but how could that happen? I'm never directly exposed to it. When we use it, it's in a syringe or enclosed in a container." Swept looked at the glass bottle over his desk, containing Compound 1040. More experiments had continued in his absence, causing a re-delineation of the fluid level in the container. Was he correct in thinking that the earlier level of fluid had been too low?

A thought struck Swept, one almost beyond comprehension. He had a sore spot over his carotid artery, a spot seemingly insignificant, but noticed by Drake. Some of the Compound could be missing. Number 1040, when combined with chloroform, caused chemical changes that were in his system. Could he conceivably have been given this medication?

"Who are the people who know about our experiment, outside the laboratory and Department? I know the NIH is aware of our work, but have you discussed it with anybody else?"

"We haven't yet published it and I haven't discussed it with anyone in the scientific community."

"Anyone else?" At a party? To a woman? Anyone?"

"No," the postdoctorate fellow said. Surely, it was not a matter for Dr. Swept's private concern that he had discussed this with the Hungarian Consulate Office. After all, he was their charge, so to speak, and they were concerned about his welfare. All Hungarian students, so he believed, reported to their respective Consulates. That was routine. He saw no reason to upset his mentor with this fact.

"Well, I have to sit on this for awhile. But something's going on." Swept picked up a lab notebook and reviewed some experimental data. The two investigators reviewed the animal maze experiments, both discussing that the NIH meeting was not far away. When the time came, the data had to be ready and Swept had to make certain he knew the structure of the Compound.

"I need all this data organized for my presentation. As you know, the meeting was put off. I go to Washington in four days. I think they'll be impressed with our concepts. We need to get this on PowerPoint," referring to the computerized slide system on Microsoft Windows.

Szeppek agreed. It was good that his mentor had taken a vacation. He knew Swept needed to be at peak performance during the NIH presentation.

Suddenly, Szeppek realized something else. "Oh, by the way, I did discuss the experiment with someone – Valerie VanDance. She was down here the day before you left, asking about our project. She said she was interested in memory from a nursing standpoint, since she had to deal with so many demented patients as a neurological nurse. I took the liberty of going over some of our data."

"Is that right? Out of curiosity, did you use the term 'mind-control drugs' with her?"

"No, but she used that term with me. I'm told I have fairly good English, but I never heard that phrase used that way. I understand what it means, but it was surprising. Is that a term Americans use for our work?"

"They ought not to. We deal with memory and the brain. We don't deal with controlling anybody or anything."

"I'm going to have a chat with her." Swept left the lab, turned left down the hall, right at the stairwell, and bounded up the stairs, looking for Valerie

VanDance. He saw her as she was leaving the Chairman's office, with Ranger.

"Valerie," taking her by the arm, "You and I have to have a talk."

Ranger looked at Swept, with a somewhat surprised expression. "How were the Caymans, Dick? I hope you had a good time."

Avoiding looking at Valerie, Swept responded, "It was a good idea, relaxing and fun. Thanks for suggesting I take a vacation. I needed it. Mind if I talk with Valerie for just a second?"

"Not at all. By the way, how's everything going for the NIH presentation?" Ranger stopped walking, Valerie at his side.

"First, you're concerned about whether I had a good time. Now, we get to down to brass tacks. Don't worry. They'll like my presentation. And, it will be ready. And, you had nothing to do with any aspect of the project. You've hindered me all the way, you won't let me work with humans, and it's only because Chippers likes me and our work in the laboratory that I was invited. Your major concern, Mr. Chairman, is that I get funding. Don't worry, I will."

Ranger, hands in his pockets, crookedly smiled at Swept, mumbled something incomprehensible, and walked toward his secretary's office. Then, the Chairman turned to Valerie. "Don't forget to meet me later this afternoon. We have to discuss the new clinic referral system we're implementing for the Department."

"Yes, sir," the nurse replied. She walked away with Swept, Ranger walking toward the secretary's desk.

"Valerie," Swept said somewhat sternly, gently taking her arm, "Let's have our talk."

"Sure, any time."

"No, I'm serious." The two entered the hallway, near the stairs.

"I just spoke to Szeppek. He tells me you've been asking questions about my work. Why?"

Valerie VanDance was unphased. "Just curious. No harm in that, is there?"

"Well, Valerie, experiments in our animals show that chloroform, the chemical I was probably exposed to during my abduction, interacts with the substance we use, causing certain chemical changes in the body. I have those chemical changes. Also, the rats have those changes when we mix the chloroform with our Compound. Further, I think some of our Compound is missing. Do you know anything about this?"

Valerie's jaw dropped slightly. Who would take the Compound? Why was it missing? Was Swept so disorganized he had lost track of the reagent's volume? More pieces of what seemed to be a puzzle appeared.

"No. Surely, you don't think I took some of your precious chemical? If I did, what would I do with it? Sprinkle it on Dr. Ranger?"

Swept's eyes narrowed, neither believing nor disbelieving. Many questions lay in his mind, but, for the moment, he had to prepare his data for the forth-coming NIH meeting.

"Well, just curious. Talk to you later." He turned down the hall abruptly, intentionally depriving Valerie of any time for aspersions or flirtatious behavior. Within a few minutes, Swept was back in his labora-tory.

*   *   *

Valerie returned to her office, shut the door, and made two telephone calls on the "Chairman's line." Now, it was decided. She would also go to the NIH meeting. She had become increasingly curious about the chemicals investigated by Swept. When Valerie told Dr. Ranger she wanted to go, stating she hoped to learn more about memory as well as the mighty NIH, he had no objections. All it meant to Ranger was a quick letter of introduction to Chippers and having his nurse leave early on a Friday afternoon. Valerie would return Sunday, in time for any assis-tance the Chairman needed when the week began.

*   *   *

The highly organized Aleksander Kostokov, with sundry mixed thoughts in his head, drove to the Washington Zoo, and waited in line to see the panda bears. When he saw them, he remembered how much his children had liked stuffed animals. People were concerned about the panda bears possibly becoming extinct. Who had concerns about his family?

Moving on, he thought about the "uniforms" he needed, as well as the explosives. The van was ready. The plan was ready. Everything was set.

Chapter Eighteen

BRIEFCASE

SWEPT ARRIVED AT Bush International Airport at 10:00 a. m., Friday, October 25th. The drive to the airport had been easy since he was driving against traffic. As he left the outskirts of downtown Houston, taking Interstate 45, he noted a slight jarring in the impeccably balanced Ferrari. He made a mental note to check the alignment.

Fortunately, there was a parking place next to Terminal B. He entered the building. Tolerating the bizarre geometric pattern that encircled the tunnel to the waiting area for the jet's takeoff, he contemplated the design of the airport, the crowded terminals, and rude personnel. Then he thought of La Guardia. Then, he changed his mind about the Houston airport – it was certainly more organized and pleasant than New York's.

As usual, he checked into the Washington Sheraton, where he always stayed when attending meetings sponsored by the NIH. However, in the past, those meetings related to grant protocols and instructions on how to work one's way through the incredibly complex system of grant applications. This time, it was different.

While in flight, the scientist rehearsed certain elements of his talk. The NIH! He would have the opportunity to present his ideas to some of the most brilliant minds in his field. Yes, he truly felt excited.

That night, Swept sat comfortably in his hotel, as he reviewed his talk for the final time. His concentration was interrupted by the telephone.

"Dr. Swept?"

"Yes."

"This is the concierge. There's a gift here for you. May I send someone up?"

"A gift?"

"Yes. Shall we take it up, Sir?"

"Sure. Who's it from?"

"I don't know. There's a card but the envelope is sealed."

"That's fine. Send it up."

Several minutes later, a bellman knocked at the door, holding a large gift, with an attached card from Cartier. Swept tipped the man and opened his present.

Enclosed was a typed message, brief and to the point.

> To Dr. Swept.
> The finest briefcase, for the finest researcher. Please take this with our compliments. It should bring good luck tomorrow. All of us wish you the best of everything.
>
> Sincerely,
> Your Friends in the Laboratory

Swept undid the wrappings, and removed a briefcase from the bag. It was gorgeous. The black calfskin, beautifully hand-stitched briefcase, with thick large brass latches was unlike anything he had ever seen. The soft supple leather contrasted with the polished brass, present not only on the latches but on the corners as well, with tiny little holes no larger than one millimeter, adding a neoclassical, textured appearance. The fresh smell emitted from the light brown suede interior was almost reminiscent of a new car.

Although no heavier than his old briefcase, this was slightly larger, offering more room. Swept reasoned, given the beauty and the Cartier card, that his laboratory colleagues must have undertaken considererable financial expense. Swept decided to take it to the meeting. He felt good about his colleagues' friendship and support as he transferred his belongings from his old briefcase to the new.

It was too late to call Szeppek and thank him. He would thank him later. Besides, for all Swept knew, the technicians had sent this or, somehow, Ranger (probably not) was in the loop. He returned to his chair, and again went over his presentation, making certain that his Kodachrome slides were available in case the computer-driven PowerPoint presentation failed. He even had his own laser pointer, having attended meetings that failed to provide them. Dick Swept felt he was well prepared.

The neurologist then poured cognac from his mini bar, noting with disdain their poor selection, and retired for the night.

*   *   *

In the morning, the doorman at the Sheraton held open the taxi's door for the Texas physician-scientist, new briefcase in hand. The shining brass reflected the Washington, D. C. sunlight as he entered the cab. The day was sunny. Swept felt prepared.

Swept was familiar with the itinerary, having stayed at the hotel many times for previous NIH meetings. However, none were as important as this. Now, he was to address the leading nidus of scientists in the area of memory, a major opportunity in his academic life. He would interact with the heavyweights. This was an opportunity to discuss with these men and women his theories and ideas, over which he had labored for many years.

As the taxi entered the NIH grounds, which has no security guards, the taxi passed over the small bridge. The modern buildings reminded Swept of his alma mater college campus. The cab crossed the small creek, turned left, and Swept stepped onto the parking lot, intending to enter Building Ten, through the side entrance. Too late, he realized that the cabbie had driven to the wrong side of the building. He walked around, and entered the building through the old metal doors.

Swept noticed a small group of antivivisectionists, ten to twelve of them, carrying various placards. Their attire was similar to those he had seen in Houston. He paid them little notice, constantly amazed at how one could hope for scientific progress without animal models of disease. Again, he remembered the pamphlet from the American Academy of Neurology, stressing sensitivity but sensibility regarding research with animals.

It was just like the Sixties, Swept thought to himself. Many people who were leftists in the Sixties still looked like leftists, with long hair, faded jeans, and an occasional headband. It seemed to be the same with the antivivisectionists. They had their own uniform, so to speak . . . jeans, cotton shirts, hair not too long, and well-kept beards. None looked too hip, and none looked too straight.

The protesters were somewhat at a distance, probably because of laws keeping them away from the entrance to Building Ten, which was a Federal Building, and they barely seemed to notice Swept. A brown van boasting a picture of a dead rabbit with a slogan against animal research on one side, a panda bear and a collie on the other, could be discerned forty feet from the protesters.

Swept also noticed that several of the protestors wore what seemed to be Walkmans. That's what the earphones would suggest to a naïve observer.

Inside the building, the elevators had an "Out of Order" sign on their front. Swept climbed the stairs, his handsome new briefcase weighing slightly heavily on his fingers. He was perspiring and tried to assure himself that the perspiration related not to anxiety, but to the Indian Summer in D. C., and the three short flights of stairs. Even when he had jogged more, he had been amazed that he became winded after climbing just a few flights of stairs. "It must be a different demand on the body's respiratory system," he had remarked to a colleague. "I can jog three miles and be only slightly out of breath. However, after a few flights, I'm dead." It was something he never understood.

In truth, he did not know whether his rapid breathing related to anxiety, curtailment of jogging since the "incident," or just being out of shape. He peered downwards at his briefcase held firmly in grip, noticing reflections on the large brass latches, and thought of the jogging incident, women, and science. He needed to muster his faculties for this presentation. The future of his laboratory as well as his own academic survival depended on it. Concentration was a must.

Reaching the top of the three-flight climb, Swept

wiped his brow with his only handkerchief, purchased years ago at Harrod's while attending a meeting on the role of acetylcholine in memory function. Swept thought of Dr. Chippers and felt nervous. He told himself to relax, reminding himself he was not expected to produce any great discoveries, simply to discuss his research. Besides, he had been personally invited by the Director of the NINDS. That was good enough for Swept and it had better be good enough for anyone else. He became slightly pleased with himself, but still felt tense.

The most brilliant men in the field would be here. Swept wanted their support, not only for future funding, but because he cared about problems of the elderly. His ideas could truly help patients with memory compromise. It was time the medical community did more than simply cogitate about the problems of dementia and Alzheimer's Disease. His theory offered therapy. He could help.

As Swept entered the main floor of the meeting, he saw scientists in the hall sipping coffee, discussing doctorate theses, funding, and the country's attitude toward research. He recognized many of the famous scientists, having seen them at previous meetings, including the one on acetylcholine.

Swept did not say hello to any of these researchers. None knew who *he* was. They were tenured, full Professors from major universities, whereas Swept was just a young Assistant Professor from Texas.

Dr. Michelo Fichmark, from San Francisco, was an expert on memory-induced chemical changes in the spinal fluid. Another, M. G. Vocalis, worked in the Sleep Laboratory at Stanford. Vocalis contended that memory patterns were consolidated during sleep and that the purpose of sleep, an active, non-restful brain state, was to consolidate memories. That explained why infants spent so much time sleeping – they had so much to learn and to remember. The theory sounded a bit offbeat to Swept, and drove Ranger crazy.

Swept recognized David Melba from the University of Washington, Seattle. Melba contended that Alzheimer's Disease was due to a slow growing virus, contracted between age six and twenty-one. Two years ago, at a closed meeting, he had vigorously opposed Swept's grant, and Swept knew it. Ranger told him about it. Melba contended that research aimed at therapy for Alzheimer patients was futile and nonproductive. All research should be oriented toward eliminating the cause, not seeking treatment, a concept with which Ranger did not disagree. However, Melba, owning great ambition and seeing in Swept a strong future competitor, insisted on telling the Study Section (the committee within the NIH having the final word on funding) that Dick Swept was engaged in trivial theories. Ranger, in that same Study Section, was not tolerant of outside negativism against a member of his own Department – an extension of Ranger's own prestige – and verbally exploded before the entire Section. Respected and admired from his Boston days, a period when his work truly was excellent, the Texas Chairman successfully defended his junior faculty member. Melba was embarrassed, holding forevermore his wrath against

Swept, a man whom he had never personally met, and felt some animosity toward Ranger as well.

There were others – brilliant scientists, and a few graduate students and postdoctorate fellows. The entire nation's bank of memory experts was in the building.

Still tense, Swept walked toward the entrance to the conference room. Nathaniel Chippers, his back toward Swept, stood at the door, talking to colleagues. Swept could see the inside of the conference room. It was a simple room, similar to old classrooms, with many chairs, writing tables, slate blackboard with chalk, a small screen, slide projector at the rear of the room, and apparatus for PowerPoint presentations.

Swept headed toward the room. Behind, he heard a familiar voice.

"Hey there, Dr. Swept. How are you?" Swept turned abruptly. It was Valerie VanDance. She approached him, leaving behind two men at the coffee table, with whom she had been conversing.

"Not again. What are you doing here?"

"Maybe I thought I was going to the Caymans," she smiled, baiting Swept to reciprocate. "I thought I'd come over and listen to your talk. Dr. Ranger said it was all right. He gave me a letter of introduction to Dr. Chippers, asking if it were okay if I sat in." She paused a moment. "It was agreeable with Chippers, okay with you?"

It was not, and he so said, but that made little difference to Valerie.

Valerie VanDance, as professional as any CIA or KGB or FSB agent had ever been, was still concerned about Swept. She intended to follow her job to the limit. Swept worked with a chemical that altered memory. He had chemical changes in his own body that reflected exposure to Compound 1040, and his behavior had changed, although it was returning to normal. Since he was going to be with leading scientists, and since she was assigned to watched his work on mind-control drugs, she had decided to hear Swept's talk. Maybe, something would unfold.

"I see you bought a new briefcase. You once told me you would never part with the old one, that it was special and had personal meaning?"

"The lab sent it to me as a gift."

"Sent it to you?"

"Yes, last night. Okay with you?"

Valerie considered this strange. Why would the laboratory send him a briefcase, rather than give it to him in person, in Houston? She looked at it, and considered letting the matter slide.

"It certainly is beautiful."

The last thing Swept needed, especially if he received NIH funding, was grief from his Chairman. There was no need to antagonize his Chairman's nurse, with whom Ranger worked most closely. He decided to make brief small-talk, keeping an eye on the entrance to the conference room, currently empty except for the technician inside working with the presentation equipment which had recently come into Swept's view. Chipper stood at the doorway, making it clear he would greet each conferee as he entered. As it happened, all of them were still at the table, drinking coffee and eating doughnuts.

"I think this briefcase is supposed to bring good luck. The lab sent it to my hotel room last night. It's roomy," showing Valerie two carousel trays in its interior, "and the brass is so shiny, not to sound like a sexist, that a beautiful woman like you can see enough of her face to comb her hair. Now," he said with a wry grin, "How's that? However, Ms. VanDance, the scientists are walking toward the door and I've got to go."

Valerie smiled, with true warmth. "Thanks, but I'm not that vain. She patted him, much as she would a puppy, and patted the briefcase as well, her hands lightly touching the corners. She was perplexed, and said to Swept, who was now beginning to stand, "What are these? Holes? These are holes! Holes! Let me see something. . . ." taking the carousels and the papers out of the interior, as well as the laser pointer.

"Valerie, are you nuts? Give me that," Swept whispered in disgusted tones as the nurse took the briefcase from him, Swept trying not to call attention to her bizarre behavior, focusing his eye on Chippers who was now greeting researchers as they entered the room.

Swept continued. "Give me the briefcase! Have you flipped? I'm going," as he grabbed his property and reached for the carousels, which Valerie had now moved behind her.

In a lightning moment, Valerie tried to piece things together: It was Dick Swept, dating Regina Bruxton back home, seeing Ricki Hardson in the Cayman Islands, strange behavior but now much better, abduction, and now, out of the clear blue sky, Dick Swept had a new briefcase, the holes of which reminded her of pictures she had seen in the past.

Valerie then made a decision, standing as Swept stood, looked him in the eye and said with thin lips and a tone he had never before heard her use: "You look! If I'm wrong, I'm wrong. But I'm not." She reached into her purse, removed a not so small Swiss pocket-knife, the presence of which boggled Swept, opened the blade, and before the wide-eyed physician made a huge deeply cut X in the bottom of the briefcase, pulling up the now loosely attached suede bottom. Beneath the suede, lay rows of wires, cellophane-wrapped material and other metal devices.

Before Swept could finish "What the. . . ." Valerie yanked the wires, tearing the flesh of her fingers as she did so, gazed down the hall to her right, focused her gaze past the doughnut and coffee table and now, with full control of the briefcase, tore out its electronic intestinal contents as she started to run to the two men down the hall. She turned to Swept, who was still dumbfounded, and screamed, at the top of her lungs, "Get out! Get out now! Just get out!"

Chippers, no more than a few yards behind her, still greeting the conferees entering the room, looked at her with puzzlement. Valerie turned to him, the two men now running toward her, and screamed, "Get out! Empty the room! Get out! Do it! Now! Do it!"

However, it was too late. Aleksander Kostokov, sitting in the brown van with the picture of the dead rabbit, had heard the entire discussion through the bugged briefcase. Even though not all the conferees were in the room, he also had to make a split-second decision, and took action. He was not going to be involved in another fiasco like the Sherpas or the Bedouins. This was it. The ball game had begun. He signaled the protestors, every one, through the head phones. "Operation Hippocampus, it's a 'Go.' Now!"

Immediately, all the protestors dropped their placards, shed their outer shirts and entered the building, barreling up the stairs, a few taking the elevators, ignoring the bogus signs they had earlier placed. None of the conferees would think to take the elevators, having all taken the stairs, because of these signs of elevator repair. This helped contain them on the third floor, hopefully making them think that the only exit, should an emergency occur, was through the stairs. They were locked in.

Each man drew his gun, loaded with glaser safety slugs. Upon impact with human tissue or objects of such consistency, the bullet would cause immediate and complete fragmentation, releasing the core particles in a cone-shaped pattern of over 330 sub-projectiles.

Each gun was a Walther Model P59MM DA autoloader, one of the finest grade 9 mm autoloaders manufactured anywhere in the world. Remarkably accurate, the centerfire autoloader was as slick as a Colt Python revolver, with a single-action pull that broke at a clean, crisp 4.5 pounds. Kostokov preferred this weapon because of one particular and unconventional aspect of the gun – the location of the ejection window was on the left topside, instead of the right, like those of standard autoloaders. Since the P5 ejects to the left, it is considered a "left-handed" gun. Being a left-hander himself, Kostokov was partial to it. It was not a problem for the right-handers, since the P5 ejects its cases nearly straight up, and its cycling rate is so quick that the action is returned to the battery for follow-up shots before the previous fired casing gets to the top of its arc.

The Russian wondered whether the Americans knew that this gun was standard FSB issue. It was quick, safe, and deadly accurate, and he and his men were now going to use it for its intended purpose: Killing.

In addition to the gun, each man also carried two grenades, and two of them carried Uzis. The pseudo-antivivisectionists and their weapons, coupled with the Semtex explosives previously placed throughout the conference room, under tables and chairs, together with the Semtex inserted into the lining of Swept's briefcase, would eliminate the entire population in the conference room within minutes.

The attack was to be simple. Just weak-ass scientists with no weapons or protection. However, this proved not to be accurate.

Kostokov and his men stormed the building after Kostokov heard Valerie comment on the wires. He told the men to rush the edifice and, en route, he detonated the Semtex, too late for the now-disarmed briefcase but in time for the conference room. A massive explosion occurred, immediately killing the technician and two scientists in the room whose last moments in life focused on their doughnuts and small talk about brain neurons. The computer-driven equipment, including slide projectors, fragmented, windows shattered, and Chippers was thrown against the wall, near Swept, killing the powerful NIH leader in a fraction of a moment, emphasizing that even the famous succumb to the common denominator of death.

The blast blew the remaining researchers, standing in line to enter the room, off their feet. Valerie and the two men running toward her momentarily lost but regained their balance. The men screamed to Valerie, "Are you okay?"

"I'm okay," she yelled, amidst the screaming of the remaining conferees, one of whom was holding his shoulder with arterial blood streaming to the other side of the hallway, another trying to keep an eye in its socket.

"How about you, hotshot? Some briefcase!" Valerie said, gasping, turning to Swept who somehow had not panicked. Then, she looked at the stairwell. "They'll come up the stairs – the elevator's broken."

Swept, the explosives and dead Chippers causing him to focus intensively, just like he had done hundreds of times at cardiac arrests, forced himself to gather composure and yelled, through the smoke and debris, "Nonsense." At that moment, as Valerie's men each held their Glock 9mm, Swept looked around and yelled, "Watch the elevator, and the stairs!" He then pulled the fire alarm, which had not gone off with the explosion, and Valerie removed a Glock semi-automatic from her purse and smiled at Swept. "Standard issue for us," as Swept stood to the side of the stairwell while one agent from the CIA stood at the opposite side and the other faced the elevator.

Men were coughing and bleeding. Valerie and her two colleagues motioned all to get low, while Swept mumbled to Valerie, "They took off the smoke detectors!"

Before she could comment, Kostokov's men were exiting the stairwell on the floor, weapons in hand but not expecting CIA Glocks. The agent opposite Swept killed the first who exited the stairwell, then killed another. A third was taken out by the second agent, facing the elevator. However, at that moment, the elevator door opened and, as that agent spun around, a bullet hit his shoulder, spinning him more, followed by his taking several more slugs, making him dead within five seconds.

Meanwhile, the man outside the stairwell, whom Swept now understood was called Frank, said, "I hope you know how to use this," tossing Swept a Glock and two clips, after the agent rolled over to his left and grabbed the gun from his dead partner's hand, subsequently shooting another man exiting the elevator. The next attacker out of the stairwell, not realizing that armed defenders were on the floor, took a bullet in the head from Swept, staring at him in disbelief as he fell.

"You know how to shoot, too?" Valerie inquired.

"A man for all seasons."

"Watch out," Frank yelled, as another exited the stairwell, grenade in hand, only to receive a bullet from Swept's gun, entering the hole in his ear, sectioning his upper brainstem, killing him instantly and making him drop the grenade, the pin now removed. Swept, closest to the dead assailant, relying more on movies and what he had been taught in Special Forces training, knew the grenade would explode in seven seconds. Swept leaped forward and tossed the explosive device down the stairwell. The subsequent explosion echoed with deafening prowess. The canyon of the stairs filled with smoke and death, and that explosion set off fire alarms on floors below. Those smoke detectors had not been tampered with by the man from the van with the picture of the panda, the collie, and the dead rabbit.

*   *   *

Things had been relatively easy, except for Swept's sojourn to the Caymans. When Swept was abducted, Kostokov, after practicing on several corpses and Ukranian prisoners, injected Compound 1040 into Swept's carotid artery, telling him several times that he would accept the briefcase in his hotel room. Having been told this several times, and being told not to call to thank anyone, he expected Swept to respond as well as Serkin. Besides, it was a way to ascertain whether the medication would work in the field. In some ways, the ploy wasn't even necessary, but in other ways it helped insure that Kostokov would know Swept's intention. Besides, there was something beautifully macabre about a man succumbing to his own experiment, a medication he had wanted to give to human beings but had not been allowed to pursue. Kostokov was fairly certain that, considering his success with Serkin, the chemical, now being injected directly in the vascular system, would be even more successful in Swept.

Chapter Nineteen

THE UNGRATEFUL DEAD

ALEKSANDER KOSTOKOV REMEMBERED his instructions. Under no circumstances should the West know that the Russians were involved. He gave the order to evacuate the building. Only he and Yorky were alive. Yorky exited Building Ten but was gut-shot, vomited blood and, holding his abdomen and smiling to his friend, uttered, "Well, we gave it a try," and then closed his eyes.

"Yes, my friend, we did," as Kostokov kissed his dead friend, leaving him on the sidewalk of the NIH grounds. Hearing sirens in the distance, Kostokov entered the van, but only after removing the magnetically attached animal pictures and the antivivisectionists logo, drove further into the NIH Complex, and exited through a side entrance, as a group of federal security officers entered the building, guns drawn, thinking that animal lovers had wreaked havoc.

As Kostokov drove away, numbed by his failure to execute defenseless egg-headed scientists, he knew he had to kill Swept. Kostokov had seen Swept alive in the beginning and presumed he was not wounded. He would check on this later, but as soon as possible. Swept knew too much about mind-control and, who knew, maybe he was tied into the CIA or some agency which had contacts with the Special Forces. Kostokov's instructions were his instructions. Dick Swept had to die.

*   *   *

Valerie and Frank spoke to the federal officers, showed their credentials – both CIA – and remained until the ambulances drove off the injured. Four of the participants, the slide technician, and Chippers were dead, and all, but two including Swept, were seriously injured.

While they loaded the dead bodies and the sick, Valerie, this time with no coyness in her voice, addressed Swept. "Where did you learn to shoot and handle a live grenade?"

"It's a long story. I just did."

"It can't be too long a story. Besides, you know, we can find out. Army records and all."

"I doubt it. Most of those records burned in a fire in St. Louis. I learned in the army. I told you I was a doctor assigned to Special Forces."

"You must have special forces, Doc," Frank said. "Your quick thinking about the elevator and that grenade, let alone your good aim, probably saved my life."

"Thanks. Just lucky, and fortunate."

Valerie and Frank easily sequestered an empty office in an adjacent building and spoke in more detail to Swept. He explained how he had received the briefcase. Frank commented that had Swept not received the briefcase and had Valerie not recognized certain nuances, they would all be dead, the explosion in the conference room killing all within its reach and the briefcase exploding as well.

Swept, more than a little puzzled, turned to Valerie VanDance. "I take it you are more than a nurse?"

"Correct. Obviously, you now know I'm involved with the Government. Years ago the Agency trained several nurses, and maybe some other health professionals for all I know, to keep tabs on anything that might be important for them. Most of what we do is to shuffle papers and provide medical contacts for agents in the field."

"Good for you. Now, what about my talk, funding, let alone the dead men and their families? What do we, or you, any of us do now?"

Valerie politely responded, feeling emotionally drained but high-spirited. "I suggest you go back to the hotel. We don't know how many antivivisectionists escaped, and we've notified the police. They suggest we haven't seen the last of them."

"Do you think these men were really antivivisectionists? They are pretty tough guys for a bunch of protestors."

Valerie smiled. "I don't think that for a moment." Frank added, "Not a chance. Those weapons are standard Russian issue. Further," turning to Valerie, "I don't know if you noticed, but all the serial numbers in the guns were filed down."

"I know, standard issue. Somehow, the Russians are here. I need to make a call."

"Who?" inquired Frank.

"Bradley Serkin. He's been involved with this since the beginning – Sherpas, meningitis, committees with the Russians. I need to talk to Bradley." A man displaying his CIA badge, accompanied by a small FBI contingent, entered the room and addressed Valerie. "Ms.VanDance, I did what you said. I telephoned Janos Szeppek. He's a post-graduate student from Hungary and doesn't know anything about any briefcase."

"I didn't think he did. Just wanted to be certain. Now, do me a favor and get me Bradley Serkin on the telephone."

"Done." The man left the room and walked down the hall.

Fifteen minutes later, Bradley Serkin was on the telephone.

"Bradley, sorry to bother you. Where are you?"

"On the other side of the globe, in Nepal. Kathmandu. It's the middle of the night here. What's up?"

"What isn't? We just had a bunch of antivivisectionists with KGB issue, maybe FSB issue, attack a group of scientists at the NIH. Several are dead, including a Company colleague."

"Sorry to hear that. Who took it?"

Valerie, noting the seemingly cavalier "Who took it?" which was not consistent with the Serkin she knew prior to her first Houston conversation with him, responded without humor. "Jasper, Bernie Jasper. Okay? 'He took it.' But, I'm calling you about another matter."

"Sure."

"Do you still think the Sherpas died from meningitis? And, what do you know about the Russian representation on that health committee?"

"Well, Aleksander Kostokov was on the committee, like he always is on matters of health, when the Russians need someone. He also had that same role under the Soviets. But, like I told you before, they died from meningitis. All the Sherpas. Oh, also, there was another guy on the committee, from Russia. I don't remember his name, something like Gamrov. I only recall it because - uh - usually the Russians have only one representative, and this time they had two. I can find out his name if you want. Are they involved in the killing?"

Valerie sighed, "I don't know."

"I can look up my notes. When do you need this information?"

"Actually, now."

"Good luck. I have to find it."

"What are you doing in Kathmandu anyway?"

Looking down at the fifteen year old Asian beauty, lithe, supple and stark naked, occasionally stirring from her hashish-induced sleep, he said, "Sometimes, I don't know myself. Why? Do you – uh – need me?"

"Can you come out here, meet us at Langely, bring all your notes, and also meet with a neurologist from Houston? How about taking the next plane?"

"Sure. Who minds being up all night? A couple of amphetamines will cure that problem." He was now toying with the breasts of his nubile lover, causing her to squirm in her slumber.

"Whatever. Just get here as soon as possible. Please."

"You got it, right away," now pinching her nipples, as she looked at him through half-damp eyes and smiled.

"Oh, and Bradley, this is 'Priority A-1, Eyes Only.'"

"'Eyes Only it is,'" as Bradley hung up the phone and gazed into Isabella's eyes, rigid as he could be, holding her hips firmly as he shoveled the debris of his life into her moaning belly, loving her as he did so.

After his amorous exploit, however brief but effective, Bradley Serkin explained to his young lover he had to leave, gave the petulant Isabella (Serkin doubted that was her real name) a crisp one hundred dollar bill that somehow soothed her aching heart, and took some Dexedrine, the dose of which he was uncertain. He swallowed two additional 10 mg tablets of Ritalin, packed, left the hotel, went directly to the airport, easily secured a flight to Calcutta, and flew to Gatwick airport in London, where he took the train into the old city. He then grabbed a cab and went to his flat where he removed several papers, then returned to Gatwick and flew to Washington, D. C..

The Dexedrine and Ritalin made him alert enough to organize his thoughts regarding which of his voluminous records stored in London he should take, but also prohibited his resting on the long transatlantic flight. Exhausted upon his arrival in Washington, he took more Dexedrine and an additional 20 mg of Ritalin.

*   *   *

When Serkin arrived at CIA Headquarters, not having slept for more than 36 hours, he found Valerie, but not without a fair degree of difficulty.

"Well, I'm here," asserted the non-shaven Serkin. "Now, how can I help?"

Valerie introduced Serkin to Frank and Swept, as well as to the others in the room, while a stenographer sat in the corner, taking notes.

"Thanks for coming. You look awful. Are you sure you're all right?"

"Sure, a little wired from amphetamines but, hey, what's a man not supposed to do for his country?"

"Quit being a cowboy! Bradley, I showed pictures and the autopsy report to our neuropathologist in Houston. He said the Sherpas had no evidence of meningitis. Why did you and your committee think they did?"

"That's why you had me come here? Look, forget about the meningitis! That's what they had. Meningitis!"

Valerie was more than perturbed. "Why, *Why* did the committee think that? Why did you, why do you think that?"

"They had meningitis. That's what they had. Meningitis."

"Okay. Why do you say that? What evidence?"

Swept joined in. "I didn't think they had meningitis. Why did you think they did?"

"That's what they had. They had meningitis. That's what they had."

"Valerie," Swept looked at her with a puzzled look on his face, "Can I do this for a minute?"

"Can you do what?" Valerie, aggravated, responded.

"Mr. Serkin, I'm just trying to understand something. I'm a neurologist and, somehow, some way or another, I'm involved in this. I even spoke to the woman, a nurse, who found the dead Sherpas."

"Good for you."

"Great. Good for me," Swept sarcastically responded. "I just have one question."

Serkin nodded for him to proceed.

"What are the abnormalities you, yourself, would expect to find in someone who died from meningitis? What are the abnormalities that meningitis causes?"

"Meningitis. That's what they had. Meningitis. They're dead from meningitis. How many times do I have to tell you?" Serkin was becoming irate, almost menacingly so.

"Okay," Swept said, now softly. "Just tell me, what would you find? Better yet, what is meningitis? What is it?"

"What is it? Meningitis is what the Sherpas died from. They died from meningitis."

"What does the spinal fluid show in meningitis? What happens to the white cells in meningitis?"

"They died from meningitis."

Valerie and her companions looked at each other, amazed. At one time, Bradley Serkin was one of the more respected men in the Agency. Indeed, that might still be the case. But his current behavior, certainly this behavior, was different.

A silence engulfed the room, Serkin having an almost insouciant attitude. Swept broke the long silence, turning to Valerie, in front of Serkin. "It's like the rats. Put them in the maze and that's what they do, go to the end, every time, no matter what. It's a learned behavior." Aghast, Swept had now studied Serkin.

Now, it was Valerie's turn. Turning to Serkin, "Let me change the subject. Can I see your file from the health committee in Nepal?"

"Sure," a wearied Serkin said to Valerie. "Here. By the way, the other guy on the committee is Jokhar Gantemirov, a Chechen of all people. The Company had nothing on him, only the background provided by the U. N., which I have here. Here's his dossier,

sort of brief. Also, I have a picture." Serkin passed
around the brief dossier of Jokhar Gantemirov and
his picture as well. The man had coarse features with
a half-hearted smile.

"What can you tell us about him," Valerie ques-
tioned, studying the photograph.

"Well, Jokhar Gantemirov is 52 years old and, although Chechen per his background description,
has lived most of his life in Moscow. He seemed like
a decent guy. Nothing special, one way or the other."

"Why is he living in Moscow, if he's a Chechen?"
Frank inquired.

"Well, this is what I know. His parents were deported from Chechnya and sent to Siberia in 1944,
when Stalin - uh - needing a pretext for disposing of
potentially troublesome nationalists, accused nation-
alist-minded Chechens of collaborating with the Nazis. Stalin deported them to Siberia. The survivors,
who must have been only a few, were allowed to return in 1957, after Kruschev gave them amnesty. That
was - uh - when . . ." Serkin looked around the room,
his face becoming flushed, made a menacing gesture to Swept that momentarily stopped. Then, his
face turned pale, his eyes rolled, and his torso fell to
the ground while his whole body shook. He had a
grand mal convulsion, with flexion and extension of
his arms, followed by tight extension of all limbs. He
was soon incontinent of urine and stool and seized
harder than anyone Swept had ever seen seize. Swept
announced the obvious, that Serkin was having a seizure. He needed help.

"Don't touch him, Doctor. We've got people of our own here." Frank pushed a button on his transmitter, which he removed from his inside jacket pocket. Within thirty seconds another guard was in the room, followed by someone from the aide station. In the meantime, Serkin continued to seize.

The agents removed the seizing body to another room, telling Swept to stay inside.

Swept called out, "Are you out of your mind? I'm a neurologist. Let me help."

The answer came from the other side of the door, loudly and with vigor. "We don't need your help. We'll take care of it."

Swept had seldom seen anyone seize as hard as Serkin. Perhaps it was because Serkin hadn't received any seizure medication. No medication was available and Swept was not allowed to touch him. Outside, the noise from Serkin's seizing announced to Swept that the convulsions had not stopped. Had he been in the room with Serkin, he would have seen his arms and legs become distorted, as the distal parts of his upper limbs began to flay in horrored forms. Within three minutes, Serkin lay dead, with black and blue marks around his eyes, giving him a raccoon-like mask.

No government physician had yet appeared.

Valerie, insisting that Swept come with her, entered the room, her face horror stricken when she saw Serkin, dead on the floor, bones broken, his raccoon mask announcing its presence to all. Valerie knew she had seen that look before, in the pictures of the Sherpas.

Swept, incredibly angry, bellowed, "You're telling me that at CIA headquarters, your Seize Team, raising his fingers as quotation marks, is less efficient than any of our hospitals, public or private? At least, you could have let me try to help."

Valerie, embarrassed and angry, responded, "We're not a medical school. We're not Texas College of Medicine. We're federal agents on federal property, CIA at Langely, no less. The Director makes it unbelievably clear in the "Directorate of Operations" that if someone is here on business, federal business, and gets sick, they can only be seen by our medical staff." Valerie sighed, threw up her hands, and muttered, "I guess."

"You guess? He died! You've got a dead agent, a dead James Bond. And, if you ask me, he looks like the dead Sherpas. Some Double-0 Seven."

"It wasn't lost on me, Dick."

"Dick. Are we now Dick, Val?"

"Pardon me, Doctor Swept. Any suggestions?"

"Sure. First, call me Dick. Second, get Szeppek on the line. Third, be certain to get an autopsy done as soon as possible on this man, by someone who knows what they're doing. But, wait a second, let me speak to Szeppek before you do that."

Janos Szeppek was on the telephone in a few minutes. "Janos, Dr. Swept here. Sorry to bother you. Do you have a second?"

"Sure. Ms.VanDance called earlier, something about a briefcase. How did the talk go?" Szeppek did not know about the killings since the media had not been informed about the killings at the NIH. "Did you get the funding? How did the talk go?"

"It's a long story. It went okay but I'm calling about something different. Please go to the laboratory, now, and give some of the rats who've received our Compound 1040 amphetamines. I need to know what it does to them. As soon as possible. Can you do it?"

"Amphetamines? Why?"

"Just do it. It's complicated. Believe me. I need to know how the Compound interacts with amphetamines. This is very important."

"Okay, but how did the meeting go?"

"Please, just do it. I'll tell you later, if you don't read about it in the newspapers first."

"The newspapers?"

"Never mind, just do it."

"What dosage should I use?"

"Whatever dose you need to see whether amphetamines interfere with the Compound. Then, call me, at this number," asking Valerie for the switchboard number and the extension of their room. "I need to know this as soon as possible."

"I'll take care of it."

"Thanks. Good-bye."

"Good-bye."

Valerie, Swept, and the other agents filled out forms, discussing how to arrange the autopsy, making certain that Swept would be allowed to be there, continually asking the neurologist multiple questions. Swept insisted that they check the dead man's blood levels of acid phosphatase and look for orange stippling in his white cells. Meanwhile, Valerie and the other agents went through Serkin's files, trying to obtain more information. In short time, Valerie had contacted CIA Research and reviewed the following information:

> The Caucasus Mountains are in Southern Russia, between the Black Sea on the west and the Caspian Sea on the east. Nestled within that region are the Chechens, most of whom are Sunni Muslims. Their reputation is that of a proud, independently minded people. Chechen means "unsubjectable" in Turkish. Stalin deported most to Siberia after World War II, for collaboration with the Nazis, and Kruschev allowed them to return in 1957.
>
> Most Russians consider Chechens to be a group of extremely brutal Mafia clans

who run a huge underworld of extortion, prostitution and illegal drugs. These gangs probably constitute only a small percent of the population, but their internecine battles are intense and make Chechnya a difficult area to rule.

When the Soviet Union began to fall apart in 1991, Chechen President Dudayev, himself a former Soviet bomber pilot and air force general, unilaterally declared independence from the Russian Federation. Within a few days of this declaration, which was not recognized by the international community, then Russian President Boris Yeltsin declared a state of emergency in Chechnya, sent in 650 troops for an allegedly easy enterprise, and was repelled by only a few hundred Chechen rebels. Since then, all hell has broken loose.

Looking at the statement, Frank asked Valerie what the above had to do with anything.

"Well, Gantemirov's uncle, according to records I just received from Research, on his mother's side is the now dead, former president Dudayev. Looking at Serkin's folder on Gantemirov, it appears that Dudayev wrote Gantemirov's letter of recommendation to several academic institutions in Russia, when they were all on better terms. Gantemirov is a scientist at the University of Moscow."

Swept interrupted. "What kind of science does he do?"

"I don't know. I'm still looking at some of this. Here's his picture and resume from the UN and WHO, and a list of some of his publications."

"Good Lord," Swept uttered. "He's published on acetylcholine receptors and antibodies that influence memory, interfering with acetylcholine metabolism. He does memory research!"

"The plot thickens," said Valerie. "That's about all we know about Jokhar Gantemirov. Also, he's never married, drinks a lot of vodka, and the Agency has reason to believe he is involved with the Chechen rebels."

Valerie continued. "Then, there's Aleksander Kostokov, who's also been on health committees, representing the USSR, and now Russia, for decades. He, on the other hand was married, his family is dead, is a big time smoker –Sobranies, and he also drinks a lot. We've known for years he's KGB, now FSB."

Swept asked for the folder. "Does he do research in memory too? What do we have here, a big memory family?"

"No, he doesn't."

Swept let out a "Wow, look at this!" Photos fell from the folder, one of Gantemirov, which held no meaning for Swept, but another one did. It was a picture of Aleksander Kostokov. "Look at this," holding up the photograph, turning to Valerie, "Look at this!"

'What's the matter?"

"What's the matter? I know him – that's what's the matter. He's my patient, or was. I'm his doctor."

Swept now had the room's attention, as he explained that the picture was of Mohammed Abdul, the patient he had treated for headaches.

"I don't know how, but everything's connected," Valerie said. "You can bank on that, one hundred percent."

The telephone rang. Valerie picked it up. "Dick, Janos Szeppek for you."

"Janos?"

"Hello, Dr. Swept. I gave the rats amphetamines, a low per kilogram body-weighted dosage."

"And. . . ?"

"You won't believe it."

"Yes I will. Try me."

"They all died. The rats can't take amphetamines with the Compound. They died, even with the low dosage. They died within an hour, with major seizures."

"They died? And, they seized?" Valerie and her colleagues were most attentive.

"That's it."

"Thanks. I'll explain later."

"Okay, I'm here in the lab. Now can you tell me about the funding? Did it go well?"

"No, I can't tell you now. But I will later. Thanks for you help Janos."

"Good-bye," Swept returned the phone to the receiver.

"Well," Swept announced. "That answers that. Serkin somehow took the Compound and, I'll bet his insistence that the Sherpas had meningitis relates to that Compound. But, how did he get it? And," leaning toward Valerie, "How do we know I didn't get it?" Raising an eyebrow, feeling the now diminished bump over his right carotid, saying to the nurse who was now becoming his friend. "No . . . It couldn't be. Inject my carotid artery? Why? Who?"

Valerie touched his arm. "I don't know, but Aleksander Kostokov and Gantemirov are involved in this." Turning to her companions, "Who else was on the committee in Nepal?"

"The usual bureaucrats, nothing of note. We have long known Aleksander Kostokov is undercover but I'll bet Gantemirov is too."

"Well," said Valerie, "We have to have some release to the media, certainly about the Director of NINDS being dead, let alone the other prominent scientists. For now, we'll blame the animal lovers but if any perpetrators got away, they'll know we're lying."

"I'll put out an 'All Points' for Gantemirov and Kostokov," Frank responded, picking up his cellular telephone.

"By the way, Dick, where is the Compound?" Valerie inquired.

"We have two bottles, a small one, basically a vial, near the maze in the lab. The other is in a large bottle, on my desk, in the lab, with lines on it."

"Lines on it. Why?"

"That's another good question." Swept explained.

Chapter Twenty

TOMORROW, THE WORLD

SZEPPEK KNEW THAT his mentor was involved in a major scientific meeting in Washington, D. C., the nation's capital. The postdoctorate student queried whether, on some level, he might get brownie points were he to call his Consulate. Maybe, Swept was in trouble. Maybe Szeppek, himself, was in trouble. Although it was late Sunday night, Szeppek knew what number to call and soon reached his Hungarian contact.

The Consulate did not know about the deaths, since the Agency had been successful in keeping the information from the media. The Consulate still did not know this after Szeppek relayed information about Swept's call. However, when Kostokov received the information, he certainly knew of the deaths. He also now knew, for certain, that Swept was alive.

*   *   *

Aleksander Kostokov rested on his flight from Washington D. C. to New Orleans, wondering how to present the details of his misadventures to his Russian superiors. After arriving in New Orleans, he rented a car, drove to Yorky's former camp near Homer, making certain no tell-tale debris remained. None did. Yorky, a professional to the end, had done his work well.

Kostokov drove back to New Orleans, flew to New York, and took the next available Aeroflot Russian International flight, business class, to Moscow. He tried to rest on the plane but found this difficult. A driver met him when he arrived in Moscow, and drove him to his flat.

It was wonderful to be in Moscow, despite his being dead tired. More than most major cities, Moscow rewards those who take the time to know it, and Aleksander Kostokov knew it well. Although Moscow seems quiet for the capital of the world's largest country, to Kostokov it pulsed with an excitement that made him dizzy.

St. Petersburgers have long contended that Moscow is just a big village, not a city. This is partly true. Moscow began life as a provincial outpost and grew slowly, different neighborhoods taking on unique identities. Today, Moscow is more akin to several thousand villages, each street, courtyard and staircase having its own character. Although Moscow has its great buildings, historic sites, broad avenues, famous theatres, busy restaurants, parks and squares, the real flavor lies within the small nooks and crannies, each individually unique.

Moscow, and Moscow alone, is the epicenter of the new Russia, offering exciting night life, shops, and restaurants that current-day provincial Russians can only dream about. Anything can happen in this city, to anyone. Unfortunately, this also includes the problems that highlight what is wrong with Russia: growing street crime, inflation, private and government corruption, all interspersed with beggars and drunks.

After resting that day and well through the night, Aleksander Kostokov spent the morning strolling through his beloved city, walking beneath the Kremlin walls, through what used to be called Red Square, and feasted his eyes on the beautiful St. Basil's Cathedral. Aleksander then took a train to Tver, 150 kilometers northwest of central Moscow.

Tver, sitting on the Volga River, was the capital of an unruly mini-state that rivaled Moscow in the 14th and 15th centuries. After that, its history was reminiscent of a soap opera, as it was punished for rising up against the Mongol Tatars, conquered by Ivan III, savaged by Ivan the Terrible, conquered by Poland, burned to the ground in a horrible fire in 1763, reborn in the 18th century after Catherine the Great made it one of her rest stops between Moscow and St. Petersburg, and more, including being the birth place of Mikhail Kalinin, Stalin's puppet president during World War II. Indeed, Tver was called Kalinin under the Soviets, a name the city changed in 1990, returning to its earlier nomenclature. Now, Tver is a nice day trip from Moscow, offering baroque classical architecture and a sense of rest.

One hundred ninety kilometers further west is Lake Seliger, nestled within a thick pine forest near the headwaters of the Volga. The lake, dotted with islands, has long been a cult vacation place for Russian intellectuals, providing phenomenal hunting, canoeing, hiking, and privacy.

Aleksander Kostokov arrived on the appropriate island, at the appropriate time, as instructed for his meeting, which was very private. After being frisked (he carried no weapon), he was admitted to a well-lit room. There they were: Yuri Lyachin, Mikhail Solokov, Liubov Usova, and Jokhar Gantemirov.

Kostokov was surprised to see Gantemirov, but said nothing.

Yuri Lyachin smiled at seeing Aleksander, gave him a floppy disk, motioned him to put it in the laptop computer, and said, "Read this. Read it once. Then we destroy it."

Aleksander did as instructed. The disk listed complaints against President Putin, ranging from failure to control the wealthy oligarchs who challenged his power, to curtailing the military budget. It also blamed Putin for the Kursk disaster.

"Well, Comrade," Lyachin said. "Tell me what you think. No harm will come to you. I promise. Tell me your thoughts."

Kostokov looked at those in the room. "Some might consider this treason."

"True. Some might. But, others might not. The disk means no direct offense to President Putin, or to Mother Russia. Just a statement of problems. Are you comfortable with what is on this disk?"

"Sure, I'm comfortable. New Millennium, New Times. Why are you asking me this? How can I help?"

"Neither President Putin nor the FSB know about us."

Kostokov froze. His face held a blank stare. "Who does? Who are you? Who are we?"

"No one knows us. We are who we are – Pi Two."

"Where do we get funds?"

"Money comes from groups wanting to help Chechens. Jokhar Gantemirov helps us." Gantemirov nodded his head in affirmation, smiling softly. Lyachin continued. "You would be surprised, but perhaps not, at how much money Islamic countries give to Chechnya, a significant fraction of which goes to us. Besides, our project hasn't been too costly. We all have contacts, and we have the drug, or almost."

"Simply put," Gantemirov chimed in, "We can give whomever we want in the Kremlin, including the FSB, even President Putin, the chemical. We can expand our base in the Caucasus. The Caucasus is fifteen million strong, including seven republics in the Russian Federation. There's no reason why we can't control all seven, including Chechnya. We can take over any country we want. Tomorrow, who knows, we could have the world."

Gantemirov continued. "Good can come from all this. Certainly, in Chechnya. Russians don't belong there. We are mountain people, all Muslims, except for the *gorskie Evrei*, the Jews, who number about ten thousand. They live in a few cities and don't bother anyone. Under the Nazis, under the Tsars, under Stalin, they'd be dead. Under us, Pi Two, no one would be. We are tolerant. We desire harmony as well as power."

Liubov Usova added her comments. "Russian politicians can't stop us. Recently, the entire Russian military budget was four billion dollars but in the United States, during that same year, their budget was three hundred billion dollars. Russia was humiliated in Kosovo and humiliated in Serbia. The world only respects power, nuclear power. Our President can't promote nuclear power – he can't afford it. Yet, the only way Russia can be a superpower is to rely on nuclear weapons. Our nuclear arsenal is substantial, and without it no one will care about us at all, but we abandoned hundreds of ships, planes and bombs to the elements. Over one hundred atomic submarines are rusting in the fjords around the Kola Peninsula, all filled with deadly radioactive material and no money to decommission them properly and dispose of their nuclear waste. Look what happened to the Kursk."

Yuri Lyachin shifted uneasily. Liubov Usova continued. "We have many decayed submarines in

Murmausk, in danger of exploding and releasing more than half the radioactive activity released at Chernobyl. What do we do about this? Nothing. What does Putin do about this? Nothing."

Jokhar Gantemirov spoke, with controlled anger. "The only reason anyone ever cares about the Caucasas is because Chechnya sits across the roots of the pipelines that carry oil from the Caspian Sea to Russia. Why shouldn't that land belong to the Chechen people? Why give the profits to non-Caucas, non-Muslim, Russian Orthodox Slavs?"

Yuri Lyachin interrupted. "Calm down. Everyone can have everything. This is do-able. It's not expensive. We can influence tribes, families, city governments, bureaucrats. We are the only ones who know about this. That is, except for Dr. Swept, Janos Szeppek, and those associated with their research."

Lyachin continued. "It's true. What we have is more powerful than nuclear weapons, and cheaper. We want to take over Chechnya, then expand our base in the Caucasas. After that. we can expand anywhere we want. When the Mongols thundered out of Asia in the thirteenth century, they were only horsemen and in thirty years had the largest land empire the world has ever known. Their leader, a Mongolian from what is today eastern Siberia, was named Temuchin. He lived from 1167 to 1227, changing his name to Great Ruler, which, translated, is Genghis Khan. But, you know what? He killed one-quarter of those he conquered. We don't have to kill anyone. We can control without killing. We can stop the muggers in the streets in Moscow, we might even get people to change religions. We can stop killing, fighting, crime. This is the greatest victory of science today."

Solokov, the premier Russian scientist, nodded his head slowly, but definitely agreeing.

Liubov Usova interjected, with stern command. "Aleksander Kostokov," who had thus far tried to avoid gazing directly at his sexual abuser, "Who else knows about this?"

Kostokov looked at her, trying to drown the disgusting memories of their sexual encounters. "Dick Swept, Janos Szeppek, and I presume Harold Ranger, although he despises this kind of research and thinks it won't work."

"I assure you, he's wrong. It will work. Trust me." The big fat woman raised both her eyebrows and snickered, enjoying the discomfort she was festering upon him. "Continue."

"I don't think anyone else knows, except for some laboratory technicians, and they probably only know a part of the puzzle."

Gantemirov interrupted. "Our contacts in FSB tell us that Valerie VanDance and Swept are at CIA headquarters, so I presume she also knows. What about the women in Swept's life, the plastic surgeon and that nurse."

"I don't know. Maybe I can find out from Szeppek, being discreet of course. I can also try to get more information on VanDance."

Gantemirov looked at Kostokov's eyes. "Are you with us?"

"Of course," said Aleksander Kostokov. What difference did it make to him? For centuries, the good had removed the bad from power, so why were there still bad guys? Nothing changes. Political life was easy when you were an existentialist.

The cabal began to leave the room. Usova told Kostokov to remain behind. "Come in the rowboat, I have something to show you. Aleksander Kostokov did as instructed. The two entered a nearby boat and Usova rowed. She then leaned back, took out a huge blanket, raised her dress, and instructed Kostokov to go under the blanket, pointing to the area between her legs, and waited for ecstasy. She held his head firmly, almost choking him, and nearly suffocating him as well. When she was done, Usova removed the blanket, sneered, and told Kostokov to jump in the water. "I rowed out here, you swim back."

Kostokov did as instructed, viewed the laughing woman rowing away, and decided to kill her. What good would mind-control drugs do in the hands of a woman like that, he thought, as he swam the short distance to shore. Then again, maybe he could change his way of thinking.

Then again, maybe someone already had changed his.

The options were powerful, potential, and not necessarily nice.

After arriving at the shore, wet clothes and all, Solokov met him. "Quite a woman, don't you think?" Solokov scanned Kostokov's wet clothes, but said nothing.

"No, I disagree."

"I am aware of her, shall we say, needs. But, I assure you, her contacts with the Kremlin go to the highest level and it is important that we maintain good relations. On a different subject, you understand, you must kill Swept, Szeppek, and anyone else familiar with that Compound. Also, we need to know the exact structure, which unfortunately Swept never revealed at the conference because of what happened."

The scientist continued. "Not only does the West probably now suspect our being interested in these drugs, but we still don't have the details that we need about the Compound."

"I seldom fail at my tasks." Aleksander Kostokov, the memory of Liubov Usova still in his mind, his clothes wet, spoke with a resolved spirit. "Surely, you understand I had no control over the NIH canceling the meeting. Otherwise, things would have gone according to plan. As for Nepal, you are aware of my lack of total authority in that mission, are you not?"

"If you want to discuss that, fine with me. You are talking nonsense. First, Swept was given too much medication when you made him unconscious. He was far too drugged after his abduction. Second, the briefcase was not as well disguised as it should have been. As for Nepal, it's over and we need not discuss it further."

At that moment, Yuri Lyachin joined the two, looking puzzled at Kostokov's wet clothes. Before Lyachin could comment, he saw Usova coming from behind Kostokov. Aleksander turned behind him, saw the huge woman, and turned back toward Solokov and Lyachin. "Comrades, listen to me. I underwent a neurological examination by Dr. Swept. He thought I had headaches and that that was why I saw him. The conversation that transpired between us is outlined in my report. I later went to the doctor's laboratory and, knowing the chemical was called Compound 1040 from our reports from Szeppek, obtained some of the chemical. There was a bottle near his desk. I took about thirty millimeters. Our laboratories analyzed it but, as you know, we're not exactly certain of the structure."

"We obtained the Compound and, having practiced with a Russian neuroradiologist, I injected the chemical into Dr. Swept's carotid artery after we chloroformed him. Our people told me the dose would go straight to his brain. I told Swept, repeatedly, there would be a briefcase delivered to his hotel room on a specific evening, the evening before the scheduled NIH meeting. He did not know the briefcase had a bomb in it, nor that there was a monitoring device. He was told he would receive this late Friday night, which I reasoned was too late to bother people in the laboratory to thank them. I told him this eighty or ninety times. It was your belief," facing Solokov directly, "based upon animal experiments performed in your laboratories, coupled with what happened to Serkin, that he would take the briefcase. As it happened, he did, even though we gave it to him later, one week later."

"The explosive is one of our best, AK-96. The researchers in your laboratory," now directly addressing Liubov Usova, "also thought the plan a good idea."

Kostokov continued. "I also told him to state in his report that he had illegally tried it on a few patients, who died. That way, if the bomb failed to kill everyone and the talk was monitored, no one would believe you could use it on humans. I also told him all this eighty or ninety times. That part, as opposed to the briefcase, we never got to test."

"The NIH calendar comes out weekly, covering the ensuing two weeks. The time of this meeting was changed after the calendar came out the week of the meeting, and no subsequent announcement was sent because so few people were to attend it. Instead of sending a regular NIH announcement to all researchers in Washington, they must have telephoned the people who were going to be at that meeting, telling them the new date. That was why we had to change plans. However, this did not significantly alter the scope of our basic plan."

"I still managed to get Dr. Swept to take the briefcase to the meeting. However, as you know, it was detected by the Americans."

Lyachin turned to Liubov Usova. "Then, the brief-case wasn't designed appropriately. You should have checked it more thoroughly."

Usova angrily answered. "The briefcase was de-signed by your Section. I was personally assured by Rensky, Head of Service, that it had been used sev-eral times. I cannot be held responsible for its hav-ing been detected."

Kostokov continued, looking at Usova with ha-tred in his heart. "I don't know how it was that the Americans noticed the briefcase. All we all know is that someone there knew Dr. Swept and was sur-prised to see him carrying a new briefcase. Evidently, that someone is Valerie VanDance. She is a nurse in the Department of Neurology, works for the Chair-man, and I presume works for American Intelli-gence."

"I don't know what else I could have done. Fol-lowing administration of the Compound into Swept's carotid artery, his behavior changed. Our laboratories did not anticipate this. The change in Swept's behavior focused attention on him and, I presume, Valerie VanDance took greater notice of him. She must have been a CIA plant, following research that had implications for American Intel-ligence. Then, as I know you know, Dr. Swept went to the Cayman Islands. The NIH meeting was re-scheduled. I touched base with our personnel to drop off the briefcase, all done through Yorky. What we had not counted on was CIA operatives at the meeting."

Liubov Usova looked him in the eye and sneered. "You alibi too much."

Kostokov ignored her. "Look at my task in a different light. Because of the briefcase and my performance on this mission, we now know that Central Intelligence operatives are aware of what Swept is doing. As best I can tell, and you have seen the transcripts, no one else is doing the work he is. I ask you, what else should I have done?"

Solokov was the first to respond. "Perhaps, nothing." The scientist then started to walk away, followed by Lyachin and Gantemirov. After they disappeared, glaring at Aleksander Kostokov, whose clothes were still wet, Usova said, "Let me show you how well that chemical works!" The giant fat woman looked around, saw no one in sight, and picked up her dress. "Get on your knees and do it again, and again after that. I'll tell you when to stop."

Kostokov couldn't believe it. Was he supposed to engage in cunnilingus with this woman? Again? Outside, in front of Lake Seliger? One look at her misty-eyed face told him he was. He started, with a sensation of nausea coupled with strange eroticism. He was enslaved himself and, to his knowledge, never received any drug. Or, did he?

Afterwards, when his female superior gave him a respite, she toyed with his neck and spoke as though nothing had transpired. "Perhaps I was wrong about you. But one thing I am correct about: You must kill Dick Swept and eliminate the Hungarian. As soon as possible. In no time at all the Americans will put together Szeppek's frequent conversations with us. Kill them both, then come back here to me."

"Won't the Americans know we're involved in mind control research if they don't already, especially if we kill Swept?"

"They probably already do. We need to be certain they get as little information as possible from one of their most valuable sources. We can't stop them, but we can sure put a brake on their activities. Besides, that's what I want done." She turned around and walked away, down a dirt path, leaving a bewildered Kostokov standing in clothes still damp.

Then, suddenly Usova turned toward him. She walked closer and smiled. "Be here, at this spot, tomorrow morning. Seven o'clock sharp. You and I are going for another ride in the boat." Without waiting for a response, the behemoth spy walked away.

Aleksander Kostokov stood there, wondering for a long time. Why did he let Liubov Usova execute sexual demands on him? Did he allow it because he feared her power? Did he allow it because he liked her? The contrast between her and his dead wife sickened him.

Why did he allow this? Then, it became all too clear.

* * *

The following morning, Kostokov was at the designated place. He walked silently to the boat,

Usova sadistically playing with his neck. Again, she rowed him out on Lake Seliger. The lake was deserted, with no sounds except songs from the dawn chorus of birds. Liubov Usova sardonically smiled at the field agent and, as she had done to him so many times before, picked up her dress and ordered him to please her. Similar to yesterday, the blanket was there, as she ordered Kostokov under it and told him to suck her. A silent Kostokov obeyed as instructed.

But Kostokov was beneath the blanket for only a moment before a gurgling sound and a whooshing gasp came from the woman's mouth and chest cavity, as Kostokov embedded a huge carving knife under the woman's left rib cage, slicing into her heart and lungs. Alive for a brief two seconds, she stared at her assassin who removed himself from the blanket.

"You gave me the chemical, you pig. That's what you did! That was why I did all this. Now, you piece of trash, you swim to shore and I'll row back." With that, he rolled the huge agent into the water, and left her bloodied body to float to shore.

Aleksander rowed to land, finding the scientist, Solokov, in his room. Kostokov knocked on the door, was granted entry, and in a matter of moments had a strip of a towel wrapped around Solokov's neck.

"I'll ask you this once and only once. Did you know that Usova gave me the chemical and was raping me? Yes or no?"

Due to lack of air, a panicked Solokov could barely speak and motioned with waving arms. Kokstokov briefly relaxed his cervical hold and the scientist answered. "No. What are you talking about? What are you doing? Are you crazy?"

"You'll find out in no time." Kostokov smashed Solokov's face against his knee, shattering his nose and left facial bones, and lit a Sobranie cigarette. Picking up Solokov, who was now terror-stricken, Kostokov impaled the burning weed against the scientist's left eye, causing blindness and immense pain, as he muffled his screams with the towel.

"I'll ask you once more. Did you know?" Seeing that Kostokov was going to impale the other eye with the burning cigarette, the scientist answered truthfully. "No, no. Not at first. She later told me to convince me that the chemical worked."

"Did Yuri know? Did Yuri Lyachin know?" Kostokov menaced his captive with the cigarette, making it clear that the man would soon be blind and experience double the pain.

"No. I don't think so. We never approved her trying it on you. It was never our intention. Now, let me go. Are you mad?"

"Hardly." Kostokov threw down the cigarette, but the momentary relief Solokov felt was only that – momentary. In three seconds, Mikhail Solokov lay dead on the floor from a broken neck.

Fifteen minutes later, an incredibly irate

Aleksander Kostokov was at Yuri Lyachin's door. Lyachin was surprised to see his field agent.

"Aleksander," said the man with his tremulous voice, holding his morning coffee. "What can I do for you?"

"Did you not wonder why my clothes were wet yesterday?"

"It more than crossed my mind, but I was busy with other matters. Is that why you are here? To tell me why you wore wet clothes yesterday?"

"No, that is not why I am here. I just killed Usova and Solokov and I want you to know why."

Yuri Lyachin squinted his eyes, sipped some coffee, and beckoned his agent to enter the room. "By all means."

"Thank you." Kostokov entered the room, asked permission to light a Sobranie, and then explained to a bewildered Yuri Lyachin why he had murdered two colleagues. A saddened Lyachin listened attentively, told him that he would contact the local police regarding what to do with the corpses, and stressed his sorrow. Quickly changing gears, he reiterated the importance of Pi Two's mission and the necessity of killing those in its path.

Chapter Twenty-One

BEHIND EVERY BEAUTIFUL THING
THERE'S BEEN SOME KIND OF PAIN

THE HUNGARIAN CONSULATE contact was as perplexed as Szeppek. Why did Swept want to administer amphetamines to his rats? And, why did they seize and die? Also, did Swept get funding or not?

The Consulate suggested that Szeppek telephone Swept at his hotel. Szeppek tried, but was told that Swept had checked out.

Swept was now staying in Fairfax, Virginia, near Langley.

*   *   *

A few days later, Valerie was back in Houston. She went to the Brain Institute and pulled the Department's records on Swept's telephone calls. Finding nothing of interest, she pulled the calls that members of his lab had made. Each laboratory member had his own billing code, and it was not difficult for her to access what long distance calls each person had made. After all, the nurse worked with the Chairman and was familiar with how this information was logged into the computer. Szeppek had a series of long distance calls. One of the often-called numbers, when Valerie phoned, resulted in someone answering, "Hello, Hungarian Consulate."

Valerie then used her contacts at the CIA to check Szeppek's calls from his apartment, screening only those over the past six months. Southwestern Bell was very obliging, providing the information within a few hours. It was soon apparent to Valerie that Szeppek frequently called the Hungarian Consulate in Houston.

Valerie decided to call Szeppek, who was not in the laboratory. She called him at his apartment. "Janos, do you often call the Hungarian Consulate?"

Szeppek, taken aback, with some hesitancy, replied that he had. "This is something all of us have to do. My country wants to be certain we are well taken care of. We often give reports."

"Which office do you call?"

"Usually, Houston. But, sometimes, I call them in different cities. It depends on what they want me to do. Why?"

"This is the most ridiculous thing I ever heard."

"We all do it."

"Do you know anyone else who does?"

"I don't know other Hungarian nationals who are students in Houston, but this *is* routine."

"What kind of things do you talk about?"

"Nothing much. They just want to know how I'm feeling, about my health, where I stand in our research. That's all. Why?"

"Janos, can I come over tonight and talk to you? There are some things we need to go over. Now. Would that be all right? It won't take much time."

Not wanting to refuse the Chairman's nurse and somewhat pleased that a woman wanted to visit him in his apartment, Janos agreed.

The Hungarian told her he needed a few hours. The more he thought about it, the more he fretted. Why had Swept not returned from Washington D. C.? Would U. S. government agencies have questions for him? Was it illegal that he had called the Consulate with such frequency? Would he be blamed for the missing aliquots of Compound 1040? What about funding? Did Swept receive or not receive the funding? Could he, Janos, stay in the United States if Swept failed to obtain funding? Szeppek had not run into Dr. Ranger since Swept had left for Washington D. C.; what would he tell Dr. Ranger? These thoughts tumbled in his head, when he heard a knock at the door, too early for Valerie.

"Who is it?"

"I'm from the Hungarian Consulate. Please open the door."

Sadly, slowly, the student opened the door. "Yes? May I help you?"

The stranger said, "Janos Szeppek?"

"Yes. Can I help you?"

"I'm from the Consulate," looking around. "Are you alone? May I come in?"

"Yes, I'm alone. Please come in," Janos turned away from the man, motioning him to enter, seeing him shut the door behind and then suddenly turning. The man rocketed his left fist into Janos Szeppek's abdomen, doubling him over, as the stranger again struck the disabled student, who recognized in his brief moment of time that death was near. A sharp chop to the neck killed him, and the postdoctorate fellow lay dead on the floor.

A few hours later, Valerie VanDance arrived at Szeppek's apartment. When no one answered, she telephoned the night manager, who curtly explained that only Szeppek had the key to the apartment. Valerie showed the man her CIA card, explained that this was federal business, and he told her to stuff it, saying that the CIA only dealt with matters out of the country.

"Really, you ignorant fool!" However, rather than argue her point, Valerie called 911.

When the police arrived, Valerie explained her concern. With some misgivings, the overworked officer broke down the door. Facing them, dead as stone, was Janos Szeppek, hanging from his neck on a noose strung over the door. A typed noted was on the table:

I'm sorry if I caused any deaths. I'm sorry.

J. S.

A Bob Dylan song was playing on the radio, in the background. Valerie heard, *"My sense of humility has gone down the drain/ Behind every beautiful thing, there's been some kind of pain."*

Valerie picked up her cell phone and called Dick Swept, still in Fairfax. The nurse explained what had happened.

Swept was aghast. "Never in a million years would Janos have done this. Never. He was a fighter, a manipulator. He never would have taken his own life."

Chapter Twenty-Two

A DOCTOR AND A SPY

AT CIA HEADQUARTERS, Swept was introduced to Major Cervantes, whose full name bore no formal relation to military rank. Cervantes reminded Swept of what some call "RA" in the army: Regular Army. Those guys played by the rules and looked it. So it was with Major Cervantes.

Cervantes looked as though he had a haircut every 20 minutes. He was clean-shaven, from his head to his neck, and spoke in clear, crisp tones, almost too rapidly. His features were sharp, demeanor formal, and evidently wanted the world to know that he was a committed patriot, as evidenced by his pictures of James Madison, Thomas Jefferson, and Ronald Reagan.

"The damn Russians, as well as the United States, have been hard at work finding a drug that controls thinking." Swept's lip began to curl, but Cervantes continued. "I know most of you scientists don't care to hear about these things, but it's a reality. If a country can control a population's thinking by administering a drug, the options are endless."

"Nuclear warfare, conventional warfare, chemical warfare would be unnecessary. Not only is mind-control more effective, it is less expensive. That's probably why the Russians, or whoever, placed the transmitter and bomb in your briefcase and the conference room. They wanted to check our level of knowledge. They knew you'd bring the briefcase into the meeting and, after recording the lectures and hearing what our scientists had to say, would have blown up the entire room, and you with it."

Cervantes did not wait for Swept to respond. "Look, Dr. Swept. It never occurred to us that Russians would infiltrate a small group of American scientists working in the field of memory research. Our error. The National Security Administration and CIA don't do enough research on these drugs. We've just been watching you scientists. We've been lax. Were it not for Valerie VanDance, our branch wouldn't even know that the NIH called you people together. We should monitor you academics more closely, you're such an independent lot. No matter, we need you. Simply put, Dr. Swept, we want you to work for us."

"You want me to work for you!? All I want to do is go back to Houston. Thanks, but no thanks. I'm tired of this. I don't know how I got into this, but I want out. I just want to work on my research."

"Dr. Swept, sometimes, this time, life gets complicated. Your work is very important to America. We need you to work with us. We need your expertise to help develop the area of mind-control drugs. You're our best option. Now that we see how intent the Russians are in developing this area, to the point of blowing up a building and killing people, including you, we can't slack off. There's no one in the area more knowledgeable than you. If you work in our laboratory, you'll have all the support you require. The carryover into the area of treating demented patients will be extensive. We'll pay you well and support your research."

Swept looked at him, giving no response. Cervantes continued. "It may also be that you're not safe. How do you know they won't try to kill you?"

"Well, if they do, I can rest assured that the United States government is watching me. That should help a lot! I hope they help me more than the services they provided for Bradley Serkin, when he seized amd died. Now, if you'll forgive me, I'm leaving."

Unphased, Cervantes continued. "Look at it this way. We're going to have someone, probably several people working in this area. It may as well be you."

"Thank you, but no."

"Well, if you change your mind and want the job, give us a call. Remember, you'll have an active laboratory with us and all the funds you need."

"Thanks, but no thanks."

*   *   *

On the jet home, refreshed, Swept read a *Wall Street Journal* editorial persuasively arguing that the would-be Turkish assassin who had shot Pope John Paul II twenty-odd years ago was financed by the Bulgarian Secret Police. The gunman was from a poor village and had been trained by the PLO. He was involved in a political murder and suspiciously escaped from a Turkish jail, only to live well in the Bulgarian Police Station and even better on a well-forged passport in Western Europe, prior to his arriving at St. Peter's Square for the assassination. The well-documented tale was derived from police records and public testimony, little being left to the imagination.

It stretched the *Journal's* credulity to be told that the Kremlin had ordered the then-KGB to order Bulgarian Secret Police to arrange assassination of the Pope. The editorial contended that Americans, having been conditioned in orderly, legal, political processes, might believe that such things only happened in spy thrillers. Whether the Soviet's leader, Brezhnev, had issued explicit orders, the world-wide KGB network of underground political manipulators certainly existed, their principal mission being the destabilization of NATO governments, partly through terrorism. Turkey and Italy were then major threats. Audacity was not uncommon in politics, as attested by wars, invasions, and multiple atrocities.

Swept sank back into his seat. A few weeks ago, he might only have glanced at the editorial. Now, he read it twice. Earlier, it would not have crossed his mind that he might one day be involved in espionage and killing. The past several days had been beyond his belief. The glory of his science was not to be, during those days. People were dead. Further, not presenting his ideas, not interacting with the other scientists, not being able to speak to Chippers – what would happen to his funding?

Dick Swept went into a near-funk. He had liked Chippers and was sad he was dead. For whatever reason, Swept felt no remorse for the people he had killed. He did what he had to do. Just as he had been trained in Special Forces.

Swept grabbed a magazine from the seat pocket. There was an article about the rare song of the Uirapuru, an Amazon bird whose melodious song was so beautiful that all the other forest birds were quiet during its singing. Unfortunately, it sang only once per year, five to ten minutes a day, during the ten to fifteen days it was building its nest.

The bird's moment of glory, its own Andy Warhol's brief period of fame, came and left, but returned in one year. The bird added something to its culture, its fellow avian civilization. What would Swept add? What could he add? Pensive, he now understood more about Harold Ranger and ordered a vodka, which he drank straight up. He then closed his eyes and slept.

*   *   *

Swept was pleased that his car was still in the airport parking lot, undamaged. He paid the woman at the exit a minor fortune with his credit card, passed two terminals, and then headed toward Highway 59. Turning on the radio, he heard a song he had never heard before:

> *Keep your chestnut mare, keep your Calico pony.*
> *Keep your lady with the golden spurs.*
> *Me, I'll take the woman from Houston, Texas.*
> *She lets the poor boy know what he's worth.*

> *I'm gonna give you a cake with some chocolate frosting.*
> *I'm gonna hand you a plump tangerine.*
> *It's been so long in this man's life*
> *That loving ever felt so clean.*

The country singer's melody changed as the song entered a minor key:

> *I ain't asking no questions.*
> *I don't want to push or shove.*
> *I don't know no magical secrets.*
> *But I know I found someone to love.*

> *Houston women . . .*

Swept turned off the radio. He was weak and thoroughly exhausted. He looked forward to seeing his dog. Ricki had agreed to feed and walk Limbic, and he looked forward to seeing her as well.

Arriving home within an hour, he felt good as he entered his home and was pleased by the attention his forsaken pet bestowed upon him.

There was a large pile of mail. Ricki must have stacked it. Only a small portion had been traumatized by Limbic. Also, there were two cards from Ricki. She wanted to see him.

After unpacking his suitcase, Swept soon had Ricki on the telephone. The bombs and the killings had been in the newspapers. She wanted to hear all about it. She would be at his house in half an hour. Meanwhile, he showered.

Having just stepped out of the bathroom, with his white terry cloth robe wrapped tightly around his waist, the doorbell rang. It was Ricki.

Smothering him with kisses, she kept saying how grateful she was that Swept was alive and safe. He explained what had happened, apologized for not calling during the events of the preceeding several days, and discussed everything with her, including Serkin's death. In no time, Ricki had her clothes off and was lying on Swept's bed, jokingly laughing about the Dylan posters on the bedroom wall.

After their lovemaking, the woman toyed with his thick hair and told the neurologist she had decided to stop smoking and abandon her Marlboro Lights. She then toyed with him elsewhere.

Before Ricki became too involved in their sexual activities again, Swept said, "Why in the world would you stop smoking now? Besides, you only smoke five or six cigarettes a week."

"I know it's not a lot, but, to be frank, I've been

smoking more since the miseries of the Sherpas. Since you've had pain and suffering, I'll go through some, too. I'm leaving the Marlboro Lights and the lighter in the bathroom. You can monitor me. We'll suffer together. Now, what do you think of that, Doctor?" She softly nuzzled herself against his chest, playing with him below.

The two engaged in another bout of lovemaking, Swept amazed that he was able to be aroused, given his state of mind. Later, as Ricki walked toward the door, accompanied by Swept, she turned to him.

"I'm in love with you, Richard. I am truly in love with you. I feel for you through all of this and I relate to you. My mind is yours. Darling, I love you."

"Look, Ricki. This isn't the time to get into this."

"I'm not asking for a Kodak moment. I'm just telling you how I feel. You can keep whatever feelings you have to yourself, and we can talk about it later. I just want you to know I love you." With that, she kissed him on the cheek and he walked her to the car.

Swept, contemplating everything that had happened over the last several days, returned to his bed, multiple thoughts in his mind.

*   *   *

At work the following day, everyone, from Tracy to hospital administrators, deluged Swept with questions. Valerie smiled hello, and told him that she was going to resign and move to Fairfax. Her cover was blown and the CIA had offered her a good position.

And, Dr. Harold Ranger wanted to see him.

Swept entered his Chairman's office and explained all that had happened, leaving Valerie out of the picture. Ranger, ever street smart, snickered, "Well, I don't know who the Acting Director of the NINDS will be, but it's good if we know him. Also, competition for you is down. The good scientists are dead. The area of mind-control," using his fingers for quote marks, "will now beckon more grants, more competition, and the NIH will probably provide more funding. As for you, I'd hate to see you go, and you're more than welcome to stay, but I must tell you that you need funding as well as a new postdoctorate fellow, one who won't hang himself. And, if you want, although it's still against my better judgement, I'll approve your application to the Human Experimentation Committee. But, you understand, it's up to them to approve it."

Swept looked at Harold Ranger, offered a half-hearted chuckle, and said, "Tough guy, tough guy."

"Just let me know what you want, Richard. And, if you go to Washington, give me some warning."

"Thanks, I'll talk to you later."

As Swept left, Ranger called out, "Oh, by the way."

"Yes."

"They offered me the position of Acting Director."

"You're joking. That's great."

"I refused. I'm too set in my ways. I'd only interfere with great young minds, like yours."

"I'm not so sure about that. Do you think you're the 'wrong person, wrong place, wrong time?'"

"No, only 'wrong time.'"

Swept returned to his lab and explained to the inquisitive technicians much of what had transpired. None knew anything about any briefcase and had not considered Janos Szeppek suicidal. Compound 1040 was now locked inside a drawer.

*   *   *

Meanwhile, Valerie had done her homework, investigating everyone, including Regina Bruxton. The plastic surgeon was not what she seemed. Valerie had secretly obtained medical records on Dr. Bruxton, which was not too difficult. Regina Bruxton had seen several doctors, including multiple gynecologists, for a medical problem that could not be successfully treated. Regina Bruxton had only a vestige of an ovary, medically known as an ovarian streak. The woman was incapable of having children. At one time, her parents had succeeded in having her see a psychiatrist regarding the depression this caused. Regina went for two sessions and quit. The money she made from her practice and, especially, the goal of pursuing it, was probably the major relationship she needed in life, aside from sexual needs which she never had difficulty servicing. She had learned, through the years, that it was easier to dislike a man than to love him, thereby avoiding the risk of her not being considered worthy, in light of her barrenness. This could explain a great deal of her behavior.

Valerie decided not to tell Swept about her discovery.

Swept returned to his office, where he had a series of messages from Regina. He found it striking that Regina now left messages at his office, whereas Ricki left messages at his home. Regina wanted to talk to him, over lunch, in her office.

*   *   *

"I'm glad you weren't harmed, but I've been giving this some thinking. I don't feel the way I should if I were in love with you. I want us to be friends, not lovers. Is that all right?"

Swept looked at Regina, a sad smile on his face. "Regina, that's all we are. Friends."

The nurse knocked on Dr. Bruxton's door, reminding her of her busy Operating Room schedule that afternoon. Regina kissed Swept on the cheek, excused herself with an "I'm sorry," and Dick Swept stared at his shoes.

Swept left Regina's swank office, filled with Monet replicas and mirrors, and walked slowly back to his laboratory. Szeppek was gone, his funding was uncertain, Ranger might leave, and he reminded himself that his funding would be unlimited at the CIA.

Swept changed his mind about where he was walking, went to his academic office and telephoned Major Cervantes.

"What are the guarantees that the CIA would let me do whatever I want?"

"Doctor, you tell us. We'll guarantee anything you want."

"Okay, let's talk."

*   *   *

Aleksander Kostokov was at the Marriott, using the same name that he had used when he had come in earlier to see Swept. He was aware that there were too many side effects from the drug. First, it seemed to interact with other medications, aside from altering white cells in some of the body's chemistry. The Russians would have to engage in more research.

*   *   *

At eleven o'clock at night, on a Thursday evening, Swept received a phone call. "This is Major Cervantes, Dr. Swept. Our offer still holds. We'll meet your requirements: Six post-doctorate fellows, eighteen technicians, twenty thousand square feet of laboratory space, and funds for travel to six meetings a year, anywhere in the world. Also, two secretaries. However, you never told us your own salary requirement."

"That, we can discuss later. I'm sure it will be competitive. I'll call you back in a day or two." Swept hung up the telephone.

"What was all that about?" Ricki asked Swept, nestled against him. "Who was it?"

"The spy system. They want me to join them."

"Wow! You know, the Washington, D.C.–Virginia area is nice. Remember, I grew up there. Besides, how do you know you won't become some big-time medical espionage figure in the CIA?"

"Come on, Ricki. They want me to do research. One thing is for certain, I'm no fancy spy."

"I'm not so certain about that. You saved lives. Besides," her hands softly scratching the lower part of his abdomen, "It might not be so bad to work in Washington."

"I don't know. It's a big deal to leave academics and. . . . ., besides. . . . . . ., to work for the CIA?"

"It's important not to let you, yourself, push you around. You could do all the research you want. What would you have done had they offered you support at the CIA, before all this? According to what you tell me, they have unlimited resources for laboratory equipment, personnel, space, and money. Isn't that what you want?"

"Well, maybe. I'm not certain. I still need time to think about it."

"I think you do, darling. Whatever you do, I'm still behind you. Right now, I think I should leave and let you get some rest. I'm still keeping my Marlboros and lighter here as a memento to my not having smoked for days. Proud of me?"

"Proud of you? Sure. It's nice to be proud of someone." Swept walked her to the door, and returned to the bathroom. He was hungry, poured a Perrier, and put some popcorn in the microwave oven. Although the instructions suggested five minutes, he had long ago learned that three minutes was sufficient time. However, before he pushed the buttons, he heard a knock on the door.

Figuring it was Ricki, not even checking through the peephole, Swept opened the door.

"Mr. Abdul? What in the world are you doing here," remembering that Abdul was Aleksander Kostokov.

"Doctor, may I come in a moment? Are you alone?"

"Why, yes. Sure. Excuse my clothes, or lack thereof," Swept said, recognizing that he was wearing only a bath towel around his waist. "Come in. I just have to make a call," dismissing himself and heading toward the bedroom, where he planned to dial 911. "I'll be back in two minutes."

Aleksander Kostokov quickly looked around the house, gathering its dimensions. "Fine, I appreciate your seeing me."

Swept called 911 and told the Houston police operator that a killer, a Russian spy, was in his home. The operator told him not to joke on the 911 line. Swept emphasized he wasn't joking. She affirmed his address and said she would see what she could do, and hung up.

Swept, fearing his life, gathered his composure as best he could and returned. "Now, Mr. Abdul. What can I do for you? Why are you seeing me here, tonight? Are your headaches so bad you couldn't call our answering service?"

Mr. Abdul, smiling, reached into his coat pocket and pulled out a revolver. He carried his Walther 9mm DA autolader with its 3.5 inch barrel. The silencer emphasized the special design feature of this gun–that no special knowledge or skill was required on the part of its user. All one had to do was aim and shoot.

"This won't take long, Doctor. Now move," as Abdul firmly encouraged Swept to move backwards.

"What is this?" Swept asked. "Who are you?"

"Don't talk. Just move." Kostokov ushered Swept backwards, past the desk on the neurologist's right, as he walked in reverse into the small hallway, and then let himself be pushed into the bathroom. With nothing but the sink, on which his shaving equipment and spray deodorant rested, together with Ricki's cigarettes and lighter, between them, Swept worried, in great earnest. "What do you want? What have I done to you?"

"Actually, Dr. Swept, you haven't done anything to me. You have your job and I have mine."

"What's your job? Killing people at the NIH?"

Kostokov then said something in Russian. Swept, not a linguist, recognized the language. "Russian?"

"No matter to you." Looking at the Marlboro Lights, Kostokov wryly smiled. "Well, Doctor, I never knew you smoked. Is this some little secret you keep from your patients and colleagues?"

Swept, trying hard to concentrate and think his way out of his predicament, said, "Yes. They're not the best brand, but do you mind if I have one? Isn't that what the bad guys let the good guys do?"

Swept picked up the lighter, just when Limbic came into the room, awakened from his sleep, now barking at Kostokov.

"The bullshit is over," and Kostokov shot the Lhasa right through his head, killing him instantly, Limbic's head disintegrating in the bathroom, leaving Swept aghast. Kostokov, remaining unmoved, smiled and slowly aimed the weapon at Swept's head, not anticipating any serious resistance. Swept, focused on his immediate problem, flicked the cigarette lighter with his right hand and, crossing over with his left at a speed he did not know he possessed, pushed down hard on the spray deodorant, a maneuver he had once seen in a movie. Depressing the nozzle with his left index finger, aiming the can across the flame at Kostokov, the flash of fire caused Kostokov to step back, prompting Swept to thrust his weight against the Russian as hard as he could, knocking him off balance, dropping his gun on Limbic's blood-soaked decapitated body. The gun was immersed in a pool of blood and fur, as Swept kicked it out of the way and ran from his assailant, into the kitchen. There, he pushed the microwave buttons and grabbed the telephone, again seeking 911. In seconds, Kostokov was at his side, pulling out the cord as Swept tried to dial the police.

It was as Kostokov was reaching for the cord, that Swept thrust an upper left under the Russian's chin, simultaneously opening the kitchen drawer and pulling a knife. The agent snarled, only to feel the blade shoved into his left thorax. Gasping, trying to pivot on his legs, Kostokov raised his left arm at Swept, momentarily surprised to hear popcorn pop in the microwave. The two then struggled on the floor for several minutes, the knife still embedded in Kostokov's chest. As each man grappled at the other, Kostokov, gripping Swept's neck, suffering pain in his hand and part of his face that were burned by the earlier flame throwing, was startled when fire burst from the microwave, again catching him off guard. At that moment, Swept, with immense anger inside him, drove his left thumb into the agent's right eye, simultaneously chopping as hard has he could at the Russian' trachea. In no time, the agent lay dead.

Swept plugged the phone back into the wall, called the police, now his third try, swore at them, and hung up. Shortly, they were there, as were his neighbors. Somehow, Ricki arrived (Had he called her? He wasn't certain.), crying. "I can't leave you alone? Are you all right?"

"Yes, unfortunately for Limbic, no. He killed Limbic."

Another night of interrogation, this time of a different caliber.

The following morning, a tired Dick Swept went to work. Swept told Ranger about the previous evening's experiences, and Ranger marveled that Swept had survived. Ranger then informed him that the International Office had insisted Dr. Ranger see a patient that day, so he had to cut his discussion with Swept short.

"That's what happened to me with Mr. Abdul. You better be careful. Who knows what's going on these days?"

Ranger listened attentively and both he and Swept, now accompanied by Valerie, walked to the Neurology Clinic. Valerie surreptitiously walked through the waiting room, and immediately recognized Jokhar Gantemirov, who had signed in under an alias. She called Hospital Security and the Houston Police. When Ranger called the patient in, Gantemirov was surprised by several law enforcement officers, who were waiting inside to take him downtown.

*   *   *

Shortly thereafter, Major Cervantes was on the telephone with the Director of the FSB. "Let's be real frank. I thought you want to combat terrorism, certainly from the Chechens. Are you supporting these derelicts?"

"Believe me, these were outside my control." The Russian, who was not stupid, knew that Solokov and Usova were dead, and found it surprising that they had allegedly died in a boating accident. In a short period of time, he would realize that Yuri Lyachin's travel roster often coalesced with those of the dead agents. "I'll look into this. I appreciate your telling me what happened."

Major Cervantes called Swept. "We're getting considerable information from Gantemirov, especially using some of the drugs we employ, as well as a lot of sleep-deprivation. Anyone else in this group will soon be caught. Now, as for you, are you with us? You should be, because the Russians are now going to look into this area and we need all the help we can get."

"Does this make me a spy?'

"Hardly. But, if you want, sure. After all, you did

kill a Russian agent with your bare hands. Not bad
for a beginner."

Cervantes continued. "Dr. Swept, you'll want for
nothing. You'll have the personnel you need, the
space you need, the money you need. Your work is
incredibly important, not only to the well-being of
people stricken with Alzheimer's disease, but also for
our nation's security. We're delighted to have you
on board."

*   *   *

That night, Swept lay in Ricki's arms. Yes, he had
decided to join the Central Intelligence Agency. He
would do his work and add something of meaning
to this crazy planet. Delighted, still professing her
love, asking no ties or commitment, Ricki said she
would move to Virginia to be with him. Planning to
live with her family for a while, she secretly hoped to
marry the physician-scientist. His science was good,
he was capable of deep feelings, and had the macho
wherewithal to actually kill a Russian spy.

*   *   *

Dick Swept sat on the Continental Airlines flight,
First-Class, next to Ricki Hardson. "It was kind of sad
to say goodbye to Dr. Ranger, Ricki. I think in some
ways he'll really miss me, but in other ways he doesn't
really care."

"I don't think that he cares about anyone, except himself. He's not normal. You would think that
he would have been more supportive to you in the
midst of your recent miseries."

"He was—sort of. I don't know whether the Agency had anything to do with it, but he received considerable funding for some of his own grants. Regardless, he told me to call him in a few weeks, and I will."

"Dick, do what you like. I just want you to know how much I love and care for you."

Swept turned to her and smiled. He picked up one of his Dylan discs, and prepared to insert the song "One Too Many Mornings and a Thousand Miles Behind" into his Walkman. After pressing the appropriate buttons, and beginning to hear the song through the headphones, Ricki turned to him and smiled. "Darling?"

"Yes?"

"Have you ever heard of the Mile High Club?"

Smiling, putting the headphones on, listening to the music but being able to hear Ricki, the neurologist answered. "Yes, and I've always wanted to join."

"I sure have come a long way from what can be called Himalayan Blues to my own personal dose of Sweptomania."

Ricki removed Swept's copy of the *New England Journal of Medicine*, *Gourmet* and *Harper's* and nuzzled against his shoulder. Swept turned to her, removed his Walkman, and said, "So have I. So have we." He gently kissed her, and thought about the Dylan song. He looked behind, and saw Valerie at the back of the plane. She smiled and winked at him. It was then that he heard Dylan's refrain, *"One too many mornings, and a thousand miles behind."*